"*Y*our fate has already been determined. By dawn, you and I will be wed." Rising on her toes, she sealed the vow with a kiss.

Ewan's senses barely registered the brush of her lips against his. Shaking his head slightly to test that he was indeed conscious, he took measure of the flame-haired woman who was calmly mounting her horse. Hitherto, she had seemed sane. Misguided, undoubtedly, but sane.

How very wrong he had been in estimating her abilities. Madlin of Dunfionn was utterly and completely mad. . . .

Gently, so as not to rattle whatever sensibility might remain within her head, Ewan cajoled with all the charm he could muster. "My lady Madlin, leave off this foolishness. Noblewomen do not kidnap men for husbands."

"This noblewoman does, if it means she can stop a war between her clan and another." Without sparing him another glance, she turned her mount toward the path leading across the glen.

When a stream of defiant protestations, punctuated with curses, started up from the golden-haired knight, the MacKendrick ordered her captive gagged. . . .

HIGHLAND BRIDE

Janet Bieber

FAWCETT GOLD MEDAL • NEW YORK

A Fawcett Gold Medal Book
Published by The Ballantine Publishing Group
Copyright © 1999 by Janet Bieber

All rights reserved under International and Pan-American Copyright Conventions. Published in the United States by The Ballantine Publishing Group, a division of Random House, Inc., New York, and simultaneously in Canada by Random House of Canada Limited, Toronto.

Fawcett is a registered trademark and Fawcett Gold Medal and the Fawcett colophon are trademarks of Random House, Inc.

www.randomhouse.com/BB/

Library of Congress Catalog Card Number: 99-90025

ISBN 0-449-00284-5

Manufactured in the United States of America

First Edition: August 1999

10 9 8 7 6 5 4 3 2 1

To Ruth Kagle, my agent, for believing in Madlin, Ewan, and me. To my editor, Shauna Summers, whose enthusiasm was infectious and expertise invaluable. And for my husband— Jim, you've been my knight in shining armor since that certain afternoon in early spring.

Prologue

1413
Castle Dunfionn, the Highlands

Sword in hand, the huge warrior loomed over the youngster kneeling on the ground. With the tip of the weapon, he tapped first one and then the other of the slender, tartan-draped shoulders. "Rise, wee knight of Dunfionn."

With great dignity, the little girl got to her feet. "Am I really a knight now, Papa?"

Baron MacKendrick, laird of the Dunfionn MacKendricks, returned his daughter's small sword with an elaborate flourish. "Ye are the protector of my heart, lass. There is no higher honor I can give ye."

Seeing the smile disappear from her sun-kissed face, he crouched low so that his ruddy, bearded face was level with hers. " 'Tis a fine thing that ye have learned to handle this wee weapon. A woman needs to know how to protect herself. But a knight must be a man full grown, not a wee lass like yerself."

Madlin started to ask if she could be a knight when she was a woman grown, but Toirlach lifted her high and twirled her around. Her question was forgotten amid the squeals and giggles her father's playfulness evoked.

Setting her down, he gave her a light push toward the keep's entrance. "Be off with ye now. Yer aunt and cousin are waiting in the solar. Elspeth has it in her mind to set ye and wee Jeanne

1

to work on a new tapestry she has designed. Best exchange yer shirt and plaid for a gown before ye join them."

"A gown! I cannot move in the silly things. And needlework?" She spat on the ground to show her disdain. "A pox on women's work! 'Tis no part of a knight's training."

"Daughter . . . !" Aimed at anyone else, Toirlach's glare would have instantly brought about a cessation of rebellion. But a pair of green eyes above a pert, freckled nose mirrored his glare. " 'Tis part of a lady's training. By the holy rood, ye'll be a lady!"

"I'm as big as Airic, just as strong, and I can move quicker," she told him without even a waver in her voice. "And, I have heart."

The silence that followed seemed to stretch out for an eternity. And then it came—her father's laughter.

"That ye have, Maddie, lass. That ye have. Yer fault lies in being too impetuous in the following of it. May ye someday learn patience so that great heart does not lead ye down the wrong path."

He narrowed his eyes on her and then caught the attention of a man just exiting the stable, a grizzled giant wearing a leather patch over one eye. "Gordie Gunn, I have need of ye."

As his cousin by marriage strode briskly toward them, Toirlach sent him a quick wink. "I have a serious quest to put to ye. Understand, 'tis one I can give over to only my most trusted man."

Gordie nodded solemnly. Neither man allowed the slightest sign of humor lest they insult the dignity of the little girl standing between them.

"This lass has passable skill with her wee sword but 'tis not the weapon of a lady. Think ye can make an archer of her?"

Scratching his whiskered chin, Gordie walked around his godchild. " 'Twill not be easy, Toirlach." He felt Madlin's upper arms. "The lass has the muscle for it, but has she the patience and the eye?"

"Her mam, God rest her soul, was an accomplished archer."

"Aye, Lady Aislinn was nocking arrows in a bow as soon as she could stand. My dear cousin was a Gunn as true as any, and we are a patient clan."

He stepped back and scrutinized Madlin with his good eye. "This one's as true a MacKendrick as was ever born."

Proud to be called a true MacKendrick, Madlin stood a little straighter. But pride in her heritage took a bit of a dent when Gordie said, "Och, lass, 'tis a sorrow a true MacKendrick like yerself cannot count patience among her virtues. Born that way, I fear. 'Tis said ye and yer brother were so impatient to see the world, ye came into it a full month before your mam's time."

Kicking at a tuft of grass, he scratched his head again. "I canna be sure, Toirlach. Mayhap this be a quest destined for failure."

"It will not!"

As if he'd not heard her denial, Gordie shook his head and said, "Och, I can but try to give ye my best attempt."

"I cannot ask for more," Toirlach said gravely and clapped him upon the back. "If ye should fail, I'll know where the fault lies."

Holding desperately to her silence, Madlin vowed she would learn patience or die trying. All her life, she'd suffered comparisons to Jeanne Gunn of Craigheade. Until recently, she'd been able to ignore them by pretending her cousin did not exist. But a fortnight ago, Jeanne had arrived at Dunfionn, and since then Madlin had been bedeviled daily. She was heartily sick of hearing praise for "wee Lady Jeanne's" patience, proper ways, and female accomplishments.

The gauntlet had been thrown down, and Madlin eagerly snatched it up. The intensity with which she threw herself into archery surprised no one, but the patience she showed in the process was a surprise to all.

Two years after she had held a bow in her hands for the first time, Madlin was hitting targets, still and moving, truer than Jeanne and even better than most men at Dunfionn. Toirlach gave her a new bow and a beautifully tooled quiver that year at the eleventh celebration of her and her brother's births.

However, she did not put aside the small broadsword that matched the one her twin used, their eighth-year natal gifts. Appealing to her older brother, Bram, for training, she increased her skill. If her father knew of it—and well she suspected he did since little escaped the MacKendrick's knowledge—he failed to remark upon it. Upon her mastery of the bow, he heaped praise.

There was little more talk of spending her days alongside her cousin under her aunt's tutelage. Except for rare formal occasions, she wore a linen shirt billowing about her slender body and a kilted plaid covering her only to the knees. Running barefoot through the heathered hills and along the craggy slopes, she was as nimble as Airic and the other lads.

But in the twins' thirteenth year, Madlin's sex betrayed her.

Airic shot past her in height and his shoulders broadened, whereas Madlin started developing soft curves, a reminder to all that one of Toirlach's bairns was female. That year's celebration of the twins' birth ended, as always, with the presentation of gifts.

Being the elder by a full minute, Airic was called first to stand upon the dais before their sire. Madlin shook with anticipation when she saw her father lay a full-sized broadsword across her brother's outstretched arms. The light from the flambeaux danced across the polished metal of the blade and set the emerald embedded in the chased hilt twinkling.

Ah, 'tis a wondrous thing, she thought, and cheered louder than anyone when her father buckled a new scabbard about her brother's waist and slipped the shiny new claymore into its sheath.

And then, it was her turn. Airic grinned and winked at her as he passed. Eagerly she moved forward, stumbling on the steps, unaccustomed as she was to wearing a gown. Beneath the yards of wool, her knees knocked, making her curtsy clumsy. As her brother had done, she stretched her arms out, palms upward. Eyes squeezed shut, she braced herself for the weight of a claymore that would match Airic's.

But the gift was feather light and rustled softly over her arms. She gasped when she looked upon yards of green silk shot with gold. A pair of silk slippers rested atop the shimmering fabric.

Disappointment choked her, smothering her reason as she turned away. Through a watery blur, she saw Airic being congratulated by the MacKendrick knights. Only the women of Dunfionn showed any interest in her gift. Disappointment turned to fury, and she hurled her gifts toward the hearth.

In her haste to run from the hall, her legs became tangled in her skirts. She would have fallen headlong upon the rush-strewn floor had her father not caught her. His touch was not gentle.

His grip around her wrists was as biting as an iron manacle as he dragged her up the stairway and toward her chamber. There, he turned her over his knee and delivered no less than a dozen sound whacks upon her backside with his broad palm. By the fifth blow, not even the yards of her hated gown shielded her from the burning pain. She nearly bit her lip in two to keep from crying out and squeezed her eyes tightly to dam her tears.

"Yer actions have disgraced yerself, me, and all of the clan. 'Tis shamed I am to claim ye as a daughter of my house."

Then the tears rushed down her cheeks like a mountain burn in spring. Deep, wrenching sobs shook her frame, but she managed an apology and followed it with a promise to do anything to make her father proud of her again.

His anger spent, Toirlach swept her up against his thick chest and held her tightly. "Och, Maddie, I've not done right by ye, so the shame is more mine than yers. Both of us must be remembering ye are a lass. Yer lady mother, God rest her soul, would not be pleased that I've let her only lass run so wild.

"Ye must start spending yer days as yer aunt thinks best. Elspeth is a stern woman, I know, but 'twas not always so. 'Tis a boon I'm asking of ye, lass, for I would again see my sister smile and laugh as she was wont as a lass before—"

A look of deep sorrow crossed his face before he brightened and tucked one of her curls behind her ear. "Elspeth is skilled in all the womanly arts. It would please her mightily to teach them to ye. But 'tis not just the pleasing of her or me that's important."

Gently he brushed away her tears with his thumbs. "Here in the Highlands we count a man or woman's deeds for more than the circumstances of birth and sometimes forget that titles are held in great store in other regions of our country. Ye've noble blood running in yer veins, lass. Mind, that blood does not make ye better than any other but brings a responsibility to put others before yerself and always to act with honor. Only then will ye be deserving of being called noble and a peeress of the realm."

Smiling, he ran his hand over her bright coppery curls. "Ye have the look of both your mam and mine. One day ye'll be a great beauty as were those fine ladies. Never let it be said that the lady Madlin MacKendrick of Dunfionn is not as fair of manners as she is of face."

That day, he wrung a promise from her that she would conduct herself at all times in a manner befitting her station and gender. Despite the sincerest of intentions, it was a promise Madlin was ill-equipped to keep.

Chaffed to distraction by the strictures of her new daily routine, she devised ways to sneak away from Elspeth's supervision. In secret, she continued practicing with her sword, sometimes engaging in a mock battle with her twin or one of the youths fostered at Dunfionn.

Sometimes her father was none the wiser. Sometimes she was caught. Each time she was found out, the threats against future transgressions grew more severe. Finally, in the spring of her fourteenth year, she went too far.

Disguised as Airic, she challenged Seamus Munro, bested him, and was found out. At sixteen years, the future laird of the Munros made up for what he lacked in size and skill with pride. The alliance between the two clans was threatened. Nothing would salve his wounded pride or that of the Munros but that Madlin apologize before an assembly of their clan.

Her cheeks stained crimson from the humiliation, Madlin nevertheless held her head high as she stood upon the dais in the great hall of the Munros. Her voice was clear as she made the demanded apology, faltering only when she forced the lie that she'd used trickery to best Seamus. Toirlach had been proud of his daughter but did not grant her complete forgiveness.

His patience at an end, he looked beyond the walls of Dunfionn for hope of shaping her into a woman deserving of her rank. He took her to Aberdeen where he placed her under the care of another aunt, the abbess, Liusadh Gunn. Madlin was to remain at St. Margaret's Abbey until such time as a marriage was contracted for her.

Chapter One

October 1424
Stirling Castle

Their sovereign's glare quieted the crowd of courtiers and noblewomen gathered in the great hall. Sensing the mood, the musicians abruptly ceased playing. With the wave of arrests and beheadings among the nobility since James Stewart's return to Scotland, many a man felt a tremor run down his spine, fearing the slightest sign of the new king's displeasure.

Furtive glances raced through the crowd searching for the source of James's displeasure. There was a collective sigh of relief when the royal gaze fixed solely upon the stranger at the back of the hall.

A tall, blond man stood at the entrance, his posture erect, his gaze unwavering as he returned the king's regard. With a barely perceptible nod, the king granted the man permission to approach the dais.

Relieved that none among them was the target of the king's dissatisfaction, the crowd parted. The unknown man, his knight's spurs jingling softly with each firm step of his booted feet, proceeded up the wide aisle created for him. The plaid draped over one of his broad mail-clad shoulders was tattered and stained. The faded colors proclaimed him a Fraser, but the elaborate hilt of the sword hanging from his lean hips bore the royal Stewart crest.

The knight stopped a few feet before the base of the raised dais, bowed deeply, then reached for his sword. The collective gasp of shock was loud. Guards on each side of the monarch sprung forward to protect their liege while others rushed to seize this man who was either crazed or incredibly audacious as to clear his weapon from its scabbard in the king's presence.

"Halt. Leave him be," was the startling order from the king.

Seemingly oblivious to all but the king, the knight balanced the great gold-hilted sword between his open palms and dropped to one knee. " 'Tis yours, sire."

"We are told you brought honor to it," said James I, Scotland's anointed king of less than one year. He made no move to take the proffered sword, nor did he direct his guards to do so. And, though it was clear to all that the position was uncomfortable for the Fraser knight, James made no gesture to give him leave to rise.

Despite the man's calm expression, perspiration began to bead upon his brow while his body swayed lightly. "I was inspired by all who carried it before me." His voice was hoarse but steady, if not quite as strong as it had been when he'd first addressed his king.

"You took your time returning it to us, Ewan Fraser," James said, at last identifying the stranger. Whispered queries and explanations rippled through the assembled. Quickly, the information spread that the man had been James's companion during the majority of his imprisonment by the English. More recently, Ewan Fraser had commanded one of the Scots battalions fighting for their ally, France, against her English invaders. That their sovereign would greet the man so coolly was cause for much speculation.

"We expected you to be with us at Scone this spring past."

"It would have been my greatest honor to have been there to witness your coronation and, if it had pleased you, your wedding some months before," the knight returned smoothly as he subtly adjusted his weight away from his leg resting on the floor. The movement caused him to wince and his handsome visage noticeably blanched. "Tardy though they may be, my felicitations for a long reign and much happiness in your marriage are nonetheless sincere, your majesties." His lips tensed briefly, then lifted as he centered his attention upon the lovely woman seated next to James. "It is indeed an honor to see you again, ma'am, and to wish you joy in your marriage. Scotland is blessed to have you."

Though her husband's features remained stern, Queen Joan dipped her head in acknowledgment and offered a soft smile. She started to say something, but her words were drowned out by the clatter of the sword falling against the stone floor. Most startling of all that had transpired since Sir Ewan Fraser's dramatic entrance was the rapidity with which the king rushed to his boyhood companion, catching him in his arms before the man's unconscious body could crumple to the floor.

A commotion at the door was Ewan's only warning of the king's arrival. "Are you strong enough to walk with us?" James asked, his angular face showing a mixture of concern and friendliness.

Rising to his feet, Ewan ignored the stiffness and burning sensation plaguing his right leg and bowed as deeply as his wound would allow. "I am, sir." He eyed the sovereign warily. After the cold reception he'd received when he'd presented himself to the king, he wondered at the warmth he now saw in James's countenance and heard in his voice.

At a slight gesture of the royal hand, a page stepped forward and offered a folded cloak to Ewan. "Wrap yourself well," the king advised. " 'Tis brisk this day, but the sun shines, and we are convinced the fresh air will do our friend good."

So regal and therefore distant was this James Stewart, Ewan thought as he settled the fur-lined woolen cloak about himself. Though James had inherited the crown within months of their capture, he'd had neither power nor responsibility until his release. During their shared captivity and youth, the disparity between their ranks had been inconsequential. They'd been so close, almost as if they were of one mind shared by their two young bodies. To think that had not changed would be foolish, perhaps fatal if all he had heard of James's short reign were true.

It was with a mixture of pride in his friend and sorrow for the loss of their easy kinship that he hastened to catch up with his king. James was already several paces down the hallway outside the chamber. Still weak from a sennight of lying abed, in and out of consciousness, Ewan was hard put to catch up with James's brisk stride.

At a flight of stairs, James dismissed his attendants and waited impatiently for Ewan to catch up. He did not speak again until they were alone atop the ramparts surrounding the royal fortress.

"Ah, my dear good friend. Yours is a most welcome face in my court." He clasped Ewan's hand firmly in his right hand and clapped him on the shoulder with his left. After but a moment's hesitation, Ewan returned the greeting in kind.

"That was quite a dramatic entrance you made," the king remarked, his eyes sparkling with mirth. "Was it a reminder of our years together at the English court or was that something you learned among the Armagnacs?"

Though he would have wished it otherwise, Ewan felt the rise of color in his neck and to his cheeks. Still, he returned his friend's grin. It was good to see the teasing light in James's eyes and the familiar hint of humor playing about the corner of his wide mouth. "From both, sir . . . save the faint."

James released him and turned to lean against the battlement, facing the wind blowing down from the North. " 'Tis good to see you after all these many years. We feared for you after we heard of Verneuil. So many of our best were lost there. What think you, Ewan? Will France be able to ward off the English invader once all our forces have returned to Scotland?"

Ewan considered his answer carefully. His years serving as a liaison between the Scots command and its French ally had taught him caution. "I believe, sir, that the French do want their independence from England and they—"

"Stop! Leave off the diplomatic sidestepping and talk to

me as you would when we were boys. Jamie Stewart and Ewan Fraser, two lads growing up together, alone and far from home in that cursed English court."

Ewan relaxed and chuckled lightly. "After my reception, I thought not to ever know my boyhood friend, Jamie Stewart, again."

James waved dismissively. "Oh that. All show for that nest of vipers that gather round me. If they think you are in my disfavor, they may be more open with their tongues when you are about."

"You would have me remain at court and spy for you?" Ewan felt a chill that had nothing to do with the brisk wind swirling about him. Now that he was at last on Scotland's soil, he wanted nothing so much as to get home to Glendarach, deep in the Highlands. Far from wars and court intrigues.

"We would if I loved you less," James admitted, slipping so adeptly between the royal plurality and the personal singular form that Ewan was hard put to discern with which persona, King James I or Jamie Stewart, he was conversing.

"Wipe the furrow from your handsome brow, you are free to go where you will," James ordered. "I would but have you keep your ears open for any talk of rebellion. I will not have my nobles warring against each other or me. After eighteen years of my uncle and then my cousin's regency, Scotland's nobles have grown used to jockeying and plotting for power whilst there is naught but lawlessness reigning throughout this land."

He slammed a fist in his palm. "I tell you, Ewan, there shall be no place in this realm where there is not law! And that includes the Highlands and your clan!"

"My clan? I have no word of trouble at Glendarach."

"Then your information is not so new as mine. We are told that the Frasers and their neighbors, the MacKendricks, are raiding upon each other, burning fields, crofts, and worse. There's been bloodshed. You will bring a stop to it, my friend."

"I am not the Fraser or the MacKendrick, but I will do what I can."

"What you can do is marry the MacKendrick's daughter," James said firmly, once again the sovereign who was determined to rule his country with an iron fist if necessary.

Sir Ewan, knight of Scotland and France, bent his knee to his king. "If that is your wish, sir, I shall present my suit at the earliest opportunity."

Like quicksilver, James's mood shifted back to joviality. "Rise, you jackanapes." Laughing, he playfully punched Ewan on the shoulder. "Do not toady to me when we are alone like this. James Stewart married the woman he loved, and so shall Ewan Fraser if God is willing. We ask only that you consider the MacKendrick lass. If she suits, a marriage would be a way of allying the two clans and stamping out at least one of the fires scattered about the Highlands."

Relaxing again, Ewan asked, "Do you know of the lass?"

"Only that she was sent to St. Margaret's Abbey at Aberdeen some years ago and has perhaps reached her twentieth year. We have been told she has not taken the veil, but there she does remain, overripe for marriage but not so long in the tooth she is past childbearing. I should think her a gentle, pious lady for her convent education and, mayhap, if the lass is possessed of any amount of wits, well versed in academics as the abbess there is a respected scholar. I know nothing of her appearance, but my sources tell me her mother was a Gunn of Craigheade and that the women of that line are more often beauties than not."

"I shall give the lady serious consideration, then."

"Would it sweeten the prospect of bedding the daughter of the MacKendrick if I were to offer you an earldom as a wedding present?"

Ewan laughed, confident James was only jesting. "Do you want peace so badly between the two clans, Jamie, that you would bribe a third son of an earl with such a prize?"

James shrugged. " 'Tis fitting that we would so reward our friend who gave so much to see us back on this throne. I need you by my side, Ewan. As one of my earls, you could not be the stranger at court I fear you will be once you journey home beyond those mountains."

The king sighed. Ewan had never seen such weariness in his friend's visage. "Too many covet this crown I wear. I have missed you, Ewan. Save for my sweet Joan, there is no one about me I can trust."

"Then I shall stay, sir," was Ewan's answer.

"Nay, you shall not. I see the yearning in your eyes as you gaze at yon mountains. Go home, Ewan. I need you more in the Highlands just now. Come back to me in the spring with an assurance that peace reigns in Moray. Perhaps you'll present your bride to me, and if it is not the MacKendrick lass swelling with Cluain's heir, we shall cast about the ladies of the court for someone suitable."

"Cluain's, sir?"

"Aye, we think it an appropriate name for a baron whose seat might be built at the center of the meadowlands between Fraser and MacKendrick lands. That land and some other properties are yours, along with a baron's title to go with it. If you present yourself next spring with the peace of Moray's banks assured, we may make you an earl despite your protests."

Ewan could not help but chuckle at his king's manipulations. "I am honored by your confidence in me, sire, and thank you for the barony but—"

"A small reward for your service and loyalty to Scotland. I'll hear no protestations against any titles or honors I think to bestow upon you."

"As you wish, sir."

"And one more thing, Ewan. . . . You must take a certain mare from my stable. I'm told your grand French stallion has quite taken her fancy, and she may pine herself into a decline if she should be separated from him. I'll expect the first foal, of course."

Ewan chuckled and tipped his head. "Of course. Anything else, sire?"

"We would stand as godfather to any son of Cluain who might carry James somewhere in his name."

Ewan matched his friend's grin when he replied, "Even if that son be the son of a mere baron?"

"You will not disappoint us in this task. We will be most pleased when Earl Cluain's son is born before Christmastide next," the king announced in a casual tone, but there was little doubt in Ewan's mind that the statement was an official royal order to bring about peace in his corner of the Highlands in the most efficient and expeditious manner possible—marriage with the MacKendrick's daughter.

Chapter Two

From the rampart high above Dunfionn's gate, two old warriors kept vigil. His companion huddled behind the battlement, but Gordie Gunn stood in a crenel and leaned into the rain that was darkening the fortress's walls. With a gnarled hand, he swiped the moisture from his face, then squinted again toward the road below.

"Damn me for having but one good eye," he muttered as he strained to see through the sheets of rain and the black of night.

"A younger man with two good eyes would not see more this night." Hugh MacKendrick pulled the end of his plaid over his head. "Ye'll not be hearing anything above the howl of that wind and the hammering of the rain against these old stones. Ye're a fool to be trying, and I'm a fool to be out here keeping ye company. She'll not be here any faster for all our waiting out here getting drenched by the rain and catching our deaths."

"*Whisht*, man, stop yer blathering or 'tis sure I'll not be hearing anything." Cocking his grizzled head, Gordie strained to listen but could hear nothing save the wind and the rain.

" 'Twas a fast horse ye sent for her?"

"Aye. Aisling, the leggy chestnut. The best in our stable. Has some of the Arabian Barb in 'er, has that one." Feeling the chill so deep in his bones, he doubted he'd ever be rid of it, Gordie wrapped the end of his plaid tighter around him.

"Damn the Frasers to perdition and for all eternity," Hugh

16

muttered as he stumbled to his feet. Leaving his shelter, he took up a position in the next crenel of the battlement.

Cupping his ear, Gordie strained to hear something above the storm lashing the walls of Dunfionn and churning the water that surrounded her. Nothing. Nothing beyond the beating of the rain and the slapping of the waves against Dunfionn's base until he detected another rhythm joining the chorus. Was it hooves on the rain-soaked causeway?

He waited a second longer to be sure he was not mistaken. The distinctive pounding grew stronger. Hugh had heard it, too, for he was already grabbing the torch sputtering in the niche behind him. Swinging it in a wide arc, he signaled the other men upon the ramparts and within the gatehouse.

The chains lifting the portcullis had just begun to creak, and hooves clattered across the wooden drawbridge as Gordie scrambled down the steps. With a speed and agility that denied the decades since he had bested every runner in his clan, he was across the courtyard and waiting at the steps of the keep just as the rider dismounted. Hugh was but a step behind him.

Both men felt the sting of tears join the raindrops streaming down their faces. Seven years had passed since Lady Madlin MacKendrick had last been at Dunfionn. The carefree young lass was gone. In her place stood a woman looking so like her mother, it was as if their beloved Lady Aislinn stood before them again. But Madlin was Toirlach's daughter, too. Her sire's mark was in the line of her jaw, the color of her hair, and her proud carriage.

For once it was Gordie who spoke first. "They're laid out in the chapel. Lady Elspeth, Lady Jeanne, and some of the other women are there now praying for their souls. Will ye be going there first?"

Only a slight pause as Madlin mounted the steps and a faint negative jerk of her head beneath the close-drawn hood indicated she'd heard the query. "Francis?"

"The bishop was at Beauly when it happened. He's been sent for."

"We'll not bury . . ." She could not finish the sentence,

could not bring herself to put voice to the image of her loved ones being lowered beneath the windswept soil. "We'll wait for Francis. He is Papa's son, too."

"Aye."

"The clan? Are they in the great hall?"

"All that are not on duty elsewhere."

"Then I must show myself in the hall first. At such a time as this, the clan must see their . . . their . . ."

Her voice trailed off again. Gordie seemed unable to form speech, so it was left to Hugh to finish the thought. "Laird," he furnished huskily.

Hugh, also, had dandied upon his knee the little girl she'd once been. Like her godsire, Gordie, Hugh had helped in Madlin's rearing. He, too, gazed with love and pride upon the striking woman she'd become.

Both men flinched when they saw her shoulders slump and her stride falter as if the weight of the responsibilities accompanying the title had literally been placed there that very moment.

The pause was brief. Her back straight and proud, Madlin lengthened her stride as she neared the great hall.

Following behind their new leader, the two old men talked softly. "Praise God, Toirlach trained all his bairns so well."

"Aye, she'll put the clan first, same as her da and his da before him. The lass knows her duty."

" 'Tis a grievous thing to lose a father and two brothers all at once."

"Och, well, I'm thinking she'll be needing us, old friend."

Dunfionn's great raftered hall was full. The men and women of clan MacKendrick stood around in small clusters, silent in their grief or speaking in hushed voices. From the gallery above came the mournful strains of a coronach played by a lone piper.

None in the hall felt scorn or embarrassment at the sight of tears streaming down another's face, be it woman or man. There was no shame in showing grief for a fallen laird and his sons, especially ones as well loved as Toirlach, Bram, and young Airic had been.

The tables fanned out from the dais at the end of the hall. There, one long table stretched with an imposing, heavily carved chair reigning at its center. It was to this chair that Madlin strode, hesitating only for the slightest moment before assuming the place of highest honor, the chair upon which only the laird of clan MacKendrick sat.

The piper's lament trailed to silence as the gathering of over four score quietly arranged themselves at the flanking tables. Gordie, Hugh, and four other elders took up their places at the high table. Standing quietly, collectively holding their breaths, all within the hall waited.

The rain-soaked hood was thrown back, revealing the burnished copper hair so like their fallen chieftain's. The intensity of the emerald gaze made many among them feel as if Toirlach had been reincarnated in this decidedly female body standing before them. For those, the uncertainty of their leadership was relieved.

For others, the uncertainty remained. Though all had recognized her as being a true MacKendrick when she'd left for the abbey, they worried that the years away might have wrought too many changes. Of further concern was that she was but twenty years, and untried as a leader.

And, she was a woman. Clan MacKendrick had never had a female at its head.

"Clan MacKendrick." Madlin's voice rung clear and strong. "To you, I pledge myself and all I have. From the strongest warrior to the weakest bairn, none who calls himself a MacKendrick or resides on these lands is more important to me than any other. If you accept me as your chieftain, 'tis I who will serve you."

Silence followed her vow, but Madlin held her head high while she waited for a response. She'd expected silence, for she knew each soul within the great hall was wrestling with his or her conscience before voicing approval or disapproval of her. Holding herself with what she hoped was a show of calm and authority, she prayed that the words she'd chosen to address the clan this first time as her father's successor were the right ones.

With each mile she'd traveled, words her father had so often repeated had rung loudly in her ears. *The clan and its welfare are always first in the mind of the MacKendrick. Ye will lead, but dinna think yerself higher than any other, for 'tis to yerself and yer personal concerns ye'll look to last.*

He'd directed those words to her brother Bram, but they'd been repeated so many times before both Airic and herself that their meaning and import had been indelibly engraved upon their hearts.

Finally, the scraping of the wooden benches against the stone floor broke the silence. Madlin felt as if her heart had stopped beating in that moment before her people raised their cups and cried, *"O Urramaich! O Urramaich!"*

For honor. All her life she had been taught the importance of honor, but never had she understood it so well as at this moment, with the clan's cry ringing through the hall.

Relieved that for the present they'd accepted her, Madlin reached for the jewel-studded goblet placed before her. Her fingers were still icy and wet from the long ride as well as from the nervousness she felt within. But she wrapped them firmly around the ceremonial goblet and took a deep draft of its fiery contents.

Uisge beatha. From toasting the newly born to toasting the newly departed, special occasions in the life of the clan were marked by the serving of this "water of life" to all who gathered in Dunfionn's great hall.

Blinking away tears the *uisge* brought to her eyes and managing, just, to keep from coughing, she rose to her feet. Fearing her legs might buckle beneath her, she took the expected second draw from her goblet. This time the well-aged liquor went down more smoothly, and she added her voice to those of her clansmen as they shouted the clan's ancient war cry, thus affirming her succession.

That done, the men and women took up their places again

at the tables. As was proper, Madlin remained standing. More was expected of her this night, she knew, for the ritual followed by each new laird of the clan had been woven into the verses sung by the bards to entertain those gathered around the great hall's hearth during the long winter months. As youngsters she and Airic had reenacted the rituals, taking turns in the role of the new laird.

At the memory a mist of tears shrouded her eyes, and through it floated a vision of happier times. A young Airic, no more than ten years, smiled and said, "Your turn, Maddie. 'Tis your turn. Be proud and strong."

In her heart, she promised, I'll try, dearest brother. I will try. Squeezing her eyes shut, she kept the tears from flowing down her cheeks.

Here in the great hall of Dunfionn, the site of so many happy times with her father and brothers, the totality of her loss struck her more keenly than when she'd first been apprised of their murders. She could almost hear her father's deep laughter, Bram's husky voice, and Airic's, too, a sound once identical to her own. She could scarcely bear that she would never hear them again, and it did not surprise her that it had been Airic's image that had appeared to her. Her twin had always been the other half of herself.

Silence now prevailed in the hall; the people gathered, thinking that she'd signaled for their attention. Realizing this, Madlin composed herself with a quick prayer for strength and wisdom. When she knew the silence could go on no longer, she began.

"My blood and that of all of clan MacKendrick cries for vengeance." Her voice rose with each impassioned word. "I would hunt down the cowardly dogs who so foully took the lives we mourn this night."

Calls for war and cries for vengeance filled the great hall. Heavy swords were loosed from their scabbards and held high over the men's heads. The lust for blood was clear on each man's face as they cried, "Death to all Frasers!"

Madlin shuddered. In her lifetime no such scene had been

played at Dunfionn, yet because of the bards' songs it was as familiar to her as if she had witnessed it many times before.

Victory and glory had been theirs when the clan MacKendrick had taken up the sword. But there had been destruction, death, and much suffering as well. The verses of lament and mourning were long and numerous.

The sight of the raised claymores chilled Madlin to the bone as her mind's eye saw the silvery blades dripping with blood. All the bloodshed would not flow only from their enemies. Her father and her brothers were not the only losses the MacKendricks had suffered in this past year. Too many dear faces were missing from this gathering.

Having been kept apprised of all that had befallen the MacKendricks by Airic's frequent letters, Madlin would've left St. Margaret's months ago if her father had allowed it. But because of the heightened hostilities between the MacKendricks and the Frasers, he had commanded that she stay safe behind the convent walls. Frustrated and helpless to do otherwise, she'd had only prayers to offer for her clan.

Now cruel fate had placed her in a position where prayer was the last response expected of her. She must take action.

War. They all expected her to declare it. But if she called for war, there would be even more empty places at the tables. More crofts would be reduced to charred rubble. More young widows would cry through the night. More wee bairns would be orphaned or worse.

Holding up her hand with a purpose this time, she signaled for silence. Her father's words of always putting the good of the clan first rang foremost in her thoughts.

"Clan MacKendrick will have justice served," she stated firmly. "But there will be no cross of fire carried through our lands or those of our allies."

Forestalling cries of disappointment and anger, she added an appeasement for those she knew to be the worst firebrands. "Not yet, at least."

Leaning forward, she spread her hands upon the table and fixed her gaze upon one man and then another. "Tonight and tomorrow we will mourn our dead and pray for their souls. On the next day we will . . ."

Fearing her throat would close from the strain of holding back her personal grief, Madlin swallowed hard and then drew in a shaky breath. "On the next day, Francis, Bishop of Beauly, will be with us, and we will bury our dead. I would have no more talk of bloodshed until my father and brothers are laid to rest."

Heaving herself away from the table, she announced, "After the burial, I'll hear the oaths of those ready to swear their fealty to me, and then I would hold council with the elders. Until that time, I pray you will allow me to be naught but daughter and sister to those who lie in the chapel. With your permission I would go now to pray for their souls."

Amid a chorus of respectful ayes, Madlin left the hall. At the small chapel's entrance, she paused. Three biers were aligned before the altar. The sight was her undoing, and she would have sunk to the floor right there had not someone caught her up in an embrace.

"Och, Maddie, 'tis not the homecoming I prayed for," Jeanne Gunn whispered as she held her.

"Nor I," was all Madlin could manage past the lump in her throat. Surprisingly comforted by the embrace of this cousin she had so often disdained when they were children, Madlin clung to her for several moments until she felt ready to stand on her own. She looked about the chapel, seeing her aunt Elspeth, several older women she recognized, and one young woman who was a stranger. Frowning slightly, she looked to Jeanne for explanation.

"Your brother's betrothed, Lady Alys Robertson," Jeanne whispered. "She was to have been Bram's wife come Martinmas. She and Bram wanted to marry here at Dunfionn with Francis blessing their vows. Your father was preparing to send for you so that you would be here for the event. Airic . . ." Jeanne had to take a deep breath before she could continue. "Airic and I hoped to persuade him to let you stay."

Madlin swiped at the tears on her cheeks. "I should have

liked to have been here to wish my brother joy. Think you the lady Alys would have made Bram happy?"

"Aye. Your heart would have warmed watching them together. Bram did naught but smile when she was near, and stars fair glowed in her eyes whenever she looked upon him. There's no small speculation that Bram's child already grows within her womb for they were much in love and slipped away often by themselves."

"If God has granted us Bram's child, it will be welcome and loved here at Dunfionn. Will the lady Alys and the Robertsons feel blessed by such a child conceived before the final vows were said before a priest?"

"I believe Alys will grieve even more deeply if it is not so. As for the Robertsons, I do not know."

"Then Lady Alys must know that Dunfionn will be her home for as long as she does want it. 'Twould be right that Bram's child be born and reared here amid his birthright if God does grant her a son.

"And you, Jeanne, how fare you? I was most grieved to hear of Donald's death. He was a braw, merry lad, and I remember him well. I know he was a good man. I am sorry your time together was so short."

Tears sparkled in Jeanne's eyes at the mention of the tall, handsome man who'd been her husband for only a few months. "Och, Maddie, you have come home to a clan with too many women mourning their men. We must pray that Lady Alys is ripening with Bram's child. Dunfionn needs bairns to bring happiness to its halls once more."

Chapter Three

Ewan breathed deeply. Pine, heather, and misty rain. The Highlands. Home. Peace.

He looked about, taking in the barren trees, the browned heather on the hills, and the bright red of the frost-kissed bracken. Winter was nearly upon them. It was sheer luck that the narrow trail he traveled was still clear. Soon snow and ice would render it impassable until spring. God willing, any hostilities between the Frasers and MacKendricks would be halted by the weather. When tempers had time to cool, the political climate would likely be more conducive to the success of the negotiations necessary to bring about peace. If marriage to the MacKendrick's daughter should prove essential in bringing that about, then he prayed the lass had a modicum of wit and enough fairness of feature and body that bedding her would prove to be more of a pleasure than a duty. But perhaps he could negotiate a peace between the two clans without offering himself up as a sacrifice.

Rain, blessedly light for this time of year, had been falling since he had started through the Grampians. The ever-present moisture had run between the plates and mail he wore, soaking the heavily quilted doublet beneath and the lighter linen shirt next to his skin. His body would have been far more comfortable traveling without his armor, but it gave him some peace of mind to wear it. If there was a war being waged between the clans, then he'd best be prepared for attack. Five years battling the English on the continent had taught him that much.

Realizing how far the packhorses had forced his man,

Lucais, to lag behind, Ewan pulled his sorrel stallion to a stop. Securing the royal mare's leading reins to his saddle's high pommel, he removed his helm and hung it there. Sweeping back the hood of his hauberk, he turned his face toward the heavy clouds.

The rain splashed on his bronzed face. Rivulets ran through his hair, darkening the gold to brown. He felt not cold rain, but a cleansing balm to his wearied soul.

While he waited, he rubbed absently at his thigh and gazed yearningly toward the silvery loch dividing the glen below. Once they traversed the glen, only another half day's journey stood between him and Glendarach, the Fraser fortress.

When Lucais caught up to him, Ewan took in the droop of his shoulders hidden beneath a drenched plaid. " 'Twill be night soon. We'll make camp as soon as we reach Fraser land. A warm fire'll set us all to rights."

"I'll welcome it, laddie," Lucais said, a roughness in his voice that worried Ewan. "Not for myself, ye understand. The horses be needin' attention."

Ewan nodded. Not by a word or the slightest grin would he let on that he knew that the rigors of their travels were taking a far greater toll on Lucais than on the horses.

The grayish pallor of the older man's face and the way Lucais's big, burly body was sunk beneath his dripping plaid worried Ewan. Frustrated with all the delays that had hampered his homecoming, Ewan had set a furious traveling pace once he'd been able to take leave of Stirling.

Lucais deserved better from him. "We'll see to them soon then." Ewan kneed his horse into motion.

Paying little mind to his surroundings, he let his mount pick his way along the trail. Ewan tried to keep his thoughts on the peaceful future he'd begun to plan as soon as the recall had been made official. But memories of the things he'd seen and been forced to do were not easy to set aside.

God's blood! He wanted no more of war. Damn the Mac-Kendricks for starting one!

Peace in his household, his clan, the Highlands, and someday all of Scotland. That was the dream that had sustained him through battle after battle. He needed not the enticement of an earldom to strive for peace in Moray and the rest of the Highlands.

Just as he reached the level ground of the glen, a heavily needled branch of a pine tree had the misfortune of hanging too close to Ewan's face. Angered that he was not yet free of war, he swatted the offending branch away with more force than was necessary to remove it from his path. A swish and a thud sounded from behind him.

Thinking he'd caused the branch to snap back and knock Lucais from his mount, Ewan reined in his horse and swiveled in the saddle.

Lucais was on the ground, but no swinging bough had brought him down. Snared in what looked like a fishing net, the man was struggling to free himself as half-naked men dropped from the trees all around him.

Like lightning, Ewan's broadsword was out of its scabbard. Wheeling his destrier in a tight turn, he prepared to set his man free when another net dropped from the heavy canopy of tree limbs above him. Slashing through the ropes, Ewan was almost free when a blow to his unprotected head sent him falling from his mount and into a black void.

As bare-legged as her men, Madlin dropped from one of the trees lining the little clearing. As soon as her soft boots touched the ground, she began shouting orders over the screams of the infuriated stallion and the shrill answers of his mares.

In truth, the warhorse was proving a greater adversary than the man who'd ridden him straight into the trap. With flying hooves and threatening teeth, the powerful destrier was determined to keep everyone away from his fallen master.

Swallowing her revulsion toward killing such a magnificent animal, Madlin calmly nocked an arrow. She'd not risk the safety of her men trying to get the captive away from the stallion's protection before the man regained consciousness.

Their success so far assured that the sentries she'd assigned to the passes had gone undetected by their Fraser counterparts. So close to the Fraser border, a force of a score would surely not go unnoticed for long. A like-sized party of their enemies would be sent to investigate. She dared not tempt the fates further by dawdling any longer at the glen's edge.

Her arm rigid and steady, Madlin was about to give the order for her men to stand clear when a heavy hand dropped upon her shoulder. "Nay, lass, not yet," Gordie implored with a grin. "Give me a chance to quiet the great beast. 'Twould surely be a sin to destroy one as magnificent and valiant as this one." He winked impishly as he gestured toward the two restless mares. "Those lassies might never forgive ye."

Madlin lowered her bow. "You have but a few moments, Gordie," she said, both relief and misgiving clear in her eyes.

"Ye'll not be sorry, lass. Such as him is not of much use here in the Highlands, but would fetch a fat purse elsewhere. Capturing this fine braw laddie and these fair lasses will likely gain us more coin than if we were to steal three score of the Fraser's sheep."

"Let us pray you are right," Madlin remarked, thinking more of the still-unconscious "braw laddie" lying on the ground than of the infuriated animal Gordie thought to calm.

Unconsciously, her hand moved to the place between her breasts where a delicate gold disk lay. Hung from a finely wrought chain of gold, its edge studded with tiny semiprecious stones, the ancient piece had been hung about her neck by the abbess at St. Margaret's the night Madlin had been called back to Dunfionn. The runes etched upon the pendant's center were faint from age and in a language unfamiliar to Madlin, but her aunt Liusadh had translated their meaning:

Value all Life
Value all Knowledge
Consider all Counsel
Trust in Yourself

While merely a dozen words, they effectively summarized all of the teachings her aunt, the abbess, had imparted to Madlin during the years of her tutelage. In the scant weeks since she had assumed the leadership of her clan, they had become Madlin's creed. The first three lines were easy for her to follow. It was the last, trusting in herself, that she struggled with, especially in this latest decision that had led to the capture of the man so zealously guarded by his mount.

Only Gordie knew her intent for their Fraser captive. Usually her staunchest supporter, he had argued long and heatedly against her plan. By nature a peaceful, gentle man, Gordie's lust for violent revenge had surprised her. Her reminder of the clan's motto, "Honor in Victory and All Things," had not at first swayed him.

Killing a captive outright was an act of cowardice and unworthy of a MacKendrick, she'd reminded him. But it was her final argument, "Would you have your godchild begin her governorship of clan MacKendrick by leading a mission fraught with dishonor?" that had finally brought him around to her reasoning.

While she watched Gordie approach the furious destrier, she prayed that time would prove the rightness of her plan and of all the actions required to implement it.

Crooning softly, Gordie carefully approached the frantic warhorse. Magically, the sound reached the animal's senses at some level, for he ceased his thrashings and turned his attention toward the source of the soothing sounds.

Taking advantage of the animal's momentary pause, Gordie tossed a plaid unerringly over the animal's head. Swiftly, before the spirited sorrel had time to shake it off, Gordie sprung, fastening the length of wool securely about the animal's head. Blindfolded, the horse stilled, and Gordie was able to grab his halter.

With a jaunty grin and a twinkle in his eye, Gordie doffed his cap to Madlin before handing the reins of the now docile animal to one of the other men. "Victory is often only in the knowing of yer adversary's weaknesses, lass. Even one so mighty as that one is still but a horse. 'Tis the same with all creatures, be they the greatest of their kind or the poorest. There be always at least one wee thing they have about them that ye can use to bring them to yer bidding."

Now that the destrier was contained, Madlin moved closer to her golden-haired captive. "You are sure he is the one we seek?"

Gordie nodded. "The lad be a Fraser, make no mistake. He has the look of his sire about him."

Gesturing toward their captive's armor, Gordie scoffed and spat upon the ground. "Poor lad. Spent too much time in France, I'm thinking. No Highlander, not even a Fraser, would be caught clanking along a trail encased in steel like that. Had we not already known when to expect him, we would've heard him and come investigating. 'Tis like the faeries scooped him up and made a present of him."

"He has been unconscious a long time. You haven't addled his brains permanently, have you, Gordie?"

"Nay, lass. 'Twas but a wee bump, and the Frasers were always a thick-headed bunch. The lad'll be coming around soon enough. If ye've a mind to hasten it, we could fetch some water from yonder burn. A good dousing would bring him sputtering to wakefulness in no time."

Inexplicably, Madlin found herself cringing inwardly at the thought of causing the man any further discomfort. "No, that will not be necessary," she said hastily, then covered her show of discomposure. "Coming awake naturally from a blow such as you gave him is far better, is it not?"

Looking around for the location of the other men, Gordie lowered his voice so that only Madlin could hear him. " 'Tis not too late to change yer course, lass. 'Twould be an easy thing to slit his throat and be done with it."

Madlin shook her head. "Nay, Gordie. I've not changed my mind, though I know my decision will not be a popular one. I've thought and thought on it, and I can think of no other solution."

She looked off across the glen. Dusk was rapidly turning to

darkness. Here and there faint dots of light could be seen, marking the locations of nearby cottages. Everything looked so peaceful from this distance. But in her mind's eye she could see the many charred ruins where soft lights had once shone and happy voices had sounded from within.

"The killing must stop." She turned her attention back to her captive. Through the mist and fading light, she could see that he was well favored. Handsome, she was sure many a maid would say.

She let her gaze wander down his long length, appraising his build. He wasn't as thick-bodied as her father and Bram had been, but he was far from being a slight man. Divested now of the plate armor that had covered him, the heavy muscles that padded his limbs and torso were revealed. Even unconscious, he looked powerful.

An odd sensation at the base of her scalp prompted her to return her gaze to the man's face. He was awake, his eyes openly studying her. A mirthless smile turned up the corners of his wide, sensuous mouth.

"Well, pretty lass, are you one of Titania's handmaidens or mayhap the queen of the faeries herself, come to take me to the Unseelie Court? Or, a mere wench along to service yon ambushing scum?"

Growling deep in his throat, Gordie cuffed the man up the side of his head. "Mind yer tongue, man," he warned. "Or, I'll be cuttin' it out of ye. 'Tis the lady Madlin MacKendrick, laird of the Dunfionn MacKendricks, who stands before ye."

Ewan struggled to his feet. He was sure that the blow to his head had addled his brains or at the very least affected his hearing. "The laird?" Boldly, he assessed her from head to toe. "Lady Madlin . . . MacKendrick?"

Tall and with an appearance of strength, she was more woman than he'd ever encountered. Her hair, a crimson mass loosely plaited into a thick rope, fell to her waist. Despite the spark of anger in her large eyes, the belligerence of her chin, and the stern set of her wide mouth, her face was lovely. Her breasts were high and full. Her hips, gently flaring, were decidedly feminine, as were her incredibly long legs. Her only garment, as far as he could tell, was a saffron shirt whose tails were tied together between her legs, the hem falling inches shy of her knees.

If he were a man given to superstition, he would have been sure his jest was close to the mark. Faery queen, nay. Before him stood the embodiment of the warrior queens of old.

Could the MacKendrick have two daughters? Surely this was not the woman his king had suggested he marry. If she were, then Jamie's information was sadly incorrect. This woman was the antithesis of the gentle, convent-bred lass James had described.

She was an ill-mannered, uncultured barbarian.

She was stunning.

He cursed his man's flesh for reacting to her appeal.

Heedless of the warning he'd been given, he scoffed then spat on the ground. "I see no lady, but a half-naked hoyden before me. Hardly the leader of a clan, even one so dishonorable and beggarly as the MacKendricks of Dunfionn."

Without warning, the woman's open palm caught him on the side of the head. Closing her fists, she began raining blows about his shoulders and chest as she railed at him. "Dishonorable? You, a Fraser, dare call the MacKendricks dishonorable? Neither you nor any of your kin know the meaning of honor! If any MacKendrick be beggared 'tis clan Fraser who has made him so."

Staggering from the surprisingly powerful assault, Ewan was thankful when the one-eyed man pulled the screeching virago away from him. The painful ringing in his head was now a loud clanging that threatened to bring him to his knees. He was saved that ignominy when his arms were roughly grabbed by a man on either side of him. One of them gruffly suggested, "We'll hear yer apology now, Fraser, or 'twill go even worse for ye and yer man."

Having previously assured himself that Lucais, save for being bound and gagged, was none the worse for wear, Ewan looked to him again. Lucais had been hauled to his feet and was being held much as he was with a man on either side. Furthermore, a man was pressing a dirk to his throat.

"Apologize, Fraser," prompted a man at his side. "And ye best be quick about it. There is not a man here who wouldna be glad to spill some Fraser blood."

In the scant light, Ewan could see a black droplet form on the tip of the dirk held at Lucais's throat. Though it felt like bitter gall in his throat, he said, "I beg your pardon, madam . . . I mean, my lady."

A painful jerk of his arms forced him to expand with, "I recant my condemnation of the clan MacKendrick. Plainly all is not as I'd expected it would be here in the Highlands. I've been away a long time. Obviously much has changed since I was a lad."

Deciding that pleading ignorance was the most direct way of finding the cause of the dispute between the clans, he asked, "Mayhap you could enlighten me as to what has happened to cause clan MacKendrick to do more than steal Fraser lasses, sheep, and cattle?"

"Later, Fraser. We've not the time." With a slight wave of her hand, the woman signaled her men to lower the dirk and ease their hold on the other captive. Sparing him not so much as a glance, she gave orders that they were to be on their way.

Despite her magnificence and the way the men followed her orders, Ewan was still disbelieving that a woman was the chieftain of any clan. But he had spied enough identifying green and black plaids to believe the band was made up of MacKendricks.

Or . . . so they would have him believe.

Suspicious that all was not as it appeared, he looked for a face similar to his own, a cockade or plaid someone had forgotten to exchange for that of the MacKendricks, anything that would give the jest away. He saw none.

But, remembering childhood pranks instigated by his brothers strengthened his belief that all was not as it seemed. What else but a prank played upon him by his brothers would explain this ambush? Who in the MacKendrick camp could have possibly known of his return and staged such a perfect capture?

Expecting to see the grinning face of any or all of his brothers emerging from the dense underbrush any minute, he began to laugh. The sound was deep and full, filling the clearing and echoing off the ancient rocks and trees that stood sentinel around it. He tried to shrug off the strong hands that still held him immobile.

"Leave off this charade," Ewan ordered. "Niall. Keith? Come out and show your gloating faces, for you've indeed bested me. Be warned, I'll plot a fitting retribution, but so glad am I to be home that I'll give you a sennight's grace before you must be on your guard."

When no man's voice, familiar or unfamiliar, offered a retort of any kind, Ewan laughed again. "Come now, brothers. Is it the twins then? Have my wee brothers grown so daring that they would meet their brother thus for the first time? Show yourselves and have your men unbind me so I can enjoy this comely wench you've been parading before me."

He grinned, his straight white teeth shining brightly in the twilight. He mistook the shudder that rippled through her as a tremor of anticipation or a reaction to the cold wind blowing across the glen. "It will not be long, sweetling, before you'll have more of a man than just his shirt to keep you warm."

His remark earned him not the laughter he expected. The men on either side of him wrested his arms back even farther, and the pain of near shoulder separation had him gasping.

"Leave off, Fraser," the older of the two men growled in his ear. "This be a virtuous lass who stands before ye. 'Tis the lady Madlin's determination to bring peace between the MacKendricks and that traitorous bunch of cutthroats ye claim as yer kin that be keeping ye alive. Left to me, I'd slip my dirk between yer ribs and throw ye over the cliff for the buzzards to find. Same as yer kin done to the lass's father and brothers."

Sickened not so much by pain but by the reality that the strife between the two clans had grown so serious, Ewan feigned innocence, still hoping for more information. "There's war between the clans?"

"Nay. War has not been declared . . . yet," the woman said quietly as she shook out the length of wool one of her men had brought to her.

Ewan felt some relief and a surge of hope. If war had not yet been declared, surely negotiations toward peace could be accomplished in a timely and successful manner. The likelihood of presenting that peace to James next spring seemed possible. Presenting the MacKendrick wench as his wife? Not even an earldom was enough to entice him to marry such a she-devil.

If he'd humiliated this Lady Madlin with his remarks, she did not show it as she busied herself securing the length of green and black wool about her slender waist with a simple braided leather girdle. When she was through, the plaid was arranged in semblance of a skirt and reached modestly to her ankles. He found he was sorry she'd covered up those shapely legs.

"I know my enemy. Your capture will prevent any more attacks," she said as she pinned one end of the plaid at her shoulder with a heavy brooch.

Even knowing that any further taunts would probably cost him, Ewan could not still his tongue. " 'Tis a fool that leads clan MacKendrick, then, if she thinks my sire will stand by idly if I am taken hostage. Glendarach will declare war, burn every MacKendrick field, and level Dunfionn in retaliation for such an insult."

Surprisingly, the woman signaled that no retaliatory punishment was to come for his latest remarks. Nor did she fly at him again for having called her a fool. Instead, she calmly mounted the leggy chestnut mare that had been brought to her.

From her perch upon her horse, she looked down at him and laughed softly. "I think not, Ewan Fraser. Cameron Fraser takes care of his own."

Matching her calm delivery, Ewan declared, "One man's life, even if that man be his son, will not stop the Fraser from seeking vengeance on an insult such as this."

"Aye, the Fraser has the luxury of many sons. He can afford to lose one or two. Still, I do not think he'll want to pay such a price for vengeance alone. He will negotiate for you."

"Never! As soon as word reaches him of my capture, he will surround Dunfionn with a force great enough to render it rubble. You would have more time to stock and fortify it if you killed me here and now, for he'll not attack you till I've been mourned and buried."

"Do you seek death so recklessly then that you advise me so?"

"Nay, lady. I but prefer a quick end to a long, suffering one. I have seen what happens to those within when a castle is under siege. Though I do not know the strength of Dunfionn's walls, nor the extent of her stores, I do know my sire's will and the strength of his resources." Ewan stated these words with a bravado he hoped was not falsely based. If MacKendrick circumstances had so dramatically changed that a woman was at the clan's head, what changes might the years have wrought in his sire and the rest of the Frasers of Glendarach?

Not allowing his doubts to color his speech, he asserted, "The Fraser will summon enough men from the clan and her allies to keep Dunfionn surrounded for months, if necessary. If you were so foolish as to attempt to outlast him, there would be none left strong enough to protect you when he chooses to storm your gates."

Kneeing her horse closer to him, she asked, "The Fraser's allies? How came the Bairds, the Grants, and the MacMhuiriches to be allied with clan Fraser?"

Frowning, Ewan looked up at her. Surely an explanation was unnecessary. Was the woman so dense that she did not understand the most basic of Highland alliances?

"Why does any clan ally itself with another? Through mutual need. Marriages."

"Marriages," the lady repeated as she dismounted and walked briskly toward him. "Remember that, Fraser, for 'tis the reason your fate has already been determined. By dawn, you and I will be wed." Rising on her toes, she sealed the vow with a kiss.

Ewan's senses barely registered the brush of her lips against his. Shaking his head slightly to test that he was indeed conscious, he took measure of the flame-haired woman who was calmly mounting her horse once again. Hitherto, she had seemed sane. Misguided, undoubtedly, but sane.

How very wrong he had been in estimating her abilities. Madlin of Dunfionn was utterly and completely mad. Everything within him cried nay! at the prospect of marrying her.

Gently, so as not to rattle whatever sensibility might remain within her head, Ewan cajoled with all the charm he could muster. "My lady Madlin, leave off this foolishness. Women do not kidnap men for husbands. Surely you do not mean what you said."

"Nay, Fraser, I mean every word. We will be wed. You have said that clan Fraser has allied itself to others through marriage. An alliance between us will end the bloodletting."

Shifting the reins to one hand, she pointed a finger at Ewan. "You, Cameron Fraser's son, will pay the debt his clan owes ours. From your loins will spring the sons we need to ensure Toirlach's line."

By the angry mutterings among her men, Ewan surmised that she'd sprung this announcement on them with as little warning as she had granted him. Yet no one stepped forward to gainsay her.

With a curt nod, she guided her mount to the edge of the clearing. "Hamish. Colin. Take his horses and as many men as you need and make for Dunfionn.

"Hugh. Gordie. See that the prisoners are bound fast and mounted. The rest of you decide if you will follow me. Since the bishop was called back to the cathedral shortly before we left, it's to the monastery by the Moray I'm headed. I would have this marriage sanctioned as quickly as possible. I welcome your escort, for I may have need of it, but I shall not fault any who choose to return directly to Dunfionn."

A murmur rippled through all save the one-eyed man and the red-bearded giant who seemed always near his side. By the looks on the rest of the men's faces, there were many who would prefer seeking the comfort and safety of Dunfionn before the night was long. However, a glare from the one-eyed man and a threatening gesture from his compatriot quelled Ewan's hopes that any of the woman's forces would be deserting her.

"Madame, leave off this foolishness." Hopeful that he could dissuade the woman from her ludicrous plan, Ewan tried one last ploy. "If you are indeed the lady Madlin, only surviving heir of Toirlach MacKendrick, a baron of Scotland, then are you not a ward of the court? Is it not the responsibility and the duty of our sovereign to find a suitable match for you?" he asked, though theirs was exactly the suitable match their sovereign had suggested.

On the strength of the love their king claimed to bear him, Ewan was sure James would not expect him to marry this woman once her character was made clear to him. "Do you dare brave James's wrath in contracting a marriage without his approval?"

She appeared to consider his words briefly before announcing, "Our king has much to occupy him since he has taken back his throne. When news of this marriage and the subsequent alliance that will follow reaches him, I've complete faith that he will approve. An alliance between our two clans poses no threat to his power, but it will stop the bloodshed here. Jamie Stewart can be naught but thankful for that."

"But, noblewomen do not kidnap men for husbands!" Ewan declared again as he was being thrown upon a small shaggy Highland pony.

"This noblewoman does, if it means she can stop a war between her clan and another." Without sparing him another glance, she turned her mount toward the path leading across the glen.

When a stream of defiant protestations, punctuated with curses, started up from the golden-haired knight, the Mac-Kendrick ordered her captive gagged.

Chapter Four

The steel flashed ominously in the dawn light struggling through the high, narrow window of the tiny chancel. A sharply honed dirk once again threatened Lucais Fraser's throat. The gag at last removed, Ewan was thrust before the altar, his wrists still firmly bound behind his back.

"Is it marriage vows or last rites the priest should be saying?" growled the red-bearded giant at Ewan's back.

Despite the blade at his throat, Lucais protested, "Do not do it, my lord."

Ewan nodded grimly toward his man. "Nay, Lucais, I'll not see you martyred." His features hardened when he turned his gaze toward the woman who stood nearby. "Madam, I yield."

Unwavering beneath the fury blazing from his blue eyes, Madlin's voice was low but firm. "A sensible choice, Fraser." Signaling for the knife to be lowered from Lucais's throat, she turned her attention to the black-robed figure huddled between two of her men.

Pale and visibly shaken, the shriveled man who'd been roughly roused from his slumbers was a far cry from the impressive figure her half brother made in his bishop's robes. Those few times she'd given marriage any thought, Madlin had always envisioned Francis performing her marriage rites at Dunfionn's chapel or even in the great hall before all the clan. Still, the simple priest would have to do, for she could not wait for Francis's return from Beauly.

Clasping her pendant, she repeated to herself the last line

of the runes—Trust in Yourself—before striding to her intended's side. "You may start now, Father."

The little man surprised all, forcibly stating, " 'Tis sacrilege to threaten lives within God's holy place. Ye blaspheme the sacrament of marriage in so forcing this man's acquiescence to your demands. It'll not be valid, this marriage. The man must say his vows of his own free will. I'll have no part of this travesty."

Madlin did not back down but stepped closer to the priest and fixed him with a glare that would have done her father proud. "Only the man?"

When the priest started to open his mouth to answer, Madlin cautioned, "Do not risk your soul with a lie upon your lips in this holy place, Father. All here know of the many lasses who have been dragged before this very altar and forced to repeat the vows under threats no less fearsome than a dirk to their throats. If a marriage is not valid when one or both of the parties are not willing, then 'tis certain bastards abound in all of Scotland."

The priest had the grace to look down, studying his shifting feet. More gently, he said, "Daughter, leave off this course, for surely forcing this man by threat of immediate death to himself and his companion shall condemn you and all your men's souls to eternal damnation."

" 'Tis lives that concern me most," Madlin stated firmly. "But I take full responsibility for the actions of this night and morning. If any soul is to be damned for all eternity, let it be mine alone."

"I shall rest easily knowing only my lifetime will be damned," Ewan announced, a bitter tightness about his mouth.

He saluted Madlin with as courtly a bow as he could manage with his hands bound behind his back. "I thank you, my lady, for taking it upon yourself to assure that my soul shall not suffer in the hereafter."

A travesty of a smile flickered at the corner of his lips, and his eyes were dark and cold as he vowed, "I shall look forward to that blissful time."

"Beware, Fraser, or that bliss may be soon in coming," the red-haired man behind him grumbled, brandishing a dirk in one of his beefy hands.

Sending both men a warning glare to be silent, Madlin returned her attention to the priest. Good. The cleric was cowed by the host of large armed men filling the chapel. Still, the arguments he had found the courage to voice indicated he possessed a certain amount of stubbornness. It would not do if he were to cling to his righteous indignation much longer. Her threat to have the throats of her captives slit would be found out for the bluff it was, and all would be lost.

She softened her tone. "Do you not ken, Father, that this union may save the lives of many?" For good measure, she loosed the leather pouch at her waist and extended it toward the priest. "To help you and your brothers with the good works you do here."

Taking the pouch, the priest weighed it briefly in his hand, setting the coins within jingling. His brows rose as he judged the worth of the contents before quickly tucking the pouch in his robes.

Quickly making the sign of the cross, he nodded his assent. "Your generosity shall not go unrewarded, daughter. We shall pray for the success of your noble sacrifice as well as for your soul."

Madlin kept her smile to herself as she bowed her head. She did not doubt that her "generosity" would be blessed far more than her soul or her "noble sacrifice" in the months to come. But it was not for her own glory that she had so graciously gifted the monastery with the pouch of gold and silver coins lifted from her captive's saddle packs. If this marriage saved the living from early graves, she'd willingly empty Dunfionn's coffers and consider the sum a small price to pay.

"Thank you, Father," she murmured, carefully keeping the triumph from her voice.

But the priest had one more show of reluctance and courage. "Surely the bridegroom will not remain bound."

Carefully, Madlin assessed the wisdom of ordering the

cords cut away from her captive's wrists. Ewan Fraser was a formidable man. He was tall and powerfully built with muscles well hewn by years of battle. And he was very angry, so angry that only a fool would not think him dangerous.

Still, she credited him with more sense than to attempt either escaping or harming her. Half a score of heavily armed MacKendricks lined the interior of the little chapel. The remainder were stationed outside with a handful scattered at various lookout points on the chance that the Frasers had been alerted and might attempt a rescue or an attack.

Yielding to the priest's request, Madlin ordered that Ewan's hands be unbound. As an added measure of safety, she shrugged the bow and quiver of arrows from her shoulder and handed them to Gordie. The small sword tucked in her girdle followed as well as the *skean-dhu*, the knife she kept in her boot. Thus, totally disarmed, she once again took up her position beside her soon-to-be husband.

The vows binding her to this man for life were said quickly. At the end of the ceremony, Madlin began to turn away for she neither welcomed nor expected the "kiss of peace" from her groom. But the priest stayed her.

"More than any other I've performed, this union needs the blessing of prayers at its beginning. Do ye not agree, daughter?"

Reluctantly, Madlin gave the priest leave to proceed. Each hour that passed increased the danger of Frasers discovering her and her band far away from MacKendrick lands. Yet she had to agree that further appeals to the Almighty for the success of her union with Ewan Fraser could not come amiss.

Not waiting for her new husband, she made the sign of the cross, knelt, and joined her hands in a semblance of prayer. An abrupt movement beside her indicated that her husband had been reluctantly forced into a kneeling position.

While the priest's voice droned over her, Madlin tried to pray. Looking beyond the altar, she concentrated on the figure of the Virgin Mary tucked into a niche. In her heart, Madlin appealed, "Blessed Mother, surely you must understand."

Och, what hae ye done this time, lassie?

Startled, for a moment Madlin thought the voice had come from the little statue. But it was not a divine response from the Virgin, only a remembered echo of the query she'd heard from Sister Agatha each time the goodly woman had escorted her to the office of Mother Liusadh.

Madlin asked herself, Indeed, what have I done this time? She closed her eyes again. Despite her fears of detection by the Frasers, Madlin hoped the priest would be long-winded in his appeals to the Almighty. She needed whatever time the priest might provide for her to collect both her faith and her thoughts.

As she'd learned under Liusadh Gunn's tutelage, Madlin removed herself from where she was. Instead of a chilly chapel on a cliff overlooking the sea, she was at Dunfionn. She no longer heard the priest nor the roar of the sea. Her father's deep laugh and the lighter laughter of her brothers played like music through her heart.

"Would I could hear them again," Madlin said to herself, the pain of the memory when last she'd looked upon their still, pale faces breaking her concentration. It had been nighttime in a small chapel, not too unlike the one where she knelt now.

Beside the three biers holding her father and brothers, she'd prayed for hours on the cold, hard stone in Dunfionn's chapel. Prayers for their souls and prayers for strength and guidance. Most of all, she'd prayed for a way to bring about an honorable peace between her clan and the clan Fraser. No solution had come to her, nothing until some of her men had returned from a trading trip to Dundee.

The port city had been filled with the latest arrival of soldiers recalled from France. Among them had been a large contingent who'd served under a Sir Ewan Fraser. Her men had purposefully lingered to discover all they could about the Fraser knight, especially if and when he might be returning to Glendarach. Only the urgency for the goods they'd been sent to purchase had hurried them back to Dunfionn before the knight had left Stirling. Else, to a man, the MacKendrick trading party had vowed they would have waited and ambushed this Fraser somewhere along the road between Stirling and the Highlands.

With a shudder of foreboding for the days ahead, Madlin opened her eyes. She chanced a glance toward the man kneeling beside her. Was this marriage the answer to her long prayers offered during that night of vigil beside her loved ones' biers?

She pledged that she would do all she could to assure that it was. The vows were said. There was no turning back from the course she'd set weeks ago.

The morning's light was growing stronger as it streamed through the chancel window. It shimmered on the gold of Sir Ewan's hair and glittered upon the silvery mail that covered his shoulders and torso. Such a glow of light surrounded him, she almost thought him a divine vision.

He's but a man, she reminded herself quickly, lest she fall prey to the ethereal image created by the sunlight reflecting off metal. Mortal like any other, and foolish at that!

Only a fool would enter the Highlands imprisoned in a full suit of armor such as the one he'd worn clanking through the Grampians. The sound had given them plenty of time to be in place to waylay his crossing of MacKendrick territory. If news of his son's foolishness got out, Sir Cameron Fraser would be the laughingstock of the Highlands, mayhap all of Scotland. And she, the MacKendrick, new laird of Dunfionn, had married this fool.

Och, what hae ye done, lassie? She heard Sister Agatha's words in her heart again.

I've married a fool, was the confession she made in her mind.

Nay, daughter. He's not a fool, and you must learn to trust yourself.

So clear were the remarks, Madlin nearly bolted to her feet in shock. Nervously, she looked again to the man kneeling beside her. His head was bowed, and his eyes were still closed. It was a pose of prayer, but Madlin was certain he was no more beseeching God for guidance and peace than she had been. Marriage or not, it was more probable that he was using the time to plot his escape. If their positions had been reversed, she surely would have been reviewing every possibility for escape.

Above her she sensed the priest making the sign of the cross and heard him intone, *"Dominus vobiscum, amen."* Bidding the newly wedded couple to rise, the priest smiled wanly at them. "May God bless this union that it be fruitful and a comfort to you both." The priest's hurried tone indicated the words of benediction were prompted merely by habit.

Turning, she faced her new husband. The hatred she saw in his eyes sent a shiver through her. Knowing much of men's pride, she attempted to soften the blow she had dealt him. "If there had but been another way."

"A man worthy of leadership would have found one," he said quietly through gritted teeth.

Stung, she managed defensively, "A man would—"

"Not have been so foolish as to sentence himself to a lifetime of hell. Pray that yours is a short lifetime, for you'll find no comfort in this union, my lady wife. May God have mercy on your soul, for I never shall!"

Any response Madlin might have had the wits to offer would have been lost beneath the roar of her men as they bellowed their rage at the threat to their chieftain. The rough benches that served as pews toppled and tumult reigned as her men moved toward her new husband.

Gordie, having stationed himself but a few feet away, was the first to reach him. Enraged, he had Ewan Fraser locked in his bearlike arms and a dirk cutting into his flesh before Madlin's cry reached through his consciousness. Stopping himself just barely before the deed was finished, Gordie lifted the knife so that Ewan could see the droplets of blood beading along its edge.

"Remember, 'twas yer lady wife that saved ye from spilling yer life's blood upon this altar. If ye should ever harm even so little as a single hair upon her head, by the holy rood, I vow ye'll nay live out the day."

The Fraser merely lifted one brow before calmly addressing them all. "I'll not harm her."

Far from appeased by his vow, the MacKendricks remained ready to spring upon him at the slightest provocation. Gathering up courage as well as his robes, the little priest stepped gingerly before the new groom. "If you value your life, repeat that vow upon the blood of Saint Peter," he said as he thrust a silver reliquary toward the Fraser's lips.

From his expression, the Fraser knight's skepticism that the blood of Christ's disciple had actually found its way through the centuries to this tiny chapel could not have been expressed more clearly. Nonetheless, he kissed the offered reliquary and vowed, "By this holy relic, I vow I'll not harm my . . . wife, the lady Madlin, the MacKendrick of Dunfionn."

Despite having a bishop in the clan, the MacKendricks were more superstitious than true believers. Still, such a vow made upon a powerful holy relic forced them to relax, if only slightly. Reluctantly, they sheathed their weapons and quieted their threats.

With a smile that did not reach his eyes, the new bridegroom turned his gaze upon the bride he had just vowed not to harm. Boldly, his eyes assessed her from the top of her head to her feet, then back again, to rest clearly upon the full breasts heaving slightly beneath the layer of linen and wool. "You are an enticing wench, but I do not intend to ever cause you even the slightest twinge of pain."

Madlin felt the warmth of relief with his promise not to harm her, for she'd dared not let herself dwell on the time when she would have to be alone with this very angry man.

The gooseflesh that rose upon her skin was surely based on fear, was it not? Surely it was relief to know that she would be able to take her rest without fear of a dirk slicing her throat. Then why did she feel a creeping unease that the victory she thought was in her grasp had somehow been snatched away?

Her new husband was grinning at her, and there was no mistaking his look of triumph. Puzzled, she looked for some explanation from Gordie and then Hugh.

His face turning as red as his beard, Hugh was studying the heavy rafters above him with inordinate interest while nervously shifting his feet. Gordie's one eye was far wider than usual, and his neck had begun to redden as if he, too, were . . . embarrassed?

Madlin started to mouth a query for an explanation, but her new husband spoke first. His grin turning snide, his tone silky, he inquired, "Could it be that the laird of clan MacKendrick has not thought out every detail of this retribution? Might I be so bold as to ask if impetuosity is a trait in my bride's character?"

The accusation stung so that Madlin quickly cried, "Nay, Fraser. Not a detail of this action was left to chance. In truth, 'tis a sacrifice I make and one offered not without great thought."

But even as she mouthed the defense of her actions, doubt sent her mind racing through every detail, searching for the flaw the Fraser seemed so sure was there. Impetuousness had ever been her downfall as a child, but she had learned to control it at St. Margaret's. Nay, impetuousness played no part in this decision.

Upon hearing what the trading party had learned of the returning Fraser son, she had spent a full sennight of days and nights thinking on how best to put the information to good use. When she'd settled upon a plan of capture and then marriage, she'd thought it through from every angle before proposing it to Gordie. Following that, she'd spent hours arguing, pleading, and finally convincing him. More time had been spent doing the same with Hugh. This was a decision more thought out than any she'd made in her lifetime.

Watching her, Ewan could almost hear her mind working. Hers was an open face, so different from the women he had consorted with in the past years.

Female Burgundian spies had heavily populated the Armagnac court. Early on, he'd discovered bed sport the best means of extracting information from them. But even naked and bucking beneath him, each had been plotting. If there had been any honesty at all in those liaisons, it was that each participant was using the other for a purpose beyond the physical satisfaction of the moment.

Had the circumstances of their meeting been different, Ewan knew he might well appreciate this apparent guilelessness about his new bride. Still, his experiences cautioned him to wonder. Was she as innocent as her puzzlement would indicate?

Sensing that the one-eyed man was about to explain the gaping error in her plan, Ewan cleared his throat. Whether it was a need for further vengeance or a sense of duty toward the woman who was his wife, he knew not. All he knew was that everything within him cried out that he should be the one doing the explaining.

"Madam, you may have wrenched the vows from me this morn, and you may still force my hand to a parchment attesting thus, but I'll not be a proper husband to you."

Seeing apparent innocence still in those wide green eyes, he fought against being beguiled. More harshly, he added, "I promise that you'll not feel the pain of a first taking or have any cause to shed virgin's blood on the sheets of a bed you think to share with me. Untried and intact you shall remain as long as you persist in this travesty of a marriage!"

Disdainfully, he eyed the skirt she'd fashioned from a plaid. Not reaching her ankles, it was a reminder of the way she'd been dressed, or rather undressed, when he'd first laid eyes upon her. A red rage flooded through him at the idea that this woman, his wife, should have regularly gallivanted about the countryside half-naked with a band of men. He rejected the immediate thought that this feeling of flaming rage was prompted by jealousy that all these men had seen his bride's bare legs and that some might have lain between her long, supple limbs. Surely his rage was for having had a harlot foisted upon him to wife.

Putting voice to the latter, he stated, "Openly displaying so much of your voluptuous charms whilst riding about the countryside in the company of men, 'tis questionable whether you are a virgin, still, and not already ripening with some other man's get you think to pass off as mine!"

His words had barely passed through his lips before Madlin's palm cracked against his cheek. "How dare you!" Her cry rose above the deeper roars of outrage from her men. A heavy cuff to his jaw from one of her men sent him to his knees with his head ringing painfully anew.

Through the din, Ewan could hear the thin shrill voice of the priest protesting the violence until the pounding in his head was joined by the torturous pain in his shoulders as his arms were wrenched behind him once again. The sights and sounds around him blurred while nausea threatened. He swallowed hard lest he embarrass himself. When his vision cleared he counted no less than a half dozen blades pointing toward his heart.

"The lady Madlin is a virtuous lass, and ye'll be losing yer tongue and then yer miserable hide, strip by strip, if ye do not beg her forgiveness afore ye pull another breath," the one-eyed man threatened.

Regretting not his accusation but that a refusal to apologize would undoubtedly end Lucais's life shortly after he'd been dispatched, Ewan managed between teeth gritted against the pain raging through his body, "I beg your pardon, my lady."

Though still angered by his vulgar remarks, Madlin regretted having struck him once again. Something deep within her rebelled against the humility forced upon the golden-haired knight on his knees before her. He was a Fraser, and for that alone she should hate him.

But Malcolm, Duncan, and Colley had told not only of the knight's return to the Highlands but the tales of him that circulated through the alehouses of Dundee. Many in the latest wave of soldiers recalled had been directly under Sir Ewan Fraser's command.

Their tongues loosened with ale and a good many drams of *uisge beatha* as well, the soldiers had painted glowing pictures of Sir Ewan's valor in battle, his devotion to his men, and the genuine concern and care he'd taken with his wounded, whether they had been noble or common. They related how, during their last battle, Verneuil, he'd suffered a sword in his own leg while blocking the back of a simple bowman.

Malcolm and the others had scoffed at the soldiers' tales, saying soldiers are always wont to bring glory upon themselves by glorifying their commanders.

Despite all her men's assertions that all the Fraser knight's glorious deeds were but false tales, Madlin was not so sure. An instinct within her told her there had been more truth than invention in the stories, and an ache developed within her breast that a warrior such as Sir Ewan Fraser should be so humbled and tortured.

Honor in all things. The welfare of the clan from the youngest and weakest to the oldest and most feeble must come first.

Her father's teachings pounded within her head. As a result of the ceremony just performed, Ewan Fraser was now a member of clan MacKendrick.

"Release him."

Gordie and the other men, each recipients in turn of the infamous MacKendrick glare, slowly stepped back, tucking their weapons away but with obvious reluctance.

Rising once again to his feet, Ewan struggled to keep from swaying. He was loath to show any weakness to the assembled, but he could not resist rubbing his shoulders and then his injured thigh.

He felt alternately chilled and overheated. James's physicians had warned him the fever might return if he did not leave himself in their care for another sennight. Damn the saints and the frailty of his own body, but he needed all his wits and strength.

Watching the lady Madlin standing so regally in the center

of the chapel, he could not disavow a certain admiration for her. She was most definitely in command and had secured the loyalty of her men.

A female laird. He could scarce credit such an oddity, but that she was, or so her men claimed, and he was married to her. How Jamie Stewart would laugh if this tale should ever reach his royal ears.

Hands on her hips, chin held high, Madlin announced, "Hear me and mark my words. No more harm shall come to Sir Ewan. He is your laird's husband and an honored knight of Scotland as well."

"Honored? A Fraser? Pah!" These and other angry denouncements of clan Fraser rumbled throughout the chapel until the lady raised a hand to silence her men.

"He was born a Fraser, but that is his only crime against our clan. Since mine is the higher title, henceforth he will be known as Sir Ewan MacKendrick. My sons will be MacKendricks no less so than if they had been sired by either of my fallen brothers."

Turning to the stunned priest, she directed, "Write my husband's name thus, priest, when you inscribe the parchment."

"You take my freedom and my name!" Ewan took a step toward his bride but stopped himself even before her men reached for him. Never had he thought himself even remotely capable of stooping so low as to strike a woman. He would not allow this vixen to diminish him even further.

"You dare too much, lady wife," he said, sorely tempted to tell her then and there that he had been endowed with a title equal to hers. Ironically, she had made it possible that he would be granted one far higher come the spring.

He glanced toward Lucais and warned him with a slight shake of his head not to divulge his new rank. If he was going to learn what was necessary to diffuse this war between the clans, he needed not the impediment of distance that his rank and friendship with the king might produce. No matter that the lady thought to thrust her surname upon him, just being born a Fraser would make his task difficult enough.

"I dare what I must, husband. I would have your parole here and now before this priest as witness and sworn upon the saint's blood you swore upon earlier."

"My parole? You jest, madam. By my honor as a knight, I cannot agree to freely remain anyone's captive. 'Tis my duty to attempt freedom."

"In times of war," was her cool reply.

"And this is not war, this hostility between your clan and mine?"

"My clan is now your clan, husband," she returned smoothly. "As of moments ago, there will be no more hostilities waged upon clan Fraser from any member of clan MacKendrick. Sir Ewan MacKendrick née Fraser, you will find clan MacKendrick does not make war within itself. Do not think to be the first MacKendrick to blot our honor by doing so."

She stepped closer to him. "Consider well before you think to deny pledging me your parole, for 'tis not only your life that would be forfeit but that of many Frasers. Until this time, we have not exacted revenge in kind upon clan Fraser for the many atrocities they have enacted upon us.

"But if you should escape or harm any MacKendrick, I will send the fiery cross through our lands and those of our allies. War will be declared, and there will be more new graves in the Fraser churchyard than there are now in the MacKendricks'. The peace is in your hands, husband."

There was much he would have liked to have said, but fearing his own temper, Ewan merely asked, "And the Frasers? Do you think by magic they will not continue to raid upon your clan?"

"Your man will be released to carry the news of our marriage to your sire, along with an invitation to spend Hogmany in celebration at Dunfionn. 'Twould be fitting, think you not, that the new year be welcomed with the celebration of our alliance?"

The wench's naïveté, or mayhap it was audacity, was beyond anything. "He'll not do it." He scoffed. "For certes, it will be a celebration if ever Cameron Fraser enters Dunfionn's hall, but not one you and your MacKendricks will rejoice in!"

She smiled impudently. "He'll come, and it will be a festive occasion for both clans."

Chapter Five

An hour had passed since the last downpour drenched the weary riders winding their way inland. Shining brightly from its zenith, the sun's rays bounced off the rain droplets still clinging to the pine boughs and then danced upon the pools the rain had left in the track.

Birds sang from the trees and glided through the blue sky above. Coming so late in autumn, such a day was a gift, all the more precious as it could well be the last before the snow and ice of winter settled over the Highlands.

Here and there, a man dozed in his saddle, trusting his mount to pick its way along the track. Those awake spoke little, too weary or too sore of heart to engage in the playful banter that usually marked the return from a mission unmarred by mishap.

Her eyes so bleary from fatigue that she could scarcely see the trail ahead of her, Madlin rode at the column's head. Though every muscle and bone ached from so many hours astride a horse, she held her back straight and her chin up.

Her new husband rode beside her. Not a word had passed between them since they'd left the monastery at dawn.

Madlin chanced a glance in his direction and was immediately sorry she had. The way he held his back and the set of his mouth and jaw left no doubt that his rage for the circumstances she'd thrust upon him had not lessened.

His eyes were directed forward, but she didn't need to see them to know how much savage rage was reflected in their icy blue depths. A frisson of cold fear snaked down her back.

She'd seen that feral look only once before—in the eyes of the animal she and Airic had dragged home, snarling and snapping, the summer they'd turned nine.

They'd spotted the young creature near a small cave and had been sure they'd found the pup that had gone missing from a litter whelped by one of Dunfionn's hounds that spring. After days of leaving food to lure him ever closer, they'd finally been able to slip a rope around his neck. Proudly, they'd dragged the animal through the gates of Dunfionn. Instead of words of cheer or applause for a deed well done, every man, woman, and child they'd passed on the way to the kennels had fled.

Only their sire had stood his ground. Arms folded across his broad chest, his expression sober, he'd asked, "What plans have ye for this wolf ye've brought home?"

Stunned by their father's identification of the animal, it had been she who'd recovered first and brashly announced, "Why, we're going to tame him, Papa."

Thinking back to that day, she realized now how difficult it must have been for her father to show such calm while his young son and daughter struggled to control the savage animal between them. But he'd managed somehow as he'd gazed thoughtfully at Airic, then at the wolf, and finally at her.

" 'Tis a wild creature ye've brought into Dunfionn that could do much harm here before ye've tamed him. I'll ask ye to think on what's best for all who live within the safety of these walls and what's best for this animal ye've snatched away from his own kind."

She and Airic had learned their lessons too well. Immediately, they'd turned around and dragged the resisting wolf back through the gates. Near the cave where they'd captured him, they'd set him free.

Against her will, Madlin found herself comparing her new husband with that wolf. She wouldn't be literally dragging him through the gates of Dunfionn snarling and snapping at the end of a rope. Still, one look at his face and even the least astute person would know that he was entering Dunfionn against his wishes.

By now, the men she'd sent back with the destrier and pack-horses would have apprised everyone at Dunfionn that their laird had taken a Fraser to husband. When she rode through the gates, would there be some who would make the sign of the cross, snatch up their children, and rush to safety at the mere sight of a Fraser in their midst? Despite her declaration that his surname would henceforth be MacKendrick, would there be any who would applaud or offer well wishes for her future with a man born a Fraser?

Madlin chanced another glance at her husband. His rage seemed not as apparent as before. Still, the way he held himself, she could not but wonder if he was indeed in possession of superhuman powers.

He, too, had lost a full night's sleep. He had spent even more of the previous day astride a horse than she and had suffered a strong blow to his head. Yet, despite all, he sat in the saddle with his back straight, his head erect, and his eyes open. He was a strong man in his prime, but how could even the strongest of men have this much endurance? That he was not human or somehow in possession of special powers seemed the only explanation.

Absently, she fingered her pendant. If a Fraser could hold himself so upright after a day and a night spent in the saddle, then so could she! She stiffened her back and set her chin more determinedly.

She was Madlin, Baroness of Dunfionn. The MacKendrick.

God's teeth, was the woman human?

Ewan's head pounded. His thigh burned. An ache had set in deep into his bones.

But for a dried-out bannock washed down with some water, he'd not eaten for more than a day. That had been hours ago during a brief respite the witch had granted. His mouth was dry, and his throat was parched. His belly felt as if a hot coal dwelled within.

The sun blazing overhead and the unseasonable heat of the day soothed when he was shaking with the chills of fever, and added to his vexations when he was not. He could barely keep his eyes open against the glare.

The weight of his chain mail made his shoulders ache. If his shoulder sockets weren't still so sore from the abuse they'd suffered the night before, he'd remove his hauberk, assuming he could move at all.

A pox on the bastard who chose this pony! Every jarring step the miserable beast took set off explosions in his head and shoulders. He doubted his injured leg would hold his weight if he were ever allowed off this cursed horse.

She hadn't slept either, not even dozed in the saddle for as much as a moment. How did she keep her seat, let alone hold her back so straight and keep that stubborn little chin up? She was like no noblewoman he'd ever known.

With her fine, straight nose, high cheekbones, and smooth creamy skin, none would ever mistake her for a peasant. Despite the stubborn line of her chin, she was quite beautiful, he supposed.

Red-haired females had never been to his taste, yet he could not help but admire the fiery mass shrouding her head. The winds and rains they'd endured throughout much of their trip had loosened most of her hair from the heavy braid stretching down the length of her back. A halo of fine gold-red curls now framed her face and called attention to the vulnerability of her slender neck.

As surreptitiously as possible, he studied her, particularly curious as to how far her braid stretched. His bride was a tall woman, but her braid brushed the saddle upon which she sat so proudly.

Unplaited, her hair would fall well below her hips. In red-gold splendor it would ripple across the fine linen of bed, brush like silk against his bare chest, his thighs, his groin. . . .

A new ache began pounding in his nether regions. To distract himself from the salacious bent of his thoughts, he shifted his gaze away from her hair.

Damn the woman!

If it wasn't her hair driving his lust, it was her enticing body. A man would have to be a eunuch not to imagine seeking his ease in her full bosom and flaring hips. Those long legs of hers could wrap around a man and hold him to her through the most vigorous coupling.

She was a witch! And despite the claims of her devoted men, she was more than likely a harlot! She'd taken his freedom, his future, even his very name!

The queen of the faeries could not be more enticing.

And she was the bride he'd vowed not to touch!

For the next league, he roundly cursed himself for the celibacy he'd imposed upon himself since leaving France, the rashly pronounced vow he'd made at the monastery, and the abnormal character of the woman riding beside him. He heaped the blame for his every pain, ache, and discomfort upon her shoulders.

A normal woman would have slumped long before now, fallen asleep. A normal woman would have whined about her discomforts and demanded a rest. And a normal woman, be she a peasant or a noblewoman, would not have kidnapped a man and forced him to marry her.

God's nightshirt! She'd not have the satisfaction of hearing him beg for rest. He was a battle-tested knight of Scotland and of France. He was a leader of men.

And, no matter what surname she declared for him, he was a Fraser. If Toirlach MacKendrick's daughter could stay in the saddle, so straight and proud, then so could Cameron Fraser's son!

At the rear of the column, Gordie tipped his face toward the sun, then squinted from the brightness. " 'Tis a good omen, I'm thinking. What say ye, Hugh?"

" 'Twill take more than one fine day to dry up this muck. Ye know it as well as me, Gordie Gunn. There will be a powerful foul odor before all's made right."

"An empty belly is making ye a prophet of gloom, Hugh

MacKendrick. Before the sun has finished its day's travel, ye'll have filled yer belly with so much food and drink, ye'll be toasting yon bride and her groom and leading the reels."

"Pah! Dancing? There'll be no merriment in Dunfionn's hall this night. Look up yonder at our lass and her new husband. Nary a word has passed between them since we took leave of the monastery. The lass is miserable, and the Fraser lad bears watching.

"I rode up there a while ago, and I tell ye, I dinna like the look in his eyes. Mark my words, no good will come of last night's business."

"*Whisht,* man!" Gordie leaned toward his friend and kept his voice low so the others could not hear. "The deed's been done. Ye had yer chance to talk her out of it and ye failed, same as me. 'Tis past time to be grumbling about it. The men are tired and in an ugly mood as it is. Best ye be thinking of something to make their hearts a bit lighter rather than feeding their miseries."

"Would ye have me play the fool?"

" 'Twould not be so hard for ye." Gordie's eye twinkled and a grin parted his bushy beard.

Hugh rode along in silence for several yards before he abruptly pulled his mount to a halt. Dismounting, he shouted, "Get down off yer pony, Gordie Gunn. We'll be having this out here and now."

Spitting on his palms, he curled his hands into fists then assumed a fighter's stance. "No man calls Hugh MacKendrick a fool."

From his mount, Gordie looked down upon his friend and shook his head wearily. "Get back on your pony, old man, before ye make a bigger fool of yerself than ye already are."

Signaling with an exaggerated wink, Hugh brandished his fists even more wildly. "Old man, am I?" he hollered and looked beyond Gordie to see if he'd caught the attention of the others. For good measure, he added in an even louder voice, "I'll be showing ye just who is the old man. Get down and fight me, ye one-eyed half-witted mucker."

Frowning until understanding dawned, Gordie leaped from his saddle with a roar. "Ye be needing some sense pounded into yer thick skull, ye great lummox!" he yelled as he swung toward Hugh's jaw, his fist brushing his friend's beard more than the solid chin beneath.

Hugh pretended to stagger and shook his head as if to clear it. Bellowing further insults, he lowered his head and ran toward Gordie. Catching him in the midriff, he knocked him off his feet. Quickly, before Gordie could recover his breath and defend himself, Hugh was upon him.

"The lads be gathering," he whispered into Gordie's ear. "A good fight ought to raise their spirits."

"Roll with me toward young Colley over there," Gordie whispered back. "The lad possesses a hot temper and has need of letting it loose more than most. We'll have us a rare, fine melee, soon enough."

The two old friends rolled around on the ground a short while longer, grunting insults at each other. Finally, they sprung to their feet and Gordie pulled back his arm and swung toward Hugh's jaw once again. Hugh ducked and Gordie's fist connected so forcefully with Colley's jaw, the younger man tumbled to the ground. Being a big man, Colley took the two men standing behind him down, too. Gordie and Hugh shared a grin. They could not have asked for more.

In the confusion that followed, the two instigators managed to make their way clear and obligingly relieved their remaining comrades of their duties guarding the Fraser knight's squire.

Holding the prisoner's horse's reins firmly in hand, Hugh leaned against a tree with a grin of satisfaction. "Ah 'tis a fine brawl the lads are having."

Gordie sighed contentedly. "They'll be bruised and bloodied some, but in far better humor for it."

His remark was answered by a sharp bark of laughter from their prisoner. "I'd doff my cap to ye, lads, if my hands were free," Lucais Fraser said with a merry grin. "I'm thinking 'twould be worth giving ye my parole, if ye was to free me and let me join in. I've not enjoyed a good friendly fray like yonder for a good long time."

Scratching his bearded chin, Gordie considered the prisoner's words for a moment, then squinted his eye at him in scrutiny. "I ken yer yearning and I'm thinking I ken you, Lucais Fraser. 'Twas more than a score of years, but were we not in a bit of a scuffle a time or two when we chanced upon a pack of Frasers trying to make away with a few MacKendrick sheep?"

"Aye, we scuffled, you and me, 'twas when we were a grand sight younger. I'd not forget a man as ugly as ye. I don't mind admitting ye gave as good as ye got. But 'twas MacKendricks doing the thieving," Lucais teased, then gave a regret-filled sigh. "It were better times between Frasers and MacKendricks than what I've brought my lad home to."

"Aye, that they were." Gordie could not stop the smile of remembrance, but he quickly sobered when images of the bloodied bodies of his fallen laird and his sons came to mind. "What spurred the Fraser to start burning and killing?"

Bristling, Lucais swore. "Could not have been himself that started it!"

"Was not the MacKendrick nor any of his clan!"

The two men's argument grew hotter as each defended his laird until Lucais shouted, "I'm offering ye my parole but ye'll be the first to feel the strength of my fist if ye take it!"

"I'll take it!" Gordie pulled his dirk from his boot and started toward the prisoner.

"Stay ye now, Gordie," Hugh cried, though he'd not missed the prisoner's eager expression. "We'd not be doing right by our prisoner if we was to let him join in."

"Ye have my word on my mother's grave I'll not try to escape," Lucais pleaded.

Hugh shook his head sorrowfully. "Nay, ye're my prisoner, and my honor as a MacKendrick would have me keep ye from harm."

"Yer honor as a MacKendrick! Ye're naught but afraid I'll bust that one's head open, maybe yers, too."

The challenge was too great. Hugh hesitated no longer before sawing through the leather bonds that held Lucais's hands behind his back. Ignoring the stiffness in his joints from the long ride, Lucais was off his pony in a thrice. He and Gordie, two old warriors, went at each other with as much vigor as the younger men in the rumpus close by.

Hugh thought to stay with the horses and stand as lookout, but his good intentions lasted only a minute before he, too, joined the melee.

At the head of the rapidly shortening column, Madlin was aware of nothing but the tense silence stretching between herself and her husband. If there was any hope of their marriage being accepted by the MacKendricks, she and Sir Ewan must not arrive at Dunfionn as enemies. Perhaps if she drew him out of his silence, the tension might ease some between them. Her cousin Jeanne was adept at conversation. More than once, Jeanne had told her it was an easy matter, naught but asking a person about himself, then sitting back and listening.

"Sir Ewan, you've been away for a long time. What adventures you must have had once you left the Highlands."

"Hmmph . . . adventures. War is not an adventure, madam."

Sobered immediately, she said, "I did not mean that war is an adventure, Sir Ewan. Too well do I understand that war means naught but death and destruction. Might I assume you hate war as much as I?"

"I cannot know what is in your heart, but I do hate war, and it was my fondest wish that I would see no more of it once I stepped on Scotland's shores."

He shifted slightly in the saddle. His chain mail reminded her of the plate armor that had encased his body when he'd been captured. "And yet you still wore the trappings of war when you arrived here in the Highlands. Why?"

"Habit, I suppose. I was warned that lawlessness does prevail throughout our land. Being ready to do battle seemed prudent."

She could not stop herself. A deep gurgle of laughter

erupted. "You have been away a long time. I venture you'll not be making that kind of mistake again."

"You laugh at me, lady?"

"No . . . I . . ." She lost her battle to be sober and laughed again. "I do beg forgiveness," she said when she could control herself. " 'Tis rare that we see a fully armored knight mounted upon a warhorse picking his way along tight and narrow trails. Up here, our warriors must be ready to fight on foot, and our ponies must be small and nimble to maneuver the terrain quickly. It was unfair to laugh at what was merely an act of honest ignorance."

"Ignorance? Now you would heap more indignity upon me by calling me ignorant?"

Madlin's breath caught at the sight of a real smile upon his face. How very handsome he was when he was not scowling. She would have to be careful lest he erase her thoughts with a mere smile. "Nay, sir, only ignorant of the ways of the Highlands."

"The ways of the Highlands," he repeated, then sent her another teasing grin. "Where the fighting is done half-naked and the women do not wait to be courted but capture hapless travelers and force them before a priest."

Madlin shrugged. "Most Highland women are courted." She looked away. "I had no such choice."

"And therefore you gave me none," he said, the bitterness returning in both his tone and countenance. "Your lineage is good, and you're not bad-looking; surely you have had suitors. Someone who could offer not only marriage but an alliance to strengthen your clan."

"None that would have assured peace so quickly."

"So you have had suitors, then?"

Suitors. The mere mention of the word made her cringe. A steady procession had presented themselves since she had ascended to the chieftainship of clan MacKendrick. Several had previously been turned down by her father during her years at St. Margaret's. Thinking her easier to persuade, they'd barely waited until her father was in his grave before presenting their suits directly to her. Upon meeting them, she'd understood her sire's reasoning and thanked God for his sound judgment of character.

Some had openly eyed her with lust. Others had coveted her lands and power. All had filled her with revulsion, and she'd unequivocally refused their offers. All but one had given up. Praise God that with her marriage to Ewan Fraser, Seamus Munro would finally desist in his senseless pursuit for her hand. She was as likely to sprout wings and fly as to ever consider marriage to the Munro.

"Aye, there have been suitors," she admitted. "Praise God this marriage will put a stop to all that as well as the hostilities between our clans."

"You are so very sure of that?"

"I have to be." She turned to look at him more fully, thinking to assure him of her honesty and sincerity. "I will—"

Out of the corner of her eye, she saw nothing. Alarmed, she turned her mount sharply. Her men were gone. The trail for as far as she could see was completely empty. She heard nothing save the rustle of a light breeze through the trees above and the piercing call of a kestrel in the sky.

While she'd been chattering blithely, her men must have been set upon. Captured one by one just as she'd captured Sir Ewan and his man—or had they suffered a worse fate? She dug her heels into Aisling's sides.

"Hold," Ewan shouted as he grabbed her mare's bridle and stopped her flight.

"Let me go! I must get to my men."

"Hold, I say," he ordered again. "You know not what you'll be riding into."

Instinctively, Madlin reached for her sword but found nothing. The weapons she'd shed at the monastery were still in Gordie's possession. With her husband's continued refusal to give his word that he'd not attempt to escape, she'd not wanted to chance his disarming her during the long ride from the coast. "Would you have me cry craven and wait here while my men are fighting for their lives?"

"Nay, I but suggest caution," he told her, his eyes burning into her with cold intensity. "You will be of little use to them if you ride unarmed into ambush and are taken prisoner or felled."

"I should think you would be glad of such an outcome, for then you would be free of me," she cried, daring him to rise to her taunt.

"I am a knight, and you are a woman. I do not take my vows lightly."

"Nor do I, Fraser. I have vowed that my clan's well-being comes before my own. Loose your hold!" Leaning over Aisling's neck, she swatted at her husband's hand on the bridle.

Already dancing nervously, the spirited mare took offense from the slap on her cheek and swung her head sharply away. Ewan lost his grip, and the horse reared, screaming her indignation and pawing at the air. Madlin remained on her back, and the mare settled her hooves on the ground, but only briefly. She bucked and writhed, shuddering to free herself. Taken unaware, Madlin was catapulted over Aisling's head and toward a huge, jagged boulder.

"No!" His heart in his throat, Ewan whipped his mount around to block Madlin's flight. When she slammed into his body, the impact nearly unseated him, but instincts honed from years of battle and tournaments served him well. Automatically, he tightened his thighs about the pony's belly and wrapped an arm around Madlin.

"You little fool, now you've lost your mount!"

With her arms wound tightly about his neck, her chest pressed against his, Ewan could feel her shaking and gasping for breath. Damn his angry reaction to the near tragedy. The woman wanted comfort not fury.

"Let me go whilst I can still call Aisling back to me."

Her voice was weak and shaky. The aftermath of such a close brush with death, he was sure. He'd seen it in others and had felt it himself. Truth be told, he was feeling it now, and far more than he would ever admit. He tightened his hold on her instinctively.

She loosened her arms from around his neck and began to beat her fists upon his shoulders. "Let me go, I say."

Her voice still sounded unsteady. Doubting she'd be able to stand, he sent her a quelling glare. "Not yet."

"Have you no sense of duty?" she demanded, and tried to wriggle from his grasp.

Color was beginning to return to her cheeks, but he was thoroughly enjoying the feel of her lush breasts against his chest. Instead of taking the sensible course and dropping her to the ground, he brought his other hand to her waist and lifted her to sit across his thighs.

"Aye, I have a great sense of duty," he said more gently, marveling at the clarity of her skin, the thickness of her long lashes, and the lush invitation of her lips.

Aided by a mischievous breeze, one fiery tress brushed across Ewan's face, and his nostrils were filled with her scent. No odor-masking heavy perfume clung to the woman in his arms. A subtle bouquet of freshness wafted gently from her, as pure and natural as the countryside surrounding them.

Utterly bewitched by this unique aspect of the woman's many physical enticements, Ewan gave no more heed to whatever danger had befallen the column nor to his oath that she'd find no comfort in this marriage.

Fearing the enchantment might be broken if he was too forceful, he brushed his lips tentatively across hers. The soft sweetness he encountered soon overwhelmed his reticence. Recklessly, he took full possession of her mouth, forcing his tongue past her lips to the warm cavern beyond, and wantonly explored. He drank of her sweet nectar and conquered her tongue's initial resistance to the intrusion.

As he took command of her mouth, she stilled her struggling and coiled her arms about his neck. Intrigued by her surrender, he gathered her closer and deepened the kiss. Where he led, she followed with an eagerness that stimulated a craving for all her mouth and lush body promised.

Though layers of mail, quilted padding, linen, and wool separated their bodies, he could feel the give of her soft form against him. Brushing her plaid aside, he closed his hand over her breast. Beneath his palm, her nipple tightened, and he was not sure if the moan he heard was hers or his own.

A chance movement of Madlin's settled her full weight upon his injured thigh. Pain shot through him and he recovered his wits instantly. Tearing his lips from hers, he repositioned her so that her weight was once again balanced on his good thigh.

The abrupt interruption sent Madlin's senses tumbling back to reality. She cried out. Frantically, she clutched at the solid breadth of shoulders beneath her hands.

Awareness of her surroundings was slow in coming, but then the emotions that had hurled her toward the heavens came to a skidding stop. If her desire had not already been doused, the expression on her husband's face would have smothered it.

The magnetism that had blazed in the deep blue depths of his eyes just before he'd kissed her was gone. In its place was a hardness and a look of such chilling repudiation, she shuddered. Humiliated by his apparent disdain, she yanked her arms from around his shoulders and shoved at his chest so forcefully he dropped his arms from about her.

"You, sir, are a knave!" she declared as she quickly slid off his horse and scurried a safe distance away. Curling her forefinger and thumb into her mouth, she blew a series of three sharp whistles.

While she waited, she willed her heart to return to its normal rhythm, her limbs to still their quaking, and her breath to calm. With his handsome face and mesmerizing eyes, the man was a devil for sure. There could be no other explanation for his having so taken over her senses that she'd forgotten her responsibilities.

Her stomach clenched with anxiety. She had to get to her men. She whistled again.

Just as she geared herself to return up the road on foot, she was rewarded by the sound of rapid hoofbeats and then the flash of Aisling's bright copper-colored coat as she cut through the forest beyond the road. The mare had not yet come to a stop when Madlin threw herself upon the animal's back. Grabbing the reins, she glanced over her shoulder, half expecting to see that Ewan Fraser had disappeared over the hill beyond, returned to the nether world of faeries from which he'd undoubtedly come.

But he remained. No unearthly glow emanated from him. No host of supernatural beings had joined him. "He's but a man, human like yourself," she muttered under her breath, burying the superstitions that had piqued her imagination to believe otherwise.

"Do not try to stop me this time, Fraser." Digging her heels into her mare's sides, she set Aisling back up the trail.

Sparing not a moment's thought to the freedom her desertion afforded him, Ewan urged his mount to as much speed as the sturdy little horse could muster. There was no chance of overtaking his bride's longer-legged mount. He could only hope to keep the tip of the animal's tail in sight.

As unarmed as she and not knowing whether it was a band of his own clan or that of another's who'd set upon the MacKendricks, Ewan knew that he had to do all he could to protect her. When he caught sight of her again, she was off her horse and wading into the very middle of the melee taking place in the clearing up ahead. His heart leaped to his throat.

Having glimpsed no unfamiliar plaids and no weapons save fists, Madlin wasted not a moment wondering why her men were battling each other. "Stop it. Stop this," she cried as she dodged flailing arms and tumbling bodies. Jostled first one way and then another, she was hard put to stay upright.

Thinking of no other means to gain her men's attention, she screamed, "MacKendricks! To me! MacKen—"

The force of the blow to the side of her head raised her off her feet and spun her around. The pain drowned out all else. It was as if a looking glass had exploded within her head. Thousands of jagged shards glittered blindingly as they cut through her brain, fighting for a way out of her skull. Blessedly, she fell into unconsciousness even before she hit the ground.

When Ewan saw her fall, the need to get to her overpowered all else. He became a man possessed. Flinging bodies to his right and to his left, he cleared a path to the woman lying crumpled on the ground.

Awareness of what had happened was not long in rippling through the MacKendricks. By the time the Fraser knight bent on one knee by his bride, he was surrounded by MacKendricks frozen into shocked silence.

With a trembling hand, Ewan brushed away the mass of red-gold silk that covered her face. The sight of blood and a darkening bruise marring the creamy perfection of her temple both frightened and enraged him. Gently, he spread a shaking palm across her chest, praying he would feel the beat of her heart and the rise and fall of her breathing.

At first he sensed nothing from the still form beneath his palm. In anguish, he pulled back his hand and pressed his ear to her chest. Faint but steady, he heard her heart beat and felt her chest rise.

Relief like none he'd ever experienced swept over him, but he was not yet satisfied. He ran his hands over her body, fearing he might find further injury.

When at last he was satisfied she had suffered naught but the blow to her temple, he dropped back upon his heels. His chin dropped to his chest, his eyes squeezed tightly closed, he begged the Almighty that the blow would soon prove inconsequential. He'd seen too many similar injuries in battle not to fear still for her wits and even her life.

He pressed his ear again to her chest and was heartened when he thought her heart throbbed more strongly within. Carefully, he turned her head, checking her ears for blood, then thanked his Creator that he saw none. When she moaned softly, and her eyelids fluttered as if she were struggling to awake, faith for her recovery began to grow.

The one-eyed man, Gordie, he thought he'd heard him called, pulled off his own plaid and made to wrap the length of wool about her. Ewan snatched the plaid from him and gently wrapped her himself.

Lifting his unconscious wife into his arms, he slowly turned, burning each man with his eyes. "This is how the MacKendricks treat their lady? 'Tis a sorry, undisciplined lot you are to have forsaken your duties for a tussle."

Not a single MacKendrick thought to take offense at the insult. Rightfully shamed, none could even meet his gaze. Tears pooled in the corners of many a man's eyes, spilled freely down the cheeks of others, and all prayed, openly or silently, for her recovery.

Spying his own man among the combatants, Ewan's eyes widened and one brow angled even more sharply in query. The response was a deep red flush spreading upward from Lucais's neck and a shrug of his heavy shoulders. "Well . . . ah . . . cap'n . . . sir, ye see, 'twas but—"

"I'll hear no excuses, for there are none." Ewan's voice cut coldly across the clearing. "Lucais, come to me and get me out of this mail." The MacKendricks were encompassed in a censuring glare. "Bring me the strongest horse for carrying both me and your lady. One with an easy gait. I'll not have her jostled more than is necessary.

"Divide yourselves into two parts, with the first half taking up the forward position of this column, and the second half behind me. Whenever the terrain allows I want a half-dozen of you to take up flanking positions to the right and left of the middle where your lady and I will be."

Silently, the MacKendricks gathered up their weapons and sought their mounts. If any man among them thought it strange to be following the orders of a Fraser, none voiced it.

The man Gordie held Madlin's hand while a suitable mount was fetched. Ewan wondered at their relationship as he watched the man stroke her with the tenderness of a mother for her babe and coax in a whisper, "Awake, my wee Maddie. 'Tis so sorry I am. Ye must awake and give us that smile that rivals the angels above. Can ye do that for auld Gordie, lass?"

Once he'd relieved Ewan of his mail, it was Lucais who tugged at Gordie's shirt and led him away. "Yer lass is in good hands, mon," Ewan heard Lucais say. "My lad will take good care of her. Come, ye have a position to take up."

The two men walked away in a comradly fashion that Ewan marveled over but briefly. The horse had arrived. Though he was loath to give his burden over to another, he knew he could not mount the horse with her in his arms. His new wife was no dainty woman, and he was not in full strength. It was a miracle that his leg had not given out during the wait, but he'd be damned if he'd let anyone else carry her. Carefully, he gave her over to one of her men, but only for as long as it took him to seat himself on the horse.

"Yer lad has the way of a commander about him."

"Aye, Gordie Gunn. The lad did Scotland proud in France." With a nod toward Hugh, Lucais gathered up the reins of his waiting mount. "There was none in his command who would not have followed him to battle Lucifer himself if my lord Ewan had asked. 'Twas the Douglas himself, God rest his soul, who granted him his spurs. Sir Ewan was the youngest of the alliance commanders. And the best."

Gazing across the little glade, Lucais watched one of the MacKendrick men lift the unconscious body of the lady Madlin up to the waiting arms of her husband. " 'Tis sorry I am that the lass caught a fist and sorrier still for the pounding in her head that she'll be suffering when she awakes. But I'm thinking it just may be the best outcome of that little bit of fun we were having."

His two companions had witnessed the transfer of their lady to her husband. They could not fail to take note of the careful way his liege cradled the bride he'd sworn would receive no comfort from him. They wore silly smiles, and he supposed he wore one, too.

Before they all fell to sighing like women witnessing a tender scene, Gordie punched Hugh on the shoulder and pointed to the sun still shining brightly above. "Did I not say that was a good omen?"

Hugh grinned sheepishly. "Mayhap the stench of last night's business will not be so strong." He soon glowered. "But winter is close upon us, and there be dark days ahead before there be a full season of bright days like this one."

Gordie shrugged, and Lucais pursed his lips. Both knew Hugh was remarking on far more than the weather.

Again taking up positions at the end of the column, the three of them plodded along for a piece in quiet contemplation. Finally, Lucais broke the silence. "If my memory serves me and I'm right in thinking I know where we be, 'twill not be long before I break with yer company and carry the messages yer lady has ordered.

"Before I go, I would ye tell me all ye know about the slaying of Toirlach and his lads and the events what led up to it. I must know the MacKendrick side of things before I ride into Glendarach."

" 'Tis a sorry tale ye'll not be liking," Gordie warned.

"Aye, but I must hear it." Lucais sighed deeply, fearing what he would find when he arrived at Glendarach and just how he was going to explain why Cameron's son was not by his side.

"And, tell me about yer lady laird. My lord Cameron and the lady Guenna will want to know what manner of lass their son has married."

Chapter Six

Danger. Madlin could feel it. She had to get to the men.

She dug her heels into Aisling's sides, but the mare refused to move beyond a walk. Crying out in frustration, Madlin tried to slap her mount with the ends of the reins, but her hands were empty. Frantically, she groped for the reins.

"Hush, my lady. All is well," came a voice from just above her.

Full consciousness was slow in coming. Madlin felt a large hand spread over her head and press it back to the warm, muscled shoulder where it had been pillowed. So comfortable. So warm and protected. Lulled by the voice, she drifted toward sleep.

"That's it, Lady Madlin. Sleep is best."

Lady Madlin . . . ? Almost no one called her that. Always, it was Madlin, Maddie, my lady, or my laird she was called.

Confused, Madlin struggled to open her eyes and lift her head.

It was a mistake. Her stomach lurched and a bitter taste of bile burned her throat. Hot, searing pain assaulted her brain. She moaned.

The voice—deep, rustling, and slightly accented—told her again that all was well. It held a familiar ring, but she could not identify it. Even reasoning caused pain, and unconsciousness threatened to envelop her again. The man began to tenderly stroke her tortured head with a soothing touch.

"All is well. Trust me."

His voice was comforting.

Trust me.

Some deep instinct told her she could.

Seeking an inner calm that might help stay the pain, Madlin breathed in deeply, then let the air out slowly. With each breath, the scent of him filled her nostrils. A blend of pine, leather, horse, and man. The scent was pleasant, intriguing, and, for reasons she could not fathom, seemed to fortify her instinct to trust its owner.

Relaxed, she sank into the comfort of the arms that held her. For the first time in what seemed like a very long while, Madlin allowed that she could escape her responsibilities as leader, if only for a spell. A laird who could not bear to open her eyes, could not hold herself upright, could not even think was of no good to those who followed her.

It was Gordie, Hugh, or perhaps Colley who held her. All were men she could trust.

The next time she awoke, sounds and motion no longer rendered her speechless with pain. Nor did any sense of anxiety claw at the edges of her consciousness. Emboldened, she opened her eyes.

Dusk had settled its gray blanket over the landscape. Without the sun, the air around her was cold and biting. But wrapped within a plaid and held in a circle of strong arms, she felt warm and snug. Slowly, she lifted her head and straightened her spine. Her stomach lurched, but only slightly.

" 'Tis still too soon, my lady. Rest is what you need."

That voice again. Who? Where was she?

Sudden recollection of all that had passed in the last two days washed over her with the force of a Highland storm. Ewan Fraser!

Everything—his capture, their marriage, the way his lips and mouth had rendered her mindless of all but wanting more before he'd thrust her away from him, the disappointment, the embarrassment, and finally the anger she'd felt—returned. She remembered bounding upon Aisling's back and whipping the mare to a punishing pace to get away from this hateful man.

What had happened that she now found herself sleeping in

his arms? And why did she remember so much pain and even now feel her head bruised and aching?

Pushing out of the arms that sheltered her, Madlin looked wildly about. Two men rode to her left. Gordie. Wavering next to him was . . . was Gordie's ghost?

Quickly, she made the sign of the cross. A prayer on her lips, she squeezed her eyes shut and looked again. Only one Gordie rode beside her now. Solid, alive, familiar.

"Och, lass, 'tis a glad thing to see ye awake," he said, concern evident in the gruffness of his voice. "Dunfionn is but yonder. Do as the lad . . . er . . . Sir Ewan says, rest yer wee head. 'Twas a powerful blow ye took to yer noggin."

Madlin raised her fingers to her temple and winced when she encountered a large bump there. Now she remembered. She'd raced Aisling back up the path, less a need to get away from Ewan than a great sense of urgency and worry forcing her to ride recklessly toward . . .

She knew not what.

"Were we attacked? Did I fall?"

Gordie looked uneasy and tightened his mouth.

"You caught a fist that was meant for someone else," her husband told her, his voice harsh with censure. "These fine men of yours were engaging in a free-for-all for their own pleasure. They are in great need of strong leadership and discipline."

"They are the best in all of the Highlands! No Fraser band could ever match them."

Struggling to free herself, she cried, "Unhand me, this instant, you . . . you . . . Fraser!"

Ewan reined his mount to an abrupt stop. Grasping Madlin's shoulders, he turned her so that they were face-to-face. He met her green-eyed glare with a matching fierceness. "Madame wife, you are not physically fit to sit a horse alone! Honor forbids me to allow you such foolishness."

"You forget to whom you speak, husband!" Fury and affronted pride raged within her until she was shaking with it. "I am the laird of Dunfionn. You will put me down this instant," she ordered imperiously, ignoring the renewed pain in her head and the shakiness she felt in her limbs.

"Do not think to use that tone with me, wife. You suffered a blow to your head and need rest it lest you lose what little sense is left within your thick skull."

With the tip of his finger he pushed at her lower lip. "Such a childish pout to your pretty mouth does not become the laird of the MacKendricks," he remarked, then had the audacity to grin at her. "Now, settle back against me like a good lass, and suffer me no more of this nonsense."

"Do not think to treat *me* like a wee bairn!" Struggling upright, she called to Gordie, "Have Aisling brought to me. I must ride at the head of this column when it passes through Dunfionn's gates."

"Do not be a fool," the hateful man said, and pulled her back against him. She felt him knee his mount into motion.

With the swiftness of a serpent, Madlin twisted and struck her husband's cheek with her palm. The speed and force of the action cost her a renewal of painful pounding and a near disastrous wave of nausea. But the result was worth the price. Gone was the smug and condescending look on his face. Anger was apparent in the tightness of his mouth and the coldness of his eyes.

Instantly she wished for a return of that softer look he'd had earlier, even the audacious grin. Words begging his forgiveness were clamoring to get past her tightened lips. Her fingers wanted so to soothe the side of his face where the imprint of her palm flamed. But something deep within her cautioned that it would be folly to so lower herself to this man and give in to such sentimentality.

"Let go of me," she ordered.

"Do not be a fool."

Given the continuing hammering within her skull, she kept her voice as calm and steady as possible. "You forget yourself. I am the Baroness MacKendrick, laird of Dunfionn. You dare call me a fool? You, a mere landless knight, a third son—"

"A man unfortunate enough to have been dragged before a

priest by you—wench!" Ewan announced through gritted
teeth. Because of the blow she'd taken to her head, he'd given
her allowances for her lack of respect but this was too much.
His blood pounded in his veins as he struggled to control his
rage, his pride.

Landless third son, indeed! Jamie had made him a baron
and given him lands richer and more vast than the MacKendrick holdings. Ironically, it would be her machinations that
would elevate him even higher if Jamie were still of the same
mind next spring. If he knew for certain the MacKendricks
would not fall upon him for being granted the lands they'd
long coveted, he'd tell her here and now.

With one smooth motion, he swept the source of his vexa-
tion from his lap and placed her none too gently upon the
ground. Despite the blows she'd dealt to his pride, when her
features blanched and she appeared to wobble, he would have
been at her side in a trice had it not been for the militant set of
her mouth.

Holding himself tightly in control, he nodded to Gordie.
"See to the laird of the MacKendricks."

Not waiting for a florid-faced Gordie to follow his directive, Ewan kicked his pony into a gallop, not caring where the
beast carried him, only that he should be away from his wife.
With no pull on the reins to either side, the shaggy animal
went to the very front of the column and a few yards beyond
before settling itself to a walk. Content to be alone, Ewan did
not think to knee the animal into a run and make a try for
freedom. He thought of nothing but bringing his rage under
control.

The MacKendricks at the front of the column kept their silence. All had heard the exchange between their laird and her
husband. Just a day before, any of them would have fought for
the opportunity to slip a dirk between a Fraser's ribs. But
today, that their laird's husband had been born a Fraser seemed
of little consequence. Respecting the man and his need for
privacy, they gave him space.

Leaning weakly against Gordie as she waited for Aisling to

be brought forward, Madlin felt him sigh heavily before he asked, "Och, lassie, what have ye done?"

Though spoken in the deep rough tones of a man, the question was too familiar not to bring a gurgle of mirthless laughter to Madlin's lips. "Mayhap I am the fool he called me."

"Will ye be apologizin', then?" he asked as he helped her onto Aisling's back.

"The laird of the MacKendricks will not apologize to that . . . that Fraser," she declared before setting her heels to Aisling's sides.

Hugh rode up to Gordie's side. "What will the lass do now?"

Nervously sliding the leather reins through his fingers, Gordie watched as Madlin and Aisling moved steadily toward the front of the column. When finally satisfied that she was going to stay in the saddle, he mounted his own pony and answered his friend's query. "She will lead us through the gates of Dunfionn, that's what the lass will do."

"Stubborn lass," Hugh said, as much to himself as to his friend. "But then, she's Toirlach's daughter." Turning a worried face toward Gordie, he said, "For all he is a Fraser, the lad doesna deserve such a waspish tongue in his wife."

"He's a MacKendrick, now," Gordie reminded.

"Well, then." Hugh sighed again, then brushed through his beard, a gesture all who knew him well understood indicated he had set his mind toward pondering a weighty subject. " 'Tis all the more reason he does not deserve a wife with such a waspish tongue. His anger before was naught compared to what I saw in his face just now. Do ye think he'll honor his vow not to harm her?"

"Not knowing the lad for long, I cannot say. 'Tis sure our lass has given him cause. He's shown powerful restraint so far, but I have not the sight to ken the future."

Rising slightly in his stirrups, Gordie could see Madlin closing in on her husband in the lead. "I'm thinking it not such a poor thing if we was to keep ourselves close to our lass and her new husband. It wouldna do if they was to still be bickering when we enter yon gates."

Hugh grimaced. "He'll not be welcomed with joy. Best we watch his back as well."

So this was Dunfionn, the fortress of his clan's enemies. Ewan gazed at the castle rising from the cape jutting toward the center of a large loch. Its crenelated walls were as white as the name implied, shining brightly against the blackness of the water that surrounded them. Large circular towers marked its four corners, with smaller turrets jutting still higher from the middle of each wall.

Dunfionn seemed not as large as he remembered Glendarach to be, but its walls were high and appeared strong from this distance. With the eye of a warrior, he assessed it and found the fortress's situation easily defended. The only access appeared to be a narrow causeway from the water's edge. Surrounding the loch were fields on the flatlands, with grazing lands dotted with sheep and shaggy-coated cattle on the rock-dotted slopes beyond. Cots, byres, and an assortment of the usual buildings typical of small villages were gathered near the end of the causeway.

A handful of small boats rested belly-up just beyond the rushes growing along the shore. A line of racks heaped with nets was situated nearby. It was obvious that the MacKendricks were no strangers to the art of netting their suppers— or their enemies. Embarrassed by the memory of the ease with which he'd been captured, he went back to assessing Dunfionn's defensive position.

But for an occasional cluster of trees, there was nothing to hide the presence of an advance force. Without the element of surprise, an assault would be difficult but not impossible. In France, he'd seen a castle situated similarly, or rather what remained of it after the English army had finished with it.

Dunfionn and all within could be thus if his sire chose to lay siege. That is, unless the MacKendricks were better prepared and led by someone far braver than the French noble who'd once resided at the annihilated castle he'd just recalled. At the first hint that his demesne lay in the English army's path, the cowardly Frenchman had taken himself and his fighting men far away. Those left behind had been left with little but his orders that the castle was not to be surrendered under any circumstances. Among those welcoming death after weeks of suffering had been the noble's wife and four young children.

Ewan glanced over to his wife, the woman who led the MacKendricks. She was young, inexperienced in both leadership and war, but she possessed pride and a loyalty that were to be admired. And she was no craven. She—

Was swaying in the saddle. The little fool! He'd spared her not a glance when she'd arrived at his side. His anger had still been too hot, and he'd feared what he might say or do if they were to engage in yet another battle of wills. Further, he'd had his own physical infirmities to deal with.

For hours, he'd been trying to ignore the throbbing, burning pain emanating from his thigh. Now he sensed a fever heating his body. *Jesu*, let that damnable wound not be turning septic again.

Despite the many ills besieging him, his wife needed watching and more than likely catching. Carefully, so as not to unsettle her nervous mount, he moved his own as close as was safe.

Out of the corner of his eye, he could see a line of men, women, and children along the roadway. He supposed the procession had been spotted long ago and the villagers had come out to get a look at their laird's new husband. He paid them little mind, though he was glad for the torches some were holding to better light the way. The light gave him a better view of his wife.

No matter how strong her will, the set of her shoulders and the line of her back were not as proud as they'd been when last she'd been at the head of her men. In the flickering light, her pallor shone white, her features strained. Her eyes were mere slits, as if raising her lids, even just a little more, would take more effort than she was capable of exerting.

And her mouth, that lush, sweet mouth he'd kissed hours ago, was set so tightly that he knew she was exercising all her willpower not to cry out against the pain in her head.

Relief swept through him when they'd cleared the causeway and their horses' hooves were rattling upon the wooden drawbridge. A few more minutes and they reached the inner bailey. Ewan was off his horse and reaching up for Madlin almost as soon as she reined her horse to a stop. "Come, my lady, let me carry you up yon steps to the keep."

Madlin allowed him to pull her from Aisling's back. But, as he made to swing her up into his arms, she resisted. "Nay, I must stand and address my people." He would have ignored her statement had she not turned her face up to his and whispered, *"Please."*

If she had ordered with even the slightest hint of an imperial tone, he would have kept her in his arms. But he could not deny her whispered plea any more than he could ignore the beseeching look in her eyes. Reluctantly, he lowered her feet to the ground but kept his arm about her waist as they mounted the steps.

"MacKendricks," she began as soon as they'd reached the summit. Her voice lacked the strength and clarity he had come to know. He tightened his hold upon her, willing some of his own waning strength into her trembling body.

"I present to you my husband, Sir Ewan of Glendarach and late of France."

Sharply drawn gasps and murmurs of displeasure rippled through the crowd. Torches stuck about the bailey lighted the faces of the people gathered there. None were happy. Some were angry, and some looked worried. At least none looked fearful as they had when she and Airic had brought home the wolf. It was as good a reception as she could have hoped for.

"Sir Ewan is an honored knight of Scotland and of France, and now he is one of us." She fixed her gaze upon one face after another. "As a member of our clan, he brings us honor, and his well-being is no less dear to me than is any other who claims the name of clan MacKendrick. Sir Ewan has—"

Madlin drew a deep breath for the courage to finish the statement and then sent up a quick prayer that her new husband would not refute what she was about to say. She had not the strength to argue nor the desire to order him subdued. "Sir Ewan shall be known henceforth as Sir Ewan of the Dunfionn MacKendricks."

She felt his arm tighten around her. She would have said something to him, but her legs began to shake and her vision to blur. She looked up at the golden-haired man supporting her, begging him with her eyes that he somehow get the two of them through the doorway behind them before she collapsed again.

Darkness was descending upon her consciousness. She barely heard someone cry, "To our lady and her new husband! Sir Ewan of Dunfionn." A silence stretched tautly before there was an answering "Sir Ewan."

My men, only my loyal band of men, she thought. A beginning. Others will follow their lead. They must.

Ewan had her in his arms as soon as the doors closed behind them. Without any preamble or introduction, the tall woman who'd awaited them at the doors to the keep said curtly, "Follow me." She led him across the great hall and up the stone steps at its back.

With each step he took, Ewan prayed the woman was not going to lead him to a chamber high in the keep's tower. What a pair we are, my wife and I, he thought as he willed his legs to carry them and his arms to retain their hold. He might have laughed had he had any strength to spare.

One step at a time, he told himself. Keep moving your feet. His new wife was taller and sturdier than most of her gender, but he'd carried wounded men, unconscious men, men far larger and heavier than the woman in his arms. He'd been exhausted from battle and still carried a man a full league to safety.

Carrying his wife to wherever that woman was leading him

was something he could do. Would do. *God's teeth, I'll not show myself a weakling to these MacKendricks.* He was born a Fraser and would be till the day he died, no matter what his wife might declare.

Cold, so cold in this great pile of white rock. Did they light no fires in this place? He could barely keep his teeth from chattering as he followed the woman leading the way.

"Here, lay her down here." He heard the woman's voice as if from a long distance. A lamp she lit revealed a high, curtained bed. He moved toward it, seeking to rest his precious burden on it and then to warm himself at the fire.

After lighting the lamps upon the mantle, the lady Elspeth turned just in time to see her new nephew by marriage collapse, part on the bed and part off.

"What ails the lad?" Gordie asked from the doorway.

Elspeth's response was a lift of a brow and a pursing of her lips before pushing Ewan's limp body aside so as to better examine Madlin. Running knowledgeable hands over Madlin's body, she said, "Mayhap you two great lummoxes can move the man and manage to tell me at the same time what has befallen your laird."

"The lass caught an errant fist to her temple," Gordie managed as he and Hugh lifted Ewan. "Och, the lad is heavier than I thought. Where do ye want him?"

Elspeth waved absently before gently turning Madlin's head from side to side. With no more directive from the lady, Gordie wrapped his arms about Ewan's chest. Hugh gathered up Ewan's legs. Together, they carried him around to the other side of the bed and laid him down. They were turning away when Hugh wiped his hand upon his shirt.

"Have ye cut yerself, then?" Gordie asked him.

Frowning, Hugh brushed again at his hand and held it closer to the lamp's light. Turning his hand over and over, he saw no cut to explain the source of the blood he had swiped on his shirt. As one, he and Gordie exclaimed, "The lad!"

Grabbing up several of the thick candles resting on the

mantle, Gordie quickly lit and stuck them in the sconces about the bed. A dark pool was widening beneath Sir Ewan's right leg. "By the saints! How?"

Having satisfied herself that the lump on her niece's head was the only thing wrong with her, Elspeth spared a glance at the Fraser her niece had married. Her brows rose when she saw the blood soaking his hose and spreading ever wider beneath him. Grabbing up a fur robe, she quickly tucked it around Madlin, then started round the bed.

A rustling at the open doorway and a slight catching of breath gave notice of Lady Jeanne's arrival. "Och, 'tis neither of them well?" She raised questioning eyes first to Hugh then Gordie, but before either could answer, Elspeth shushed her, "Stay your prattling, lass, and fetch my medicine chest."

Laying her hand upon Ewan's brow, Elspeth raised her brows again and tightened her lips. Shaking her head, she quickly and efficiently cut away his hose, then the soiled bandages wrapped round his right thigh. Pressing skilled and knowing fingers to the edges of the wound, she said, " 'Tis a deep wound and not recent by the looks of the poison pouring from it. Some fool has had a clumsy hand in it before me."

She took a deep breath and let it out audibly as she stood back and studied the wound. Then, pushing up her sleeves, she began issuing orders worthy of a battle commander.

For the next hour, Hugh, Gordie, and the lady Jeanne were sent scurrying to do her bidding. They toted buckets of water, some for refilling the cauldron hanging over the fire and some for a large bowl that was kept well away from the fire to keep the water as cold as when it had been drawn from the well. Mindful of Elspeth's zeal for cleanliness, Jeanne discreetly removed her cousin's garments and cleansed her body before tucking her between the fresh linen sheets.

Hugh and Gordie were busy tending the Fraser knight. First, they stripped him of his remaining garments and sponged the travel grime from his body while Elspeth prepared her medicaments and set out her tools. Throughout, Sir Ewan drifted in and out of consciousness, muttering unintelligibly from time to time.

It was when a hot liquid passed his lips that Ewan came fully awake. Spitting the bitter taste from his mouth, he looked wildly about the room. He recognized nothing about it, save for the two men hovering nearby. Their names, however, were lost somewhere in the fog shrouding his brain.

"Ye're at Dunfionn, lad," the man with the patch over one eye supplied. " 'Tis the lady Elspeth, yer wife's aunt, who's tending ye. She be as fine a healer as be had in all of Scotland. She'll be settin' ye to rights, lad. Never fear."

The man's words came as if from the bottom of a well, and at first Ewan could scarce credit their meaning. "My . . . wife?"

Closing his eyes, he sank back against the pillows, waiting for his brain to clear. "Ah . . . yes, my wife." Images flashed through his mind of the bare-legged Amazon who'd captured him, forced him before a priest, and tasted like the sweetest nectar.

Another image flashed. A red-haired woman lying crumpled upon the ground. Her lovely features, too quiet and still. Her skin, too white and fragile against the rain-soaked ground. Dark blood making an obscene trail against the creamy skin of her temple.

"Where is she? How does she fare?" He made to get out of the bed, but dizziness and weakness engulfed him.

"She is resting and should be much herself by tomorrow. Now swallow this," Lady Elspeth ordered, pressing a cup to his mouth. " 'Twill help you withstand the pain when I see to your wound."

Having only regained his senses, Ewan spurned dulling them again. His leg throbbed with an ache that carried deep to the bones. But he'd experienced that before. Part of the healing process, the royal leech had told him. Turning his head away from the offending brew pressed to his lips, he saw Madlin at last.

"How came ye by such a grievous wound, lad?" came a man's voice as if from some distance.

"Verneuil. And it has been seen to. By the king's own physicians." Rising on one elbow, he studied his unconscious wife lying the breadth of the wide bed away from him.

"So still she is." Tentatively, he caught up her hand, the only part of her he could reach. He stroked her limp fingers and lightly caressed her palm with his thumb. He was not surprised to find small calluses there. A strong hand, but graceful, too. Capable of many diverse tasks was this new wife of his.

He pressed his fingers to the inside of her wrist. Her skin was warm, but not overly so, he noted with relief. A steady, strong pulse beat beneath the fragile skin beneath his fingertips.

"She will wake soon," a dainty dark-haired maiden told him as she replaced the cloth draped across Madlin's brow. "For now, Lady Elspeth has said sleep is the best healer for my cousin's bruised head."

"And will be a help to you, sir." Lady Elspeth tugged at Ewan's shoulder until he was forced to let go of Madlin's hand and settled back into a more prone position.

"Drink."

Immediately, a cup was pressed firmly against his lips.

God's teeth! There was no denying this woman was kin to his wife, he thought as he was given no choice but to swallow the evil-tasting brew steadily filling his mouth. He recognized the sickening sweet taste for the opiate it contained and knew it would be but a few minutes more before he would become oblivious to all around him.

He was helpless to do more than glare at the stern-faced woman. As his brain succumbed to the soporific mixture, he was not sure whether he had spoken or merely thought, "MacKendrick women! Stubborn, the whole lot of you. Had the Douglas a battalion of you at Verneuil, for certes 'twould have been the English that would have been routed."

Heedless of her patient's mutterings or the blisters rising on her hands, Elspeth wrung cloths from a small steaming cauldron over and over again and laid them upon the ugly gash. "King's physicians! I know of their remedies. Ground gems to dried dung. No telling what manner of contaminants those fools sprinkled into this wound. Pray this Fraser is held in some esteem, for the gem dust would likely do less harm than dung from the royal stables." She dropped yet another soiled cloth to the heap forming on the floor beside her.

At last, the hot cloths had done their work. Yellow-green pus oozed from the gash and mixed with the blood pouring again from the opened wound. She nodded in satisfaction when only blood flowed.

The stench and sight were too much for Hugh, who had been holding Sir Ewan's leg steady. He turned and rushed toward one of the empty buckets near the hearth. There, he lost what little had been in his stomach.

At the knight's head, Gordie began to sway. "Out with the both of you," Elspeth cried as she pushed him away lest he fall across the bed and add more injury to her patient. "Jeanne, come, I have need of you here."

Neither Hugh nor Gordie needed any further enticement to absent themselves. Glad to leave the two women to their work, they took up positions outside the door to the bedchamber.

"That woman is a tyrant in the sick room," Hugh grumbled as he settled himself against the stone wall.

"Say yer prayers that yon tyrant and her witch's brews heal the lad."

"Ye thinking the same as me, then?"

"Aye, there's more to that lad than being Cameron Fraser's third son returning home from the war in France."

Hugh shook his head slowly. "Och, we shoulda known as soon as we took his sword. 'Twas no ordinary knight's sword."

"Aye, that crest is Royal Stewart or my name is not Gordie Gunn."

"Does the lass know?"

"I have not had the chance to tell her."

"Och, what has our lassie done?"

Gordie rubbed a hand over his head and down his face. "By

marrying that man, she has either made or destroyed this clan."

"Mayhap, we'd best spend the night on our knees in the chapel."

"God will have to hear our prayers from here. I'm not moving from this spot." The sound of voices and activity rising from the great hall increased the worry lines on Gordie's face. "Go on to the chapel if ye must, but see to the cause of that commotion yonder first."

Chapter Seven

Danger. Darkness. Cold.

I must get to the high meadowlands beyond the loch. The sun shines there, and I will be warm and safe.

He is waiting for me. A golden knight, his arms open wide in invitation. Sunlight glows all around him.

I must get to the sunshine. To the warmth. There is safety there, in the knight's arms.

At first, Madlin could not move her legs. Something was wound snugly about them. Moaning in frustration, she kicked and struggled against the confining layers.

When at last she was free, she moved toward the heat and the safety. Her knight had shed his mail. His smooth, muscled body was bared to the sun and her touch. Wrapping her arms around him, she pressed her cheek against his warm, broad chest and was comforted by the steady heartbeat within.

Strong arms enveloped her and drew her even closer. "Mmmm . . . safe," she murmured. Breathing deeply, she filled her nostrils with the enticing blend of pine, sunshine, rain, and man. The scent reminded her of the day the golden knight had kissed her until she'd been soaring far above the earth, reaching for a place even higher and brighter.

Yearning for that mysterious but enticing place, she pressed closer, desperate to fill an emptiness she could not define but that instinct told her the golden knight could appease. She brushed her lips across his. His response was immediate.

As she remembered, he took possession of her mouth,

plunged his tongue inside of her, and explored, sipped her taste, and conquered her will. Where he led, she followed.

Her skin tingled more intensely with each brush of his hands over her back and buttocks. When he moved his hands to her breasts and began kneading their fullness, a warm melting began in her belly and nether regions. She felt herself begin to soar again. She strained to reach that place she'd glimpsed just once before and whimpered in protest when he released her mouth. But her whimper quickly turned to a moan of pleasure when he nuzzled her ear and trailed his lips down her throat.

Writhing in the pleasure of his kisses and caresses, she still wanted, needed more. She moved atop him so that their bodies were pressed together, chest to breast, belly to belly, thigh to thigh.

Something hot and hard prodded her belly. She reached between their bodies to push it away. Her palm encountered the heated rod, and by their own volition, her fingers wrapped around it.

Such power and life throbbed within her grasp. The hard male body beneath hers shifted, and she thought she heard a low moan before a harsh gasp.

"God's teeth, woman. Unhand me!"

Startled into full wakefulness, Madlin opened her eyes, surprised by the sight of the icy blue eyes of her husband so close to her own. Realization that she lay completely naked atop his equally naked body came next. Then, that his broad hands cupped her buttocks and that one of hers was wrapped firmly around his very aroused manhood.

"Oh . . . oh!" Shock kept her locked where she was during the most humiliating moment of all her twenty years. Finally, she gathered her senses, loosened her fingers, and scrambled to the far side of the bed.

Still on all fours, she crouched there, gasping for breath as her sleep-muzzled mind tried to separate what she'd thought had been a most pleasurable dream from the horrifying reality.

But, knowing how she'd come to be in such a scandalous position was inconsequential when her husband set loose a string of stinging epithets ending with, "Be gone with you. Naught of your body nor your harlot's ways tempts me to stand stud for you!"

Scrambling off the bed, Madlin fled to the farthest wall of the chamber, grabbing up a plaid along the way. "Blessed Virgin, what have I done?" she muttered as she wrapped the plaid about herself, never taking her eyes from the wide bed that dominated the center of the chamber.

Pressed against the stone wall, her body still vibrated with a kind of excitement she did not understand. Her skin felt so taut that she feared her body might explode at any moment. If not that fate, she would surely die of humiliation the minute Ewan Fraser appeared from behind the curtains surrounding the bed. Quickly, she confessed her sins.

"Holy Mary, Mother of God. Pray for this sinner now at this the hour of my death," she muttered beneath her breath and then waited a few moments in anxious anticipation of her imminent demise.

Death would surely be preferable to enduring more humiliation. "Now, Lord. Now would be a good time to pluck my spirit from this earthly body."

When no emissary from either heaven or the other world came for her, Madlin eyed the bed nervously.

Several long minutes passed with no sound or movement from the bed. Madlin began to relax her guard. Sensing that the immediate danger was past, her limbs began to quiver until she feared they would no longer hold her. Slowly, she slid down the wall and sat upon the floor.

The floor was cold. She pulled up her knees and tucked the plaid about her toes. She judged it barely dawn from the faint light coming through the shuttered window.

She would be expected in the hall to break her fast soon. She needed to show herself to her people, assure them that she was well. And . . . explain her reasons for marrying their enemy's son. Undoubtedly, the council of elders would descend upon her sometime today. They would not be happy that she had taken such a drastic action without first consulting them.

Rubbing her head, she winced when she grazed the lump on her temple. Had Aunt Elspeth given her a sleeping draught? Perhaps it was merely the aftereffects of the blow to her head that accounted for her being so woolen-brained. Either could have made her sleep so deeply, made her think herself in a dream when she'd—

"Oh, dear God! I am the harlot he called me."

With one arm flung over his eyes, Ewan lay on the bed willing his body to relax as he listened to the sounds his wife was making on the other side of the chamber. What on God's earth was she doing? All he could hear was indistinguishable mutterings and the sound of heavy breathing.

Heavy breathing. Bigod! Even the sound of her breathing set up a torture in his groin that was worse than the pain throbbing in his leg. Had it not been for that damnable wound, he would not be lying here alone in the throes of frustrated lust. Should he be praising or damning the fates that had brought him to such a sorry state?

Untried and intact you shall remain as long as you persist in this travesty of a marriage! The vow of a prideful fool.

Awakening with his wife's sweet taste on his tongue, her voluptuous body in his arms, and her fingers wrapped around his throbbing rod, he would have broken that vow with enthusiasm had it not been for the failings of the rest of his body. Far easier to come up surly and send her scurrying away from him than to admit that pain and weakness prevented him from completing the act.

God's teeth, the woman was a temptress! Even in the scant light within the enclosed bed, he had seen enough to know that his fantasies about her body paled in comparison to the reality. Save for a peculiar pendant nestled between her breasts, there had been nothing to hide the naked splendor of the woman.

Her hair. Released from its plait, it was the embodiment of his fantasies. The wild tangle of silken curls tumbled over her creamy shoulders and down her back. Her breasts were high, full, and filled his large palms to overflowing.

She was Aphrodite, Helen, and Titania, too, all melded together to create a banquet for a man's most lustful appetite.

Ewan Fraser, you are a fool! It had not been his wife who'd sentenced them both to a life of living hell, but himself. Vowing never to touch her, never to give nor take comfort from her siren's body, was the vow of an idiot! If lunacy was sweeping the Highlands, he had succumbed immediately after the marriage ceremony.

He heard the sound of bare feet padding upon the wooden floor of the chamber. His body tensed. He half feared she'd return to the bed and half feared she would not.

Stealthily, Madlin moved about the chamber, the laird's chamber. In the weeks since she'd returned, she'd not been able to bring herself to take it over, preferring instead to use the small chamber at the top of the tower that had always been hers. She'd given orders that this chamber be left undisturbed, everything left just as it was and had always been when her father was still alive.

In the weeks since his death, she'd crept into the chamber late at night, long after the castle folk had sought their beds. By touching her father's personal possessions, wrapping herself in one of his plaids, she'd sought strength and wisdom. And in this chamber, closed away from the clan, she'd wept.

Looking about her, she saw that the chests where her father's clothing had been stored were gone. All the weapons and personal items, too. The room had been cleaned and aired. Aunt Elspeth's doing? It had to be. No one else would have taken that authority upon themselves.

The woman dares too much! More reason Madlin needed to dress and leave this chamber. She would confront her aunt first thing.

Her stomach growled, a reminder that close to an entire day

and night had passed since last she'd eaten. A talk with her aunt would come second.

Spying her own clothing chest, Madlin quickly lifted the lid and rooted through it for a clean shirt and plaid. Finding nothing but the few feminine garments she had in her possession, she would have sworn long and loudly had it not been for the occupant of the bed. Since there had been no indications otherwise, she had to assume the man had fallen back asleep. If for any reason Elspeth had poured some of her potent brew down his throat, Madlin could only be thankful.

As for having placed them in the same room, the same bed? The woman had that decision to answer for as well. Elspeth was not laird of clan MacKendrick! It was past time that she had it out with her father's sister as to just who was in charge of Dunfionn.

Madlin began rehearsing the speech she was going to deliver to her aunt as she slipped a chemise and a woolen gown over her head. She wound a woven girdle about her waist and then hiked up her skirts to pull on a pair of heavy woolen stockings, cursing as she fumbled about tying the ribboned garters. She was relieved to discover that she had more than just a pair of fragile slippers to wear on her feet. Her aunt had provided her with a pair of sensible low boots of the kind that Elspeth herself favored.

Spying the MacKendrick brooch resting upon the mantel, Madlin grabbed it and the plaid as she made for the door. Her hand on the latch, she hesitated and turned back toward the bed. Why would her aunt pour a sleeping draught down Ewan Fraser's throat? Holy Mary! What had befallen him that her aunt would drug him so heavily that he had not left the bed?

Concern for her captive's well-being obscured her trepidations of further taunts from him. Moving quickly around the bed, she yanked open the bed hangings.

"God's holy rood, you are a relentless wench!"

Her husband's grab for the bedclothes was not fast enough to prevent Madlin from glimpsing his arousal. She swallowed hard and felt a flood of heat through her body. Squeezing her eyes shut to block out the sight was of no use as the image of his long, heavily muscled body, with his manhood jutting proudly from between his thighs, was imprinted on her memory.

"Have you returned to take advantage of my weakness?" he asked as he covered himself. "Or is it your aim to torture me further?"

"Torture you! Holy Mother, 'tis worse than I thought." Madlin gripped the bed hangings for support. "What has been done to you and by whom?" she demanded. "I assure you, whoever it was, they will be punished. It will not happen again."

Nervously, she began twisting the bed hangings. "I will protect you. I must. 'Tis not honorable that a captive, I mean my husband, be treated ill. I'll tolerate no such conduct. MacKendricks do not fall upon each other. Whoever has done you harm shall be punished."

Closing her eyes, she dropped her head backward and began muttering again. The pattern and occasional decipherable word reminded Ewan of the muffled mutterings he'd heard from her earlier.

He frowned at her confusion and then realized she could not have known about his lingering wound. Honor compelled him to explain, but he stayed his tongue. For all the indignities and frustrations he'd suffered at her hands, she deserved at least a few moments of torture.

Honor. Pah! In his experience, few women knew the meaning of the word. He doubted Madlin MacKendrick was among those very few, even though the word *honor* was liberally sprinkled amid her ramblings.

"Cease, woman!" He was gratified when his order was actually followed. " 'Tis an old wound that plagues me and 'twas from an English sword not a MacKendrick's."

"Praise God," Madlin said in a rush of obvious relief. Her face flushed so rapidly with color that Ewan nearly chuckled. "I . . . I mean not that you were wounded, but that it was not a MacKendrick sword that felled you."

"Honor does mean that much to you?"

"Of course," she answered firmly.

Not a hint of guile could he detect in her gaze. Only puzzlement was reflected in the deep green depths of her eyes and in the furrow between them. "Pardon me," he found himself apologizing for insulting her with his question. "I have been long away from the company of honorable women."

With a slight tilt of her head, she appeared to grant him forgiveness. "If the sword was English, then 'twas in France, and it has been festering for a long time untreated. 'Tis a miracle you still live."

He hitched himself up to lean against the dark wood of the headboard. "If I do die, the fault lies in the witch's brews poured down my throat and in whatever mischief that woman performed upon me once she rendered me helpless."

Leaving off wringing the bed hangings, she pulled herself up as straight and proud as ever he'd seen her in their short association. Every voluptuous inch was Lady Madlin, the MacKendrick, as she announced, "That woman you so wrongfully condemn is my aunt, a woman of great skill in the healing arts! If anything could be done for your wound, she would do it."

Despite his admiration for her, he lifted a skeptical brow. "Even a Fraser's wound?"

"My aunt is a MacKendrick! A woman of honor! No man shall question that! Especially not you—*Fraser!*"

Noting his wife's clenched fists, Ewan inquired snidely, "Will you beat me again whilst I lie here all but helpless to defend myself? 'Tis a habit of *honorable* MacKendrick women? This preying upon helpless men?"

As soon as the words left him, Ewan braced himself for a torrent of blows, for surely his errant tongue was now guilty of far worse than that which had sent his quick-tempered wife's fists to pounding upon him once before. God's blood! What kind of spell had this rowan-haired minx cast upon him? Never, through years of political imprisonment, war, and then as a liaison to a royal court whose capriciousness would surely try the patience of a saint had he found himself so reckless with his comments. What was there about this woman that set him to goading her so?

"Nay, 'tis not the way of a MacKendrick to prey upon the helpless. Pray forgive me. I . . . I did not mean . . ."

Sucking in her lips, she blinked her suspiciously bright eyes. She looked away, but not before he saw tears spill onto her cheeks. Gently, he caught her chin in his fingers and turned her face toward him. The bruise on her forehead stood out obscenely against the backdrop of her creamy skin. He felt himself bruised just looking upon it. "Your head. Does it pain you so?"

"Nay, I shall recover. But you. You have suffered far more, and I have added to it. I . . . we . . . did not know."

"Would knowing I was coming home wounded and weak have made a difference? Would you have let me pass?"

"I . . . I could not have. Capturing you had to be done. But 'twas not a fair fight, and I cannot feel easy about that."

"Wars are seldom fair, my lady, else there would never be a winner. And I am not so very weak that I am beyond protecting myself," he told her, though it was more a lie than he cared to admit. He caught one of her tears on his thumb. "Like you, I shall recover."

She raised her tear-laden lashes and looked him squarely in the eyes. "Will you?"

"From the wound in my thigh, aye."

"But the wound to your pride? What of that?"

Taken aback by the question and her sincere concern, Ewan could not answer immediately. How very open she seemed, he noted, marveling anew at this refreshing quality in this most unusual of women. Confessing that James had all but ordered him to marry her would relieve the guilt so clearly reflected in her eyes. But years of diplomatic experience had taught him caution. Better to gather up more information about the MacKendricks and this war with his clan before divulging his association with the king and the mission James had given him.

"That may take longer," he told her with a sheepish grin, hoping to lighten her guilt if only a bit. Given the indignities she'd thrust upon him, he was well within his rights to let her suffer for at least a little while longer. So why did it pain him to see her anguish?

He grinned more widely and shrugged. " 'Tis not every day I find myself trapped in a fishing net. I hope you can appreciate what an embarrassment that is."

He was rewarded by a sparkling smile that nearly took his breath away. "Do the English not have fishing nets, then?" she asked, all innocence itself in her voice, but not in the saucy piquancy in her eyes.

Chuckling, he nearly kissed the tip of her nose. Fearing he might not stop with her nose and unwilling to risk finding himself in the same frustrating situation he'd suffered earlier, he settled for merely tapping her nose with the tip of his finger. "I trust you'll not tell Bedford of their uses."

"That Sassenach butcher will receive no aid from me or any of my kin." Indignation fairly bristled from her as she went on to declare, "I would not aid those who kept our king in prison all these years. I and all the MacKendricks are true and loyal subjects to James Stewart and enemies to any who would challenge his reign, be they from beyond our borders or within."

You, my lady, are more loyal than you suppose. He shifted toward the middle of the bed and patted the space he'd made. "Calm yourself, wife. I was but teasing. I was not questioning your loyalty to the crown, but your answer does intrigue me. Do you expect some to challenge James for the crown?"

"Mayhap not for his crown precisely," she said slowly as she lowered herself to the edge of the bed. "Already this summer there was grumbling in Aberdeen against some of his new laws and the severity of their enforcement."

"In Aberdeen, you say," he remarked, more interested in the play of the morning light on her hair and the way it rippled across the pillow. "How come you to know so much about the grumblings in Aberdeen?"

"I have spent the past seven years at St. Margaret's Abbey outside of Aberdeen."

"So long cloistered behind those walls and you did not take the veil?"

Madlin sighed and plucked at the fur beneath her hand. "I . . . I have not the temperament nor the self-discipline necessary to be a good nun."

"And yet you stayed there seven years?"

"Becoming a nun was not why I was sent there."

The blush staining her cheeks piqued his curiosity. "Why were you sent there?"

Her blush deepened, and she took a deep breath before answering in a rush. "My sire did think my aunt, the abbess, his only hope of making a lady of me after I challenged and bested Seamus Munro in a fight with swords."

"How old was this Seamus Munro?"

"He was sixteen, and I was but a lass of thirteen years."

Ewan could not help but laugh. "And for this you were sent away? I should have thought the lad's sire would have punished him for scrapping with a lass and losing."

Madlin shrugged. "Well . . . Seamus did not know he was fighting with a lass until afterward. I . . . I disguised myself as Airic, my twin. In those days we were shaped so much alike, I had but to tuck my hair into a cap and wear a shirt and plaid to look like a lad."

Remembering her voluptuous curves, Ewan found it difficult to imagine any time in her life when she'd been mistaken for a lad. "Ah . . . it must have been quite a blow to the lad's pride." Enough to make him a lifelong enemy? Could it be this Seamus Munro who was behind the war between the MacKendricks and the Frasers?

"Aye, Seamus was ever a prideful lad, as was his sire, the Munro. To save the alliance between our clans, I had to apologize before the Munros and say I'd used trickery to best their heir."

"But you did not, did you? Use trickery to best this Seamus Munro?" he asked, knowing her answer before she gave it.

"Nay, but it was best for the MacKendricks that I say so."

Knowing how prideful she was, he could imagine what a sacrifice she had made for her clan. Duty, honor, loyalty. She apparently possessed them in abundance. It would seem she was indeed worthy of the leadership that fate had thrust upon her. "This Seamus Munro, where is he now, and have you still an alliance with his clan?"

"Och, Seamus. He is the Munro, and, aye, we are still allies. He . . . he—"

The sound of the door opening put a stop to whatever else Madlin had to say about the Munro. As if caught in a guilty act, she moved quickly off the bed. Her turn was so brisk that her long, unbound hair whipped about, caught on his whisker-roughed chin, and then trailed down his chest before she was away. As the luminous strands brushed his flesh, Ewan could not suppress a moan.

"You are in pain, Sir Ewan?" Lady Elspeth inquired as she opened the bed hangings fully and secured them to the posters. Noiselessly, she swept around the bed and placed her hand upon his brow, then caught up his wrist.

Needing to see for herself just how badly her husband had been injured and how the wound fared now that her aunt had tended it, Madlin trailed along in her aunt's wake. Her interest was piqued no more or less than it would have been for any in the clan, she rationalized. It was a chieftain's duty to know the condition of each and all under her protection.

"Your skin has cooled some, but I like it not that your heart is beating so rapidly," Lady Elspeth said. "You shall stay in this bed until I tell you otherwise."

"I am not that weak," Ewan declared, but the lady Elspeth either did not hear or did not believe him. Without so much as a by-your-leave, she swept the bedclothes aside.

"God's teeth, have a care!" He made a grab for the sheet to cover his groin. Though his sex had relaxed some during his conversation with his wife, it had risen to full attention once again when his wife's hair had briefly caressed his chest. Like a youth caught dallying with his first woman, he felt the heat of embarrassment flood his cheeks.

"Make yourself useful, Madlin, and fetch my chest from the corner," Elspeth said as she unwound the strips covering his thigh. If she'd noticed aught else she made no comment.

Curious himself as to how his wound fared, Ewan strained to look over the woman's shoulder. Though the skin around the gash was still reddened, the streaks he remembered spreading away from it had all but faded. The lady bent her face to it and sniffed.

" 'Tis good," she announced, then began a gentle pushing along the line of fine stitches she'd made the night before. "And you, Madlin, how fares your head this morn?"

"I am well, Aunt." Madlin placed Elspeth's medicine chest next to the bed. Not for anything would Madlin admit to a throbbing in her head or a dizziness when she moved too quickly. Holy Mary, she'd not give her aunt reason to strip her of her clothing and tuck her back in that bed with Ewan Fraser. Sitting on the edge of the bed, fully clothed, and conversing with him had been pleasant and safe. She'd not chance being dosed with a sleeping draught and awaking to find herself playing the harlot again.

"I'll not swallow any more of that sleeping draught," Ewan announced, and Madlin wondered if he feared it for the same reasons she did. They had taken a step toward some understanding between them. Sharing a bed as husband and wife would take a while longer, assuming he should ever recant his vow against consummating their marriage.

Seemingly unfazed by the Fraser's adamant refusal, her aunt continued mixing powder into a cup of wine. "If you wish to get well, you'll drink every last drop." She thrust the cup toward Ewan's tightly closed mouth. Impatience marked her voice as she explained, "Nothing more than a mixture of feverwort and goosefoot."

"To cleanse and strengthen the blood," Madlin supplied to reassure him. Her aunt's head spun around to look at her, and there was more surprise in her expression than Madlin could ever remember seeing there. Madlin shrugged. "I may have been a reluctant student, Aunt, but you are a good teacher."

The admittance caused yet another expression she rarely saw on her aunt's face—approval. Madlin narrowed her eyes on her husband. "Stop being such a *gomeril* and drink it down!"

Ewan's expression at her show of authority was merely a raised brow. He didn't enjoy being ordered about, but he was hard put to keep a smile from forming. God take him for a fool, but he enjoyed this Madlin MacKendrick whose eyes flashed with mischief and fire.

He relaxed his lips just enough to test the mixture being offered. He might be a fool, but he was not a totally trusting fool. When he was satisfied there was nothing in the cup that would render him senseless, he drank it down.

His stomach welcomed the mixture with a loud growl for more. The sound seemed to be a reminder to Madlin's that it, too, was empty, for it chose that moment to grumble as well. "We are both in need of food. I shall leave you in my aunt's capable care, Sir Ewan," she said as she started from the room. "I will make certain food is sent up to you immediately."

"Wait, Madlin," Elspeth called. "You cannot mean to show yourself in the hall with your hair all a tumble. 'Tis not fitting for the lady of Dunfionn to appear so. Further, you are a married woman now. Your hair should be bound and your head covered. There should be a wimple or square of silk in yon chest. Fetch it."

"Nay!"

The bellow from the bed stayed Madlin in her steps. Shocked, she turned toward the bed. Her aunt turned as well, her expression speculative.

"I . . . ah . . ." His cheeks decidedly flushed with color, he recovered to say smoothly, "Surely a chieftain should not appear as other women. She should be instantly recognizable by her people, and for certes my wife's hair is a most distinguishable feature, would you not agree, Lady Elspeth?"

The lady Elspeth's raised brows remained in place, though she allowed a reluctant-sounding "aye" before encompassing both Ewan and her niece with a mildly censuring gaze. "But there are proprieties a lady must honor, and the laird of the MacKendricks is a lady."

"Perhaps, a small piece of silk secured by a simple chaplet would satisfy propriety but yet not shield her hair from her people's view," Ewan suggested.

"That would be acceptable," the lady Elspeth said. "But still her hair must be bound. It is most unfitting that she wear it loose, as would a maiden."

"Plaited and coiled in two great loops on each side of her face is quite a fashion among the ladies on the continent, but I do not think it would suit her. A single plait seems more appropriate for her and more in keeping with a small adornment."

"You have an eye for fashion, sir." Elspeth nodded approvingly. "Madlin, fetch your comb from your chest. I believe there is a lawn kerchief that will do quite nicely. There is no chaplet in that chest, but we can make do this morn with a ribbon to secure the linen."

Madlin, who had remained silent throughout the exchange, moved forward. Her hands on her hips, every line of her body crying out with irritation, she demanded, "Have I, the Mac-Kendrick, nothing to say in this matter?"

"No," was her husband's immediate and most authoritative reply.

Chapter Eight

"How dare he decide how my hair is to be worn," Madlin muttered beneath her breath as she finally escaped the chamber. "Sweet Mary, what has happened to Aunt Elspeth? Meekly following his orders as if he had every right to deliver them."

That she was wearing her hair in its customary single plait had no effect in softening her anger. That the small scrap of linen secured atop her head would have been her choice carried no weight either. He had no right to order any changes about her appearance. Or, to order her about in any way.

"This will not do." She slammed her fist into her palm and ran squarely into the broad wall of a man's chest.

"Lass? Er . . . I mean, my lady?" Gordie Gunn asked as he steadied her.

Madlin felt the rise of color in her cheeks. "Oh . . . Gordie. Forgive me for not looking where I was going. Good morrow, and to you, also, Hugh."

Both men were eyeing her curiously.

"Are ye well?" Hugh asked.

"Oh yes, quite well, thank you." With unsteady fingers, she brushed her brow, wincing a little when she grazed the raised bruise. "I have a hard head, which, of course, you both already know. 'Twill take more than one fist to the head to lay me low." She was babbling like the idiot they probably already thought her to be. "Have you broken your fast? I am on my way to the hall. I . . . I am quite famished. Would you care to join me?"

Gordie gave her a long measuring gaze that made her even

more uncomfortable. But it was Hugh who said, "We have been down already this morning. Not together, but in turn so as not to leave the door unguarded."

"You spent the night guarding the door?" Her flush increased. Had they heard Sir Ewan's shout at dawn? "That was not necessary. The Fraser . . . I mean, my husband, Sir Ewan, is in no condition to attempt an escape."

" 'Twas not his escaping that was worrying us," Gordie said.

"You ought to have sought your beds. There was no need to spend the night on duty out here in this cold hallway. Ewan Fraser will never hurt me. He is a man of his word."

Her husband's angry words echoed through her mind. *I do not intend to ever cause you even the slightest twinge of pain.* Certain the recollection of that vow would show on their faces, she was momentarily saved further humiliation by the opening of the door behind her.

"Madlin, Gordie, Hugh," was Elspeth's simple greeting before heading toward the stairway. Briefly, Madlin considered following her aunt, but the serious expressions on the two men's faces stayed her.

" 'Twas not yer safety but yer husband's that was heavy on our minds, lass," Gordie said quietly when Elspeth had disappeared from view.

Any embarrassment still lingering within Madlin was quickly superseded by alarm. "You cannot mean that anyone at Dunfionn would harm Sir Ewan? I charged the clan with his well-being, did I not?"

"Aye, ye did, my lady. But old hatreds are hard to let go and other than MacKendricks were inside the keep last night."

"We have visitors? Who? Why was I not told?"

"Och, 'twas Seamus Munro. Rode in late last night long after ye was abed," supplied Hugh.

The ache that had been plaguing her for the past hour changed from a dull throb to a sharp pounding. Squeezing her eyes shut, Madlin rubbed her forehead, wincing when she encountered the bruise there. "Seamus." Rolling her eyes, she muttered beneath her breath, "What more, Lord? Have I not had enough travails already this morn?"

"Ye'll not have to deal with him," Gordie informed her. "He left with the dawn. I do not think he'll be back for a good long while."

"Praise God." Some of the tension created by the mention of Seamus Munro left her. "Why was he here? What did he want?"

Gordie scratched at his beard, squinted his eye, and then shook his head. " 'Twas queer, him coming so late. Said he'd been traveling and stopped here to spend what was left of the night before going on home."

"Was he alone?"

"Aye, and that does bother me some," Gordie admitted. "Seamus Munro is not a man to travel all alone, not even so short a distance as from here to Dubhfireach."

"Wasn't all fit out like a strutting peacock like he usually is when he comes calling on ye," Hugh inserted. "Wearing all black and looking a mite tattered and a whole lot dirtied. I don't mind telling ye, I didn't like the look of some of the stains."

"Blood, or my name is not Gordie Gunn. Up to no good is that Seamus Munro, and it may come to worse. The fool did not take the news of yer marriage well."

Madlin raised her brows and took a deep breath. "No, I suppose he would not, but 'twill put a stop to his endless proposals of marriage."

As good as it would be to be relieved of Seamus's petitions for her hand, she did not think her problems with him were at an end. The suspicions forming in her mind were not ones she liked, for the Munros had traditionally been the MacKendricks' closest ally. Even less to her liking was asking, "Have we anyone at Dubhfireach we can trust to keep an eye on Seamus and report to us?"

"We can send someone."

She considered her order only briefly. In all her lifetime,

she had not once been given any reason to trust Seamus Munro. "Do it, but for the moment, do not let our concerns go further than the three of us and whoever is sent to spy on the Munro. I trust the two of you will know of just the right man whose arrival and stay at Dubhfireach will not be at all suspicious. I would not insult even Seamus Munro with such an act of distrust if there is not cause."

A look passed between Gordie and Hugh, then a short nod of agreement before Gordie announced, "Beatha."

"Beatha!" Madlin could not believe they'd think to entrust the chattering Beatha MacKendrick with such a serious mission. "That woman's mouth does not stop wagging from dawn till dusk."

"Aye," Gordie agreed, but his grave expression did not alter. "But she's sweet on one of the Munros and has a sister married to one of 'em who's expecting a wee bairn soon. 'Twill not be strange for her to visit her sister. Being known as a talker is the best disguise of all. No one will believe the lass has a brain in her head and does ever use her ears a tenth as much as her mouth."

Throughout the conversation, Madlin could not stop shaking her head. "I cannot believe this, and I have known Beatha MacKendrick all my life. Beyond that, I do not think she's up to such a task. I'll not risk putting her in harm's way if we do, in fact, have cause to set a spy on Seamus and she is found out."

Gordie patted her shoulder reassuringly. "Our Beatha will come to no harm. She knows how to handle herself. She is Daidbidh's granddaughter," he reminded her. "In her own way, Beatha is as good a warrior as her grandsire was in his prime."

Madlin raised her brows at that kind of praise for Dunfionn's most notorious gossip. Full of misgivings, she cautioned, "This must be her choice, not an order. And, if she agrees, tell her to be cautious and to put her own safety above all else."

Assuming her interview with the two men was over, she said, "If you'll pardon me, I'm off to break my fast."

"There is one more thing ye should know," Gordie said.

Frowning, Madlin turned back. Whatever else they had to tell her must be even more serious than Seamus Munro's strange behavior. Both men looked so uneasy, she felt the rise of an irreverent giggle. Not so many years ago, she had frequently been the one shifting from one foot to the other, studying the floor below and then the ceiling above, struggling for just the right words to explain a transgression of some sort. "And what would that be?"

"Well, my lady. It's about something Sir Ewan was carrying when we captured him. I think it best that I show it to you and that we talk about it someplace more private." With a nod to Hugh, who quickly stationed himself once again in front of the door to the laird's chamber, Gordie motioned for her to follow him.

A few minutes later, they were sequestered in her father's estate office. There, Gordie extracted a scabbard from a pile of packs heaped in one corner. Carefully, he drew the sword from the scabbard and laid the impressive weapon across the top of the heavy desk. Pointing to the crest engraved upon the hilt, he asked, "Do ye recognize it, lass?"

Madlin did not have to look too closely, for the engraving was large and the design unmistakable. A lion rampant with the motto *Bi Glic*, "Be Wise," was emblazoned within a double border of counter fleurs-de-lys. "Royal Stewart," she said softly.

Running shaking fingers lightly across the crest, she could not credit that such a thing was lying in front of her. The temptation to test the weapon's weight and balance proved irresistible. Obviously well crafted, the gleaming blade was made of Toledo steel and the overall balance finer than any she'd ever held. Feeling almost reverent toward the sword, she carefully laid it back upon the desk.

"Sir Ewan was wearing it when we captured him."

"But he is a Fraser. How? Why would he have this sword?"

" 'Tis what Hugh and I have been wondering. Sir Ewan

muttered some last night that his wound had been seen to by royal physicians."

Stunned, Madlin's gaze was drawn back to the crest. Her knees began to shake and she abruptly sat down. "Oh Gordie, what have I done?"

"Ye've captured a man in high favor with the crown, I'm thinking. 'Twas why Hugh and I thought to keep a close guard on the man. 'Twould not go well for us if he were to come to harm."

Gordie's comments seemed to be coming from far away as her mind raced through all the details she had heard of the man who lay in the laird's chamber. Stirling. He'd gone first to Stirling and had stayed there nearly a fortnight before beginning his trip home. The king was often in residence there. She was a dolt for not investigating the precise reason for the Fraser knight's journeying to Stirling.

"Who else besides you and Hugh know of this?"

"I cannot be sure. No one has said anything, and 'tis possible no one has looked closely at the sword. Hugh and I bundled it up quickly before Sir Ewan's belongings were sent here."

"And you did not see fit to tell me my prisoner was most likely a friend of our king?" she asked in a tone dangerous in its calm and quiet.

"In truth, lass, we did not have time to think much on it that night, and with all that happened, we forgot. 'Twas when he talked of the royal physicians that we were reminded, and ye was sore wounded yerself and—"

"Enough!" Madlin stood and gestured toward the scabbard. "Tell no one about this," she directed as she resheathed the weapon. Though she was loath to face her husband again this morn, she could not avoid it. With the scabbard cradled in one arm, she approached the hearth and carefully pushed on one of the leaves carved in the mantelpiece. A hidden door in the paneling beside the fireplace opened, and Madlin started through it.

Gordie handed her a lighted candle. "I would not have ye taking a tumble on that narrow, winding stair."

Needing a moment of lightness to break the tension stiffening her body, she teased, "Are your fears for this great sword in my arms or for me?"

Her Godsire's slow grin and the twinkle in his eye did more to shore up her confidence in the rightness of the confrontation ahead than anything else he could have said or done. "Och, ye'll heal, lass, but that sword . . . 'Tis a treasure to be sure and not one to be handled carelessly." He sobered measurably. "I can come with ye."

"No, but I thank you. It's best I do this myself." As much to reassure herself as Gordie, she added, "I'll be in no danger."

"Och, Sir Ewan, you tease me. No woman could manage with such a monstrosity upon her head." The lady Jeanne burst into another spate of musical laughter.

"I swear it is the truth. As many as four pointed cones soaring so high, 'tis a marvel the women could hold their heads erect. Perhaps the French noble ladies are not blessed with slender graceful necks as are the lovely ladies of the Highlands such as yourself."

He was rewarded for his boldness with an enchanting blush coloring her flawless skin. He doubted the vivacious lady Jeanne would be a widow much longer. Surely her charm and beauty would capture another man's heart soon, if it had not already.

"Have you nowhere else you're needed, cousin?"

"Och, Maddie!" The lady Jeanne pressed her hand across her heart. "You gave me a fright."

Ewan's gaze followed Lady Jeanne's to the opening in the paneling beside the fireplace. It was not the sudden appearance of his wife through a hidden passageway that startled him. Keeps like Dunfionn usually had them. It was what she carried that made him uneasy. *The sword.*

"I . . . I believe I shall be on my way. Good day to you, Sir

Ewan." Lady Jeanne gathered up her skirts and hurried toward the door. "And good day to you, Maddie. Are you feeling well this morn?"

"Aye, Jeanne. Thank you for your care last night and for seeing to Sir . . . my husband's well-being this morn."

Though her words were pleasant and polite, her expression did not soften for so much as a brief moment. Not at all the discomfited woman who'd fled this very chamber earlier.

With a flourish, she unsheathed the sword and swung it high. Such drama was certainly intimidating, for the woman knew well how to brandish a sword. He refused to allow the slightest flinch, though his every muscle bunched in readiness to roll to safety if that sword began a downward arc or a forward thrust. "You do that very well, my lady."

Seemingly ignoring his comments, she tossed the scabbard aside. Carefully, she balanced the sword across her palms before laying it across his thighs. It was an act of either naïveté or trust. Or, perhaps returning his weapon was a test.

Suspecting it was both an act of trust and a test, he made no move to pick up the weapon. Frasers were as honorable as MacKendricks claimed to be. He'd give her no proof that it was otherwise.

"How came you, a Fraser, to have this Stewart sword, my lord?"

A diplomat this woman would never make. She was far too direct. But it was a directness he admired. Knowing it would be an insult to both her and himself if he were to claim that the crest was other than Stewart, he stated simply, "It was given to me by a friend."

"A very good friend who would gift you with such a fine weapon."

"Aye."

"A royal friend, perhaps?"

"Aye."

"James Stewart, King of Scotland, is your friend."

It was not a question but a statement, and Ewan chose neither to confirm nor deny it. He'd not lie to her but thought it better not to offer more information than she asked for directly. However, he had a strong feeling she would ferret out all. How she went about this interrogation would tell him much about her. As would her reaction to the information she extracted.

"When did your friendship with our king begin?"

"When we were mere lads."

Carefully, he watched her reaction as he answered her questions. Surprise was evident from the slight widening of her eyes, but only surprise. Not shock.

"You are of an age with our king, are you not?"

"Aye." God's teeth, she would have it all from him if he did not at least make an attempt to divert her mind's path. His new title, Jamie's orders, even the promised earldom would have to come out sooner or later. He preferred later, after he knew more about the attacks and how the MacKendricks would react to a Fraser being given the disputed lands.

He reached for an oatcake on the tray her cousin had brought for him. "Would you care for one of these, my lady? Perhaps some of the porridge or kippers? There is surely more than enough for two."

Her gaze immediately shifted to the tray beside him, confirming his suspicion she'd not yet broken her fast. The tip of her tongue crept across her lower lip, eliciting an immediate tightening in his groin.

Good lord, she's bewitching.

Though the lady Jeanne was as lovely and charming as her cousin, she had not aroused him in the slightest. But one glance from the lady Madlin's green eyes, the sight of just the tip of her tongue, even just watching the way she moved, and he was all but panting after her. The sooner he ended this interrogation and sent her from the chamber, the better, he told himself. Then, knowing himself a fool to flirt with temptation, he found himself setting the sword aside and making room for her beside him.

"Come." He patted the spot he'd just vacated and beckoned

when she still demurred. "Sit and break your fast." He shifted himself a bit more toward the middle of the bed and surreptitiously tossed one of the furs over the sword. If the sword were out of sight, perhaps he could divert her thoughts entirely and buy a bit more time before she discovered all the details about his relationship with James. "The laird of Dunfionn should not faint from hunger."

Madlin eyed the spot on the bed for a moment before her gaze strayed to the man himself. Had he no modesty whatsoever? Remembering the easy chatter she'd overheard between her husband and her cousin, she supposed not.

If Jeanne hadn't been disconcerted by the sight of a man's bare chest and the certain knowledge that the rest of him was equally as bare beneath the covers, then why should she? She'd seen male chests before. Ones just as muscular and just as broad.

It wasn't the sight of Ewan Fraser's naked chest that was making her feel so warm. It was hunger. Madlin promptly sat down on the edge of the bed and reached for one of the oatcakes.

"Would you care for some ale?" He handed her a mug.

"You're feeling a bit better?" she managed around a mouthful of oatcake, grateful for the ale. Her mouth had gone suddenly far too dry when his bare arm brushed against her shoulder.

"Aye, your aunt is a good healer. Already I'm feeling much stronger."

Refusing to appear the coward, she remained where she was, took another long swallow of the ale, and reached for a piece of dried fish. "You had best stay abed until she tells you otherwise," she warned him. "She does not like her orders ignored."

He dipped one of the oatcakes in the pot of honey on the tray. "I'm told you would know, as you have frequently disregarded her orders."

"My cousin does talk too much." She belied the sharpness

in the tone with a mischievous grin before admitting, "I was not an easy lass for my aunt Elspeth to raise."

The sound of his laughter was infectious, and eased her trepidations. It felt good to laugh and talk of her childhood, when her greatest concern each day had been how to avoid her aunt's instructive sessions. Between the two of them the food on the tray disappeared as they shared stories of childhood pranks.

It wasn't until later when she was hurrying across the bailey that she realized she'd been neatly outmaneuvered. She'd discovered no more about her new husband's connection with the king—and had left the man with a weapon.

Whirling about, she'd taken a step back when she halted. She'd done much to wound the man's pride in the past two days. Could she not allow him at least his weapon, the most important symbol of his knighthood?

He's a prisoner and must be disarmed.

I've insulted the crown by capturing the king's friend. If I give back the sword, tear up the marriage lines, and send him on his way with my most sincere apologies, perhaps my head will remain on my shoulders.

And the war between Frasers and MacKendricks will continue. I cannot let him go. Lives depend upon this marriage.

As my husband, he will not wield that sword against a MacKendrick nor bring the royal wrath down upon us. He is one of us now.

He is Fraser-born.

There'll be no peace between us until we learn to trust each other.

The arguments warred within her head until at last she decided to trust the honor she believed marked her new husband's character. She would not insult the man again by taking away his weapon. *Holy Mary, I pray I am not placing hopes for my marriage and my own head above the welfare of my clan.*

She quickly made the sign of the cross, turned, and started toward the stables. After only a few steps she halted again.

Restoring one man's dignity was not worth risking the safety
of her clan. Spying Gordie at the stable door, she hailed
him. "Take Hugh with you and return the Stewart sword to
safekeeping."

Chapter Nine

"Madlin, might I have a private word with you? In the solar, if you please."

"Of course, Aunt," Madlin replied without enthusiasm. "I shall be up shortly."

But at the top of the steps she hesitated, uncertain as to whether she should go. She'd been wanting to have a confrontation with her aunt. Now that the chance was at hand, she was reluctant to agree to the woman's request.

Pausing before the heavy-banded door of the solar, she wiped her dampened palms on her gown and smoothed her hair as best she could. She was barely inside the room before her aunt inquired, "The elders have called a council. Are you prepared?"

"I have given it little thought, for I have had many things to see to this morning. You will attend, Aunt?" Madlin dropped her weary body onto one of the cushioned settles flanking the hearth.

"I shall be there, but I wanted to talk with you beforehand." Elspeth thrust a goblet in Madlin's hand. "Drink it down. 'Twill ease the pain in your head some without altering your wits. You will need them when you face the elders."

Madlin drank down the herb-laced wine, not surprised her aunt had already guessed that she was suffering a steady ache in her head. The woman was uncanny in her ability to detect the source of a person's discomfort merely by looking at him or her. Some thought her a witch like Old Meta, though of a type they were glad to have among their midst when sickness or injury befell them. Madlin wasn't sure whether she believed or disbelieved the notion.

"You have chosen a Fraser to husband. I would hear your reasons." As she spoke, Elspeth selected a needle and thread and began to work on a piece of deep green silk shot with gold threads.

The fabric looked vaguely familiar to Madlin. She frowned as she stared at it momentarily, trying to remember where she'd seen it, before forcing her attention to the subject at hand.

"You heard the stories about him that Colley and the others related. At first I thought merely to capture him and use him as a tool to force Cameron Fraser to meet with me."

"Hmmph." The rhythm of Elspeth's stitching did not alter. "Cameron Fraser was ever a proud man, as was his father before him. He would not have bargained with you whilst you held his son captive."

"So I've been told," Madlin admitted dryly. "But 'tis well known the Fraser does take care of his own."

"And so you married his son."

"It seemed the best way to ally our clans and thus stop the bloodshed. But . . . um . . . there is more about him that you should know." Madlin took a deep breath, then confessed in a rush, "He is a close friend to our king, and I fear in kidnapping him I have insulted the crown. If there is any more bloodletting, I fear it will be James calling for my head."

Calmly, Elspeth snipped a thread, rethreaded her needle, and resumed stitching. "I doubt 'twill come to that."

"That's all you have to say? Have you no suggestions for what I should do? No reprimands for my thoughtless actions?"

Still attending to her needlework, Elspeth asked, "Do you still believe your marriage to Sir Ewan will bring peace between our clan and his?"

"Well . . . yes . . . I believe there is still a chance."

"Then, I suggest you do what you must to ensure this marriage lasts."

"And that would be?"

Elspeth put aside her sewing and crossed the chamber to a

cupboard. From it, she extracted a cloth-wrapped wedge of cheese, a pair of apples, and a small loaf of bread. "First, you will eat. You should not meet with the elders on an empty stomach."

Around the wedge of cheese she'd popped into her mouth, she said, "Some here at Dunfionn think I have betrayed my loved ones' memories by bringing a Fraser to Dunfionn. They fear he'll open the gates one night and let in his clansmen to kill us all in our beds."

Elspeth placed a mug of watered wine near Madlin's hand. "Aye, some would fear that."

"I met Alys in the garden, and she would not talk to me." Madlin tore a piece of bread into a pile of crumbs as she remembered the look on the lady's face when she'd hurried past her. It had been a look of such horror, as if Madlin were a viper. "A Fraser!" was all she had said before dashing away. "I fear I've lost a friend and that Alys will now wish to return to the Robertsons."

From the other side of the chamber, Elspeth told her, "The lass is still grieving. She has a well-schooled mind behind that pretty face. She'll come around when she has time to think on it and to understand your reasons."

Madlin was not so sure, but she could not afford to think long on the lady Alys Robertson. She'd met with many of her people in the few hours she'd had this day. Some were as distressed as her brother's betrothed. Most were skeptical, but some, all women, had thought she'd made a fine choice.

So intent was she on the conversations she'd had that Madlin gave the food she was pushing into her mouth little thought. Once her stomach was filled, she wiped her mouth and fingers with the soft snowy cloth that appeared just as she finished.

"Thank you, Aunt Elspeth."

The simple words were for once spoken with true feeling and a smile. For perhaps the first time in her memory, Madlin found herself genuinely appreciative of her aunt's care.

"Problems are best solved on a full stomach. Now, let us

prepare for your meeting with the elders." Elspeth seated herself upon a settle facing Madlin. Again, her hands reached for
her needle and thread.

"Before we do," Madlin began, "I must confess you have
surprised me."

Elspeth slipped her thimble back upon her finger and pushed
a stitch through the shimmering silk before responding.
"How so?"

Madlin hardly knew where to begin. "I came here expecting
a severe scolding for being rash, for racing about the countryside dressed as a lad, for forcing a man, the king's friend no
less, to marry me, and thus making a mockery of one of the
holy sacraments. For any number of the mistakes I seem to
make nearly every day which cause you such displeasure."

Elspeth's fingers stilled. "Madlin, you are not a wee lass in
need of such lectures. You are a woman now, and you have
gained much knowledge and patience during the years you
spent away from us. Toirlach was wise to send you to Liusadh
Gunn. She did well by you.

"But you are also very much my brother's daughter. Every
day I see evidence of how well you listened when he was
teaching Bram what he needed to know to be a good chief.
Yours is a rare mind, niece. I have always thought so, and if I
was sometimes overly cross with you in the past, it was because I feared you might allow that mind to shrivel up for lack
of good use."

Madlin laughed in self-derision. "I gave you much cause to
think so."

Elspeth graced Madlin with one of her rare smiles. The expression gentled her features and put a soft light in her eyes,
giving evidence of the pretty young lass she once had been.
What's more, as Madlin studied Elspeth more closely, she
realized how young her aunt still was.

Few lines marred her creamy skin. Her hands were smooth
and strong. Her figure firm and nicely curved. Three and
thirty, was she? The years that separated their births seemed
not so very many now.

"I will not claim to have been pleased when I was told you had married a Fraser, " Elspeth began. "But I think your reasons are both admirable and sound. Sir Ewan seems an honorable man who must surely want peace as much as you do."

She paused to thread a needle with glittering gold silk. "As a former soldier, Sir Ewan should appreciate that fate provided you with an opportunity for peace and you did exactly what a good leader should. You acted upon it. And I should not worry overmuch about his friendship with the king. Sir Ewan will not want his wife to come to any harm."

How her aunt had formed such a favorable opinion of Ewan Fraser Madlin could not imagine, nor did she fully agree.

Still, Madlin was as relieved by her aunt's words as she was fascinated by the skill and speed with which Elspeth created a winding vine of stitchery along an edge of the silk. Recognizing what a fine garment it was, far more fine than was practical, curiosity spurred her to ask, "For whom are you making that gown?"

"You."

"Me! I have no need for such finery. 'Tis a waste of funds we sorely need elsewhere. I can scarce credit you would spend precious coin on silk. With the crops and livestock lost these past months, we will need the price of such as that to help feed our people this winter."

"Calm yourself," Elspeth advised gently. " 'Tis the length your father gave you years ago. Only a wee corner of it was singed before I could rescue it. It would be a waste to leave it to molder when it could be put to good use."

"A good use, you say?"

"Aye. I would you appear the baroness you are when you are presented to the Earl of Glendarach and his countess. I hope 'tis done in time."

"Did not Gordie or Hugh tell you I invited the Fraser to come for Hogmanay? There are many weeks left before then, Aunt. Given the speed of your needle, you could fashion gowns for all the women of clan MacKendrick by then."

Elspeth looked up and toward the window beyond Madlin, noting the angle of the sun's rays. "The elders will be gathering below," she said, carefully laying aside the silk gown. "Think you that Cameron Fraser will wait eight weeks before presenting himself and a full contingent from Glendarach?"

"You think they will come sooner?"

"Aye." Elspeth stood and moved to a chest beneath a far window. "I doubt he'll wait so much as a fortnight. I expect a messenger from Glendarach any hour. Come." Elspeth beckoned. "We have more immediate concerns than meeting with Cameron Fraser. We must prepare you."

She lifted the lid of the chest and sorted through it. "Take off that old gown. You look like a serving wench. You are the lady of Dunfionn, chief of clan MacKendrick and married to a good friend of King James. You will appear the part when you stand before those men."

This was an Elspeth with whom Madlin was familiar. After the rare camaraderie of the past hour, she felt almost comforted in being ordered about. However, old habits are hard to break, and for a moment Madlin considered resistance before reaching for the laces at her sides.

Consider all Counsel. Elspeth knew the elders better than Madlin. Her aunt had sat on countless councils in recent years. While far from an ancient like the others, Elspeth was daughter, sister, and now aunt to the MacKendrick. Madlin would be wise to abide by her advice on how she should be attired for such an important occasion as the first real confrontation with the elders since her becoming laird.

"It was your mother's. You are built much as she was when she wore this, and it should be long enough for you," Elspeth said as she dropped a gown of black velvet over Madlin's head. "Who among the elders can you count on for support at this meeting, Madlin?"

"Gordie and Hugh, of course," Madlin said as she struggled to push her arms through the snug sleeves of the gown. "I talked with Dag and Hardwin some when I visited the stables and kennels this morning." She told her aunt of the conversations she'd had with the two men and then all she'd learned from others she'd talked with throughout the morning.

"I believe I was able to allay Dag and Hardwin's concerns. They will stand with me today, at least."

"Good, good, you have done well so far," Elspeth muttered as she fastened a girdle of gold links about Madlin's waist. "Meta will seem to swing her support back and forth, but in the end, if you are firm, she will stand with you. Sit down now and let me rebraid your hair."

"Who among them do you think the worst firebrand?"

Elspeth chose a vial of fragrant oil from the cupboard and poured a small amount of it in her hand. "That would be Daidbidh. He has grown stiff and bent with his years and thinks if he calls for war the others will think him still the fearsome warrior he imagined he was when he fought alongside my sire, your grandsire."

The scent of rosemary filled the air as she rubbed her palms together, then began working the oil into Madlin's hair. "You must stand tall and look him straight in the eye when you tell him this marriage will bring peace to the Moray," she advised as she reached for a comb. "Do not flinch. Do not so much as blink an eye at whatever that old blusterer may say. And above all, do not shout."

"But Papa often shouted during council meetings," Madlin argued. "Airic and I could hear him even though we'd been banished from the hall."

"Aye, Toirlach had a mighty voice and could outshout any man of Dunfionn. And you have a strong set of lungs yourself, but you'll be no match for Daidbidh or Airdsgainne if either of them should argue overlong," she said as she began fashioning Madlin's hair into a tidy braid with ribbons of black and emerald silk twining through it. "You must not raise your voice. Be calm, but firm."

"But—"

"Did you not learn the power of quiet talking from Liusadh Gunn? The woman is a master at it. Your mother could quiet a room with a single calm word. 'Tis a skill few have. Think on it and use it."

Elspeth dropped a diaphanous wisp of pale ivory silk atop Madlin's head, arranging it so that its hem barely brushed her brows in the front and fell only to her shoulders at the back. Mindful of the bruise at her niece's temple, she carefully placed a narrow gold chaplet over the silk to secure it.

Not used to wearing such ornaments, Madlin was uncomfortable with the band of precious metal riding in the middle of her forehead. At her frown, Elspeth handed her a small mirror. A stranger blinked from the piece of polished metal, but a rather regal-looking stranger, Madlin thought.

" 'Tis a symbol of your rank. Much the same as are the golden spurs your husband is entitled to wear. If you prevail in forging this alliance with clan Fraser, you will have earned this circlet of gold no less than your husband earned his knight's spurs," her aunt said firmly before ordering her to stand.

"Today is your first battle." She secured a small plaid of MacKendrick colors at her left shoulder with the elaborate ceremonial brooch of the MacKendrick.

Backing away a few steps, Elspeth studied her creation. "Turn. Good. Good. Och, your half-boots. Take them off."

"I am meeting with our clan's elders, not Jamie Stewart," Madlin announced, glaring at the pair of dainty velvet slippers her aunt had pulled from the chest. "I cannot think if my toes are pinched and the soles of my feet are cold. These boots will do."

"Ah, use that tone and just that look when you talk to the elders," she said with a slight smile as she tucked the slippers back into the chest and closed the lid.

A light knock sounded at the door before it opened. "They are gathered below," Jeanne announced as she entered. "Maddie! How beautiful you look. Like a queen you are this day."

"Hardly that." Madlin scoffed.

Jeanne walked around her. "Just as I remember your dear

lady mother. Did I never tell you how when I was a small child I thought Aunt Aislinn was the queen herself? So tall and beautiful she was. You are like her, you know."

"Enough prattling, mistress."

Madlin was exceedingly grateful for her aunt's stern order, for she was growing embarrassed under Jeanne's fulsome comments. As beautiful as her lady mother . . . By the Virgin! 'Twas a blasphemy to say such. She remembered her mother well. Aislinn had been a goddess, so beautiful, graceful and accomplished. Perhaps it was a blessing she had not lived to see her only daughter grow to womanhood. She would have been deeply disappointed.

"Come, Madlin, we must not keep them waiting overlong."

"Och, I almost forgot," Jeanne cried. " 'Tis your husband, he is demanding his packs. He is threatening to march into the council wearing naught but a sheet from the bed, or even naked, if he is not allowed his clothing."

"He should not be out of bed," said Elspeth.

"He cannot attend the council," said Madlin.

"I am and I will," Ewan announced from the open doorway.

Chapter Ten

Looking remarkably fit, Ewan Fraser strode into the room. With a cord from the bed hangings, he'd wrapped a sheet about himself as if it were a ghostly plaid. Despite the ridiculous attire, he appeared self-assured, which was far too disconcerting for Madlin's peace of mind.

One of his shoulders was bare as was a good expanse of his chest. With his slightest movement, the muscles rippled beneath his firm flesh.

Madlin had seen him in less, but even this much was enough to heat her body anew and numb her brain. She thanked God his attention turned first to her cousin.

With a dazzling smile that showed the evenness of his teeth, he swept a flamboyant bow. "My dear Lady Jeanne, who saved my poor body twice in the last day from wasting away for lack of sustenance and my mind from wasting for lack of stimulation." Bringing one of her hands to his lips, he declared, "You are an angel in looks as well as in deeds. I shall be forever in your debt. You have refreshed my body as well as my soul."

Releasing the lady Jeanne's hand, he turned his charm upon Elspeth. "Lady Elspeth, I owe you much. As you see, my strength has returned, and my much-abused limb is bearing my weight. I salute your skill and beg your forgiveness for my surly behavior."

Not a woman to be easily swayed by fulsome compliments, Elspeth did not return his toothy smile. "Sir, you should still be abed."

"Ah, but you underestimate your skills." He paused to grace Jeanne with yet another smile that set Madlin's teeth on edge. "Your vast knowledge and this sweet lady's tender care have worked magic."

Madlin watched him wield a courtier's charm with suspicion. She'd been given a detailed report of what had transpired when her men had confiscated his sword once again. Though he'd not lifted it against them, he'd not given it over without a spate of invectives against both the action itself and her for ordering it that had sent Gordie and Hugh scurrying from his company. That extreme a rage was not usually set aside so quickly. Whatever he was playing at now made her decidedly uneasy.

And Jeanne! Did she not realize how she embarrassed herself with such fawning? Actually giggling and blushing from the knave's compliments.

Intent on putting an immediate stop to whatever Ewan Fraser was about, Madlin cleared her throat to gain attention. "Sir! You should not—"

"And yet another lovely lady," Ewan interrupted, looking for all the world as if he had just now noticed Madlin's presence. He graced her with an even more flamboyant bow than he'd given Jeanne. "You do look familiar, my lady. Have you a sister?"

Before she could prevent it, he captured both her hands in a vicelike grip. Holding her in place, his smile was no longer charming and his eyes were once again filled with the icy disdain with which she was familiar. "Surely a lady of such beauty and grace as yourself would not think to strip her poor husband of all his possessions so that he must wander about wrapped in a bedsheet. No *lady* would do such a thing."

His sarcasm stung. Her palms itched to slap the smug look from the face bending over them. Doubtless the miscreant had anticipated such an action, for his grip tightened. "For certes, your fever has returned and has weakened your brain. My aunt is correct, sir, you should be abed before you do yourself harm."

Pulling her steadily closer he asked, "Is your concern for me, wife?"

"Of course it is."

Still keeping her hands imprisoned, he curled his free arm around her waist, trapping her against him. "Really?" he drawled. The single word dripped with sarcasm. "Perhaps it was concern that I might do myself an injury that prompted you to have my sword taken away . . . again."

Caught up so close to him, her forehead grazed his chin. His smooth, too smooth chin! A cold dread spread through her. While this beast played the courtier, were Gordie and Hugh lying in pools of blood in the hallway, their throats slit by whatever he'd found to scrape away two days' worth of stubble from his chin? "What have you done to the men guarding your door?"

"Guards? There were no guards outside the door when I left the chamber."

His moderate tone was too clearly a thin veneer shrouding the rage emanating from him. Her fear rising so that she could almost taste it, Madlin looked to her cousin. "Were not Gordie and Hugh in the corridor when last you left Sir Ewan?"

"Nay." Her cousin's soft brown eyes skipped rapidly from Ewan to Madlin. "They were so very tired, I sent them off when I took Sir Ewan his noon meal. Poor Hugh could barely stand, and Cousin Gordie's eye was so red and bleary that the poor man could scarcely see from it. Their weary appearance fair tugged at my heart. They are not young men, Maddie. I thought 'twas best they seek their rest."

Relief that the two men she held so dear were not hurt, or worse, swept over Madlin. Then, just as quickly, her relief was replaced by anger. "You thought!"

Wrenching herself from Ewan's grasp proved an impossibility, but it did not prevent her from admonishing her too trusting cousin. "You dismissed them, cousin? Did they send replacements?"

"We . . . I . . . saw no need." Jeanne's pretty countenance drained of all color in the face of Madlin's anger. " 'Twas not thought that Sir Ewan was capable of leaving his bed," she offered meekly, dropping her eyes. "I . . . I am truly sorry if I erred, and take full responsibility for having no one else assigned to the post."

Before Madlin could further reprimand her cousin, Elspeth insinuated herself in front of Jeanne in a surprisingly protective manner. "I believe it was an assumption based on sound reason." The pointed look she gave Ewan indicated clearly that she thought his reasoning otherwise. "Jeanne and I shall leave you two to discuss why Sir Ewan's presence at the council is neither appropriate nor wanted."

She bent her head in deference to her niece's rank. "If it is acceptable to you, niece, I shall have Sir Ewan's packs sent up straightaway. Since he is determined to be about, it simply will not do for the MacKendrick's husband to be seen in naught but a length of bed linen. I shall delay the others a bit, but I would advise you not to tarry long before joining us in the hall."

The heavy door was not yet closed behind Jeanne and Elspeth when Ewan remarked with a grin, "A sensible woman is your aunt. Quite pretty, too, when she allows a smile. I believe I like her."

He released his hold on her, and Madlin quickly moved several feet away. "You will have your clothing, but you must return to your . . . our . . . the chamber and stay there." Gingerly, she moved to skirt her husband and make for the door. "I have important business to attend to. Clan business. 'Tis none of your concern."

"Ah, but surely it is my concern, for by your own vow, clan MacKendrick is my clan now, *n'est-ce pas?*" Adeptly, he kept himself between Madlin and the door. As they engaged in a sort of comical dance to gain the advantage of the door, frustration grew on her face. The sight was a delight to his pride.

Vexed, are you, sweetling? 'Tis but a taste of what you deserve.

"Surely the husband of the MacKendrick should attend this important gathering of his new clan's elders. I should think it expected."

" 'Tis not expected. Your presence will not be welcome." Gathering her skirts about her, she made a quick feint to the right and then to the left, but Ewan deftly cut off her escape once more.

"Surely they will have questions about me. Who better than myself to assure them of my loyalty?"

Her patience clearly at an end, Madlin fisted her hands but planted them firmly on her hips. He had little doubt that she was struggling to keep from pummeling him with them.

"Impossible! Step aside. I can tarry here no longer."

Ewan folded his arms across his chest and leaned against the door. She'd have to go through him to escape the solar. He wasn't at the peak of health, but bigod, he had strength enough to keep a woman from passing—even one as formidable as his wife. "Impossible that I could be loyal or impossible that they would believe me?"

"Your loyalty is not at issue."

"If my loyalty is not at issue, why did you take away my sword?"

"It was merely a precaution. For . . . for your safety."

"*My* safety? You think me so inept and clumsy I cannot handle my own sword?"

Her response was a rolling of the eyes and a most unladylike huff before repeating, "It was a precaution, nothing more. It is too soon after the last raid for a Fraser to be seen parading around Dunfionn armed. I prefer to err on the side of caution. Better a wound to your manly pride than to your body or a MacKendrick's if you were forced to defend yourself. Now, I ask you again to put aside this notion of attending today's meeting. You have not earned the right to sit on the council."

Holding his temper in check, Ewan decided it best to drop the issue of his sword for the time being. "I do not expect to sit on the council, merely to present myself to that august body so they may determine for themselves whether I am suitable for begetting sons upon their lovely lady laird."

Her gasp delighted him, perverse mood that he was in. "What would you have me do first, sweetling? Recite my bloodlines? No, 'tis certain they are aware of them. Best not remind them I am the devil's spawn . . . eh?"

"I . . . you . . . this is quite enough!"

"Mayhap they will wish to make sure that I have all my teeth and that my limbs are sound." Tipping his head to the side, Ewan lifted the sheet dangerously high to expose his bandaged thigh, then remarked with some regret, "Ah . . . well, both my legs are not sound as of yet, but with Lady Elspeth's magic and Lady Jeanne's tender care, this one shall soon be as strong as the other."

He lifted the leg in question and turned it from side to side. The movement made the hem of his makeshift plaid ride even higher, giving Madlin a view of his lean hip and a hint of the muscles that corded his belly. The sight sent a rush of heat through her body. She remembered all too well the feel of his hardened body beneath her palms, her naked breasts, her belly. . . .

To her great relief, he dropped his foot to the floor and allowed the makeshift garment to fall back in place as well. But the light in his eyes was unmistakably one of battle, and of a kind for which she was completely unprepared.

Swallowing hard, she managed, "Why are you doing this?"

He shrugged. "Since you brought me to Dunfionn to stand stud for you, I thought it only logical that you would want to prove to the elders what a good choice you have made," he continued in the mocking tone that was steadily eroding what little composure she had left.

"Is that not why this meeting has been called? To convince the clan elders of the rightness of your decision to marry a son of clan MacKendrick's worst enemy? Have you in mind a better strategy than parading me before them so they can assess my manly attributes?"

A good cuffing was what was called for, but she'd vowed not to resort again to violence with her husband. She took a deep breath, relaxed her hands, and crossed them loosely before her. "Leave off this foolishness. What is it that you are truly about?"

She could not be sure, but the smile spreading across his face appeared almost genuine. "I would know the nature of my position in this clan with which I have been forced to ally myself. Am I merely to lounge about in our chamber as a prisoner held for your . . . ah . . . pleasure? Or have you other tasks and responsibilities planned for me? Mayhap you think to set me to counting the linens, inventorying the spices, casks of wine, and other stores. 'Tis surely what was expected of my predecessors, the espoused of the MacKendrick."

If it was possible, her cheeks flamed hotter than she felt they already were. Just how her husband might spend his days had not been a consideration to which she had given even a moment's thought. Her imagination was nearly her undoing for a picture formed of him bedecked in full armor, sitting quietly in this very chamber, doing needlework.

Calling upon any reserve of dignity she had left to stay the laughter that threatened to gurgle forth, she straightened her back, lifted her chin, and met his gaze straight on. "What skills beyond the battlefield have you that would be of benefit to clan MacKendrick?"

He moved close enough to lift one of her errant curls and gently place it behind her ear. "What is your most immediate concern, my lady?" he returned smoothly, his voice softer, more intimate.

Just where this moment might lead if you were to hold me close and kiss me again, Madlin almost blurted. Startled, she swallowed hard and took a step backward. "That . . . that I am lingering overlong talking nonsense with you."

"Nonsense. What kind of husband might I be if I were not interested in my wife's concerns?"

"One who does not interfere in his laird's duties," she

snapped, just as a scratching sounded at the door. "Your clothing has arrived. I shall leave you to dress in privacy while I proceed to more important matters."

Ewan did not move from his position closer to the door. "Just one more request, sweetling."

"And what other request might you have?"

"That I may have the freedom to roam about Dunfionn at will."

"Granted. I shall instruct your guards that you are to be allowed to go wherever you wish. Now, sir, open that door and let me pass." Gathering her skirts, she prepared to take flight the moment the door opened. But still, Ewan did not budge. "Well?"

"No guards."

Nonplussed, she could but gape at him and blink for a moment. Finding her voice at last, she stated firmly, "You will have guards. This matter is at an end. Now step aside before I order the door stormed."

Calmly, Ewan patted the bar behind him. "I think this will withstand much. I should think a battering ram and several men would be needed to break through."

"You have to let me go now!"

"We will go when I am properly attired as befits the husband of the MacKendrick when attending a meeting of the clan elders," he announced.

"You cannot!"

"I will." His voice boomed louder than hers. "Lady, do not engage in a shouting match with me over this. I will shout louder than you, and I will be heard by the elders either calmly in their presence or bellowing from here."

For the second time in the course of a day she'd been warned against engaging in shouting matches with men. Her temper high, she gave a moment's thought to reaching for the dirk she carried in her boot before discarding the notion.

Less than the length of one full day had passed since she had declared that his well-being was no less dear to her than any in the clan. It would be the worst kind of dishonor if the MacKendrick herself were to carve this newest member of the clan into ribbons.

Quiet talking. If her lady mother could quiet a room with a single word, surely she could calm one man by the same means. Willing her limbs to relax, she asked very quietly, "Why?"

"The passing of each moment is of some import to you, I gather."

Praying for patience, Madlin crossed her hands once again. "You know it is."

"Do I have your word you will not fly by me as soon as I lift this bar?"

"In return for?"

"My speed in attiring myself so that we may attend the gathering of the clan elders with little further delay. That is, unless you'd prefer that I appear as I am."

By the implacable set of his jaw, Madlin could but surmise that any further arguments on her part would be met only by further rebuff. "You have my word. I will not attempt to get by you."

When he did not immediately remove the bar, impatience stormed the shaky dam of her serenity. "Retrieve your garments, pray, with all speed," she said as she moved further from the door.

To afford him some privacy, she turned her back. When she heard the deep-chested rumble of a chuckle, she nearly reached for the closest object to hurl at him. But, before her hand closed about the stem of a heavy candlestick, she heard the grating of the bar as he slid it across its brackets and then the swish of the door.

"What do you know of me?"

"Beyond that you are a stubborn, ill-humored madman?"

"Nay," he said with another chuckle that had her palm itching to wrap itself around the candlestick once more. Only the continued soft rustle of fabrics kept her right hand firmly trapped within her left.

"You seem to know that I have been in France and was knighted by our ally as well as our own country. I admit curiosity as to your source of that information."

Quickly, Madlin told him of all that Colley and the others had heard of him.

"The tales contain some exaggeration, but hold enough truth that you should know I am a man of action, a leader as well as a man forced upon occasion to play the diplomat," he remarked when she'd finished.

"Given those experiences, why should it surprise you that I might insist upon being present at this council meeting that will decide the rightness of your plan to bring about peace?"

"It is right!" Madlin cried, whirling about. "An alliance between our two clans will stop the . . . stop the bloodletting . . ." Her voice trailed away with her breath.

She'd thought him well favored when he'd been unconscious, and even when he'd been surly. Except for the horrid Fraser colors falling from one shoulder, he was attired all in black velvet. The severity of the outfit was relieved only by a delicate line of silver down the front and on the cuffs of his knee-length jacket. He was startlingly handsome.

"Are you so very sure it was Frasers that have raided your lands and killed your clansmen?"

So mesmerized by the way his hair waved across his broad forehead and away from his face, Madlin did not immediately register his query. Gathering up her scattered wits, she revealed, "There were bits of their plaids left at the scenes of their crimes, sometimes even whole ones. 'Twas as if they wanted to taunt us with the identity of the perpetrators."

She paused and glared at the crimson-and-green plaid crossing his heart. "You cannot be thinking to wear those colors."

"I am, and I will," he said firmly. "I shall not skulk about Dunfionn. You may take my name away from me, but a Fraser I am and always will be. And was it not a Fraser you needed to sire your sons, sons your clan is owed?"

"I . . . I . . . yes. But I have trouble enough ahead of me just trying to convince the clan of the rightness of that decision."

Worried that he would endanger the peace for which she was sacrificing their very lives, Madlin entreated, "Please, do not add insult by wearing that plaid here."

"I shall wear this plaid with no less pride than you wear yours until it is proven irrefutably that there is no honor in clan Fraser."

The set of his jaw and the intensity that darkened his blue eyes was proof that he would not be easily dissuaded to leave off his plaid, any more than he would be to let go of his insistence on attending the council meeting. "For both our sakes, I pray your loyalty is not misplaced."

He held her gaze for a long moment. "No less than do I, my lady. No less than do I."

Breaking off the intimacy of the shared moment, he headed for the door. "Come." He beckoned and offered his arm.

She hesitated before allowing him to take her arm and lead her toward the stairs that descended to the hall. "Tell me more of this feud. Have you directed retaliatory raids?"

While his touch was light and separated from her skin by the heavy velvet of her gown, she felt the imprint of it through her entire body. Needing not the distraction of the melting sensations swamping through her lower regions, she pulled away from his grasp.

"We have retaliated, yes. But we have not slaughtered livestock nor murdered people. The need for revenge has been great, but my father sanctioned neither murder nor reckless waste. Nor have or ever shall I."

Halting, Madlin turned and grasped Ewan's arm. " 'Tis only my word I can offer, but we are an honorable clan."

"Just as I offer only my word that the Frasers, too, are an honorable clan," he said gently, and brushed a soothing finger across her brow. "I vow I know of no reason my sire would suddenly set the Frasers upon the MacKendricks in such a vicious manner. 'Tis not his nature."

They'd reached the balcony that surrounded the hall. Voices rumbled from the floor below. Pausing, Madlin squeezed her eyes closed and sighed heavily. "Is there nothing I can say to dissuade you from going down there with me?"

"No," he said, threading her arm through his and starting them toward the stairs once more.

The closer the stairs loomed before them, the more Madlin's trepidations increased.

" 'Tis Daidbidh we're hearing now," she remarked as they drew closer. "He was a mighty warrior under both my grandfather and my father." Her husband's response was but a grunt . . . or was it a low moan?

She looked sharply to his face, noting a paleness at the edges. A dull pain had begun in her own head, a reminder of the blow she'd taken as well as the tension and worry assailing her. Given the grievousness of his wound and recent fever, 'twas more than reasonable that he would be feeling ill and weak.

"Elspeth is correct. You should be abed. You'll do yourself harm being up and about so soon." Despite her misgivings, she tucked her shoulder beneath his arm and lent him some of her strength.

"Mayhap, but lying abed is a luxury I can ill afford," he allowed, leaning heavily upon her as they began their descent.

"A luxury . . . ? I shall think it no luxury if you tumble us both down these stairs and I crack my head once again," she chided.

" 'Twould be most unchivalrous of me, would it not?" His words were teasing, but his features were strained.

"Indeed it would," she muttered, taking note of the white-knuckled grip he had upon the stair rail. She doubted he could make it to the hall without her aid. Now was her chance to foil his plans to attend the council. As soon as the thought formed, she dismissed it. Chivalry was not exclusive to her knightly husband.

"Upon your honor as a knight, tell me exactly why you must meet with the elders of clan MacKendrick this very day? You can barely stand. Could you not wait until another time?"

"Time is another luxury we do not have, wife. I suspect my father will be at Dunfionn's gates before many more days pass. Today is none too soon to begin our quest for peace between the clans. A meeting of the elders is a good place to begin the process."

"*Our* quest? You do want peace, too?"

"Aye, I would be a fool not to want the rewards to be had from peace between our clans."

"Rewards? You speak as if there is more than just the cessation of the carnage and destruction to be had from peace."

When he merely smiled but gave no further explanation, Madlin's curiosity was aroused. They were at the entrance to the great hall, but as of yet their arrival had gone unnoticed. Madlin halted and demanded, "Just what do you mean?"

"There is not time to explain, lest you insult your elders further with your tarrying."

"*My* tarrying! I—"

Infuriating her even more, he placed a quieting finger upon her lips and had the audacity to grin. "I suggest we present a united front, wife. 'Twould not do for the council to see us at war with each other if there is any hope of convincing them that our marriage will succeed in its purpose."

Madlin cast a quick glance at the small gathering before the hearth. Lowering her voice, she asked, "What has happened to so quickly change your anger to acceptance of our marriage?"

"Suffice it to say, madam, that I have had time to analyze the situation. There are many rewards to be had from this union."

Again he spoke of rewards, and Madlin opened her mouth to demand explanation. Promptly he inserted, "Trust me, my lady wife, all will be explained to you in due course."

"I shall hold you to that, sir."

He lifted his arm from her shoulders and tested his weight. When she started to reach for him again, he shook his head. "Allow me some pride, woman. I shall walk into that den of lions without aid."

He smoothed the frown from her forehead with the tip of his finger, then winked. "A prayer from my wife that I shall not collapse and embarrass myself would be most appreciated."

Chapter Eleven

" 'Tis what comes of havin' a woman for our chief."

Walking up behind him, Madlin asked, "And what exactly would that be, Daidbidh MacKendrick?"

His back still turned, the silver-haired patriarch seemingly ignored the startled gasps rippling through the assembled elders. A mug in one hand, he paused in lifting it toward his lips. "Ye've not the stomach to call for the cross of fire and declare war on the Frasers as ye—"

His mouth dropped open when he saw Ewan at Madlin's side. His rheumy eyes widened. The mug wobbled, then tipped, splashing ale down his chest. "Aiii . . . aiii!" The ale pooled in his lap.

With a string of expletives, Daidbidh jumped to his feet. Dripping with ale, he teetered uncertainly while pointing an accusatory finger at Madlin. "She brings . . . him here. He dares wear those colors in our midst!"

Coming to the elderly man's aid, Ewan moved to place a steadying hand on the man's back and started to swipe at the ale with the nearest thing at hand—a corner of his own plaid. Daidbidh's eyes widened dangerously and he staggered backward before Ewan could touch him. "Nay! Nay! Away . . . away from me."

"Ye'd best leave him be, Sir Ewan," Hugh remarked with a chortle as he rose to aid the man. A broad grin on his face, he helped Daidbidh back to his seat. "Och, Daidbidh. 'Tis only a scrap of wool. Ye faced far more dangerous weapons in yer day."

A glazed look upon his face, Daidbidh babbled, "A Fraser at council! Crimson and vert. 'Tis an insult."

Meaning to calm and reassure, Madlin placed her hand gently on Daidbidh's shoulder. "Aye, 'tis no secret my husband was born third son to the Fraser of Glendarach. And a proud clan they are, like the MacKendricks. Would you have him denounce his heritage?" she asked with no small amount of guilt haunting her thoughts.

"I denounce it and all his murdering kin!" Daidbidh shrugged off her hand and rose to his feet again. Though his back was bent and his muscles slackened by time, he was still a commanding figure.

"Daidbidh, you do not—"

"I do! And I denounce your marriage to him. No good will come of it. Ye be laird of Dunfionn, Madlin MacKendrick, but ye show yerself naught but a foolish woman for taking a Fraser for husband. Yer father, God rest him, would be ashamed of ye."

"You'll not impugn my wife, sir," Ewan said as he quickly moved between her and the old man. "Lady Madlin has found the most expedient and likely means to bring about a cessation of the hostilities between MacKendricks and Frasers. 'Tis a wise leader who looks to a way to save lives, not send them off to their deaths. Clan MacKendrick is fortunate, indeed, to have Lady Madlin as its chief."

Startled more by her husband's defense of her than by Daidbidh's condemnations, Madlin was momentarily speechless. How closely his words echoed her aunt's prediction. *Aunt Elspeth, perhaps you are a witch.*

She was saved from having to say anything by the sound of palm striking palm and a crackling voice tinged with laughter. "Och, Daidbidh, sit down and hold yer gab. We've all of us heard ye bluster long enough. Have ye no manners left in ye? 'Tis time we heard from our laird and perhaps a word or two from her new husband."

Daidbidh narrowed his eyes once more on Ewan, made a

huffing noise, then turned his attention to the wild-haired old woman seated close by the fire. "Meta MacKendrick, ye're daft and have been all yer long life." He growled deep in his throat but lowered himself onto a bench beside Hugh. "Never should've let the witch on the council," he muttered as he arranged his sopping plaid about him.

"And ye, lad." Meta beckoned toward Ewan. "Come sit yerself here by the fire before ye fall down. I'm told ye are not well and should still be abed."

"Wounded at Verneuil," Hugh said, nudging an elbow in Daidbidh's ribs as Ewan limped by. "The man's a hero. Did Scotland proud in France, he did. Ye best be giving him yer respect as 'tis a friend to—" He grunted and scowled at Gordie.

"Was knighted by Buchan, himself, Sir Ewan was," Gordie inserted smoothly, looking totally innocent of sharply jabbing his friend in the ribs. " 'Tis proud I am to be in his company, even if he was born of Glendarach. The man has had enough of war and wants only peace, same as all of us."

"Peace? There cannot be peace between MacKendricks and Frasers now. Not after all they've done to us," announced another of the silver-haired men seated in the circle. "Daidbidh has the right of it. 'Tis war we should be declaring and should have done the very day they murdered Toirlach and his lads."

"Now Airdsgainne, Daidbidh," came a calmer voice. A tall, lean-bodied man rose slowly to his feet. "Ye're not alone in feeling bitter toward the Frasers. I'm asking ye to put aside yer anger and listen to what our lady has to tell ye. There will be enough time after to decide if it's war what's wanted."

"Thank you, Hardwin." Madlin smiled her gratitude. More comfortable in the company of the hounds and shepherd dogs than with humans, for Hardwin this had been a lengthy and difficult speech.

Clasping her hands together for a moment, Madlin gathered her thoughts before beginning. " 'A good laird looks to the needs of the clan before his own.' Those are my father's words. I will not dishonor him by forgetting them. The lessons he taught my brothers and me are why I will not risk the lives of others to satisfy my personal need for revenge. Peace is what our clan needs most. Through my marriage with Sir Ewan Fraser, an alliance will be struck between the Mac-Kendricks and the Frasers, and peace will reign in our part of the Moray."

Though some of the elders nodded and even smiled, one made a disgruntled sound and slowly rose to make his statement. "Peace for a time may come from this marriage. Mark my words, 'tis the lands that lie between us that's at the root of all our troubles with the Frasers. Now and in the past," Dermott supplied. That he'd been silent until now was Madlin's only surprise.

"Even if King Jamie himself was to give title of them to one, the other would be angered. 'Tis like a wound that will not heal, those lands, and only when one clan is killed off by the other will it ever be healed. That's what's behind all the killings and burnings now. The Fraser has it in his head to be claiming those lands and then to take ours, too."

"We do not——" Ewan rose to his feet and tipped his head to Madlin. "With your permission, my lady, I would like to address this august body."

Trust me. He was saying it again with his cool, clear blue eyes meeting and holding hers in thrall. Deciding at least the appearance of unity was best, she sent him what she hoped appeared an affectionate smile. "If it is agreeable to the council." She looked about the circle. There were a few frowns, but no one voiced an objection. "You may speak, Sir Ewan."

"Thank you, my lady," he said with a deferent bob of his head. "And I thank the elders of clan MacKendrick."

Throughout Madlin's speech, he'd wrestled with revealing his new title and the holdings that accompanied it. But after the elder's statements, he knew now was definitely not the best time to announce that James had titled the disputed lands over to their laird's new husband. No matter what surname

Madlin thought to attach to him, he was still a Fraser in his own heart and theirs. He had to gain their trust first.

"I have been away from Scotland more years than I have spent here. However, Scotland was always my home, and returning to live in the Highlands was a dream that sustained me during the darkest hours while I was away. That dream was of a peaceful place where I could retire my sword and concentrate all my time and energy on the breeding of fine horses, and watching my children grow to adulthood, perhaps jounce their children on my aging knees."

"Och, 'tis a pretty dream and one dreamt by many," Daidbidh growled. " 'Tis yer clan what's made it impossible for ye and snatched it away from us."

"So it would seem," Ewan said, unable to keep a tightness from his voice as he strove to bank his anger. "I beg your understanding that 'tis hard for me to think the loving father I knew being capable of committing the atrocities attributed to him of late."

"Time changes all things, including men," Airdsgainne inserted. "And a man can be many things. Even a wolf is gentle with its young."

"Aye, but I will tell you true that I cannot condemn my sire until I hear it from his mouth that he has wreaked such vengeance upon his neighbor and his reasons for it."

Airdsgainne started to remark, but Gordie interrupted him. "Loyalty to family is an admirable thing; we cannot fault ye for that, Sir Ewan."

"Aye, a fine thing if it is not blind or ill-deserved. I pledge to you here and now upon my honor that . . ." Ewan paused and wiped sweat from his brow. "Be it my father or any of my kin, I condemn the instigator of these raids and shall do all that is necessary to stop these acts of slaughter and destruction. I have seen too much of war to think there is ever a true victor. Lives and property are lost no matter who claims the victory, and in the end, pride is perhaps the only prize."

A tremor began in his wounded leg that threatened to

topple him. "Pri—" The room tilted slightly, and he felt himself sway. "Pride cannot fill an empty stomach nor provide shel—"

A tug on his sleeve halted him. "Sit down, laddie, before ye fall down." Without further warning, the old woman beside him hauled him down to the bench and then hailed a serving woman hovering at the edge of the gathering. "Fetch Sir Ewan a tankard of water. Mind that it is fresh from the well, and do not be lagging about it."

Her surprisingly sharp eyes turned fully upon him. "Ye have the silver tongue of a diplomat, Ewan of Glendarach. Fate has not been as cruel as ye have thought. It has been the making of ye."

Peculiar words which he had not the time to puzzle out before she placed her hand over his and a comforting warmth spread up his arm and through his body. "Ye have overcome much of it and will overcome what's left." Lifting her hand, she ordered, "Get on with it. I ken ye have more to say."

Nonplussed, Ewan hesitated before continuing. "I cannot believe the man I knew has become so unreasonable that he would choose war over peace. I knew him to be a proud man, but also a practical one possessing a logical mind. Those elements cannot have changed in the years since I last saw him. If the marriage between Lady Madlin and myself does not assure an alliance and therefore a permanent peace, it will at the very least force the Fraser to speak with the MacKendrick. Perhaps then a peace agreement can be reached and a compromise worked out regarding the ownership of the disputed lands."

A silence hung over the group when he finished. A movement at Ewan's shoulder signaled the arrival of the requested water. Murmuring his thanks, he grasped the tankard and drank eagerly of its contents.

"We'll not be sendin' this laird to meet with the Fraser in some distant place. Not even with an armed force accompanying her," Daidbidh vowed.

"Nor would I," Ewan agreed quickly. "Baroness Madlin MacKendrick is your laird, but she is also my wife, and I will protect her with my life."

The vehemence beneath his pledge startled everyone, most of all Madlin. Though they'd vowed to work for peace together and she knew he would never harm her, she had not trusted that he did not still wish to be rid of her. Not by murder, for he had too much honor to cause the murder of a woman. But if she were to be captured by his clan, what better means to rid himself of an unwanted wife than to have her spirited away to a distant convent and have the marriage annulled?

Or did his pledge have something to do with the mysterious rewards he had alluded to? Puzzling over her husband's reasons for making such a pledge could wait; she needed to diffuse the tension and assert her authority. "I am chief of the MacKendricks and shall decide whether I meet with the Fraser."

Grumbling met her statement, as she'd expected. "But I assure you, I shall not repeat my father's error," she stated firmly.

"I have invited Glendarach to Dunfionn for Hogmanay in the hope of celebrating the beginning of a new era between our clans as well as the beginning of a new year. My husband assures me that he will come and most probably far sooner than stated in my invitation. Negotiations for peace will be made within the safety of these walls."

Raising one brow, she fixed a scathing gaze upon one, then another and another of the known firebrands within the group. "That safety will extend to the Fraser and all who accompany him. Further, Glendarach's and his party's safekeeping will not stop at the gates of this fortress but will extend to the very edge of MacKendrick territory. Both during his arrival and departure, even if a peace is not struck while he is here."

For good measure she walked to the mantle and placed her hand upon the shield hanging above it. "Upon my father's and grandfather's shield and the honor with which they led their lives, I so vow. Who is with me in this pledge?"

Hugh and Gordie were the first to place their hands upon the ancient shield and give their pledges. She had expected as much, counted on it. Hardwin, Elspeth, and Meta followed, and finally, after a pause, the others followed suit. "What of the safety of the MacKendricks?" Daidbidh growled as he returned to his bench. "Who's to say the Frasers will not be cutting our throats as soon as we let them inside the gate?"

"Their honor as Highlanders," Madlin quickly stated. "They know as well as we do that hospitality is not to be repaid with violence."

"Hrumph . . . honor! 'Tis not honorable to lie in ambush and fall upon a chief and his sons who were coming in good faith, unarmed and unescorted, in answer to a call for talks, but they done it!" Airdsgainne folded his arms across his chest and cast a belligerent glare toward Ewan. "What say ye to that, Ewan of Glendarach?"

Ewan tightened his lips. "If 'twas as you say, I will personally haul my sire before James and insist that justice be exacted upon him in the most severe method known."

Doubt that he would keep his word, or perhaps that he had the means to do so, was clear upon Airdsgainne's face as well as several of the others. He knew of only one way that he might gain any measure of trust from them. It was a gamble, for he was not certain where their loyalties lay.

Rising slowly, he asked of Madlin, "Would you have my sword brought? I would pledge upon it and the friendship I hold most dear with the man who gave it to me."

"You did well, Madlin," Elspeth informed her hours later after the meeting was finished. Before Madlin could respond to the rare compliment, her aunt turned her attention to Ewan.

"You, too, sir. I thought it was wrong for you to attend the council meeting, but I was mistaken. Facing them and you, yourself, revealing your friendship with the king was the right thing to do. You earned a measure of admiration and moved a bit closer to earning their trust. Your divulgence had just the right blend of reluctance and humility. They would not have responded so well had you boasted of it."

Humility? Madlin rolled her eyes heavenward at the very idea of Ewan Fraser being described as humble. Prideful, he was. So much so, she could not think there was room for an ounce of humility in his body. His angry statements after his capture and, worse, after their marriage ceremony had certainly attested to that!

Despite his avowals that he wanted peace as much as she did, she was not convinced that he was fully reconciled to his present circumstances. Most assuredly, he was playing at something. Once she had likened him to a wolf. Now she wondered if a serpent was not a more apt description, and she vowed to keep a close watch on him.

Barely mindful of the inane pleasantries being exchanged between her aunt and her husband, Madlin analyzed the council members' reactions after Ewan had presented the Stewart sword. It had been a brilliant move, for once he explained how it had come to be in his possession, even the worst of the firebrands showed signs of changing their attitude toward having at least this Fraser in their midst.

While neither Airdsgainne nor Daidbidh had precisely voiced approval of the marriage, they'd indicated it more subtly. As the meeting progressed, it had been abundantly clear that they were more comfortable dealing with a man, even if that man was a Fraser, then with the woman who was their laird. How easy it would have been for him to have taken over leadership of clan MacKendrick then and there, if not in title but in practice. And yet, Ewan had repeatedly deferred to her, reminding them that it was his wife who was the laird of Dunfionn, not him.

Madlin could not stop herself from commenting, "This has certainly been a day for revelations, has it not?"

"Indeed, it has." Reaching between them, Ewan grasped

her hand and brought it to his lips. "You are a remarkable woman, lady wife. Proposing that the king decide the amount of any recompense owed to the MacKendricks was most wise. Then, shifting the discussion to the harvest and the possibility of new storage methods effectively diverted their attention. You may have a struggle convincing some of their validity, but I found your ideas for next year's planting season most intriguing. Where did you hear of such things?"

"My aunt, the abbess, taught me many things that I hope to implement here. The abbey's fields and livestock are models of good, sound husbandry."

"I would like to hear more about the methods incorporated at the abbey, but first, might I ask a boon of you?"

"If it is within my power," Madlin allowed graciously while struggling to pull her hand away. The brush of his lips and the warmth of his large hand encasing hers was wreaking havoc with her thoughts. If asked right then, she doubted she could explain a single reason for the abbey's high crop yields.

Apparently unfazed by her struggling, Ewan rested their clasped hands upon his good thigh. Moving his free hand to the hilt of the sword resting at his side, he said, "I thank you for your trust in allowing me to wear this again. When I am recovered, might I join your men in their daily training?"

"Train with my men?" Unsure of his motives, Madlin narrowed her eyes on him and finally succeeded in freeing her hand from his grasp. "Why?"

"I believe it would be wise if I were to learn Highland warfare methods."

For added measure, he patted his sword's hilt once more and reminded, "I did pledge to guard your life, my sweet. I need to feel better equipped to do so if I am to keep that pledge. Hence my need to train with your men."

Madlin glanced at her aunt, almost hoping for a word of advice. If Elspeth had an opinion on Ewan's request, she was keeping it to herself. Madlin hesitated a moment, then said, "I suppose it would not come amiss."

"Naught but those old fools' stubbornness was amiss this day," Old Meta announced as she joined them. Relieved by the interruption, Madlin was slow in turning her attention away from her husband.

Cackling merrily, the old woman gestured toward Ewan's plaid. "Och, lad, but ye are an audacious one. I feared that old fool Daidbidh would expire on the spot when a Fraser plaid came so near his manly parts. 'Twas certain he thought his cock would shrivel to a nubbin."

She punctuated the bawdy statement with more crows of glee as she settled her plump body next to Elspeth on the settle opposite Ewan and Madlin. "Ye have the look of yer da, Ewan of Glendarach, but I ken a good bit of yer grandda in ye, too. Ever the prankster was that Niallie Fraser. Like ye, he were fair and braw."

A dreamy smile softened the creases of her face as she sighed. "Och, 'twas Niallie Fraser who was settin' the lassies' hearts aflutter in these parts and beyond when I was still a lass meself. Ye have a brother by that name, do ye not?"

"Aye." Ewan lost much of the merriment in his eyes with the articulation of the simple reply. "Niall is the eldest of my father's sons. I believe he still lives."

Old Meta sobered as well. "I've heard naught that the Fraser has lost another son," she said. "Only the one wee lad those years ago."

All color drained from Ewan's face. Sitting so close to him on the narrow seat of the settle, Madlin could swear she felt his body chill. Alarmed, she started to reach for one of his hands, but Old Meta's were there first.

Cradling his large hand between her two small palms, the old woman said so softly that Madlin could barely make out her words, "Let go of it, lad. 'Twas his time and yer mam's, 'twas naught ye did or did not."

Madlin puzzled over the implications but not over the fact that Meta somehow knew there was something troubling him. The old woman was said to have "the sight." Her visions were not always of the future but often of what dwelt deep within someone's soul. For those gifts and the "healings" she performed, she was highly revered by the MacKendricks.

Madlin looked nervously about the hall. It would not go well for Meta if an outsider were to happen upon this scene, for the Church frowned upon such practices. Francis could well arrive at any moment, and Old Meta's special powers were kept secret from her half brother, the bishop, for fear he would be honor-bound to report the old woman as a witch. It was a kindness they did him, keeping such knowledge away from him. Surely it would be unfair to place a man of the cloth in such a position where he must choose between his clan and the Church.

Madlin kept a vigilant eye on the entrances and noted Elspeth was doing the same. Unaware or heedless of the danger in so public a demonstration, Meta's attention was fully upon Ewan.

Her mind racing with as many questions as worries, Madlin waited impatiently as several more moments passed. At last the old woman sighed and let go of Ewan's hand. "Yer will is too strong, lad. Ye'll have to come to it by yerself."

In a twinkling, the old woman turned a mischievous grin on Madlin. "Full of questions, ye are, lass. Answers will come in their own time. Patience is what's still needed in ye, though ye've come home with more than what ye took to St. Margaret's."

"Unusual women appear rife among the MacKendricks of Dunfionn," Ewan said, his voice rougher and softer than Madlin had yet heard from him. "I thank you for trying, Meta. My man, Lucais, told me of you. Sister to his grandmother, Fey Fionna, are you not?"

Old Meta's familiar cackling laugh broke the serious atmosphere. "Aye. Fionna was my sister, older than me by more than just a few years. Gone now, she is, like our mam, who was called Strange Sileas." She cackled again and clapped Ewan on his sound knee. "Mam lived in a nice little cot high in the meadows of the lands 'twixt Fraser and MacKendrick. Built it with her own two hands, she did. Didn't like living close to folk and didn't claim or disclaim either MacKendrick or Fraser. Some said she was neither and was of the Glencaries, but Mam never told us either way on that.

"Buried her up there, we did. Behind her cot. 'Tis a pretty spot with a burn gurgling through it and a good dependable spring. I doona think she'd mind if someone was to build a fine manor house near it," she remarked with a long look toward Ewan.

He merely raised a brow at the comment, to which Meta nodded almost imperceptibly. 'Twas a queer exchange, but Madlin let it pass. Having sat at Old Meta's feet many a time during her childhood, she recognized the signs that a lengthy, rambling tale was forthcoming.

Out of the corner of her eye, Madlin glimpsed Alys hesitating at the main entrance of the hall, prompting a reminder that she needed to reassure the young woman. Or at least make the attempt, for it was unthinkable to allow their friendship to fail and for the lady to return to her family.

As she geared to move, she discovered that the tensions and exertions of the past few days had taken a toll from her body's store of strength. How alluring was the thought of resting her head against the settle's back, and basking in the warmth of the crackling fire.

She shook off her languor. Move she must, and quickly, lest Alys escape to the far reaches of Dunfionn. Mumbling her excuses, she made her way across the hall.

"Good eve, Lady Alys," she called.

"Lady Madlin," the fair-haired lady replied, gratifying Madlin that she had at least chosen to acknowledge her greeting. However, the formality of the greeting and the utter lack of regard in her face wounded, as did the tears that sprung to her blue eyes.

Madlin hardly knew where to begin making the amends she so desperately wanted with her brother's betrothed. "Och, Alys, how formal we are," she said at last, and impulsively she reached for Alys's hand. Alys did not jerk away from her touch. Madlin took it as a sign she would not be opposed to hearing her out.

"Come, let us talk a while, as we have done so often in these past weeks. How are you feeling? Is your belly still unsettled?" Madlin asked. 'Twas certain now that the lady was carrying Bram's child, though few knew about the babe. She had not been having an easy time of it so far, though Elspeth had assured her all was perfectly normal.

"Mornings are the worst," Alys admitted. Her eyes were downcast, but Madlin could see tears sliding down her pale cheeks. "I . . . I must apologize for this morn. 'Tis—"

"Forgotten," Madlin finished for her. "You are my dear sister, Alys. Never think otherwise," she said from her heart, along with a string of other assurances when Alys's tears turned to sobs. Slipping an arm about her, Madlin led her away from the eyes and ears of others.

From across the hall, Ewan watched the tableau between his wife and the fair-haired young woman with only mild interest. He could not allow his thoughts to stray far from Meta's discourse. It was just possible the old seeress might provide a clue or two that might help him solve the riddle of just who had stepped up the feud and why. It appeared there was neither a soul nor a happening at either Glendarach or Dunfionn that Old Meta did not know of.

"Poor lass. 'Twill not be good for her or the babe if she keeps holding her grief and bitterness so tightly."

Her babe? God's blood, the wench and her henchmen had deceived him! To think he'd come to regard her as exactly what she presented herself as. An innocent. A woman of honor, completely without guile.

"Settle yerself, laddie!" Meta chortled. " 'Tis not our lady who's carrying, though I s'pect 'twill not be much longer before she be quickening with yer babe."

The old woman's words brought the level of his rage down by several notches. God's blood. Instant fits of rage were not his way. Or had not been until that redheaded vixen had captured him.

A speculative glint sparkled in Meta's eyes as she studied

him. "There be a powerful strong pull betwixt the two of ye. Even pride as big as yers and hers will not stop it."

"You see too much, Meta MacKendrick," Ewan grumbled.

"Sometimes, and not enough others. Too often 'tis only feelings and naught to explain them."

"These killings between the two clans? Have you clear feelings about who started it all?"

Meta sighed and rubbed her head again. "Och, I fear I do not, no more'n I knew that day when Toirlach and the lads rode out that they wouldna be riding back. But I tell ye, no MacKendrick started it up and no Fraser, neither. Ye can ease yer mind on that, laddie."

While Ewan spent much of the next hour sifting through Old Meta's diatribe, Madlin and the lady Alys repaired to the chapel. It was the one place in Dunfionn where quiet and solitude could be achieved.

Madlin helped Alys to one of the benches that served as pews and settled herself beside her. "Do not weep so, Alys. 'Tis not good for the bairn or yourself. Bram would not want you to be so sad. My brother was a man full of life and laughter."

Between intermittent sniffles, Alys got out, " 'Twas why I loved him so. And your father and dear Airic. Even with all the raids this summer, the hall was often a place full of joy. Especially when your father and brothers joined us for the evening meal."

Alys's tears were not the only ones running freely. Madlin swiped at her dampened cheeks with the heels of her hands and took a deep, shaky breath. "Och, the laughter. 'Twas what I missed so powerfully when I was away all those years. I yearn to hear the sounds of joy again in Dunfionn's hall."

"And yet you brought a Fraser to it?" Alys's tears began afresh. "Oh, Madlin, how could you?"

Both young women were startled when a man's voice inquired, "And what pray has my little sister done to bring such a gentle lady to tears?"

"Francis!"

Feeling much like a guilty child caught with a stolen sweet-meat in her hands, Madlin jumped to her feet. Just how much had he heard? She had hoped to explain her marriage to her half brother herself. She relaxed some when she detected nothing about him that would indicate he had heard more than Alys's last question.

Crossing his arms over his chest, Bishop MacDonald's usual stern expression softened slightly, for one corner of his mouth did seem to be attempting to turn upward. "A mischievous chit you were as a wee lass, and I think you have not changed, sister. What have you done to sweet Lady Alys, imp?"

"Oh, 'tis naught she's done to me, my lord bishop." A protective hand over her still-flat belly, Alys rose gracefully. Dropping a hasty curtsy, she kissed the ring on Francis's extended hand. "The lady Madlin is naught but kindness itself to me."

" 'Tis sweet of you to say so, Lady Alys." Madlin quickly added, "But I am at fault. I should have been more careful with your bracelet. I shall do my best to find it and return it to you immediately." She jabbed Alys lightly in the ribs and was prepared to step on one of her slender feet if the lady attempted to refute her lie.

" 'Twas just a trinket of no real value." Alys's quick wits supplied yet another lie that added some credence to Madlin's. " 'Tis I who am embarrassed for going on so."

Curtsying again to Francis, she said, "How very good it is to see you again, my lord bishop. I beg your leave, for I have promised the lady Elspeth that I would help her with the evening meal."

Alys had barely disappeared beyond the chapel's entrance when Francis raised a speculative brow. "And what was that really all about, Lady Madlin, laird of the MacKendricks?"

Madlin could not help but giggle. "Lady Madlin, laird of the MacKendricks. How strange that title sounds coming from you, Francis. You must be vexed indeed to call me such."

Francis chuckled lightly, though Madlin noted that, as always, no merriment was reflected in his eyes. How terribly sad never to feel total joy. Perhaps it came from having been born a bastard.

Dark of hair and eye, of less ruddy complexion and of smaller stature than the other sons her father had sired, she supposed it was not surprising he would think himself an outsider. Though she'd never thought of him as anything other than her eldest brother, she supposed Francis was an outsider. Born in Inverness, he carried his mother's name and had been given to the Church when most barons' sons were sent to foster with an ally.

On impulse, she hugged him as she used to as a child during his rare visits. Since his appointment to Beauly, he had been at Dunfionn more frequently. So much so, the chamber beyond the chapel was no longer thought of as the priest's chambers but as Francis's.

"I am still your little sister, the imp who tries her best to coax a smile from your sober face." Toward that end, she sent him a warm grin.

Scarcely returning his sister's embrace or her smile, Francis quickly stepped away. He gestured toward her gown. " 'Tis no imp that stands before me, but a fine lady."

He tapped her beneath her chin and smiled, though faintly. "I thought never to see you attired thus. Is this a special occasion?"

"Aye, a meeting of the elders. Aunt Elspeth thought it wise for me to appear so." Growing nervous under his dark gaze, she turned and walked slowly toward the front of the chapel.

At the altar, she fussed with the cloth, smoothing its heavily embroidered edges with her palm. Stalling for time was not her way, and doing so made her nervousness increase. Her hand moved by its own volition to the place between her breasts where the pendant lay.

Trust in Yourself.

She had faced the elders and won them over. Francis had ever been her gentle brother, the friend to whom she had confessed her many sins. Surely it should not be so difficult to explain her marriage to him.

"A serious meeting, sister?"

"Aye." Madlin fingered the pendant's edges but a moment longer. Better to get it over with. Folding her hands loosely before her, she said as calmly as her pounding heart would allow, "Yesterday at dawn, Sir Ewan Fraser and I were married at the monastery by the Moray."

Chapter Twelve

Francis stared at her, opened his mouth as if to say something, then quickly closed it. Closing his eyes, he took a deep breath through his nostrils, which seemed to do nothing to ease his shock. In a somewhat strangled voice, he asked, "You married a Fraser?"

Madlin nodded.

His hands pressed together, he began tapping his chin. "And yesterday morning, at the monastery by the sea? Why the haste, sister? Seems overly impulsive, even for you."

"It was not an impulsive act, but one given weeks of thought and planning."

"Weeks? And you said nothing to me? Had someone else conduct the ceremony?"

"You were not expected back so soon from Beauly and . . . and it was important that the marriage take place immediately."

"Again I would ask why such haste?"

Madlin was hard put to keep from squirming beneath Francis's piercing gaze. Keeping her chin up and her back straight, she met his gaze unblinkingly. Once he heard her reasons, surely he would support her decision. Francis had always been the most understanding of her brothers. "I gave much thought to marrying Ewan Fraser. I—"

"Your father's murderer!"

"Sir Ewan had nothing to do with Papa's death or any of the other atrocities our clan has suffered," she said before relating Ewan's history and how recent had been his return.

Unimpressed, Francis condemned her marriage in increasingly more vehement terms. "You are an unnatural woman, Madlin MacKendrick, if you think to continue leading this clan. God did not fashion woman so that she should dominate men. 'Tis a sinful position our father's and brothers' deaths forced upon you. Would that I could serve the clan in your stead and thus save you from the fires you will surely suffer if this doth prevail overlong. But I cannot forsake my vows. I shall ask God to remember that this role was thrust upon you and beg Him not to punish you overseverely."

"But surely God does understand, Francis."

He shook his head as if overcome by a great sadness. "You are still such a child, sister," he said with a sigh. "Impulsive as always, but then you are a female. Your sex is commonly in possession of a large measure of that weakness." He used such a placating tone that the words were insulting.

"If you had married more wisely, you could have given up this unnatural role and handed over the clan leadership to your husband. Then, you would have been able to retire to the life God planned for you. One of obedience to a husband chosen for you and if God pleases the bearing of children."

His hands clasped together in an attitude of prayer, he began to pace across the chapel's rough-planked floor. As he moved back and forth, the motion both mesmerized her and made her dizzy.

"Perhaps it is not too late to repair the damage your foolhardiness has brought upon the clan. Several men petitioned our father for your hand. I'm told the Munro was among them. With their land marching alongside the MacKendricks', it would be a good match. He's a young man, not ill-favored, and of suitable wealth and rank. I cannot think why Father refused his suit. As your closest male relative, I shall do my duty by you and approach the Munro."

"Nay!" she cried, horrified at the very idea. "I already have a husband, brother. Even if I did not, I would not marry Seamus Munro! Papa knew we would not suit and turned him away for good reasons."

Pausing, Francis narrowed his eyes on her. "Then if not the Munro, what of Malcolm MacKay? Perhaps he could be persuaded to renew his suit. A good man is MacKay. Devout and wealthy."

Madlin rolled her eyes and folded her arms across her bosom. "The MacKay has five grown sons and has buried that same number of wives. No!"

Francis named several of the other suitors, all of whom Madlin flatly turned down. In contrast to the anger evident in the penetrating light in his eyes, Francis's tone was smooth and gentle when he suggested, "Perhaps God would be more pleased if you were to take the veil. After all, 'twas by His hand that our father was guided to send you to St. Margaret's."

"And who would lead clan MacKendrick then?" Madlin asked, matching her anger to his. "I am my father's successor, and as laird I have chosen a husband who will aid my quest for peace and therefore the well-being of all."

"Clan MacKendrick will not accept a Fraser at its head. You will damn yourself beyond redemption if you persist in this marriage! Have you lain with him, yet?"

"I . . . I—" Shocked by his bluntness, Madlin found forming any sort of answer difficult. "We . . . we were put in the same bed but . . . nothing—"

What happened at dawn was far from nothing, but she was not about to relate the details of that incident. "We were both unwell when we arrived last night. Elspeth and Jeanne spent much of it attending us."

It was only a small lie, but she steeled herself from giving it away beneath her brother's probing gaze. She nearly collapsed with relief when Francis turned his attention elsewhere.

"Good, good," he said. "Though it is an abomination that a woman should do such, you must refuse your husband's rights to your body."

Madlin had a hysterical urge to laugh. If she told him of her husband's vow that he'd never touch her, she'd have to reveal how she'd forced her husband to the altar and threatened a life in a holy place. More sins heaped upon her soul, and no good would come of confessing them to Francis. They were between her and God. "That would negate the possibility of children, the very purpose of marriage, according to the Church."

Her statement earned her another dark glare and the sharp order, "On the grounds of coercion, you will petition the Church for an annulment immediately."

"No, Francis, I will not. This marriage is for the good of clan MacKendrick." When he started to argue, she held up her hand to stop him. "Hear me out, brother."

The way he sucked in his breath left her with no doubt that she had insulted him. Staying any words of apology, she kept her voice as calm and low as possible in hopes of calming him. Surely it was the shock that made him so uncharacteristically unreasonable. "The elders have approved my marriage. Even King James will approve it, as surely our sovereign wants peace throughout his kingdom."

"If, and there is no guarantee, but *if* peace should be achieved between the two clans, what of within the MacKendricks? I say it again, sister, our clan will not accept a Fraser as its chief. I could not bear it if any harm came to you, but it could if you anger the MacKendricks by turning over the chieftainship to this husband."

"Francis, Francis." Madlin slowly shook her head. "Put aside that worry, for I shall come to no harm from the hand of a MacKendrick. Further, you are mistaken in thinking Sir Ewan or any man I married would become laird of clan MacKendrick. I am the chief and would be so even if my husband had been chosen for me."

"But you are a woman. Women are not suited to lead."

"History proves otherwise. Mabh, Carimandua, and Boudica were leaders in their day. And the Amazons were an entire race with women as—"

A loud hissing noise from Francis interrupted her. "Do not blaspheme, sister! Never even mention that time when darkness was upon the earth. Those were pagan women ruling a pagan people. All are even yet burning in the fires of hell for their transgressions. You are fortunate to have been raised in the true faith and should know that God fashioned woman to serve man.

"You must set aside this marriage, Madlin. Not only *your* soul but those of all the MacKendricks are at stake. They will spend eternity in purgatory or worse if they must live out their lives under the leadership of a woman."

Though every part of her wanted to scream at him, she said very quietly, "I learned to read at the abbey. I, too, have read the Holy Scriptures. Nowhere do they state anything of the sort, nor do they even imply that women are not suited to lead."

Tears stung her eyes, and her body was shaking with a mixture of anger and pain that her own brother should rail at her with such priestly condemnations. With a deferent dip of her head, she turned away. "Perhaps it would be best if we said no more this day." Pausing only long enough to make the sign of the cross as she passed the altar, Madlin started from the chapel.

"Sister, do not turn your back on me." She halted just as her hand touched the door's latch, but did not turn to face him. When his hand touched her sleeve, she flinched.

"Forgive me," he said softly. "Speaking to you thus has been the worst of ordeals. Can you not turn and look at me?"

Swiping the tears from her eyes, Madlin did as he bid. "Ah, sister, I have made you cry. I shall pray for God's forgiveness for having lost my temper. I fear I must make amends for succumbing to shock that my very own sister should take the son of our father's and brothers' assassin to husband."

"Oh, Francis, then you do understand?" she asked, hope warming the chill left from his rantings. "Will you give my marriage your blessing?"

His lips tight, he shook his head. "I have not yet been able to find any forgiveness in my heart for the Fraser or any of his blood. I cannot approve this marriage."

Finding it difficult to merge this dogmatic priest with the gentle brother she thought she knew, Madlin let her annoyance show when she said, "As a man of God, I should think you would be in favor of anything that might bring about peace."

As soon as the words left her mouth, Madlin knew she'd insulted him once again, but she no longer cared, for this was not a Francis she understood.

"Do you add chastising a bishop to your list of sins, sister?"

"No, my lord bishop. I am merely attempting to understand."

"You dare much, sister. I shall spend this night praying you will yet learn humility, for the souls of all MacKendricks may depend on it. Then perhaps you will admit your mistake and see that annulling this marriage is God's will."

The implacable set of his features warned her that further discussion would be of no use. "I leave you to your prayers then, brother. You will need the whole night if you are to convince God of all you desire. I will be praying as well, that nothing and no one will stand in the way of peace and the well-being of the people of clans MacKendrick and Fraser."

Turning on her heel, she left the chapel as quickly as she could. Hiking up her skirts, she took the steps two at a time in her haste to put as much distance as possible between herself and Francis. Lord, forgive her, but she did hope his visit would be short.

She'd expected some disapproval from Francis for what he would see as an act of impetuosity, but never had she expected to be subjected to such a diatribe of condemnations and dogmatic drivel. After the funeral, Francis had been the first to place his hands within hers. He'd not knelt and pledged fealty like those who'd followed, for as a bishop he was pledged to God and the Church. But he'd done what he could, in the most dramatic way possible, to lend his support. That he should now be condemning her as unfit to lead merely because she was a woman was such a turnaround she could not make sense of it.

When she arrived in her chamber, it was dark, but she did not light any of the candles. The glow from the embers banked in the hearth was enough for her to find her way to her destination. She sat down upon the floor in a corner and wrapped her father's plaid about herself. Alone in the dark and quiet, she could think, cry, or indulge in any sort of misery she cared to. This was most definitely one of those times.

Where was she?

According to Lady Alys, the bishop had arrived and she'd been closeted in the chapel with him ever since. At first, Ewan had thought little of it, especially after Lady Jeanne explained that Bishop MacDonald was Madlin's half brother and the pair were quite close. But when people began to gather for the evening meal and neither Madlin nor the priest appeared, Ewan grew uneasy. Deaf to the conversations going on around him, he considered searching her out.

Elspeth paused long enough in her duties to remark, "You are not looking well, Sir Ewan. I insist you return to your bedchamber immediately. I shall have a tray sent up, and later I will want to look at your wound and change the dressing."

Relieved for an excuse to go in search of his wife, he smiled and said, "I'd be a fool to argue with you, Lady Elspeth." He started to rise but had to make a grab for the back of the settle. Taking several deep breaths, he waited for the world to cease its shifting and the painful stab in his thigh to subside.

Leaning heavily on a stout walking stick, he took a few tentative steps. A bit shaky, but at least he'd not fallen down. He sent a rueful smile to his companions Meta and Lady Jeanne. "Ladies, I bid you good eve."

As he began to limp away, Meta called after him, "Ye've no need to be rambling anywheres but to yer chamber."

If Ewan had any doubt as to her meaning, it was dispelled when she nudged Jeanne and said, "See to it there's enough food for two on that tray. There's a good lass."

In front of his chamber, Ewan leaned against the door to rest a moment before entering. God's teeth! How did he expect to start courting his wife when he could scarcely stand?

He pushed the door open and peered about the chamber.

No candles or lamps had been lit. Only the glow from the embers in the hearth and a torch shining from the hallway aided his search until he heard a snuffling sound and then a sniff.

"Who goes there?"

"Go away." The voice was definitely Madlin's, and was that weeping he heard?

The MacKendrick weeping! His brave, audacious, utterly exasperating, and altogether too tempting wife was weeping as if her heart were broken. The sound was like a sword to his heart.

Quietly, he closed the door behind him and waited until his eyes grew accustomed to the darkness. Her face pressed to her knees, she was coiled into a tight ball of shuddering misery in a corner near the hearth. Lost in utter despair, she appeared unaware of his presence.

Compelled by an instinct he could not resist, he started across the chamber, intent upon pulling her into his arms and comforting her. His attention fully on his wife, he'd taken a mere three steps when the tip of his walking stick skittered on something on the floor. Thrown off balance, he flailed ineffectually at nothing but air before he landed sprawled full out on the floor with a loud "oof" as the air left his lungs.

"Wh . . . who?"

He could do nothing but groan. From his ignominious position in the darkness, he could only sense her movement.

The light gradually increased, and he assumed she was lighting a brace of candles or perhaps one of the oil lamps set upon the mantel. "Ewan?" she asked as she dropped to her knees beside him and gently touched his shoulder.

His lungs just beginning to refill, Ewan rolled to his back and managed a weak, rasping, "Aye."

"My lord, what has befallen you? Can you sit up?" She ran her hands over him searching for new wounds, broken bones, or whatever her facile mind was imagining. "Wait here, stay calm, I'll fetch my aunt."

"No . . . need," he gasped out, and clutched at her skirts to prevent her flight. Holding fast to a handful of velvet, he pulled himself to a sitting position.

At last realizing his plight, she started rubbing his back, "Stay calm. You just had the wind knocked out of you."

So much for comforting his disconsolate wife! At least she'd stopped weeping. "I . . . I'll be fine." Severely wounded pride made him shrug from her touch.

Spying the walking stick lying several feet away, he heaped blame on it with a string of colorful epithets. Apparently unfazed by his show of temper, Madlin slipped an arm around his waist. "Come, I'll help you up. I know what a frightening thing it is to lose your breath. Makes one feel so helpless. You're still weak. I'll help you to the bed."

Her placating tone, her very strength in the face of his weakness ignited his fury. "Get your hands off me!" Stumbling to his feet, he wrenched out of her grasp. "First your aunt and now you. Must you MacKendrick women continually order me to bed? I'm neither sleepy nor ill!"

Madlin's gasp followed him as he lurched toward a chair by the hearth. Even when she'd captured him and forced marriage on him, he'd not felt so unmanned. God's teeth, he sounded like a petulant child.

Panting and sweating from the exertion of merely maneuvering a few feet, his humor didn't improve when he looked at his wife. Though her eyes were red-rimmed and swollen and tears still glistened on her cheeks, she stood tall, tight-lipped, and glaring with a force he could almost feel.

And then the corners of her lush mouth began to twitch.

"Don't you dare laugh," he growled.

His warning cracked the dam of her control. Her musical laughter burst forth, filling the room.

Desperate to hold on to his righteous anger, he folded his arms across his chest and tried to look anywhere but at his wife. But her laughter wrapped around him and plucked at a chord he'd not played in years. Soon his own laughter joined with hers.

Their laughter did not break its steady chorus until Jeanne

appeared between them. At their startled silence, she blushed. "I knocked till my knuckles were nearly bruised, but you did not hear me above your ruckus." She smiled brightly as she placed a linen-draped tray upon a small table near Ewan's chair. "You're feeling fair better then, Sir Ewan?" she asked, adjusting the handle of the basket swinging from her arm.

Swiping at some moisture in his eyes, Ewan sobered but dared not look at his wife for fear he would begin again. "Aye, much better, Lady Jeanne."

Turning her smile on her cousin, she exclaimed, "Och, Maddie, 'tis good to hear such laughter again from you." Setting the basket before the hearth, she expressed shock at the lack of a fire. Quickly tossing several blocks of peat on the grate, she reached for the poker and stirred the embers to life.

"Lady Elspeth was called away. 'Tis Maud's time, and she'd promised she'd be there when the new bairn was coming," she explained, naming the blacksmith's wife. "Lady Elspeth asked that I change the dressings on your wound." When she was satisfied with the fire, she dropped to her knees and began extracting rolls of linen and several small earthenware pots from the basket. "Mind, I'm not the healer that is Lady Elspeth, but she has taught me how to assess a wound, clean, and redress it."

Finished laying out her supplies, Jeanne sat back on her heels. "Och, you're still wearing your trews. Can you peel them off yourself or do you need help?"

"I believe I—"

"Would prefer this be done later," Madlin finished for him. A squeeze to his shoulder effectively stilled the hands that had started to move to the tapes at his waist. "My husband and I are quite famished and would prefer to eat our supper first. I, too, have been instructed by my aunt and can see to his wound."

Was this a show of wifely possessiveness? Brushing his hand across his mouth, he hid a grin before craning his neck to get a look at his wife. From his angle, he could see nothing of her features except the rather obstinate set of her chin.

"Of . . . of course. How foolish of me not to . . . ah . . . realize that . . . um . . . not to realize." Vainly hiding a piquant grin, Jeanne jumped to her feet and hurried to the door. "Good eve to both of you."

As if to validate her statement, Madlin dragged the table before him and whipped the linen from the tray. Looking over the contents, she nodded approvingly, then pulled the other chair closer. Sitting down, she popped a piece of meat into her mouth with one hand and reached for one of the spoons and a bowl of potage with the other.

Ewan raised his brows at the zeal and remarked, "You really are famished, aren't you?"

Madlin halted her spoon midair. "Why the surprise? I said I was famished. Aren't you?"

Not sure he believed hunger was her only reason for stopping her cousin from attending his wound, he still felt a stab of disappointment that it might not have been wifely possessiveness that had prompted her. "Aye, I am," he said, and reached for the other bowl of potage.

With the first spoonful of the creamy mixture of peas, leeks, turnips, and barley, he realized he was as famished as his wife had claimed. "Delicious," he exclaimed between spoonfuls. "I've not had the like since I was a lad."

"They did not feed you well in London?" Madlin asked, spreading a piece of dark bread with honey.

"Not badly did they feed us, just different." Sopping up the last of his soup with a chunk of bread, he looked over the other platters on the tray. "Then in France, much of the time I was forced to survive on a soldier's rations."

Spearing a piece of meat, he savored the tender morsel. "A soldier's fare is not good under the best of times, and the worst is . . ." He grimaced and feigned a shudder. "Suffice it to say the worst is best left undescribed."

Light laughter met Ewan's statement. He noted that her eyes were not so tear-ravaged now and an intriguing light twinkled in them. "Your cousin is right, my lady. Your laughter is quite a joy to hear. Far more to my liking than the sound of your weeping. Tell me, sweetling, what was the cause of all that blubbering when I entered?"

Chapter Thirteen

"I was not blubbering!" Her denial sounded peevish even to her own ears.

"Forgive me. I have been too long in the company of rough soldiers," Ewan returned smoothly with only the barest touch of sarcasm. "Blubbering is perhaps not an appropriate description of the sounds a gentle lady makes when her shoulders shake and tears fall from her lovely eyes. What or who was the cause of your gentle weeping, my dear?"

"I . . . ah . . . fear I am much fatigued from this day and—"

"Fell to uncontrollable weeping?"

" 'Tis not uncommon among women, you know."

From beneath her lashes, she chanced a quick sidelong look at Ewan. He did not look at all believing of her explanation, which was no surprise. She'd never been very good at prevaricating, and Ewan's gaze was as intense and probing as had been her father's. She felt as much guilt avoiding the absolute truth now as she had those rare times she'd attempted evasion with her father.

"Just womanish tears," she stated with what she hoped sounded like honest conviction. " 'Twas a strain, the meeting with the elders. And I was already much fatigued from the previous two days, and, of course, the blow to my head does still cause me pain."

"Ah. Reasons aplenty for many a woman to fall into tears. Come." He pushed the table aside. Pulling the pillow from beneath him, he tossed it to the floor between his feet. "Sit here with your back to me, I'll try to ease the tension you most probably are suffering in your neck and shoulders. 'Tis the least a husband can do for a wife with so many responsibilities."

Warily, Madlin eyed the pillow, then his hands. How long are his fingers and broad his palms, she thought. A warrior's hands. Strong. Strong enough to snap her neck in an instant and be rid of her.

Och, but that would be foolish, for his own life would be forfeit the moment her body was discovered. And any hope of peace between their two clans would be destroyed. He wanted that peace as much as she did, of that she was certain.

"Drop your head forward," he ordered as soon as she'd settled herself upon the pillow. He lifted her braid and draped it over her shoulder. "Let your head hang loose, and place your hands in your lap. Close your eyes, take a deep breath, and let it out slowly."

Madlin did as he directed and found that some of the pain in her head disappeared immediately. But at the first touch of his hands upon her shoulders, her eyes flew open and she tensed.

"Relax. This is no battleground. Trust me. I am not going to hurt you, only offer a wee bit of comfort."

His vow that she'd not find any comfort in their marriage rang clearly in her mind. Unable to refrain, she asked, "Comfort, sir?"

The pressure of his hands and the motion of his thumbs altered not a whit when he answered, "Aye, 'tis comfort I'm offering. Don't expect me to take back vows in the future, but that one regarding no comfort of any kind in our marriage, I do beg you to forget."

The brush of his thumbs between her shoulder blades was easing the muscles there, and already she felt her hold on her wits loosening. Before they left her completely, she had to be sure of how he viewed their marriage. "If offered the chance to put aside our marriage, would you?"

"Those vows are not easily set aside."

"But if an annulment were made easy, would you agree to it?"

He stopped the massage and gently turned her to face him. "Why this line of questioning, madam? Having second thoughts? Now that we've had a day to better know each other, is there something about me you find so intolerable that you wish an annulment?"

So close was his face to hers, she felt as if she could drown in the blue of his eyes. His was perhaps the most handsome visage she had ever encountered, both of face and of figure. Though she knew him to have a temper and an abundance of pride and stubbornness, there was nothing she disliked about him.

"No," she answered. The very thought of living her life without this man who was holding her chin so tenderly in his large hands caused an ache in her throat. His handsome face blurred, and she quickly slid her gaze away, hoping he would not see the tears in her eyes.

"No?"

"No," she repeated. "But . . . but it has been pointed out to me how very unfair it is to you and . . . and since our marriage has not yet been consummated, and you did not make your vows freely, an annulment would be quite easily obtained. I cannot in all honor force you to endure living your life with one such as myself."

"What is there about you that would make living with you so unbearable?"

"I . . . I am an unnatural woman."

Caught completely off guard, Ewan fell back in his chair and studied her for a long moment. "Unnatural? I cannot fathom such an appraisal. Abnormally strong, most unconventionally educated, and exceptionally beautiful, yes. But unnatural? Have you the sight, or other supernatural gifts?"

Madlin shook her head and pressed her teeth into her lush lower lip. "I am not like Meta. 'Tis . . . 'tis . . ."

She took a deep breath but did not finish. Hearing a catch in that breath, he grew more unsettled by her hesitation along with the way she kept her eyes focused away from him. "Whatever it is cannot be of any import."

Instead of comforting her as he'd intended, her eyes filled with tears again. The sight of them pained him but not as much as the words that began tumbling from her. " 'Tis a sin for a woman to lead men. 'Tis unnatural and . . . and . . . all those who must follow me are eternally damned."

"What drivel! Who has filled your head with such nonsense?"

"I did not believe it either at first. But Francis is a bishop and should know about such things." Tears were running down her cheeks and her nose had grown red. Fishing into a pocket of his jacket, Ewan extracted a square of linen and handed it to her.

"Thank you." She mopped her face and nose. "After I left him and came up here to think, I began to understand that it was not anger that caused him to speak to me so, but fear— fear for my soul and all the MacKendricks. He has always been so kind and gentle with me. The way he lost his temper was most uncharacteristic of him."

With a small amount of urging, she detailed the audience with her brother, continually making excuses throughout for the man's malicious attack on her. He wanted to howl his outrage against her loyalty to the bastard as much as the offal that had spewed from the priest's mouth. By the rood, bishop or not, he'd run the bastard through at the first opportunity. The man was not worthy of his title or of calling himself her brother.

Unnatural woman! The only thing that was unnatural about his beautiful, brave wife was her loyalty to the bastard!

"Perhaps he's right in that I should turn clan MacKendrick over to a man for leadership."

He snorted. "And that man would logically be your husband, except we both know the MacKendricks will not accept me, a Fraser, as their chief." He grinned and tapped her on the nose. "So, clan MacKendrick will just have to remain under the very capable and wise leadership of their lady laird."

She didn't return his smile. If anything she looked even more miserable. Shifting her eyes away from him, she said dully, "Perhaps you should not dismiss annulment so quickly, sir. Since we have not consummated this marriage, it should be quite—"

"Irresponsible! That's what it would be. Irresponsible." He couldn't believe his ears. What kind of hold over her did this priest have to make her doubt herself? "What of the feud between our clans? I seem to remember you telling a priest that you were more interested in the living than in the souls of the dead. Have you given up on the living?"

"I . . . I do care about the living," she cried. "Stop yelling at me! I've had enough of men yelling at me. I'm the laird of this clan and by the Virgin, I do want peace."

"Praise God!" The fire was back in her eyes, and her chin was firm and belligerent. "So what do you suggest we do, Lady Madlin, laird of the MacKendricks?"

"We keep this marriage intact! We assure that it cannot be annulled. We . . ." Bright spots of color appeared on her pale cheeks. "We must consummate this marriage, but . . . but . . ."

The way her eyes slid to the bed and her cheeks flamed even brighter told him exactly what she was thinking. "Wounded pride can lead a man to say many foolish things, my lady. Did I not already tell you that my pride would heal?"

"Aye, but—"

He stopped her with a gentle finger against her lips. "I have already begged you to forget my foolish vow and I would now ask your forgiveness for my anger this morning. 'Twas not you I was angry with but myself, or rather, my own weakness."

The look of puzzlement on her face indicated he would have to swallow even more pride and explain. "My wound and the fever, my lady. I feared I would not be able to . . . ah . . . perform my duty properly."

Though her expression revealed a small element of relief that his anger had not been toward her, she still looked confused. Her confusion revealed much about her. Her utter innocence delighted him. "You have no real idea what goes on between a man and a woman in the marriage bed, do you?"

"I . . . I know that . . . that you . . . I mean the man must . . . must . . ."

Chuckling lightly, he said, "Yes, a man must do many things to please the woman who shares his bed. When I am more recovered, I will happily demonstrate. God willing, madam, you will bear the sons you desire from my body, and we will both take a lot more than comfort in the begetting of them."

He did not think it was heat from the fire burning close by that caused her skin to redden further. "Where did that bold chieftain who captured me and announced she would have sons from me go?" he teased.

She sighed and turned her face away from him. "Mayhap she should apologize for her boldness. 'Tis unseemly for a lady to talk of such things with a stranger."

"Mayhap with a stranger, but not with her husband."

She turned back to him, her eyes wide. "Truly?"

He smiled wickedly. "Truly. I assure you I quite enjoy your boldness and look forward to experiencing it often when we are alone. You, my lady, are a precious gem with many facets. All of them quite dazzling, I might add."

"And you, sir, are a most accomplished flatterer."

"Nay, I am but a simple man who speaks but the truth. Now, my lady, I would extract a promise that you will leave the priest to me. Avoid him if you can, and let me inform him that there are no grounds for annulment."

She started to reply but was overcome by a wide yawn. "It has been a long day, and we are both tired. Go to bed, Madlin."

"Aye." She rose and shook out her skirts. "I beg you not to judge Francis by what I have just told you. He has always been most kind and loving to me. I am sure he is even now repenting his words and will be most supportive of our marriage by the morrow. As a priest he has to want peace, but he is a man, too, and one still grieving for our father and brothers. He was but giving vent to that grief."

"He vented it most wrongly and shall—" At her look of dismay, he softened his tone and promised, "I shall try to keep an open mind."

She yawned again, and he repeated, "Go to bed, Madlin."

"You too, sir." Her foot encountered the basket of medicaments as she moved toward him. "Och, your wound. I must see to it."

She dropped to her knees and removed his spurs, then tugged off his boots. "Can you stand and peel off your trews, or will you need some help?"

Tension gripped him at the very thought of her hands upon his body. He did not relish ending the day the same way it began. "I can take care of the wound myself. Off with you, now. Ready yourself for the night, and get into bed."

"Do not be foolish. I am fatigued but no more than you are. I shall do it and then help you into bed."

She reached for the hem of his jacket, and he caught her hand. "No!" Through clenched teeth, he ordered, "Go to bed, Madlin. Now!"

With a gasp she spun away from him. Sorry he snapped at her but not wishing to torture his loins by calling her back, Ewan rose unsteadily to his feet and began undressing himself. From another part of the chamber, he could hear the rustle of her clothing and her mutterings beneath her breath.

He had stripped down to his shirt and was sniffing at the various pots in the basket when she called out, "Have you a preference for a side of the bed?"

"Aye, the side closest to the door." Satisfied he'd found a salve he recognized as a healant, he began unwinding the bandage from his thigh. "Do not worry about that this night. I shall sleep here on a pallet by the fire."

"You will not!" In a blink of an eye, she was in front of him once more. "You will share that bed with me this night and every night."

The way the light from the hearth's fire shone through her thin chemise, she might as well have been standing before him naked. Not daring the temptation of her lush body, he forced his eyes to focus above her neck. "Ah, the bold wench shows herself again." He grinned at her. "I am flattered by your eagerness, but I must beg your patience for at least another night. I promise I shall do all possible to regain my strength and agility so that tomorrow or the next night I can accommodate you. But if you think it might appease your outrage, bend down close and I'll be happy to give you a goodnight kiss."

"I had nothing of the sort in mind," she told him with the righteous indignation he'd hoped to provoke. "It is only that you are in more need of a good night's sleep than I am. 'Tis you who are recovering from a grievous fever and injury."

She grabbed the pot of salve from his hand, placed it back in the basket, and lifted out another. "You shall take the bed as soon as I tend to your wound."

This time she would not accept his refusal of aid and efficiently went about seeing to his wound. Keeping up the argument over who would sleep in the bed and who would not kept his mind distracted from the brush of her fingertips along his thigh. He won the battle over the bed but not the battle with his groin. By the time she tied the final knot in his bandage, he was as hard as a rock and dangerously close to tipping her backward and taking her no matter how clumsily he might perform.

"Thank you, and now to bed for you," he managed between gritted teeth.

Her pretty mouth set in a hard line, she sent him a glare that might have felled a lesser man before she trounced away. Seconds later, a well-aimed pillow hit the back of his head, followed in rapid succession by two balled-up furs and a plaid. A MacKendrick plaid.

"Good night, Sir Ewan of *Dunfionn*. Rest well," she called with exaggerated sweetness.

"Good night, my lady Madlin, laird of Dunfionn," he growled as he stumbled about making up a pallet before the hearth. Wrapping himself in colors he thought never to encounter so closely, he murmured, "Rest while you can, MacKendrick minx. You'll have little when a Fraser shares that bed."

His threat was answered by what sounded suspiciously like a muffled giggle. A moment of silence followed and then the query, "What will your friend, the king, think of our marriage? Will he approve?"

"I'm quite certain he'll approve."

"That's good. I have worried that my treatment of you might be considered an insult to the crown. And . . . Ewan?"

"Yes, Madlin."

"Is sharing a bed one of the rewards you mentioned?"

"I fully expect to make it so. Go to sleep, Madlin."

"You, too."

It took him a long while to calm his body enough to sleep.

Chapter Fourteen

When Ewan wakened, Madlin was already gone from their chamber. She'd evidently stoked the coals and added more fuel, for a pleasant fire burned in the hearth. But even with a warm fire close by, his muscles were stiff and his bones ached from a night spent on a thin pallet spread over a bare floor.

Rising, he tested his legs, finding his wounded thigh complaining no more than the rest of his body. He'd just finished the most pressing of his morning ablutions and was rummaging through his packs when a knock sounded on the door. Finding his woolen bed robe, he slipped into it before calling out, "Enter."

Hugh came through the doorway, carrying a large crockery bottle of what Ewan dearly hoped was warm water for shaving. "Thought you might be of a mind to be wakening about now."

Gordie was right behind, a tray in his hands. "Elspeth has sent some food up for ye. Said ye was to take it easy today. She'll see to yer leg later on."

The bottle was filled with hot water. Ewan poured it into a basin and, using a pot of soft soap, lathered his face. Peering toward the window, he noted the gloom and the promise of snow in the dark clouds hovering above. "And my wife?"

"Rode out early this morning," Hugh supplied. "Got word some folks was short of rations for themselves and their stock. Wanted to get to them before the weather made it impossible, so she had some wagons loaded right quick with supplies. Said she'd check on all the crofts and herds as long as she was going."

In the act of applying his blade to his face, Ewan nicked himself. The blood seeping through the white lather inspired a chilling image of blood on snow. Madlin's blood. He quickly wiped his face clean. "And you let her go? With snows about to come in and God only knows who waiting for the chance to snatch the MacKendrick or worse?"

What Madlin had done was admirable. In fact, it was the duty of a good laird, but knowing it a necessary action and accepting that it was his wife doing it were two very different things. Fear for her warred with anger that she'd taken herself off without a word to him.

"Ye're not to be worrying yerself." Gordie's words didn't slow Ewan as he started pulling on heavy woolen socks and trews. "She left hours ago. Ye'll not catch up with her, if that's what ye're thinking. Best ye stay here and let that leg heal. The lass is no fool. She took half a dozen men with her, along with the drivers of the three wagons."

"And just how long does she expect to be gone?"

Hugh handed him a tankard of ale. "All day, perhaps even some of tomorrow."

While he finished getting ready, Ewan queried the two men as to the caliber of the men Madlin had taken with her. Not having met many of her men, he could only take Hugh's and Gordie's word that they were capable of protecting the lady. "The cowards what's been raiding have never attacked a force of fighting men," Hugh assured him.

"Yet." Ewan buckled on his sword and grabbed up his heavy cloak. His anger blocked out all other feelings so that he was almost to the stairway before he felt a painful cramp in his leg. His stride shortened, slowed, and finally he was forced to stop and lean against the wall.

Gordie handed him the walking stick. "If ye've a mind to see to yer horses, we'll show ye to the stables."

With a tight grip on the stick, Ewan started down the steps. "And wherever else I may wish to wander, no doubt," he muttered under his breath. That his wife had left her two most trusted men to serve as his watchdogs in her absence served to stoke his anger further. "Tell me, gentlemen, might I ride out those gates and over the causeway, or did my lady wife instruct you to keep me within Dunfionn's walls?"

"I s'pect that stallion of yers be needing a bit of exercise." Gordie reached for a cloak hanging on a row of pegs near the keep's outer door. "The mares, too. Fine animals ye have, Sir Ewan. Don't see the like around here too often. We'd be honored, Hugh and me, to give the lassies some exercise for ye."

"Treise and I will enjoy the company," Ewan said, full well knowing he had no choice if he expected to ride out of Dunfionn's gates.

Once they were outside, Ewan noted that snow was falling heavily. He wasn't sure if it was a good omen or a bad one for his wife's sojourn through her territory. Perhaps she'd turn back. Assuming she could, that is. If the weather worsened, a horse like Treise or even the mares could make it easily through deep drifts. But Madlin's flashy mare and the Highland ponies her men would be riding? He wasn't so sure.

The only thought that gave him some peace of mind as he walked toward the stables was that if the weather worsened, the raiders would likely stay close to wherever their den was. Madlin should be safe from attack. But would the weather prove to be a greater adversary?

It was late afternoon of the third day since Madlin had left for the far reaches of MacKendrick territory, and the weather had finally cleared. Ewan pounded a gloved fist against the battlement. Still no sign of her! The light would be gone within the hour.

With the gathering darkness, a bitter wind had begun blowing in from the loch that surrounded the fortress. He was chilled to the bone but loath to leave his vantage point high above the gates. The weather that had stranded his wife God only knew where had also kept the bishop in residence. Ewan wasn't looking forward to the man's company at table for even one more evening.

The bastard was pleasant enough. Or was attempting to be, for not once had he suggested annulment directly. Instead of the threats of damnation the man had rained upon Madlin, he had subjected Ewan to hour upon hour of lectures on the holiness of marriage and the importance of entering into a marriage freely, with purity of heart and intent. That is, when he was not wringing his hands and adding to Ewan's own fears by expressing grave concern that Madlin and her men might be attacked.

Exactly what the bishop's game was, Ewan was not yet sure. At the edges of his mind was the niggling thought that Madlin had manufactured the entire tale. As soon as the thought formed again, he dismissed it. She was completely without guile, he was sure of it. The lady was incapable of such dissembling. It was the priest who was the dissembler. But why?

"I'm for the hall, lads," Hugh announced. "Ye may freeze yerselves here if ye like, but I'm for a warm fire and a wee dram or two to warm my bones."

"Auld woman," Gordie growled under his breath as his friend passed.

"The lass and the lads are not coming this day," Hugh growled in return. "Fine sight they'll have when they do return if the two of ye stay up here much longer. A pair of frozen carcasses looking down on 'em from the ramparts is what they'll likely be seein'."

Shifting his weight from one foot to the other, Gordie stood before a brazier where a fire burned fitfully. "For once, that man could be right, lad. Our Maddie and the lads are likely to be holed up nice and warm somewheres waiting for first light tomorrow. Might as well tell the men to let down the gate. Not likely to see man nor beast comin' across that bridge any more this day."

Tearing his gaze from the causeway, Ewan stretched his hands toward the meager heat of the brazier. His leg grew stronger by the day. He'd pushed it a little harder every day and now felt it strong enough to spend a day in the saddle. If Madlin didn't appear by tomorrow morning, he was going to mount a search party.

Over his shoulder, he gave the causeway one more glance before following Gordie. By the time he reached the bailey, the chains were just beginning to creak. The portcullis was halfway down when shouting could be heard from beyond. Ewan didn't let himself hope it was Madlin and her cadre until he heard the clatter of many horses on the drawbridge.

The leggy mare, Aisling, was the first horse through the barbican. Ewan raced across the bailey and lifted the rider off the mare's back even before she'd reined to a stop. Gripping her shoulders, he shouted, "Where have you been?" and gave her a shake. Not giving her a chance to answer, he shook her again. "How dare you ride out in weather like this. Have you no sense?"

Madlin's smile of greeting died. Wrenching out of his grasp, she gave him her most imperious glare. "Must I remind you that I am the MacKendrick and I must do my duty?"

Not sparing him another glance, she issued orders for the care of the horses and for her cadre to warm themselves inside and fill their bellies. Tight-lipped and straight-backed, she mounted the steps to the keep and strode inside.

Ewan started after her, but Gordie placed a staying hand on his shoulder. "Pardon an old man who's known her since she was a babe, but I'd give her a little time. She is not a lass to hold her temper long."

Still staring at the door where she'd disappeared, Ewan shook his head and admitted, "Never have I lost my temper so often and my sense so completely as I do around that woman."

Gordie chuckled and clapped him on the shoulder. "She was not raised like most lassies of her station, so stands to reason she's a mite different than the ladies I s'pect ye've known."

"That, my friend, is an understatement."

Chapter Fifteen

"Send whoever that is away, Edella," Madlin said when a knock sounded at the door. "Tell him . . . I mean whoever it is . . . that I'm enjoying a bath and do not wish to be disturbed by anyone. And I do mean *anyone*."

It was Ewan, but Edella barred his entrance effectively, delivering her message as firmly as Madlin had anticipated. Edella was the cook's daughter, and like her mother, she could be a formidable force. But after he'd gone, Madlin was not sure whether she was relieved or disappointed that he had left so quickly and without a single argument.

To think I wanted nothing so much as to get back to Dunfionn and that odious man!

Madlin's open-palm smack sent a spray of herb-scented bathwater in her face. She was glad, for it hid the tears of disappointment and hurt she'd felt since her husband's angry greeting. Sinking farther into the water, she tried to relax and let the heat and herbs work their magic on her tired, aching muscles. But what of her aching heart?

Three days, she'd fought the elements and her own impatience to return to Dunfionn and *him*. And what had braving the wind and cold earned her? Harsh words and a shaking. *A shaking!* The man had actually shaken her as if she were a bairn in need of a reprimand.

"Will ye be wanting the black velvet or the green wool to wear down to supper?" the serving maid asked, spreading the gowns across the bed.

"Neither, just lay out my bed robe. Once I am warmed

again, I think I'll not stray beyond this chamber until morning." It was cowardly to avoid the hall, but she had no desire to confront Ewan or Francis this night.

"Och, ye must be frozen clear through for riding in that wind." The maid handed her a tankard of wine she'd just heated with a poker from the fire. "Lady Elspeth said I was to see that ye drink all of it. 'Twill chase the chill from ye, she said."

Madlin dutifully took a deep draught of what she expected to be a mixture of spiced wine. The concoction was far more potent. Her throat burning and her eyes watering, she declared, "By the Virgin, she's laced it with *uisge*! Or was that your own addition, Edella?"

"Only a wee dram," the woman admitted. " 'Twas me mam's idea as ye was out in bad weather all the day. A little *uisge* be good for a strong Scot like our laird, 'twas what she said when she added it to the drink yer aunt mixed up fer ye."

More cautiously this time, she took another sip. In small measures, the mixture was very good and was already warming her from the inside. Seeing a hint of worry on the maid's face, she quickly assured, "It's good. Just what I need. Thank you and thank your mam for her thoughtfulness."

At least someone cared about her well-being. After that last evening she'd spent with her husband, she'd eagerly anticipated comfort from him upon her return, and even more "comfort" when they were alone once more in this chamber. Obviously, she'd been mistaken, or perhaps he'd changed his mind again about their marriage. In her absence had Francis swayed Ewan to the idea of setting her aside?

She'd drained the tankard by the time she stepped from the tub and into the warmed length of linen Edella held for her. "I've changed my mind, Edella. I feel quite recovered. I'll wear the green. 'Tis only supper, and no reason to dress so fine as the velvet."

Feeling much like she was about to go into battle, she added, "I believe I'll wear a circlet." *No knight went into battle without his spurs, did he?* She didn't have spurs, but the circle of gold would do quite nicely. "You'll find it in that trunk. Do you think you could tackle this great mop of mine and put it in some order?"

Edella slipped a fresh chemise over Madlin's head, quickly followed by the woolen gown. "Oh, aye, 'twill be a pleasure. 'Tis glorious hair ye have, my lady." She made short work of the laces and was reaching for the brush when she remarked, "I always thought so, even when ye were still a wee lass with it all tucked up in a cap most of the time. Sit yerself by the fire and we'll have it dried and fashioned in no time."

An hour later, when Madlin descended to the great hall, she was quite transformed from the bedraggled and totally dispirited woman who had climbed up the stairs. Every inch the lady and laird of Dunfionn—or so she did hope that was the image she presented. Everyone was already at table, and, as she made her way through the hall, she did not risk another glance at the dais. She'd spied Ewan, seated beside the high, carved laird's chair, the moment she'd entered the hall.

Francis was beside him. The two seemed to be in deep conversation. From her vantage point, Francis looked quite congenial. And Ewan? Ewan looked irritated. Was that a good sign or bad that he was of the same mind regarding their marriage as he'd been before she'd been called away? Or, perhaps he was still angry with her.

"I do hope, Sir Ewan, that in our short acquaintance you have come to look upon me as someone you can turn to. I am first and foremost a humble priest, and 'tis my calling to bring comfort and guidance to those in need."

Ewan took another long draught from his tankard, eyeing the man over the rim. "I shall keep that in mind, your lordship, should I feel in need of such."

"I would hope we have come to know each other well enough and, being related by marriage as we are, you would call me Francis."

Serpent, comes to mind. A serpent garbed in priest's robes. "As you say, brothers by marriage."

He took another swallow of his ale to wash away the distaste of the words.

The priest smiled, but it was a smile that set Ewan further on alert. "I see my sister has finally arrived. I must confess I was surprised you have not been with her since her return, being newly wedded as you are. Bridegrooms are usually so . . . so . . . shall we say . . . eager?"

Ewan had been aware of Madlin's every move since she'd crossed the threshold of the great hall. For all the weariness she must be experiencing, she stood no less straight and proud than she always did as she talked with her people. The heavy brooch of the MacKendrick at her shoulder, Madlin of Dunfionn wore the mantle of leadership as admirably as Jamie wore his crown. If he didn't fear a most public dismissal of his efforts to apologize, he would be already at her side.

Eager was a mild word for what he felt about spending time alone with his bride. But he saw no need to explain that to the priest. What happened or didn't happen in his chamber was no business of Francis MacDonald's.

"My lady wife was understandably cold and tired when she arrived. A little quiet and a good long soak in a hot tub was what she needed more than her new husband's company."

How much of that miserable greeting I gave her do you know, priest? Given the snubbing the ladies Jeanne and Alys had given him, he was sure his outburst and rough handling of her had been trumpeted throughout all of Dunfionn.

"Perhaps, you would care to talk with me about this woeful station. It is well within my power to provide a solution to your plight."

"Woeful station? My plight? I fear I do not understand. Exactly to what are you referring?"

Francis calmly folded his hands and smiled faintly. "Your fortitude is admirable, but it is not necessary that you endure your present circumstances forever." Pausing, he looked heavenward with closed eyes and moved his lips soundlessly as if in prayer.

When he'd finished, he looked beyond Ewan to where

Madlin was lingering, talking at length with a group of young lads at one of the lower tables. "I had hoped we could discuss this before she returned, but there never seemed to be the time as you spent so much of each day beyond Dunfionn's walls. We have not much time now before she joins us, so I shall speak bluntly.

"I understand my sister forced you to say the vows against your will. Lest you be unaware, that is grounds for annulment. If you wish I can compose the petition myself. You need only sign it and be on your way to take up the life you intended before my sister . . . ah . . . interrupted your progress to Glendarach. Free to then marry a woman of your own choosing."

Ewan schooled his features and tone to a blandness he was far from feeling. "I do appreciate your offer, but setting aside a wife and repudiating vows made before God, no matter the circumstances, is a grave matter and should be granted the benefit of much thought . . . and, of course, prayer."

Francis smoothed a hand down his chest where it came to rest over the large cross he wore. "Your reverence for the sacraments is well noted, my son." His sharp gaze shifted to Madlin, who was moving slowly toward the dais. "Would that such respect were common to all God's children. But alas, there are weaker vessels among us who are incapable of such understanding of honor and the reverence owed the Church's holy sacraments."

Weaker vessels? Only a pompous idiot would consider such a magnificent woman as Madlin the weaker vessel. Nor were any of the other MacKendrick women for that matter. *Jesu!* 'Twas difficult to manage civility with this man.

He'd seen his like on the mainland and the burned corpses left in their wake. In the name of God they exacted their foul deeds. It was not to His glory they scourged their little realms of so-called heretics but to the glory of their own aspirations.

He'd wager all he owned that Francis MacDonald was of that ilk. Ambition hung about the man as clearly as the heavy pectoral cross hanging about his neck.

Having little else to do during Madlin's absence, he'd explored Dunfionn, the village, and some of the territory beyond. He'd learned much from the MacKendricks, especially from the two guard dogs Madlin had assigned him. It was openly acknowledged that this slender, dark-eyed priest was Toirlach's baseborn son begotten before he'd married the lady Aislinn Gunn of Craigheade.

More to the point than the man's circumstances of birth was that Francis MacDonald, Bishop of Beauly, was a bastard in character. Unless he misread the expressions used by some he'd talked with this day, he was not alone in holding that opinion.

"I do love my sister, but as her spiritual guide I worry that her subjugation of you is not acceptable to God. Being a man, you better understand these things. An annulment will put this unfortunate episode behind both you and her. In time and with guidance, I have faith she will find her way back to a path more in keeping with God's plan.

"Perhaps she will return to St. Margaret's, take the veil, and devote her life to doing God's work. I have long harbored the desire for her to be my sister in Christ as well as blood."

The veil? Madlin? I think not, priest!

"There are many ways to do God's work," Ewan began instead. "Bringing about a lasting peace between two great clans would surely seem one. Your sister and I are in total agreement that our marriage is the most likely means of achieving such a peace."

Ewan was gratified to see a flash of anger in the priest's dark eyes before Francis dipped his head and answered smoothly, " 'Tis a noble gesture, sacrificing your personal happiness in the name of peace. I shall pray that God grants you guidance in this matter."

"Sometimes God does move in strange and mysterious ways. We mortals must accept each day He grants us and have faith all is part of God's plan. Is that not true, my lord bishop?"

"Of . . . of course." To Ewan's great satisfaction, bright spots of angry color rose on the priest's pallid cheeks. "But—"

"Ah! Here is my bride at last." Rising, Ewan turned his back on the priest. Catching both her hands in his, he held her before him. "Madlin, my sweet, you do brighten the hall and my heart with your very presence. Your duties took you too long away."

She struggled to loosen herself from his grasp as he knew she would. It would take more than one pretty speech for her to forgive him.

He brought both her hands to his lips, kissing each in turn, then leaning forward he brushed his lips against her cheek. Softly, for her ears alone, he said, "I do most humbly beg forgiveness for my behavior earlier. 'Twas worry and fears for your safety that set my tongue on such a rampage. I pray you do not cuff my ears before all assembled here but wait until we are alone to deliver the blows I surely deserve."

Rising on her tiptoes, Madlin gave the impression of returning his kiss. But, between clenched teeth, she hissed, "You deserve a good thrashing and in front of everyone."

"That and more, but we have our duty to our clans to think of, and I do apologize, most sincerely."

"Duty, sir? I wonder that you understand the meaning of it." She tried to free her hands, but he refused to let them go. "If I smile, will you let go of me and let me take my chair?"

Against her cheek, he whispered, "I do understand duty most well, and look forward to taking up any and all duties appropriate for the husband of the MacKendrick. You may count on it, and now, since you have smiled so sweetly, you may sit down." He punctuated his statement with a quick kiss on each of her hands before freeing them.

Once he'd seated her and himself, he leaned toward her and said, "I must offer yet another apology, my dear."

Her eyes wide, but no longer stabbing him with anger, she asked, "Another?"

"Aye," he smiled and placed his hand on her arm. Atoning for his bastardly behavior would begin at once. A bit of wooing could not come amiss, either. That it might tickle the priest's ire was but a small bonus. "For failing to remark that you're looking especially beautiful tonight. On you a woolen gown is as silk upon a queen, and that simple circlet a royal crown. And I thank you most heartily that you did not cover your glorious hair with more than a wisp of silk. To cover such beauty would surely be a sin."

She graced him with but the barest of smiles. Fulsome compliments of her person were clearly not the way to this lady's good graces. He would have to try a different tack.

"And you, husband, are looking quite well. How does your wound? Does it pain you when you walk, still?"

"I am quite recovered, my lady. It bothers me hardly at all," he said, then grinned devilishly. "I assure you I am once again a very able man, prepared to assume all duties expected of me."

She blushed and shifted nervously in her chair. Ewan took heart. "And your head? The bruise has faded, but does it still cause you pain?"

"Nay, I am well, also. Fatigued, some, but well."

Leaning around Ewan, Francis inserted, "A most taxing trip, I am sure, dear sister. God be praised you are home again, safe and uninjured. After I heard you had ridden out, I spent much of my time praying you would not be attacked by Fra—" He sent Ewan a sideways glance. "Raiders. The outlying crofts? All was well there?"

Madlin sighed. "No, there had been a raid a week past on a herd, but it was a minor one. Only a few cattle stolen in the dead of night. No one was hurt, nor property damaged."

"We are lucky it was not more."

"I do not expect any more killings, brother."

Stiffening almost imperceptibly, Francis offered, "The weather, I suppose."

"Nay, Sir Ewan's and my marriage. By our union, we shall forge a peace between our clans." She placed a hand over Ewan's. "But until the earl and I can agree together on the terms of that peace, I took the precaution of convincing the herds and cotters to move into the village."

"Very wise of you, sister."

"I agree, sweetling, a most wise leader, you are. Any and all under your leadership are blessed indeed."

Madlin's response to his praise was a brief, very pointed rise of one brow before her attention was pulled away by her aunt's mild admonishment. "You have not touched your food, niece. You must replenish your body after such strenuous days, lest you fall ill."

Smiling gently, Ewan said, "Lady Elspeth is most correct. Think of the clan, my lady. Clan MacKendrick must have a strong leader at its head, not one wasting away for lack of sustenance."

Leaning toward her, he pressed his mouth to her ear and whispered, "And I would wish a strong, eager wife in my bed this night." His audacity was rewarded by her gasp and the return of the blush he found so utterly enchanting.

Spearing a savory morsel from her trencher, he lifted it to her lips. "You cannot refuse such delicious fare. Your cook is to be complimented on her methods. I have tasted none better in my travels."

He watched her chew and knew the moment the tasty cube of expertly seasoned mutton awakened her appetite. A smile of sheer mischief preceded, "And sweetmeats and comfits? Do they weaken you as well, Sir Ewan?"

Ewan chuckled, delighted to see once again a light shining in the green depths of Madlin's eyes and smiles frequenting her lips. His gaze unwavering on her lips, he said, "I've a weakness for all things sweet. And you, my dear, are the sweetest of all," and was rewarded with the rise of another blush on her cheeks.

He waved a second cube of tender mutton dripping with fragrant juice beneath her nose before pressing it to her mouth. When her tongue licked the juice from her lips, he nearly groaned aloud. The fever caused by his wounded thigh had been but a trifle when compared to the heat throbbing in his groin.

Primed by the steady presentation of food to her lips, Madlin began to feel her strength return and a tingling exhilaration fill her with each glance and smile from her husband. She'd been too hasty in assuming he and Francis had spent her absence plotting Lord only knew what.

Trust. If apologies were in order, perhaps she should be apologizing for not trusting him. Later, perhaps, she would.

Her belly full, she leaned against the back of her chair and shook her head when he offered her another spoonful of custard. "How are you finding Dunfionn? I am told that during my absence you have ridden and walked much each day."

Ewan gave her a wry smile. "My . . . ah . . . escorts did allow me to wander whither I wished."

Madlin heard the frustration in his voice and was sorry she'd asked. But she was not swayed in her conviction that it was best he be accompanied by men she trusted at all times. Not forever, just for these first few weeks until she knew he'd been accepted.

"I trust you were satisfied with the care your horses are receiving?" she asked, in an attempt to direct his attention toward a subject close to his heart. If this knight, who could slip so easily from courtier to fire-eating combatant, possessed any genuine affection within his body, it was for his stallion. In her progress through the hall, a group of stable boys had hailed her, fair bubbling over with descriptions of the reunion between horse and master. So effusive had been their praise of his horsemanship and ways with his animals, Madlin had thought she might never be able to move from their table.

"Gordie Gunn is a fine stable master. Treise has known no better care even when in the royal stables, and our monarch does value his animals."

"Treise is as fine a destrier as any Gordie has ever seen. Is he French-bred?"

"Aye, he was bred in Anjou. A gift from a distant cousin."

"And the mares . . . ? Are they also French-bred and gifts?"

"The bay is French, and I purchased her. The white-faced chestnut is from a strain being developed near the Clyde here in Scotland." He shrugged lightly as if embarrassed to admit the next. "She was a gift from James."

"You are indeed held high in our king's favor if he has gifted you with such a fine sword and a valuable breeding mare." And what else, husband? Madlin wondered. She sensed Ewan's answer had been carefully worded. She gauged him too honorable to lie openly, but would he withhold information? The sword he carried and a fine animal like the white-faced mare were indeed valuable, but as reward for choosing to remain in captivity with the king all those years? She thought them paltry for such loyalty and service.

"The mare is like all fine Scots ladies, a spirited lass but gentle and biddable when treated well," he remarked, and placed his hand over hers. The way he was looking at her made her think he was not talking about the mare's temperament at all.

"Has she a name?" Madlin asked, reaching for her goblet to quench a throat suddenly gone very dry.

"Perhaps you would care to name her."

He began a light stroking of her hand that sent a quiver along her flesh. "Oh, but I could not. She is yours and—"

"Nay, I give her to you." Smiling, he brought her hand to his lips and pressed a kiss to her palm. "I think the mare an appropriate bride's gift, if you will have her." He winked at her before adding, "And me."

Madlin reached for her goblet again, glad it contained only watered wine and spices. More *uisge* she did not need to warm her body.

At a table below the dais, Gordie nudged his elbow into his companion's side. A merry glint in his eye, he tipped his head toward the couple. "Ye'll be handing me yer purse when we break our fast on the morrow, my friend."

For a man in peril of losing what little coin he owned, Hugh's expression was remarkably cheerful as he watched his laird and her new husband. "How is that ye'll be knowing ye've won? Are ye thinking to be pressing yer ear to the door all through the night? Or have ye fashioned a peephole some-wheres so as to observe the goings-on?"

Gordie's smile disappeared in a flash. His heavy brows came together, and the look in his eye was thunderous. "*Whisht,* man! Another word and I'll be running ye through for just thinking me so depraved."

After cuffing Hugh more heavily than was purely congenial, his expression lightened considerably. He gestured with his mug. "Just look at the poor lad, will ye? Fair shaking with excitement, he is, sitting up there next to her. Mark my words, he's as randy for her as that great stallion of his is for his fancy mares."

Hugh saw Madlin try to stifle a yawn and the way her shoulders were beginning to droop. He shook his head slowly. "Do not be thinking overlong on spending my coins. Horses is horses and men are something else again, no matter how much alike ye think they are. If ye've enough mind left in that old head of yers to know the difference, turn yer eye on the lass. So worn out is she, next time ye look she may well be resting her head in her trencher."

Gordie took a long draft from his mug. Over the rim, his eye was clearly directed toward the head table and his expression thoughtful. "Mayhap she is a mite fatigued, but our Maddie was ever a lass full of vigor. A wee bit more of them victuals he's stuffing down her and she'll be revived."

Grasping his tankard of ale, Hugh started to rise. "I think 'tis past time for a toast to our newly wedded couple."

Gordie pulled him back to the bench. "Nay, not yet. Best not break the spell the lad's casting on our lass. He be wooing her right and proper as sure as I'm sitting here next to ye."

Hugh watched as Ewan pressed a soft kiss to Madlin's wrist, then he swept his gaze about the hall, taking in the expressions of all. "Some of the good folk of Dunfionn are not so pleased to see a Fraser wooing their laird. More'n just the bishop is unhappy about the marriage. There could still be trouble. Wouldn't hurt for you and me to continue staying close a wee bit longer."

"Aye," Gordie agreed, sobering. "Made some friends, he did, these past three days, but 'twill take a while longer for some. You, me, and most of the others what was with us when we took him have been spreading the word that he is a fine man and blameless in the killings and raids."

"According to Sir Ewan, all the Frasers are blameless of the killings. Do ye believe him?"

Gordie thought for a bit before answering. "I'm beginning to think there be a powerful stink about all them Fraser plaids laying about after every murderin' raid. Too obvious, and what Scot would leave his plaid behind and ride back home bare-legged and bare-assed? Could be we was a bit hasty in our accusing. How think you?"

"The same. But if not the Frasers, who?"

Leaning close to Hugh's ear to ensure no one heard his answer, Gordie said, "Seamus Munro."

Startled, Hugh jerked upright on the bench. "*Whisht!* The lad has not the balls to do such a thing. More's the point, there'd be none of the Munros what would follow him. 'Twas never a leader, that one."

" 'Tis a right powerful grudge he bears our Maddie. His pa died but a few weeks before Brianna and her bairns was killed. Without Nairn Munro to control the miserable whelp, could be Seamus is finally getting retribution for the insult our lass gave him. And ye saw him the other night. Powerful angry he looked 'bout our lass marrying a Fraser."

"Och, well. Always was powerful strange, that one." Hugh eyed his friend with open skepticism, then shook his head. "No, only an old fool like ye would think the whelp any kind of leader. Ye know as well as me, that lad couldn't lead a band of wee lassies to pick berries and have any success."

"Once that was true, but some years have gone by. He's a man growed, now, and he is the chief of the Munros. We'll know when Beatha comes back."

"Och, ye be losin' yer mind, for certes, if ye think Beatha will tell us the man's changed that much."

"You was for sending Beatha, same as me. I'll not be listening to any more foolery like ye're not worried about the Munro." Gordie gestured toward the high table again. "Look at the way the lad's holdin' her hand and the way she's looking at him, will ye?" Smiling, he remarked, "Ye might as leave give over yer coins right now as wait until the morrow."

Watching the color rise in his laird's cheeks as her husband whispered something in her ear, Hugh swore beneath his breath. But the expletive not only lacked conviction, it was accompanied by a silly smile.

"Och, well, all the same, I'm holding my purse a while longer. There be many hours betwixt now and the dawn of tomorrow.

"But I've another wager to put to you. Sir Cameron is not a man long on patience, and you know it as well as me. Lucais Fraser shoulda been at Glendarach long afore this and told all. I'll wager there'll be a whole column of Frasers led by Sir Cameron himself tapping on Dunfionn's door by . . . hmmm . . . say midday on the morrow?"

Gordie eyed his friend, rubbed his head, then winked his eye at him. Offering him his hand, he said, "I'm thinking I'm as foolish to take that wager as ye were to take mine, but I'll do it. Since I'll be having all yer coins by then, what are ye putting up to back yer claim?"

"The same as always," Hugh replied as the two friends shook on this latest wager. The two had been losing and winning each other's purses for so many years that neither one was sure which leather pouch was his own. And when one was purseless, the collateral offered was always the same. His broadsword. Somehow neither man was ever without his weapon. Leastways, not for long.

Chapter Sixteen

Madlin poked at the embers glowing in the bedchamber's hearth, awakening the fire. The sight of the flames conjured an image of the hot and consuming pair of eyes that had been gazing so intently into hers throughout the evening meal.

She poked again at the fire, sending a cloud of sparks rising up the chimney. When the flames settled to their task again, their blue color freshened the memory of Ewan's gaze when, at meal's end, he'd said, "Come, I believe we are agreed that duty does come above all else."

Duty. A wave of heat shot through her body at the new twist circumstances had placed on that simple word. Perspiration beaded between her breasts as her imagination ran with images of just how this particular duty would be executed.

Moving away from the fire, she rubbed at her arms to ease the tingling in them. Too much of her body had reacted so to his wooing. And too much of her yearned that it was more than duty that compelled him to share her bed. Not for just the much-needed heirs or the peace so necessary to her clan did she want this marriage to succeed.

She understood the rudiments of what happened between a man and a woman. But she sensed there was a magic to be found in the act and that it was Ewan Fraser who could best reveal it to her. If with but a touch, a glance from his eyes, or the sound of his voice, he could elicit such heat to surge through her body, what might it be like to merge with him? Not just her body but her soul as well. To love and be loved.

She dismissed the idea as quickly as it formed. Love was

rare between couples of their rank, where most marriages were arranged for political or monetary gain. Like this one. That she and Ewan could manage to learn to trust and respect each other, perhaps develop an amount of fondness, was the best she could hope for. It was the height of foolish feminine dreaming to expect love. She'd never indulged in such before. Why now?

When Gordie had stopped them in the hallway and asked for a moment of Ewan's time, she'd been glad for the respite. Relief had been momentary, for the waiting was heightening her anxieties.

Why had Gordie detained her husband in the hallway and urged her to go on ahead? A thread of alarm slithered through her consciousness, but she pushed it away. If there was trouble, they would consult her first. Gordie's and Hugh's loyalty to her was unquestioned.

She shivered in reaction to the sound of voices murmuring in the hallway. Not all of them. Just one. Her husband's.

She could not discern his words, only the timbre, that low, rustling quality that distinguished Ewan Fraser's voice from any she'd ever heard. The sound set her skin to tingling again and her limbs weakening. In truth, that had been her state since his first touch when she'd joined him at the high table.

The thick oaken door swung inward. Not yet ready to face her husband, she kept her gaze upon the fire. "What was it that Gordie needed to discuss with you?" She could not disguise the suspicious tone of her query.

"A messenger is expected from Glendarach any day. Mayhap as early as tomorrow. He thought to assure me of my clansmen's safety." He lowered the bar into its brackets before coming up behind her.

"Cold, sweetling?" he asked, covering her hands with his own. He curled his palms about her forearms and ran them lightly down to her wrists and back up to her shoulders.

"Yes . . . no . . . I . . ." Her mind seemed to lose its focus as she floated from one sensation to the next. His touch, his scent, the mere sound of his voice, were like sweets at the end of a meal—tantalizing the senses to savor and enjoy.

"So sweet," he murmured against her head and buried his nose within her hair. The warm dampness of his breath filtering in and out of her hair set her body atingle all the way to her toes. When he loosed the heavy mass from its plaited coil, all her worries fell away as quickly and easily as the silken curtain drifted to her buttocks.

"Mmmm . . ." she moaned softly as he winnowed his fingers through the tresses and massaged her scalp. His ministrations chased away the last vestige of the megrim that had been threatening around the edges of her consciousness on and off throughout the evening.

He swept her hair to one side and began pressing kisses along the column of her neck from shoulder to ear. Moments later, Madlin was barely aware of her gown and chemise sliding down her body and pooling around her ankles. Other sensations—pleasurable, exciting, and frightening, as well—drew her attention.

Puckering first from the exposure to the chill air, her nipples peaked and thrust against the broad, masculine palms that had quickly covered them. Warm, liquid heaviness pooled in her breasts, her belly, and between her legs as he alternately caressed her and gently plucked at her nipples.

Drawn so fully into the mist of sensuality he created, she gave no thought to modesty or the foreignness of the intimacies he was taking with her. Involuntarily, she arched her back. Squeezing her eyes shut, she pressed her palms against the top of his hands to ease the aching in her breasts.

But when she felt him cup her mons and press a finger against the button of pleasure she had not known was hidden there, she cried out. Frightened by the intensity of the pleasure that bolted through her body, she jerked away from him.

"Wh . . .what are you doing to me?" Scarcely could she recognize the voice as her own, so soft and breathless was the sound.

"I'm trying to seduce you," he answered, pulling her back against him, this time her breasts against his chest, her belly against his, thighs against thighs. "Remember our duty? There will be no annulment, sweetling. Least ways, not instigated by me.

"And you?" he asked, nibbling at the lobe of one of her ears. "Have you second thoughts as to whom you wish to sire your sons?"

"No . . . I . . . am but still surprised to hear you say such," she managed. The rasp of his clothing and the touch of his lips against her suddenly oversensitive skin made her tremble and alternately chill and overheat. "Did . . . did you not declare most . . . ahhhh—"

Madlin's knees buckled with the sweep of his tongue around the shell of her ear. She might have crumpled to the floor had Ewan not been holding her. "You . . . did once declare you would not stand . . . stand stud for . . . me," she finally got out between gasps.

"I do not intend to stand." He left off teasing her ear to take up a tender seduction of her mouth.

Gently, with only the barest whisper from the tip of his tongue, he traced the outline of her lips. Sensations, at once fascinating and alarming, rushed through her. When his tongue pressed against the seam of her lips, she yielded easily, craving the exotic flavor of him.

Pressing against him, she felt the hard thrust of his sex at the juncture of her thighs. When he retreated, she instinctively did the same, then just as instinctively started to meet his thrust again and was lost in him until memories intruded. Layers of memories, spinning dizzily through her head.

Ewan's blue eyes, cold with condemnation. Francis's brown eyes, almost black with anger. Papa's green ones, first alight with humor, then darkening with serious intent.

Her head began to pound as the voices swirled and superimposed upon each other. Shouting. All of them shouting at her.

"You are an unnatural woman."

"Naught of your harlot's ways!"

". . . marriage an abomination."

"Hoyden!"

"A wolf ye have brought within these walls."

"Another man's get."

"Must learn patience lest yer great heart lead ye down the wrong path."

"Your people shall suffer eternal damnation."

Too weary to make sense of them, or battle, she began to shake. Frantic to be free and away from the torment, she pushed against the strong arms that held her. "Nay! Cease," she cried, covering her ears with her hands and taking several steps backward until she was pressed against the wall. "No more condemnations and rejections."

"Condemnations? Rejections? Before you stands a man burning for you, not rejecting or condemning you."

When Madlin remained pressed against the wall, Ewan started to close the space between them. He'd taken but two steps when he saw how glassy and wild her eyes were. He froze, his desire replaced by a fear as great as when he'd seen her crumple to the ground their first day together.

Carefully, he took a step closer. He'd seen thus in the eyes of men either from complete exhaustion or when the utter horror of battle had so insulted their sensibilities, they'd lost their wits for a time. Even the strongest and most experienced of warriors had his limit. Clearly, Madlin had been pushed to the very edge of her endurance.

"Shhh . . . shh . . . sweet lass," he crooned, moving slowly toward her. Seeing the way she continued to shake, he paused to pick up a fur robe draped over the back of the settle. Slowly and carefully, keeping up a litany of soothing nonsense, he approached her.

Though her body was still racked by deep shuddering sobs, her eyes held more life and she did not flinch when he settled the robe about her. The tears streaming down her cheeks and the dark shadows beneath her lustrous eyes assailed him. It was rest his lady needed most. Only a beast would insist they do their "duty" this first night after the grueling three days she'd just endured.

Sweeping her up in his arms, he went only so far as the settle before the fire. For a long, long while, he rocked her as if she were a babe. Sensing she'd been holding far too much inside her for too long, he urged her to let out all that troubled her. It came in an anguished torrent that left her breathless and him aching for her.

"I am not worthy of leadership. You said it true, I have no sense. My clan is ill-served with a woman at its head." She brushed angrily at the tears flowing down her cheeks. "I cry too much! A good laird should not be weeping all the time, and, of late, it seems that's all I do. 'Tis so . . . so . . . womanish!"

"Ah yes, they are womanish, and you are very much a woman. Tears do not make you any less strong or less wise. I'll hear no more that clan MacKendrick is ill-served by the woman who is their laird."

"Hmmmph." She sniffed. " 'Tis not only my clan that is ill-served, but you, too. I've ruined your life and the plans you must have had for your return."

"Nay, 'twas I who had no sense to shout at you so when all I wanted to do was hold you in my arms and thank God you were safe returned to me."

"But I have ruined your life," she insisted on a shuddering breath.

"Nay, you have not. I planned to marry as soon as I found a suitable lass, and you did that for me." Brushing his lips across her brow, he returned to rocking her. This nurturing of a woman was becoming a most satisfying pleasure. A contentment he'd not known in his adult life settled over him as he held her.

When she started to argue and repeat the prideful words he'd flung at her after their wedding, he pressed his forefinger against her lips. "We discussed this our last night together, remember? And I did beg you to forget that vow. 'Twas pride, sweetling. Naught but foolish pride that formed those words."

"My cousin, Jeanne, has told me men have an overabundance of it," she managed between sniffles. Though red-rimmed and still tear-filled, her eyes reflected once more the lively intelligence he'd come to enjoy so greatly. "And . . . and you, Sir Ewan Fraser, knight of Scotland and France, are of a kind with even more than most."

Whether he'd just been complimented or insulted, Ewan was not sure. Still, he could not help but chuckle. " 'Tis the nature of men, I fear. And, mayhap I am guilty of possessing more than most."

"She says I have unmanned you . . ."

Ewan controlled the self-derisive laugh that statement prompted. A slight shift in his position would have proved how wrong was the lady Jeanne's assertion. Since awakening that first morning with his rod surging hotly within his wife's grasp, he'd been in a perpetual state of arousal whenever she'd been near. 'Twas a miracle he could walk at all.

Unaware of the struggle he was having, Madlin relaxed further, resting her head in the crook of his shoulder. " . . . and 'twill be a long while before you would forgive, if ever you can."

Ewan smiled. Her open honesty was a delight to his soul. "Not so long, for I have already forgiven you," he said with a shrug. " 'Twas unmanning, mayhap, to be overcome and left with no weapons save words to hurl in my defense."

"Would you have hurled a sword or dirk at me had you still had them?"

He did not give voice to his response immediately, for the answer that had sprung to his mind startled him. Slowly, he admitted, "Nay, for when I saw you crumple to the ground from that blow, I died a little. You are a woman; I could not have wielded a weapon and brought you down." He pressed his lips against her temple. "I could not suffer that kind of guilt again."

Jerking upright, she turned to face him. Her eyes wide with horror, she clutched the fur about her like a shield and began scooting off his lap. "You, a knight, have slain other women?"

Before she could put the breadth of the room between them, or worse, flee the chamber, he reached for one of her hands. Keeping his grasp light so as not to frighten her, he closed his large palm around her slender one. "Upon my honor as a knight, you have my word that I have not nor will I ever raise my hand or a weapon against a woman," he declared solemnly.

With bated breath, he watched every tiny nuance play across her face while she considered his declaration. God's blood, it was important that she believe him. Trust was needed between them—and now, if his suspicions for tomorrow should prove true.

"You told me once that you take your vows seriously, and I do believe you are a right and honorable knight."

Ewan let out the breath he'd not known he'd been holding. "Thank you."

"What is this guilt you would not suffer again? Surely 'tis not for enemies slain in the heat of battle?"

Such a look of grief came over him, Madlin nearly cried out. His voice was so soft, when he began speaking, she returned to the settle so that she might better hear him.

"My brother Alistair was younger than me by more than a year," he began, and described the fun and closeness he'd shared with this brother, how alike they had been. Listening, she thought how common had been their early childhood, hers and Ewan's, with a brother to run the trails with and practice against with a wooden sword. And, like her and Airic, they were teased but watched over as well by an older brother. Or, in Ewan's case, two older brothers, Niall and Keith. Life at Glendarach sounded not so very different from that at Dunfionn.

"Our father warned us many times to keep off the narrow trail along the cliffs until we were older. But, prideful even then, I was hell-bent on catching a hare that had escaped our snare, no matter where the tracks led. I led, and Alistair always followed." He paused and took a long, shaky breath.

"We were running, our attention more on the chase than on where we were putting our feet. And, we . . . we slipped off the trail and went over the cliff."

Madlin squeezed her eyes shut to stem the tears threatening. The roughness in Ewan's voice revealed how painful the memory still was for him. Madlin could feel the terror that he had experienced as he described how he'd desperately clung to a tree root to keep his footing on the narrow ledge where he'd landed.

"I called and called throughout the night. 'Twas not until the next morn when we were found that I knew why Alistair had never made a sound. They found him at the base of the cliff. He . . . he . . ." He paused and took a shuddering breath. "It was my fault. He would still be alive if he had not followed me."

"No . . . no." Madlin wrapped her arms around him, returning the comfort he'd given her. "You cannot know that. 'Twas long ago and 'twas not your fault. You were but a lad and doing the kinds of things young lads do. You must believe that."

His voice was flat when he said, "Our mother could not. Alistair was her youngest and her favorite. She was dead from her grief within a fortnight. I carried guilt so heavily that even the loving care of my new stepmother could not assuage it. Finally my sire and Guenna decided it best that I be fostered far away from home. And so I was sent to France."

He stretched out his legs and leaned back against the settle with a deep sigh. "They thought to send me to a quieter place, a gentler land, free of the cliffs and narrow trails that reminded me so fiercely of that night. You see, I could not bear to go near them and cowered like a bairn inside the walls of Glendarach." He made a noise that sounded like a chuckle but was without humor. "But, of course, it took me many years to complete that journey to France, and when I did finally get there, 'twas not so peaceful."

"But you survived and became a twice-knighted warrior, a leader of men." Unable to meet his gaze, she turned her face toward the fire again. Her tears had begun anew. She wept for the little boy whose night of terror left him so fearful of heights that he was sent to a land faraway, known for its gentle, rolling terrain.

"And returned home only to be forced to marry the hoyden who captured you," she said, not meaning to voice that thought aloud.

Cupping her chin in his palm, Ewan dried the new tears dampening her cheeks with a brush of his thumb. " 'Twas no hoyden who stood with me before a priest. My bride is a brave warrior with a great and gentle heart, and one who has a purpose I cannot fault," he said as he smoothed her hair away from her face. "I find her very much to my liking."

Guilt for his capture and all the rest lightened considerably, and Madlin yawned widely. "Truly?"

"Truly."

She yawned again. "You should be in bed," he stated, scooping her up and starting across the chamber.

A sparkle of laughter glimmered in her eyes. "Now who is it that is ordering another to bed at every chance? Nay, sir. I will not take the bed this night unless you share it with me."

"I will not, for it's rest you need most, and you'd not be getting it if I shared this bed with you." He lowered her upon the down-filled mattress, carefully tucking the fur robe around her before turning away.

Immediately, she started to scramble off it. Remembering too late that she was practically nude, she grabbed for the fur and wound it about her. "I . . . I will be comfortable upon a pallet near the fire. 'Tis unfair for you to sleep upon the floor again. You have been most ill and—"

Putting a hand on each of her shoulders, Ewan held her where she was. "Stay," he ordered firmly, and she ceased her mutiny. Bending more closely, he brushed his lips lightly across hers to seal her silence. "No more arguments. We both need a good night's sleep."

Slowly, he loosed his grasp. "I shall be very comfortable tonight, I assure you. I was a soldier, remember? I have endured far worse than a night on a pallet in front of a warm fire." Freeing the buttons marching up his chest, he shrugged out of his jacket and tossed it toward the chest at the foot of the bed.

Chapter Seventeen

In rapt wonder, Madlin watched her husband strip off his clothing. Her eyes still stung from another bothersome bout of weeping, but she refused to close them to ease the dryness. Not for anything would she tear her gaze away from her husband.

As more and more of his body was revealed, she felt none of the embarrassment she'd suffered their first morning together but instead a growing excitement. It was fascinating to watch the flickering light dance upon his head. He was again the golden knight of her dream and more.

Used to seeing men stripped to their waists while working or practicing in mock battles, she was familiar with men's chests. But not chests like that of her husband.

MacKendrick men tended to be heavily furred across their upper chests and even toward their bellies. Along with the broadening of shoulders and a deepening of the voice, the sprouting of body hair was yet another sign that a man was fully grown. Or so she had thought.

For certes, her husband was a man fully grown, yet the skin above his waist was as smooth as hers. But oh so wonderfully different. With every movement he made, the muscles beneath his skin rippled and bunched. Such power showed in his arms and shoulders, more than enough to wield that great sword with the royal Stewart crest.

There was so much to discover about this man, and she was eager to learn all. But, try as she might, it was a struggle to hold her eyes open, let alone give voice to all the questions she had for him. Her lids were growing heavier and heavier while her mind grew fuzzier at the same rate.

His back to her, Ewan was untying the points of his hose when he heard her yawn again. "You wound me, my sweet," he teased as he tossed the hose upon the heap growing upon the trunk. "My disrobing does not usually bore a woman."

He turned to see that his bride's eyes were closed, and, from the soft sound of her deep, even breathing he knew she was fast asleep. "Nor has it ever put them to sleep," he remarked softly as he approached the bed. "A prideful fellow I am, for thinking to arouse your desire by baring my body to you."

He laughed at himself as he went about removing his wife's slippers and stockings and rearranging her sleeping body beneath the covers of the bed. In the act of covering her, he paused briefly to study the curious pendant she wore. He had noticed the chain about her neck before but had assumed it held a cross or perhaps a jewel.

Carefully, he lifted the pendant from its customary resting place between her breasts. An ancient piece, he guessed. The workmanship was exquisite, unlike anything he'd ever seen. In the dim light he could not make out the etchings on the face of the disk. Perhaps tomorrow he would ask her about it. Gently, he replaced it and then covered her.

After blowing out the lamps scattered about the chamber, he looked with dread at the pallet he'd made for himself on the floor. Madlin was right. He should not spend another night there.

Loosing the bed hangings from their posts, he joined his wife in the intimate confines of the bed. He swept one arm around her, then winced when she nestled against him.

The soft press of her full breasts to his side was a torment, but when she brought her thigh across his groin, he was in utter agony. His sex rose to throbbing attention, and no amount of willpower on his part could will it into submissiveness.

"Pride is not the only thing a man like me has in overabundance," he muttered as he lay in the throes of frustration.

"Mmmm . . . thank God you did not cling to that pride and spend the night on the floor again."

"Why, you little minx! I thought you were asleep."

"I was until you pulled me against your cold body."

"Cold? Perhaps you might care to warm me," he said, pulling her more fully upon him.

"I suppose that would be the duty of a wife, wouldn't it? Warming her husband." She began brushing her palms up and down his sides, then inched her hands between them, closer and closer to his throbbing shaft.

A low agonized moan escaped him when she touched his manhood. Catching her hands, he brought them back up to his chest. "I'm quite warm enough, any warmer and I'll explode."

"Then I suppose my duty is done," she said, then made a loud sighing sound as if totally bored and started to slide off his body.

"Not yet, sweet wife, not yet." Wrapping his arms around her, he rolled and reversed their positions. With his groin nestled comfortably between her thighs, the tip of his sex nudging the nest of curls there, he was barely able to curb the impulse to drive himself deeply into her.

Levering himself up to shift into a safer position, he told her, " 'Tis time I did my duty to you."

"Will it be such a chore?"

"Oh, aye, one I hope will take most of the night," he said before starting a shower of light kisses upon her face. First her brows, then her cheeks, her nose, and finally, when she grew restless beneath him, he took her mouth.

Madlin opened her eyes at the thrust of his tongue within her mouth, then closed them again to concentrate more fully on the sensations he was evoking throughout her body. Responding to the way his tongue swept through her, she sent her own tongue exploring, savoring each new and thrilling taste and texture.

That there was so much to learn about this man had been her last thought before she'd fallen asleep and was foremost in her mind now that she was awake. She needed no light to see the very male body that held her. She saw it again in her mind's eye and satisfied her curiosity about it with her lips, tongue, and hands.

How smooth, even silken, was the skin stretched so tautly across the hardened hillocks of muscle upon his chest. Silkier still was the skin further down, across his belly. She wanted to explore further, but he caught her roving hand and brought it to his lips.

"Not yet, sweetling," he murmured against her palm as he alternately kissed and licked it. " 'Tis a pleasure too great, I fear. 'Twould be over far too soon if you hold me once again."

Placing her hand upon his shoulder, he returned to tantalizing her mouth before she could offer a protest. With new territories and textures teasing her fingertips, she did not rise to the challenge he had unwittingly made by stopping her questing hand. But hold some part of him she would. Pushing her fingers through his golden hair, she trapped his head exactly where it was with his lips and tongue pleasuring hers.

His deep-chested chuckle vibrated against her breasts before she felt the touch of his hand upon them. As desperate as she was to satiate her appetite for his taste, her other senses clamored for satisfaction. Arching beneath him, she brought her aching breast more fully into his hand and the relief she instinctively knew his touch could provide.

Her soft cry when again he lifted his mouth from hers was quickly followed by a moan of pleasure when he drew one of her throbbing nipples into his mouth. His other hand skimmed down her body, curled briefly at the curve of her hip, then moved farther. His fingers traced a steady pattern on her thigh, a circle growing wider and wider until it included the moistening crease at the juncture of her thighs.

This time she did not thrust his hand away when he sought and found the center of her desire. Restless and craving more, she lifted herself toward his roving fingers and welcomed the gentle invasion.

Ewan could bear it no longer. Her sheath was too warm,

moist, and welcoming. Already the walls were undulating with passion, and, selfish or not, he wanted to feel them tighten around him when she reached her pleasure this first time. That it was her first time with a man, he doubted not at all. Passionately responsive she was, demanding, too, but there was an innocence and curiosity in the touch of her hands and lips that testified to her inexperience.

Exerting all the control that he was able, he entered her slowly, giving her as much time as he could to adjust to his fullness. Withdrawing only slightly, he returned, more deeply, until he met the delicate barrier that proved her innocence. He wanted to hesitate, but she shifted and thrust upward, and he was fully inside her. He caught her cry within his mouth.

He tried to go slowly, but she met him thrust for thrust. When she wrapped her legs around his plunging hips, he nearly lost all control. "Come with me, sweetling," he murmured against her throat as he increased the pace until their mating melded them into one being, one mutual possession that carried them closer and closer to an explosive climax. Hearing her cry out her pleasure, he sought his own release.

Totally spent, he collapsed into her arms with a satisfied sigh. "You are an extraordinary woman," he managed as he struggled to bring his breathing under control.

"That . . . was most extraordinary," she said between ragged breaths.

Ewan chuckled. "Most extraordinary, indeed." His lips pressed against her throat, he waited for her pulse to return to normal and his own heart to slow its rapid pounding. He thought to move off her, a reflex born of habit to relieve the woman beneath him of his crushing weight, then his smile increased.

Her thighs were still clamped about his hips and her arms locked about his waist. This was no dainty woman gasping for breath beneath him, but his warrior queen, as voluptuous and strong as any of myth or history. In this, a most vulnerable moment for a man, she held him tightly. Had he the strength,

he would not have sought freedom from her arms, for this was
a capturing too sweet to struggle against.

"Jamie, you are a right and just ruler," he murmured, not
realizing he'd said the words aloud. She was a gift, this
woman. Like so many others from his friend and sovereign,
he'd tried to refuse it. Ever the fool.

Madlin wondered briefly at his remark. But, her heart drum-
ming so loudly within her chest, she was not sure she had
heard correctly, or even that she'd heard anything at all. Not as
large as before, that part of him that marked him male was
still a foreign presence throbbing deep within her. Stretched
out upon her, his body surrounded her most pleasantly. From
the way his breath was deepening and evening, she guessed
he was already asleep, and was relieved.

Self-conscious as to how utterly wanton was the arrangement of her limbs and the incredible intimacy of their joining,
she eased her legs to the mattress. He remained nestled comfortably between her thighs, his breath blowing gently against
her cheek, one hand cupping her buttocks, the other cradling
her breast. Trapped she was, and trapped she was most surprisingly contented to stay.

Lightly circling her fingertips against his hard, muscled
back, she thought in pleased wonder about what had just occurred between them. A curious thing was this mating between a man and a woman, and most exhilarating. No wonder
so much of it went on between the men and women of Dunfionn. Indeed, it was a miracle any work ever occurred.

She giggled at the thought and was immediately rewarded
for her mirth by a stirring of his manhood within her. The feel
of him thickening and stretching toward her womb once more
sent a delicious ripple of pleasure through her body. She
raised her knees and dug her heels into the mattress as she
rose to take him more deeply within her.

Ewan's deep and long moan of pleasure was all the encour-
agement she needed. Grasping his buttocks, she surged upward to take him more fully, then retreated, mimicking the

actions that had set her on fire and sent her soaring to some-place beyond herself.

Suddenly, he rolled them toward the middle of the bed. She registered a moment of surprise to find herself astride him, and saw the glitter of his grin in the darkness. "Your turn, sweetheart," he murmured.

While his hands did wondrous things to her breasts and the tiny button of pleasure hidden between her thighs, he raised and lowered her upon him until she learned to set the pace herself. It was as if a door had opened for her. Toward the sun-light she rushed, as the torrents of heat rippled through her again, increasing in intensity until she cried out his name. She hovered there until the intensity was so great she could bear it no longer. The rush to the pinnacle had taken all from her, and, in the sweet aftermath, she pillowed her head upon his chest.

Utterly spent, Madlin drifted toward sleep. "This marriage is *not* an abomination," she muttered, nestled comfortably within the circle of her husband's strong arms. God would not grant such pleasure in mating if He thought it an abomination. Ewan Fraser was her husband, and she would remain his wife. They would have fine sons to carry on Toirlach MacKen-drick's line.

It was a pleasing thought that drifted through her mind. As were the visions of golden-haired sons, hers and Ewan's, laughing and playing in Dunfionn's hall as she, Airic, and Bram had before them. God willing, Bram's son would be there, too. She must assure that.

With that task tucked into the back of her mind, and the steady beating of Ewan's heart beneath her ear, she finally closed her mind to consciousness.

Hours later, the sound of pounding interrupted her pleasant dreams. Thinking it was but her husband's heart beating so strongly, she strove to soothe it to a more gentle rhythm so that she might rest longer. Rest, they both needed rest.

More asleep than awake, she patted his chest but to no avail. The pounding grew louder and stronger. Alarmed at the unnaturalness of a heart beating so strongly, Madlin crooned, "Ease, dear heart. Ease," smoothing her palms across his chest.

Ewan caught her hand and brought it to his lips for a quick kiss. "I fear 'tis not I who needs ease, my sweet," he remarked as the pounding continued, more forcibly and louder if that were possible.

Yanking the bed hangings open, he bellowed, "Leave off that assault on our door!" Both he and Madlin squinted against the bright sunshine streaming through the window.

" 'Tis past terce," Madlin said, her horror at being still abed at such an hour reflected clearly in her eyes. As was true every day, there was much to do and never enough hours, even rising before dawn as was her usual habit.

A string of curses delivered in a mixture of French, Gaelic, and English rent the air as Ewan left the bed and crossed the chamber, stumbling on the garments, his and hers, littering his path. By the time he'd lifted the bar and yanked the portal open, the man standing in the hallway had been informed in no uncertain terms of Ewan's opinion of his ancestry, sanity, and even his virility.

"And 'tis glad I am to see ye, as well, milord Ewan," Lucais Fraser said with a twinkle in his eyes and a wide grin upon his face. "I trust 'twas yer comfort not illness that has ye still abed when the sun has been shining already so long in the heavens this day."

Doffing his cap, Lucais swept it to the floor as he bowed. "And a most hearty good day to you, my lady. Last I saw of ye, ye'd been foully struck and my lad . . . er, I mean, Sir Ewan was cradling yer unconscious body in his arms. If I may be so bold, let me say what a bonny sight ye be for these old eyes. By the saints, 'tis a joy to see you looking so fine and well."

Feeling a blush heat her body from the top of her head all the way to her toes, Madlin clutched the blanket she'd hurriedly wrapped about herself. Had she known it was a Fraser at their door, she might well have cowered within the bed. Swallowing, she nodded. "Master . . . ah . . . ?"

"Lucais, my lady. I fear we were not properly introduced

when last we met." His cap resting across his heart, he sent her a look of such joy, Madlin found herself smiling in return. That is, until she saw the glower on her husband's face.

"Ah . . . it is a pleasure to meet you, Lucais," she said, but took a step backward, wishing she had more than just a blanket covering her. Worse, Gordie and Hugh were peering over Lucais's shoulder. Curiously, silly grins broke across each of their faces, and more curious still, each reached to his belt, extracted a small pouch, and handed it to the other.

"I believe the great hall would be a far better site for a conference," Ewan remarked, and stepped through the portal and slammed the door behind him. He'd taken three full strides when he heard hearty laughter behind him, joined by a trilling giggle that could only be that of the lady Jeanne.

Extracting one of the sheets from the armful of clean linens she carried, Jeanne offered it to Ewan as she approached. "My cousin has not taken all your clothes away again, has she?" Not waiting for an answer, she sailed on past, a twinkling grin wide upon her face. "You are a bonny braw man, Ewan Fraser. My cousin is a fortunate woman."

It was then Ewan realized he'd been striding totally naked toward the hall. Shaking out the crisp linen, he quickly wrapped it about his middle. The stormy glare he sent the three men standing in the hallway silenced their laughter.

"You have messages from my sire, Lucais?" The set of his jaw and the clipped tone of his speech indicated he would tolerate no jocularity.

"Aye, sir." Pulling himself to full attention, he announced, in a tone that indicated he had rehearsed the speech, "It is my pleasure to announce that Sir Cameron Fraser, the lady Guenna Fraser, Niall, Keith, Andrew, and Alexander Fraser accept the MacKendrick's invitation to celebrate your marriage."

Ewan's expression remained thunderous. If anything, it had grown more so by the end of Lucais's little speech. "And that was so urgent you must pound upon my door as if the wolves of hell were at the gates? Hogmanay is weeks away, man."

Lucais shifted his feet and relaxed his posture but slightly. "Well, ye see, lad . . . er, my lord. Yer sire and . . . um . . . the lady Guenna are most anxious to see ye. Himself and the rest of the party was to leave an hour or so behind me. I expect they'll be here some time around midafternoon."

Chapter Eighteen

"Today."

Standing at the steps of the keep, Madlin repeated the single word for perhaps the hundredth time since Lucais Fraser's announcement that the Fraser's arrival was imminent. Immediately upon hearing of it, she'd wanted to dive into the center of the bed and pull the covers up over her head.

But she had not. Instead, she had swallowed her apprehensions and begun issuing orders. However, throughout the preparations of Dunfionn, she had had to remind herself that she was the MacKendrick. Her position, if not her title, was equal to that of her visitor. As an equal, she would meet the earl, Sir Cameron Fraser.

Elspeth had outdone herself in assuring that her niece would indeed meet the Frasers in an impressive fashion. The final stitches were placed in the gold-shot emerald silk. The design of the garment revealed Elspeth's astonishing knowledge of the styles currently sweeping the courts of all Europe, knowledge gained from the many letters she received from friends scattered about the kingdom and even beyond. It was a reminder to all that Elspeth had for a short time in her youth led a very different life than the one of reclusive industry she'd chosen since her husband's death.

The excessively full skirt was gathered to a fitted bodice with a deep V neckline and very full sleeves falling beyond Madlin's wrists. The *houppeland* style would overwhelm a dainty figure but was well carried by a tall, generously endowed woman like Madlin. Atop her head was the gold chaplet, securing a wisp of gold *sendal*. In deference to the bitter cold and wind of the season, she wore a dark green velvet mantle lined with marten.

Unaccustomed to wearing such finery, Madlin had at first felt self-conscious, but the heated look her husband had given her, as well as compliments from others, had bolstered her confidence. Even Francis had relaxed the embittered aloofness he'd shrouded about himself and complimented her appearance.

Having finished giving last-minute assurances and directives to her people gathered in the bailey, she had nothing left to do but wait. It was a respite from the flurry of frantic activity that had marked the day, and not particularly welcome. She had time, now, to contemplate the butterflies battling frantically in the region of her stomach.

"You look magnificent and will overwhelm my family," Ewan said quietly, effectively pulling some of her attention from this attack of nerves. He gave a reassuring squeeze to her hand. "The earl is merely a man. He does not usually eat MacKendricks for supper and never ones as lovely as you."

"I am not at all nervous about meeting him," she lied, though in truth only part of her nervousness was for the upcoming confrontation. The rest was from an unsettling excitement that shot through her every time her husband turned a heated gaze toward her. Or brushed against her. Or spoke within her hearing. Or moved in a way to send the scent of his body to her nostrils. The mere mention of his name jumbled her thoughts and disrupted her nerves in a way she could ill afford this day.

" 'Tis concerns for his safety and that of the rest of the party that troubles me. There was so little time to send out sentinels. Truly, it is a miracle your Lucais arrived safely."

"Not so miraculous. Sentinels were sent out last night. They had plenty of time to be in place before Lucais rode onto MacKendrick lands."

Madlin turned her head so quickly, the edge of tissue-thin silk caught in the corner of her mouth. Brushing away the bothersome ornament, she sputtered, "Last night! How do you know that, and who gave such orders?"

"The possibility of a messenger, mayhap even my sire, stepmother, and brothers arriving this day did occur to Gordie Gunn, and was the reason he detained me in the hallway last night," Ewan confessed. "You were so very weary." He paused to grin. "And a bit anxious as well. We thought not to bother you with such a simple matter."

"Simple matter? The Fraser coming to Dunfionn is no simple matter, sir. 'Tis a monumental event! As laird of clan MacKendrick, weary or no, I should have been the first to be consulted."

God be praised, Ewan mused, his warrior queen was once more herself. Exciting her anger after a night of mind-boggling lovemaking was a sure way to put the roses in her cheeks and the fire in her eyes. He'd remember that in the future whenever her worries and responsibilities weighed her down and drained the vitality from her lively mind and luscious body.

The smile of raw male satisfaction spread easily across his face, for he'd been wearing it often throughout the day. Involuntarily, his gaze dropped from her eyes to her lips and beyond. He stifled a groan as he saw how the soft fur trimming her mantle brushed her ivory throat. It was too great a reminder of how she looked wrapped in nothing but one of the fur robes piled upon their bed.

Glad for the concealment his jacket's knee-length skirt afforded, he breathed deeply of the chill air, hoping to douse the fire building in his groin. "And what would have been your orders, sweetling?"

Madlin raised a curious brow to the strangled sound of his voice. "Post sentinels and guards at intervals along the most logical route your clansmen would take. And send messengers throughout our lands to announce the impending visit, and charge all that the Frasers are to pass through safely."

"And that is exactly what was done," he replied, effectively spiking her indignation as he'd hoped it would. She was far too logical and pragmatic, this chieftain of the MacKendricks, to dwell on indignation for its own sake. But taking in the stubborn set of her jaw and mouth, he decided more smoothing of her justifiably ruffled feathers was in order.

"More than a score of men were sent out just as you would have ordered. Your lieutenants, Gordie and Hugh, are most impressive. A wise leader you are, my dear, for gathering men about you who are capable of initiative. I would have been the better for having such as them at my side whilst fighting in France."

Madlin sent him a narrow-eyed glare, a clear indication she was not at all placated by his compliments. "We were all in agreement that a good night's sleep was what you most needed before such a momentous occasion as negotiating a peace with clan Fraser," he told her in such an insouciant tone, her teeth were set on edge.

Before she could form a suitable response, the blast of a horn sounded beyond the outer wall. Good night's sleep, indeed, she thought as she lifted her hand to the circlet to assure it was in place. The man had kept her awake through a good half of it. Despite her anger, she felt a warm pleasure radiate through her body at the memory of just how they had spent the night.

That pleasure was short-lived, for the sound of hooves across the drawbridge set the butterflies to battling again. Involuntarily, her right hand sought her pendant, while her left spread across her stomach to settle the turbulence within. "Holy Mary, the Fraser is here," she said beneath her breath. "And perhaps his countess. I do not even remember her name."

"Guenna," Ewan supplied.

"Guenna, Lady Guenna," Madlin repeated. "And your brothers' names, again?"

"Niall, Keith, and the young twins, Alex and Andrew, born after I left, so strangers to me as well."

His admittance only heightened her nervousness.

A ripple of unease spread through the crowd gathered in the bailey. Out of the corner of her eye, Madlin saw more than one young mother clutch her child more closely to her bosom and step behind a stalwart male. Anxiously, she scanned the crowd to assure herself that all were abiding by the policy of peaceful hospitality she had demanded. For insurance, Gordie, Hugh, Dag, and Hardwin were scattered about the courtyard.

The clatter of more than a score of horses upon the drawbridge drowned nearly all else as they passed through the barbican. So loud was the sound that when Ewan brought his mouth close to Madlin's ear, she only heard him remark, "I trust 'twas not just sleep that has put such a sparkle in your eyes after such a truly good night we spent in that vast bed."

It was the radiant blush upon the MacKendrick's face that greeted the Earl of Glendarach when he rode into Dunfionn's inner bailey. "The lad's a complete fool if he is not happy with a wife such as that one," he said under his breath as he helped his own wife down from her mount.

"You have no fools among your sons, my love," Lady Guenna whispered back. Once her feet were upon the ground, she did not hesitate to move briskly toward the handsome couple advancing down the steps. Though she presented a dignified image in her double conical henin and ankle-length cloak of sable, the countess dropped all pretensions, opened her arms wide, and cried "Ewan!" then promptly burst into tears when her stepson enveloped her in a warm embrace.

The earl maintained his dignity, though a glistening at the corners of his eyes indicated he was deeply affected, too. If not an actual smile, it was a pleasant expression he directed toward the striking young woman who stood hesitating at the base of the steps.

"Cameron Fraser, at your service, my lady. I fear it will be some time before my wife lets loose my son so that he might effect the proper introductions."

Glad for the voluminous skirts that hid her shaking legs, Madlin advanced. Far from the fork-tailed ogre of her childhood imaginings, the Fraser was indeed merely a man, reassuring in his remarkable likeness to his son. It was like peering into the future and seeing her husband thirty years hence.

His golden hair was slightly silvered. Perhaps his forehead was a bit higher, his face a bit more weathered. His waist a mite thicker, his shoulders not quite as square. But he was unmistakably Ewan with the passage of time.

Holy Mother, pray for me that I might reach an accord with this man, she beseeched as she executed a curtsy. "Madlin MacKendrick, my lord. Welcome to Dunfionn."

Sir Cameron bowed over her hand and brushed his lips lightly across it before helping her rise. " 'Tis a pleasure to meet the MacKendrick of Dunfionn and welcome her as a new daughter of my house."

Madlin heard the collective gasp of reaction to the Fraser's statement. *A daughter of the house of Fraser.* Sweet Mary! It was not an aspect of her marriage she had considered. She'd thought no further than making a Fraser a son of the house of MacKendrick.

"I—I thank you." In a voice loud and clear enough to be heard throughout the bailey, she expressed the goal foremost in her thoughts. "I do pray that the marriage between your son and myself will promote peace as well as an alliance between your clan and mine."

To her disappointment, the Fraser merely tipped his head slightly and tightened his lips. "He dares refuse our lady's plea for truce," someone shouted from where she knew not, any more than she recognized the voice.

At first there was a mere murmur of displeasure undulating through the crowd. Then, here and there were shouts of displeasure, and a line of MacKendricks stepped forward. Hands on the hilts of their swords, they moved quickly to form a ring around the visitors.

In reaction, the Frasers formed a tight protective circle around their lady. No swords slid from their scabbards, but like their MacKendrick counterparts, to a man they were ready with their hands upon the hilts. Shoulder to shoulder, they started backing toward the gates.

Horrified that this chance for a lasting peace might be so easily destroyed, Madlin raced back up enough steps to make sure all could see and hear her. "MacKendricks! Your Honor!" The appeal was her only hope to diffuse the disaster that was so close to eruption. "The Frasers are our guests and have come in peace."

Somehow Ewan extricated himself from the throng of crimson and green that had surrounded him as well. Shaking off the staying hand of one of his brothers, he started toward the steps, but his sire was already there before him.

"Frasers!" Sir Cameron's voice was deep and rumbling, carrying more easily above the mounting tumult. "We shall not insult the hospitality of the MacKendrick!" So like his son's when angered, his blue eyes were cold and intense as they centered upon one then another of his own men.

His gaze never wavering from the cluster of Frasers sheltering his wife, he quietly announced from the side of his mouth, "My lady, as an act of good faith, I will call for my wife to join us here. But I warn you that if one hair of her head is touched, your bailey will run red with blood until the last of us is cut down by yon archers."

"Archers?" Madlin jerked her attention to the ramparts of the inner wall and could scarcely credit the proof of his assertion. At regular intervals all around them stood MacKendricks, arrows nocked, strings drawn taut. She spared hardly a moment's thought to who had ordered them there and when they had gathered.

"On the walls! Stand down! Drop your weapons." The men scattered about the ramparts did not move fast enough. A fury like none she'd ever known possessed her. Narrowing her glare, she placed her hands on her hips and bellowed with a power and rage not heard since her sire had been laid to rest, "Now!"

Relieved to hear the clatter of bows upon the stones, Madlin turned slowly on the step, to assure herself each had dropped his weapon. Not until she'd studied each man did she turn her attention to her guest. "Sir, I beg your forgiveness for that dishonorable show of aggression. There is no excuse for such a threat to a guest of this house, and hence I shall offer none."

The slight quake in her voice revealed clearly the fury and embarrassment raging inside her. "If you will permit, I and three of my kinswomen will descend these stairs and personally escort Lady Fraser into the keep. No MacKendrick would dare assault us or the guest in our midst."

With no hesitation, Elspeth quickly ushered Jeanne and Alys to the forefront of the small group gathered before the keep's door. But before they could begin their descent, Francis materialized at Madlin's side and grasped her arm. "Sister," he admonished sternly, "you cannot mean to put yourself and the other females in such danger."

Far too angry to be cowed by anyone, not even a priest arrayed in full bishop's glory, Madlin glared pointedly at the hand wrapped around her forearm, then directly into his face. "My lord bishop." Her tone was cold and commanding, her choice of address, purposefully formal, lest he use their blood relationship to attempt any further intervention. "I thank you for your concern, but you will stand back and stay out of this. *I* am laird of clan MacKendrick, and it is *my* duty to set the example. If you wish to offer aid, let it be as a man of God—with prayers."

Francis flushed. For a moment he looked as if he would challenge her. Finally, he loosened his grasp and stepped back with a deferential dip of his head. "I shall indeed pray for your safety," he said tightly.

"Your prayers will be most needed for the traitorous fool who gathered those archers upon the ramparts," Madlin told him through gritted teeth. Having neither the time nor the inclination to placate the bishop's affronted sensibilities, Madlin turned her attention to the Fraser.

Sir Cameron's assent came in a quick bob of his chin, but the rigid set of his shoulders indicated he was ready to spring to action at the first sign of any trouble. His hand was no longer resting upon the hilt of his sword, but his cloak was thrown back and the way clear if there was need to unsheath his weapon.

This time when Madlin descended the steps, Alys, Jeanne,

and Elspeth were in her wake. The foursome presented a panoply of color and richness, the likes of which had not been seen since the day of Madlin's mother's arrival as a bride.

Proud and awed by their ladies, the MacKendricks were silent. Frasers, too, stood frozen in silence. Only the whisper of soft kid slippers upon the stones could be heard as the four women approached the solid wall of Frasers.

The sea of crimson and green–clad Frasers parted to reveal a stately raven-haired woman, perfectly composed in contrast to moments ago when she'd wept so joyously in her stepson's arms.

Immediately upon sighting her, Madlin swept a deep curtsy. The rustle of silk behind her indicated that her ladies had done the same. "My lady countess, you are welcome to Dunfionn," she said in a voice that rang clear and true. Following Elspeth's lead, Alys and Jeanne glided gracefully but quickly to positions surrounding the countess of Glendarach, effectively shielding her with their bodies.

"Lady Madlin of Dunfionn, you are all and more than I hoped when we rode through your gates," Guenna Fraser stated with a radiant smile as she dipped in a reciprocal show of respect. Friendliness shone in her warm eyes as she rose and linked her arm within Madlin's.

"Well met, my dear," Guenna said loud enough for only Madlin to hear. She patted Madlin's arms approvingly. "Your Gunn bloodlines are showing clearly. Mother Liusadh would be proud of you and so would have been your mother if she were here today."

Startled that Ewan's stepmother should know so much about her family, Madlin could barely keep her mouth from falling ajar. Guenna quickly supplied, "Long ago, when you were but a wee bairn in your mother's arms, I was a student at St. Margaret's. I believe we have much in common, you and I. I am looking forward to having a good long chat with you.

"But that pleasure shall have to wait. For now, we must protect ourselves with the weapons God in His infinite wisdom has granted us. Smile, my dear, and continue to hold your lovely head as the proud chieftain you are."

Guenna started toward the steps where her husband and stepson waited, smiling all the while. Madlin marveled at the lady's outward show of poise, for she could feel the tremor in the soft arm linked with hers.

"Niall, Keith, Alex, Andrew," Lady Guenna called out. "Where are your manners? Do offer your arms to these lovely ladies who have come to welcome you to Dunfionn."

As Madlin moved with her, she scanned the crowd and finally found Gordie. Catching his eye, she rolled her eyes toward the ramparts and lifted one brow in pointed query. His answer was a slight shrug and a shake of his head. She could but pray he ascertained the culprit's identity quickly and ensured there would be no further "surprises" remotely akin to this incident.

Once inside the keep, Madlin sighed with relief. The expressions on the Fraser men's faces and the clipped syllables of their speech gave evidence that they were still angry. Before Madlin could summon a thought as to how to soothe her guests, Elspeth smoothly took charge.

Leading the way into the great hall, Elspeth directed their guests and a contingent of MacKendricks to chairs and benches arranged before the hearth. Adeptly, she guided the countess to a cushioned chair nearest the fire.

Like captains on a battlefield, Alys and Jeanne waged a kind of attack with friendly chatter and bright smiles. Victory was not yet won when Madlin joined the fray, but the enemy's defenses were softening.

The soothing scent of rosemary and lavender rose up to meet her with her every step. Madlin chuckled inwardly. Fresh herbs. The art of pleasing scents. Yet another weapon in her aunt's arsenal. As she advanced toward the cluster of Frasers gathered around the hearth, she noted that their expressions were considerably more relaxed than when they'd first arrived within the hall.

Och, Papa, would that I had but recognized it then, but you did gift me with a weapon as powerful as Airic's sword. This day, 'tis silk and the womanly arts that have won the first battle.

A hand on her shoulder halted her progress.

"Sister, I would have a word with you."

Chapter Nineteen

"Perhaps later, Francis. I will not insult the Fraser further by suddenly absenting myself from his company." She looked pointedly at the hand on her shoulder.

Francis had the good grace to remove his hand immediately. In a show of unease, so different from his usual confident pose, he shifted from one foot to the other. "I will not detain you long, but what I need tell you must be said before you meet with the Fraser."

Madlin let out an impatient huff. "I'm listening, but be brief."

Nervously, Francis glanced toward the hearth where clustered the Frasers and a like number of MacKendricks. "Perhaps in a less public place," he suggested, and made to take her arm.

Angry that he would presume to detain her again, Madlin shrugged from his grasp with more determination than was necessary. " 'Twould waste time I do not have. You will tell me here and now, and quickly, or save it for another time."

"Woman, you will not—" Clearing his throat, he used a more conciliatory tone. "Pardon me, milady. I do forget that my little sister is no longer a wee lass whose days are filled with naught but mischief making."

"More than mischief making did occupy my days, and you would do well to remember that, Francis. And that when you are at Dunfionn, I am your laird. What is it that you have to say for yourself?"

"I . . . I . . . am responsible for the men assembled on the ramparts. The men must have misinterpreted my suggestion, for I meant their presence there with their bows only as a precaution. I did truly fear for your safety." In a more plaintive note, he added, "I could not have borne it had you been harmed . . . or worse."

Madlin felt her body sway. She took several deep, fortifying breaths. "You had neither the authority nor the knowledge to issue any order for the defense of Dunfionn, Francis. You will remember that in the future. Lest you forget, the men will be instructed to ignore any future suggestions you may have for the security of Dunfionn."

By the way the color drained from Francis's face, she knew her remarks had struck deep. She was glad for it. His meddling had nearly undone all she had worked for. Might still, for the earl had been deeply affronted.

He started to move away, but she was not yet finished. Grabbing his arm, she spun him back to face her. Her voice low and husky from the strain of containing the bellows she would have preferred, she let loose all the anger she felt toward him. "When you are in residence here at Dunfionn, you will confine yourself to its spiritual needs, for that is what you were trained for. I was trained to lead the MacKendricks and see to their well-being and defense. And that, brother, was what did fill my days and occupy my mind whilst you were studying God's holy words."

Slowly, as if she did not quite trust what he might do when freed, she uncurled her fingers from his forearm. She did not relax until he dropped his eyes and, with a dip of his head and a flourish of his robes, strode from the hall.

"Bravo, sweetling. Bravo," Ewan whispered in her ear as he slipped an arm about her waist.

Madlin could not yet give up her stiff-backed stance. For certes, she feared she might fall into another bout of tears if she gave in to the lure of her husband's comforting arms. She would not face the Fraser across a conference table with evidence of such weakness. "How much did you hear?"

"Enough to know that the priest is most fortunate that his back is not now being striped with a whip for such an act."

"He does deserve it and more. Only his raiment does protect him from such. 'Twas a dishonorable thing he did and nearly ruined the peace between our clans before it was even born. He does not carry our father's name, but he does carry the blood and has spent enough time here to know the meaning of MacKendrick honor. There is no excuse."

Ewan chuckled, and a glint of merriment shone in his eyes as he caught up her hand and pressed a lingering kiss upon it. "You are laughing at me?" Madlin asked. "I do not take honor lightly, nor the peace between our clans."

"I do not laugh at you or your honor, my lady warrior," he said as he tucked her arm through his. "But at myself forever thinking 'twas a quiet biddable lass I would seek to marry." With a mischievous wink, he added, "I'd thought perhaps a convent-educated lass of gentle ways and a modicum of wit. Someone with respectable bloodlines and sound body, who would be a good breeder. 'Twas all I thought to need in a wife."

A most unladylike snort was Madlin's first response. " 'Tis typical of a man to liken a wife to a broodmare."

"Or a woman to liken a husband to a stud," he returned neatly. *"N'est-ce pas?"*

Madlin's cheeks warmed with embarrassment, but she recovered quickly. *"C'est autre chose,"* she returned smoothly, not giving an inch. They were most certainly another matter, her reasons for marrying him. His ability to sire her children was not truly the issue.

" 'Twas for peace above all else," she said softly as they neared Ewan's father.

Against her ear, Ewan said, "I would then we have more peace between us, as we did last night."

The rush of his warm, moist breath against her ear sent a tingling tremor down her spine. The thoughts she'd been organizing for the upcoming conference with the Fraser jumbled and danced with the memories of his lovemaking. "Knave! You would say such things to me now?"

Unrepentant, he declared, "I would say more, but there is not time right now to tell you of all the ways I plan to make peace with you. Later, sweetling." He kissed her hand and turned her over to his sire. "The MacKendrick, sir. I believe you and she have much to discuss."

Madlin was far from feeling peaceful as she attempted pleasantries with the Fraser and his countess. She sipped at the goblet of mulled wine Edella handed her. It calmed her nerves so that she was able to smile at the earl and countess. But each time her gaze happened to fall upon her husband, it narrowed with warning against any further intimate remarks. Though he kept his tongue, the more pointed her gaze, the wider his grin grew, until she chose to ignore him altogether.

"My lord, if it should please you, I think 'tis time you and I adjourned and discussed the alliance between our clans." Meeting the Fraser alone, one chieftain facing off with another, was how Papa would have conducted such a meeting. She saw no reason to do otherwise.

Extending his arm, Sir Cameron announced, "Where you lead I will follow." Hearing the clatter of goblets hastily placed upon tables and trays, he cast a meaningful glance toward his sons. "Only I."

Madlin took his arm with a smile of satisfaction. It was a good omen, she thought.

There was a veritable explosion of protests from Frasers and MacKendricks alike. "Sir, you cannot mean to hold such an important conference without us. At least Keith, Ewan, and I should be a part of this."

"No, you should not, Niall. I shall meet with the MacKendrick as I would meet with any other laird. Alone." The Fraser's voice was low, no louder than it had been in conversation. But the force behind it, coupled with a stern look, stilled their tongues.

Following the Fraser's example, Madlin quelled the MacKendrick insurgence with a glare so like her father's, her clansmen immediately closed their mouths. Daidbidh dared return her glare but only briefly. Relenting, he shook his head and mumbled as he walked away, "Himself is there within that lass, make no mistake."

"Pray 'tis so, Daidbidh," Madlin said to herself as she led Sir Cameron down a hallway to a small corner chamber with a fine view of the loch. It was called the counting room as business was conducted and the estate accounts were kept here. But it also served as a sort of sanctuary for MacKendrick lairds during those times they needed most of all to be alone. A policy had been established by Madlin's great-grandsire that no one entered without the express consent of the laird.

"I envy you this room, Lady Madlin," Sir Cameron remarked as he looked about him with appreciative eyes for the view of the loch beyond, and the comfortable furnishings within. A cheery, warming fire burned in the grate of the small hearth, adding further to the relaxed atmosphere of the room.

"I thank you, my lord." She indicated the wide-armed chair on one side of the heavy desk that had served her father and grandfather. She waited until the Fraser had seated himself before taking the high-backed chair on the opposite side. "I have found it most comfortable and a good place to think, as did my father and his before him."

"And read?" he asked, nodding toward the extensive collection of books on the shelf behind her.

"Aye, it would be a fine place to read, but I fear I have not had the time since I left St. Margaret's." Unable to stop herself, she ran a hand along the precious volumes she'd arranged so carefully between the stacks of heavy ledgers. An atlas, books of poetry, philosophy, history, mathematics, and science.

"My lord, tell me of the raids that have been made upon your clan," she began.

Sir Cameron retained a pleasant expression on his handsome face. "Lady Madlin, I do admire your directness. I believe we shall deal well together."

Madlin smiled, "I do hope so."

"The raids began last spring, shortly after the snow and ice melted in the passes," Sir Cameron began. His demeanor changed. His entire body seemed to stiffen, his features nearly expressionless.

"The first was an old shepherd, Aiodh. After his wife died, he lived all alone on the very edge of our border along the disputed lands. A gentle soul, caring for hardly more than a dozen sheep, with naught to protect him or keep him company but a dog. Dubh, he called the collie, and the animal was a loyal friend and helper to him."

He cleared his throat, and his voice grew a bit harsher as he continued. "His hut and the fields around it were torched. We think perhaps during the night. The smoke was what alerted us that something was amiss. When we arrived, 'twas too late. Aiodh, the dog, and every single sheep in their small flock lay slaughtered upon the ground."

Sir Cameron did not spare her as he detailed the terrible carnage exacted upon the lone shepherd and more. Such horror was visited upon other Fraser crofters in the weeks and months following. Old men, young men, women, and children. Animals slaughtered and left to rot. Crofts and fields burned.

When he had finished, Madlin could barely speak beyond the lump clogging her throat. "And did you lead or order a raid for revenge when you found Aiodh?" Her voice was barely a whisper.

Sir Cameron tightened his lips and swallowed hard before answering, "Not immediately, though 'twas difficult not to ride directly from that croft onto MacKendrick lands and treat the first cotter we encountered in like fashion."

"How did you know for certain it had been MacKendricks?" she asked, though she feared she knew his answer.

The Fraser extracted a scrap of wool from a pocket within his jacket. He tossed it upon the desk. "That was stuffed down Aiodh's throat when we found him. Evidently, he did not die quietly enough for the miserable curs who attacked him," he added bitterly.

The scrap was ragged, faded, and bloodstained, but the colors and their arrangement were too familiar. It had clearly been manufactured right here in the weaving shed of Dunfionn.

Madlin could not bear to touch the scrap. Bile burned in her throat as she stared at it. Blinking tears, Madlin pushed away from the desk.

"We have lost many, as well. The first was Brianna," she said, crossing on shaking legs to a cupboard across the room. "She and Tavis had two wee bairns, a little girl just beginning to walk and a wee boy born with the new year."

Opening the cupboard she extracted a folded length of woolen—worn, tattered, and stained. She held it gingerly, touching it no more than was necessary.

"Their croft was near the edge of our lands also, where our border lies along the disputed lands. 'Twas a pretty little cottage they had. Tavis built a snug and sturdy shelter for his family and Brianna made it a home.

"She was forever digging up plants from the hills and meadows, carting them home, and coaxing them to grow. In the summer bright color continuously surrounded the cottage, for Brianna had a true gift for life."

She dropped the piece of tartan wool upon the scarred desktop. Though she was facing Sir Cameron again, her eyes were focused inward. "I was still at St. Margaret's when it happened. I'm told Brianna and the children were alone that day and much of the previous night, for Tavis was out with the others retrieving the livestock Frasers had stolen from him. Brianna's garden had not yet begun to push new shoots through the ground."

She brushed the tears from her cheeks with the heels of her hands. "Tavis found that plaid on the ground near their bodies, Brianna's, wee Lucie's, and the babe, Alain. They . . . they did not die gently. 'Twas Shrove Tuesday, a day for sport to some."

Sir Cameron brushed a hand down his face and breathed deeply but shakily when she'd finished. A muscle ticked in his jaw as he stared at the crimson and green tartan. "That is one of ours. Or looks to be, but no Fraser dropped it there. We did cut a score of sheep from a MacKendrick flock at the edge of your lands," he admitted, his voice carefully controlled.

" 'Twas the number of sheep slaughtered with Aiodh, plus five. 'Twas all we did, I swear. We took four extra for Aiodh and one for his dog. All were given to his grandson, a start for a young lad, wanting to follow in his grandsire's footsteps."

Madlin nodded, understanding the reasoning. Her sire had led raids in kind.

"We do not kill women and children," the earl declared, his hands curled tightly into fists upon his knees. "Shrove Tuesday is not a day celebrated with such vile sport by any who calls himself a Fraser."

"And MacKendricks do not make vicious sport upon old men and their dogs," Madlin declared just as firmly. "Nor do we murder women and children."

Blue eyes met green and held. Madlin studied the man across the desk. Though his image was blurred by the tears she could not stem, his face looked so like Ewan's, and there was an air about him, so like his son's. Indescribable though it was, something set her every instinct screaming, Here was a man to trust, a man of honor. And further, she saw pain in his eyes, pain for the suffering and deaths of his people. And perhaps there was pain there for the MacKendrick dead as well.

Beneath the rich silk of her gown, the ancient pendant seemed to warm, a reminder of its presence against her heart. *Trust in Yourself.* She felt the words, heard them in her mind as clearly as if Liusadh were before her now, translating the ancient runes sketched upon the disk's worn surface.

"An evil has come to the hills and meadows of our lands, Cameron Fraser. MacKendricks and Frasers must be allies. 'Tis our only hope against the forces striking down our people."

Standing, she reached her hand across the desk. Sir Cameron did not hesitate to rise to his feet and enclose her slender hand within his larger one. "From this day forward, Frasers will ally with MacKendricks against all foes, and have naught but peace between ourselves." He placed his other hand atop their clasped ones. "On behalf of the Frasers, you have the word of Cameron of Glendarach."

Madlin placed her hand atop his. "On behalf of the Mac-Kendricks, you have the word of Madlin of Dunfionn that it will be so."

They held on to the solemnity of their pledge for a long moment before Sir Cameron smiled and relaxed his hold upon her hands. "My son has suffered no hardship being captured and married to you. You are a most extraordinary young woman, Madlin of Dunfionn," he remarked as he sat down again.

Flustered by such praise, Madlin sat down quickly and said the first words that popped into her head. "They simply must stop."

"I assume you mean the raids."

"Yes, ah . . . of course, the raids. Together, we will stop the murders. In anticipation of an alliance with clan Fraser, I ordered a cessation of all raids upon the Frasers the very day I married your son."

"As did I after I was apprised of the marriage." Sir Cameron cleared his throat. "Given the opportunity for alliance and the peace we have just agreed upon, the unusual circumstances in which you brought my son to the altar are understandable, mayhap even applaudable."

He rearranged his body slightly in the chair. As he settled one leg across the other, she was uncomfortably aware that he was taking her measure.

"However, as you might well expect, I cannot be pleased that your marriage contract calls for Ewan to give up his very name."

"It has been done before when the bride holds the higher title and is the sole surviving heir," Madlin responded, and was prepared to cite specific precedents.

" 'Tis rare even under those circumstances, but aye, it has been done," Cameron allowed. "But never when they are equal."

"No, never then," Madlin agreed, choosing her words slowly. It was important that she not give on this detail of the marriage contract. Her clan would never stand for the barony's heir to bear the name of Fraser.

Ignoring the warnings ringing inside her head, she rushed to say, "I and all of my clan do appreciate Sir Ewan's standing as a knight whose spurs were won most honorably upon the field of battle. But, he is a third son who—"

"Has been granted the barony of Cluain by James Stewart, King of Scotland, in appreciation for Sir Ewan Fraser's years of friendship and outstanding service to his king and his country," the Fraser stated smoothly.

Her voice was an embarrassing squeak when she at last found it at all. "Cluain?" In a daze, she repeated the earl's statement.

"Aye, Cluain. 'Tis the name our king has given the meadowlands between Fraser and MacKendrick lands. 'Tis a far better name than the 'disputed lands,' think you not?"

"Aye . . . better than 'disputed lands,' " Madlin echoed. Why had her husband not revealed his true status immediately or when he'd been taunted for lacking a title beyond knight?

" 'Tis a fine name," she managed, though the words were hard to form. *Cluain,* the Gaelic word for meadows. Such a gentle name for lands her clan and his had shed so much blood over throughout the years.

Sir Cameron's voice did not rise in volume or pitch, but somehow it fairly shook the walls when he declared, "As is Fraser, the name the first baron of Cluain was born with and his heirs will carry."

"And so they shall," Madlin agreed. Though the very idea brought a stab of pain in her heart, duty and honor forced her to say, "I cannot give him those heirs. Clan MacKendrick does need heirs that bear its name. Honor commands that I release Cluain from his vows. Bishop MacDonald has already volunteered to present a petition of annulment to the Church. 'Twill not take so very long before Sir Ewan is free to marry a woman more suitable."

"More suitable!" Cameron Fraser exploded from his chair. He rounded the desk and loomed over her, his expression so thunderous that Madlin shrank against the back of her chair. "Young woman, my son already has a most suitable wife. You!

I will accept no other, and, bigod, neither will he! This business of surnames will be dealt with in some other way."

"But . . . but I am my father's only heir. 'Tis my duty," Madlin said in a small voice. She may have misjudged Sir Cameron. Never, even as a small child, had she quailed so, even beneath Papa's glare.

His hands braced upon the arms of her chair, Sir Cameron held her trapped. "Male MacKendricks appear to be in adequate supply. Are none of them suitable?"

Madlin shook her head. "And there has been no one who has challenged my ascension." She breathed a sigh of relief when Sir Cameron moved a few feet away.

His hands folded behind him, he began to pace. "God's teeth, this is not the royal house of Scotland. 'Twould be simpler if it were, for there are always legions awaiting to claim the crown whenever a sovereign dies without male issue."

He continued to pace back and forth, until, at last, he halted by the hearth. There he studied the flames. "We shall think on this, you and I. We *will* find a solution," he declared, his voice far calmer than before.

Turning away from the fire, he gazed for a long moment at her. "Lass, only a fool would set you aside for another. I assure you I have no fools among my sons."

Like the sun sending a sudden shaft of light through a dark-clouded sky, he smiled. "You have my word and, mayhap more importantly, that of my wife's on that. She has assured me of such, and I do believe her for she is a woman of truth and honor as assuredly as are you."

His smile changed subtly and became the mischievous grin she so often saw on Ewan's face. " 'Tis possible my son had a reason for keeping his identity from you. Still 'twas most unwise not to have apprised you before our meeting. It put you at a disadvantage. I suggest you take him to task for it at the earliest opportunity. Deception holds no place in either alliances or marriages."

Chapter Twenty

Madlin shifted uncomfortably in the large carved chair on the dais. Edana had outdone herself preparing a suitable feast. Apparently she and all her kitchen staff had been apprised of the possibility of the Fraser arriving this day.

Trays laden with capons, poached salmon, roasted venison, lamb, braised vegetables, stewed fruits, and cream tarts had paraded from Dunfionn's kitchens. Edana had to have been at work long before dawn preparing such fare—with all the village wives alongside her! Had she, the MacKendrick, been the only one in the entire clan who had slept last night away in blissful ignorance of the Fraser's imminent arrival?

She hid a yawn behind her hand. Her night had been blissful, aye, but little sleep had been involved. Beneath her lashes, she watched the man seated to her left. That his expression was strained gave her some comfort. He deserved to suffer for all the deceptions he had practiced in the past day and night—nay, since the moment of their first meeting!

After her audience with his father, there had been no time to have it out with her husband, beyond letting him know her displeasure and disappointment. Later, when they were alone, there would not be bliss prevailing in their chamber, that was certain. She was going to get a full explanation for his deception if she had to hold him at sword point to get it.

Though a truce had been declared between the two clans, a kind of war was being fought in the gallery overlooking the great hall. The Fraser "weapons of choice" were the lute and the recorder. The MacKendricks had "armed" themselves with a psaltery and a vielle, the beat steadied with a bodhran. In reserve, each clan's favorite piper stood ready and eager.

The opening duet from the Frasers had been charming, a sweetly rendered tune for the pleasure of the diners gathered below them. Equally pleasant had been the host musicians' selection. But, as each group took its turn, the rhythm escalated and the volume increased, making conversation impossible.

The inability to converse through this interminable meal and entertainment was a blessing, Madlin decided as she sat between the Fraser and her husband, Baron Cluain. *Baron Cluain!* She mentally repeated the name again and again and all that the title carried with it.

Oh, dear God, the disputed lands have been granted to a Fraser. Holy Mother, pray for me that I may find the words to announce this to my clan. The alliance is new and fragile. May I not be the one to break it by skewering with his own sword the deceiver who sits by my side.

Ewan cringed when he saw his wife squeeze her eyes shut and bow her head. He yearned to curl his arm about her and comfort her. Clearly, the noise level was paining her greatly. But the chair she sat upon was wide, the arms high and solid. She was imprisoned within it and untouchable.

Or was it that the great chair of the MacKendrick shielded its current occupant? God's teeth! After last night, he'd thought they'd reached an accord. Nay, there was more than just an accord.

Passion. Aye, there had been plenty of that. But more. Affection and understanding. Perhaps the beginnings of a true bond based on a far, far stronger emotion. What had happened in that small chamber where she closeted with his sire that should so chill her affections toward him?

An alliance between the two clans had been worked out. And, by the attitude his wife and sire had displayed when they emerged, a mutual respect, even a fondness for each other had begun. She'd been full of smiles until her gaze had fallen upon him, her own husband. Bigod, she'd been cold. He needed to talk to her.

Madlin gazed about the great hall. She might have smiled, even laughed, if she, too, were not suffering so. Everywhere she looked, the diners' expressions had at first been masks of polite enjoyment of the music to cover their wariness of sitting down with those they'd thought of as enemies for generations. But as the musical battle had escalated, MacKendricks and Frasers alike had become united in common strain and finally pain from the assault upon their ears.

Leaning close, Ewan almost shouted, "God help us all when the pipers step into this fray."

Madlin groaned. That she had allowed the musical battle to continue was a discourtesy born of her own cowardliness. No longer could she put off calling for a cessation of the music and making the announcement she'd been rehearsing since she and Sir Cameron had emerged from the counting room.

Rising, Madlin lifted her goblet high, praying all the while that she could catch Dermott's eye and cease the cacophony before her shaking knees gave way and she crumpled onto her chair. When the noise came to an end, she felt equal parts of gratitude and trepidation. Sweeping the jewel-studded ceremonial goblet of the MacKendrick in a salute encompassing all the assembled, she called out, "MacKendricks. To our guests and allies, the Frasers."

The sounds of benches scraping backward and feet shuffling upon the stone floor were not forthcoming. After a moment of silence, so long, Madlin was prepared to repeat her salute, a deep voice fairly roared from a far corner, "To the Frasers!"

Airdsgainne. She could scarce credit it, but his voice was unmistakable. His silvered head held proudly, his shoulders set more squarely than had been seen in many a year, he stood alone but briefly. Throughout the hall, others gradually followed suit until all MacKendricks were on their feet, their goblets and tankards held high.

So startled that Airdsgainne had been the one to lead the response, Madlin's senses barely registered the burn of the *uisge beatha* as it slid down her throat. She tipped her goblet toward the old warrior in gratitude and took another swallow of the well-aged brew.

Beside her she felt a brush of movement. Sir Cameron had risen to his feet, his goblet held aloft for all to see. His gaze was steady and pointed as it swept down the length of the head table, sending a clear message to each of his sons.

The twins, Andrew and Alexander, were first to their feet, Keith and Ewan quickly following. Niall, the eldest, was slower, hampered in his movements by the sling encasing his right arm as well as an obvious reticence in his demeanor.

"For certes, the faeries are spreading magic this night," Madlin said under her breath as she watched in wonder as Elspeth graced Niall with a glittering smile and tucked her hand beneath his good arm to help him to his feet.

"Or the *uisge* flowing so freely," Ewan said with a grin.

Madlin steeled herself not to respond even faintly. Clearly disappointed, Ewan's expression was solemn.

Once his offspring were standing, Sir Cameron turned toward Madlin, "To the MacKendrick! A lady whose wisdom, daring, and leadership has brought peace to our clans."

If the sprinkling of Frasers at the lower tables was slow in joining their laird in the toast, their reticence went unnoticed, for the MacKendricks responded so immediately and enthusiastically, the walls resounded with their voices.

Sir Cameron waited until the din had lowered to a few scattered murmurs to add, "And now, may we all wish happy, Lady Madlin of Dunfionn and Sir Ewan, Baron Cluain."

A hush swept through the assembled, then the title was repeated here and there, softly at first reflecting incredulity. Into the breach of relative quiet, Madlin stepped. Sparing not even a glance toward her husband, she nodded at Gordie seated at the head of the nearest table. Immediately, the man was on his feet, across the great hall and disappearing into the corridor beyond.

"In gratitude for his years of service in the cause of our old ally, France, in her fight for freedom against England and for the years of friendship shared with him, our good and wise King James has awarded Sir Ewan the newly created barony, Cluain."

Applause and shouts of congratulations rang out. Heartiest were from the Frasers, but a goodly number of MacKendricks joined in, for Ewan had already earned the friendship and respect of many of her clansmen.

Despite her own anger toward her husband, she praised God for the looks of gladness on so many of her clansmen's faces. Elspeth, dignified yes, was on her feet, turned toward Ewan and clapping her hands. Meta, Hugh, even Colley were urging their kinsmen to rise and pay homage to her husband for his reward.

Jeanne. Bless my cousin, Madlin thought for not the first time that day. Ever quick with the bright smiles and enthusiasm, the dainty woman tugged on Francis's cassock sleeve until he, too, was on his feet. Some remark from Jeanne even chased away the sullen expression he'd been carrying throughout the meal.

While she waited for the display to quiet enough for her to speak again, Madlin tried to still the tumult within herself. *Holy Mary! Give me the right words for what I must next announce. I fear it more than when I introduced the blackguard as my husband.*

"Along with that title, our king has awarded Sir Ewan the meadowlands that lie between Fraser and MacKendrick lands and given him permission to build a fortified manor upon them to serve as the seat of the barony, Cluain, from this time forward." Murmurs rippled through the assembled as she'd expected.

Sheltered meadowlands fed by springs and bubbling burns. Forested ranges teeming with game and fruit and nut-bearing trees. The territory touched the shores of Moray Firth near a deep inlet that would serve as a natural harbor. A large and prime territory, indeed.

Fixing her gaze upon those with the darkest glowers, she announced in a firm voice, "Henceforth, those lands we have all come to call the 'disputed lands' shall be known as Cluain and will serve to further unite our peoples as does our common desire for peace and the marriage between myself and Baron Cluain." Madlin forced herself to turn to her husband, smile, and applaud him.

Bowing over her hand, he offered softly by way of an apology, " 'Twas never quite the right time to tell you of Cluain."

She lifted a skeptical brow before turning away and stepping slightly behind her chair. The high, wide back of the laird's chair hid Ewan's view of the exchange between Madlin and Gordie. When she returned to the fore, she was clutching his sword.

Blade down, the ornately carved gold hilt level with her heart, she held the heavy weapon firmly before her. There was no need to call for attention. Every voice was silent, every eye was upon her.

"Most of you have seen Cluain wearing this sword and know it was a gift from our king as a token of the friendship begun eighteen long years ago when their ship was overtaken and Scotland's prince as well as Sir Ewan were taken captive. What you do not know is that Sir Ewan could have been released at almost any time during those years but so steadfast is his loyalty and love for our king, he chose to remain by James's side."

An approving murmur rippled through the assembled, and Madlin waited until all was quiet again before continuing. "Finally, James implored his friend to choose freedom and represent him with this sword in our ally's fight for her freedom."

Turning to Ewan, she extended the sword to him. "Though this sword has already been returned to you, today I ask your forgiveness for ever having taken it, and your freedom, from you."

Ewan took the sword but announced, "My lady, I *cannot* accept your apology."

A collective gasp of shock punctuated his statement. Over the murmurs, Ewan declared, "I cannot, for there is naught to forgive. You were right in taking away my weapon, for surely I would have used it against your men that night. 'Twas their safety you considered as a good leader should."

Holding the sword much as Madlin had, so that it formed a cross before him, he pledged, "Upon my honor as a knight and the sanctity with which I hold our marriage, I pledge to you and all your clan that this sword will never be raised against a MacKendrick." He sealed the pledge with a kiss upon the hilt, then carefully placed it upon the table before them.

His vow went far to appease the MacKendricks. At first, there was but a ripple of approval. Gradually, it swelled throughout the great hall. Catching up Madlin's hand, Ewan pressed a kiss upon it before raising their clasped hands aloft. Turning, he presented her to the assembled.

"Frasers and MacKendricks, I pledge to you that Cluain will be a land of peace for the people of both clans. As my wife so eloquently stated, Cluain will be a land that unites, not divides, clan MacKendrick and clan Fraser. Will you join with me in toasting the first Baroness Cluain, Lady Madlin, the MacKendrick—my lovely and most treasured wife."

His declaration was a step toward assuring full acceptance of the alliance and their marriage by both Frasers and MacKendricks alike. Too many issues, foremost being the name the next laird of Dunfionn would carry, were still unresolved for the hall to echo with cheers. To fill the void, the pipers filled their bags and began to sound the drones. At a signal from Elspeth, serving maids hurried along the tables with heavy pitchers to replenish the tankards and goblets.

Madlin barely heard the commotion reigning about her. Since she'd discovered his deception, she felt as if a layer of ice had encased her heart, numbing her to everything around her. *Trust.* How many times had he asked her to trust him, and yet he'd not trusted her enough to reveal his true identity.

When her husband curled his arm around her waist and

swept her up against his side, she felt like a figure on a stick being bounced about for a crowd's entertainment at a fair.

"Bravo, sweetling," he murmured against her forehead. "Not even James could have addressed his subjects so well." He brushed his lips across hers. "No husband could ever be so proud of his wife as I am at this very moment."

She wanted so to believe that he was sincere in all he had said, most especially in that she was his "most treasured wife." How much she wanted that to be true startled her. And frightened her.

More frightening was the voice sounding inside her that said, "You love him, Maddie. And, you want to believe he loves you."

It was her heart talking, the part of her that led her to do impetuous things. With the peace between the clans so new, she must lead with her head. She'd believed Ewan to be a man of honor, a man to trust, and where had it led her but directly into a trap neatly laid by his father—another man her heart had told her to trust.

"Your compliments are too fulsome, sir," she said, pushing out of his arms. "Your eloquence did cast mine in shadow."

"You were both eloquent," Lady Guenna said from behind them. "I did not mean to eavesdrop, but I could not help but hear much of your exchange." She hugged first Madlin and then Ewan.

"You do sound the courtier, Ewan dear, too full of compliments to be believed by a woman of strength and wit like Madlin." The sparkle in Guenna's eyes gave the lie to the rebuke. "But I shall not scold you, for you did speak only the truth. Madlin, my dear, you are indeed all and more than Ewan did declare. 'Tis safe to believe him today, but wise of you to let him know that his pretty words will not always sway you."

She had more to say, but Sir Cameron interrupted her. "I believe I shall take this troublesome woman away before she offers any further advice that might make future trouble for you, Ewan. You have trouble enough to set straight, without my wife giving yours more fuel to hurl at you."

With one arm curled about his wife, he bowed to Madlin and said, "My dear, you were articulate and most brave. There was an explosive climate when you explained Cluain's lands. I could not have diffused it better myself."

Playfully, he punched Ewan on the shoulder. "You were passably good. Now, I suggest you find a way to apologize to your wife. Not telling her of your new title put her at an unfair disadvantage when she and I were negotiating the alliance. No harm has been done, this time, and she has learned an important lesson in negotiating with an adversary. However, I strongly advise you not to deceive this young woman in any way, large or small, ever again."

Tugging on her husband, Lady Guenna laughed. "Come, my love, we are advising these young people overlong." She winked at Madlin before casting a stern look toward her husband. "You have some explaining to do, yourself. How dare you even consider taking any kind of unfair advantage of your own daughter by marriage."

"But, 'twas with the MacKendrick I was negotiating," Sir Cameron explained as his lady began leading him away.

"The MacKendrick and our Madlin are one and the same," Guenna told him.

Madlin could not still a giggle as she watched Ewan's parents move away. "A formidable force is your stepmother," she remarked.

"Aye, that she is," Ewan agreed, a grin upon his face. " 'Tis both the bane and the joy of his life that she does take him to task so severely. Just as I—"

The force of a heavy blow to his back sent the breath from Ewan's lungs. He stumbled but was righted by the brother who had nearly felled him. With a mischievous grin, Keith asked, "Little brother, have you the strength and grace to dance with your wife, or will you be stepping aside so a better man can partner her through the first reel?"

Still gasping for air, Ewan responded with only a glare. At

last managing a deep breath, he bowed to Madlin. "My dear, would you do me the honor?" Not waiting for her answer, he cupped his hand beneath her elbow and pushed her toward the steps leading from the dais.

"We do not have to do this."

"Aye, we do. 'Tis expected, and we must do our duty."

Madlin moved her feet slower and slower. Usually the first sound of the bagpipes set her toes to tapping, but not today. Dancing was for celebrating and should be done with a light heart. She felt neither.

" 'Tis a sprightly tune, the spinning and twirling could be too much for you. All here know you are newly recovered from a great wound to your leg. 'Twill be no disgrace in saying nay to dancing."

"I will dance the bride's dance with my wife." He started moving her toward the dancing floor, but she planted her feet.

"Your pride may well send you toppling to the floor, Ewan Fraser."

"Nay, it will keep me on my feet." The teasing light in his eyes almost brought an answering one from her, but she was not quite ready to forgive all.

"Have you any more deceptions to confess? You have spoken often of rewards to be had from our marriage; is that a clue to more you are withholding?"

"I withheld nothing from you last night," he answered glibly. "Was not that a reward?"

Madlin gulped and felt every inch of her body grow warm and damp at the memory. "What of today? Will you promise never again to leave me ignorant of such an important event as the arrival of an enemy at Dunfionn's gates?"

"I do solemnly promise never to withhold that sort of information from you."

His words were all she could wish, but his face was full of too much merriment to give credence to the vow. "I believe this subject of deception needs further discussion."

"As you wish, my lady. Later, perhaps, there will be time, when there is no dancing to distract us."

Her eyes shone with the joy prevailing all about her. Ewan decided that seeing that smile was worth the agony he was going to suffer executing the fast and difficult steps of a Highland reel.

Grabbing a cup from the tray of a passing serving woman, he drained it quickly. The *uisge* warmed him all the way to his belly. *God's teeth, let it numb me to any pain this foolishness causes in my cursed leg . . . but not so much that I cannot perform later—abovestairs in that grand wide bed.*

Ewan's step was brisk and his own smile broad as he led Madlin through the arch made for them by the other couples. "Do not tire yourself overly with the dancing, sweetling," he said against her ear. "I would you have strength left for later when your lush body is joined with mine. 'Twill be my given name you cry out, not my title, I guarantee, if it takes all night of pleasuring you."

"Cluain, you are a wicked knave; completely without shame."

His grin was unrepentant. "Aye, I am, and are you not glad?"

The flash in her eyes warned him he was fortunate that they were required to separate with the next steps. While he caught up the next lass about the waist and twirled her, Madlin was sent down the line of men. By the time she was returned to him, she was too breathless to utter a coherent word. He caught her around the waist and lifted her aloft.

The skirl of the pipes, the hoots and cries of the dancers, the clapping and stomping of feet overwhelmed all else. Ewan turned in place, still holding her high so she was head and shoulders taller than any in the hall. Her gaze swept about the room. Once, twice, three times.

From her vantage point she could see and be seen by everyone gathered. A veritable sea of faces turned toward her, all smiling and enjoying themselves . . . save one. Flanked by two of the MacKendricks assigned to guard duty, the newcomer stood rigidly at the doorway, a black scowl upon his face.

"Seamus Munro."

Ewan barely heard Madlin breathe the intruder's name, but already it was being echoed throughout the hall as others spied him.

"Let me down, now."

The urgency in her tone and the sudden change in the mood of those around him warned Ewan that something was gravely amiss. Slowly, he lowered her. Her feet had barely touched the floor when she spun away from him and headed toward the entranceway. Without hesitation, Ewan followed at her heels.

Chapter Twenty-one

The sounds from the pipes, so gay and bright but moments ago, dwindled with a mournful wail as the drones slowly gasped to silence. "My lord Seamus," Madlin greeted as she neared the newcomer. "The Munro is welcome at Dunfionn, and we are pleased to see you."

Every MacKendrick within the hall knew the falseness of her greeting to her father's former foster son. If there was one soul in all of Christendom she would less like to allow past Dunfionn's gates, she could not imagine who it might be. But she could not turn the chief of an allied clan away.

"Lady Madlin." He sneered her name just as he had been prone to do when he'd fostered at Dunfionn. The disdainful sweep of his gaze up and down her person was familiar as well. During her childhood when her bare legs and feet had been exposed to his censuring gaze, she had never quailed nor felt embarrassment. This eve, when his gaze stayed overlong on the deep V of her gown's neckline, it was not embarrassment she felt, but a deep revulsion. Now, as in years long past, she did not shrink but met his gaze straight on until he looked away.

"I see I have chanced upon a celebration." Narrowing his eyes first upon the man to his left and then the one to his right, he remarked, "These ruffians would not divulge the reason for celebration, nor would they allow an ally and close friend such as myself to enter unescorted."

Close friend? Never had Seamus been a friend, and the alliance between their clans had been shaky since the spring when Seamus had become the Munro chieftain.

Clearly miffed to have been treated so unfamiliarly, he looked to her for explanation, apology, or perhaps both. He would wait until Judgment Day, Madlin decided, for if an offense had been committed, it was the laird of Dubhfireach who was responsible for it. For more than one offense he owed an apology. He'd not attended nor even sent a representative in his stead to his foster father's and foster brothers' funerals. Never once in all the times he'd come since to press his suit had he even expressed condolences for their deaths.

While he waited, he shrugged out of his cloak. Absently, he tossed it at one of his escorts. Madlin hid her smile when the cloak fell to the floor by the guard's foot and remained there. "We suffer uncertain times, and I have ordered caution with the admittance of any—be he stranger or friend—who arrives at Dunfionn's gates."

Dismissing her explanation with a snort, he ran a smoothing hand over his dark locks and straightened the bright blue velvet jacket he wore atop particolored hose of blue, gold, and red. Vanity ever colored his character and bright plumage his appearance. A peacock, she and Airic had called him.

"Aye, well . . ." He brushed at his sleeves. " 'Tis wise, I suppose. 'Tis clear a strong man is needed here. 'Twould dissuade any who think the MacKendricks vulnerable since the death of your father and brothers."

Whether unaware or uncaring of the reaction of those within hearing to his affront, the peacock left off preening his plumage. Smiling, he stepped forward and reached a hand toward her. " 'Tis why I am here, dear lady."

Madlin stepped backward, recoiling from even the idea of being touched by her old nemesis. Involuntarily, her hand went to the hilt of the only weapon at hand, a small eating knife dangling from the gold girdle circling her waist. Beside her, Ewan had stiffened. Praise God, his great sword still lay upon the table.

"I must beg your forgiveness, Seamus, in being so slow in making introductions," she said in a soft, breathy voice. "I owe 'tis the surprise at seeing you that has sent this poor female mind in flight. I do pray you will understand." She paused and linked her arm through Ewan's. "Baron Cluain, may I introduce Seamus, the Munro of Dubhfireach. I may have mentioned him to you. Seamus once fostered with my father," she explained, knowing such an introduction would take some of the air from beneath the peacock's wings. "Seamus. Cluain, Sir Ewan Fraser, is my husband."

The smug expression upon the Munro's face was replaced by shock. His dark eyes widened to a dangerous point, and bright color rose from his neck. He opened his mouth, but no words came forth. He looked much like a salmon flipped upon the bank of a burn, gasping as it flopped about. Indeed, Seamus's arms flailed helplessly at his sides as he sought support.

Heretofore, he'd not bothered looking beyond her to the occupants of the great hall. He did now, his color heightening further when he saw the Fraser colors liberally sprinkled among the crowd. "Then 'tis true! You married one of Toirlach's murderers."

"Nay, Seamus," Madlin said calmly but forcibly. " 'Twas not Frasers who murdered Papa, Bram, and Airic, or any of the others we grieve here at Dunfionn. 'Twas an evil whose name we do not yet know."

"Grieve? Woman, I see no grief here at Dunfionn or upon your traitorous face. If an evil is visited upon clan MacKendrick, 'tis the evil of the hellish bitch who dares call herself its chief and insults the memory of all who went before her by spreading her legs for a Fraser!

"O Urramaich!" The MacKendrick battle cry was a blasphemy upon his lips as he lunged toward her. But, he was so blinded with rage, it was easy for Madlin to dodge the clawing hands aimed for her throat. The peacock went sprawling upon the floor.

Sprawled on his belly, Seamus embarrassed himself further by venting a stream of vitriolic curses while pounding and kicking his frustration against the floor. Seamus had changed little over the years. This scene had been played before whenever he had been thwarted. Beginning with a nervous chuckle, then a laugh, soon whatever curses Seamus still spewed were drowned beneath a veritable tidal wave of laughter.

No humor brightened Ewan's eyes as he swept Madlin into his arms. "Give me leave to put him out of his misery for you," he said, his voice tight with rage.

"Nay. I have no fear of him." But the tension of the confrontation gave way to a release of nervous giggles within her.

"His life would be forfeit had he laid a hand upon you."

Help for the blubbering man came in the person of Francis. Bending over Seamus, he placed his hand upon his shoulder and said quietly, "Come, my son. 'Tis a shock you have suffered, and for that your actions are understandable. God forgives you, and I'm sure so does my sister and all here. Come now, come with me."

Seamus ceased his thrashing. His wailing and cursing diminished to inarticulate mutterings.

Not wanting to chance enduring further antagonism from any quarter whatsoever this night, Madlin nodded to her men. "Carry the Munro to wherever Bishop MacDonald directs. Stay nearby, lest he should need you for protection."

"Nay!" Francis's declaration was surprising in its forcefulness. "I need no protector, save God. Seamus deserves the right to the privacy the Church assures all who seek counsel through her servants."

With some misgivings, Madlin acquiesced to his wishes. "So be it, then. Return to your posts once you are finished."

The order seemed to take the last of her reserves. Feeling utterly drained, she leaned more heavily against Ewan. Behind her, she heard a sharp clap of a pair of hands, quickly followed by the sound of a piper filling his bag. Whether the signal to resume the festivities came from Elspeth or another, she did not know. Or care, only glad that it had come. "I . . . we must return to the celebration," she murmured without conviction against her husband's chest. Beneath her cheek, she felt the steady thrum of his heart, as reassuring as the strong arms wrapped around her.

Tears had begun to clog her throat and stream from her eyes now that the shock had worn away and the ugliness of Seamus's words and actions had settled within her mind. " 'Tis in our honor and your father's. And all your clan. We celebrate the alliance and your good fortune. I am the MacKendrick, I cannot fall to womanish weeping. 'Tis a silly, silly thing these tears and babbling now that the danger is past."

"Nay, it is not, sweetling," Ewan assured, his lips brushing her forehead. "Think you warriors do not fall upon their knees at a battle's end? Tears in their eyes and a prayer upon their lips that, but for the grace of God, they are not among the dead or dying all around them?"

"Truly?" Her eyes searched his face and saw the truth reflected in his gaze.

"Truly," he affirmed. "Trust me, for I have indeed done that myself." He smiled gently. "Come, quiet is what you need." Tucking her arm in his, he turned her toward the staircase.

Madlin tried to plant her feet, but Ewan's will was stronger and she was near-dragged along beside him. "But . . . the celebration."

Ewan sent her a wicked grin. "I have in mind a kind of celebration far more worthy than dancing to laud the strong leadership of the MacKendrick."

"Do not be so certain, Cluain," she warned with a lift of her brow. "I have not forgotten the matter of the deceptions you have practiced since first we met. With no dancing to distract us, the rest of this night will best be spent in discussion."

Ewan groaned. "The entire night?"

"That would depend upon how much you have yet to confess and how satisfying are your explanations," she said as they skirted past the two pipers on the balcony.

Slipping his arm about her waist, Ewan bent his head close to hers so that his lips brushed her brow when he spoke. "You have my word that you will be well satisfied before this night is through."

* * *

Belowstairs, Niall chanced to look up in time to glimpse his new sister and his brother crossing the balcony. The corners of his mouth twitched slightly, and his brows rose when he saw the way his brother snuggled his wife close to his side and bent his head to hers before they disappeared down a corridor. " 'Twould seem my brother is not averse to this marriage, after all."

Still gazing toward the balcony, a soft smile warmed Elspeth's eyes. "So angry he was when he first arrived here. I did not expect him to give it up so soon." She smoothed her hand across the linen tablecloth. "Nor my niece, either. She was very angry with your brother when this banquet began. I cannot say I have ever seen her that angry. I venture her anger is but set aside temporarily."

A sound almost like a chuckle came from Niall. A faint light, perhaps reflecting a small amount of enjoyment, flickered in his eyes. "I do not know your niece, nor, for that matter, the man my brother has become. As a lad, our Ewan, for all that he felt so deeply, was not one to hold anger overlong. But a more prideful and stubborn lad was hard to find."

"I am only coming to know the man, but I venture he has not changed so very much. He is, I think, a good match for our Madlin." She gestured toward his bandaged arm. "It pains you very much. If you would allow it, I would see to it while you are here at Dunfionn."

Niall did not answer readily but studied her as he considered her offer. His perusal of her features was steady, overbold, and bordered on insulting. She did not alter her expression beneath his inspection but met it with a serene calm.

"I'm told my brother was quite ill when he arrived here and that you have wrought miracles with his wound."

"Not a miracle, for only God can work miracles. But, aye, I did tend his wound."

Niall nodded, then glanced at the balcony before fixing his gaze upon her once more. "You did more than tend his wound, dear lady. You saved his leg, perhaps his life. For that you have the gratitude of all my family. We were so long without him, it would not have been borne to have lost him when at last he was returning to us. I would be grateful if you would tend my arm."

Elspeth rose gracefully. "Come then," she invited. "We shall make our excuses and proceed to the solar where I keep my medicines. Time, I have found, is not something in great supply when a wound needs care."

Not a man given to showing much humor, Niall's smile came slowly, as if his face had had little practice at it. But there was a teasing lilt in his tone when he asked, "Will you have me healed by the morn? I'm told a hunt is planned."

"I am no sorceress, sir."

He shrugged, then sighed regretfully, "Perhaps another time I will have my chance at the deer and boar in the MacKendrick forest."

"Perhaps," Elspeth allowed, then waited patiently while he rose to his feet. Folding her hands loosely before her, she kept them there, for she did not want to wound his pride by assisting him. More than his wound pained him, she was as sure of that as she was that his arm needed tending.

After making their excuses to the others, she led him toward the solar. Later, as she tended his wound, she was relieved to find it had festered far less than she had suspected.

As she applied a healing poultice to the gash in his upper arm, she found herself wishing she had some of Old Meta's powers that might allow her to see into this man's soul and heal whatever festered so steadily there. Ewan was not the only one of Glendarach's sons who felt deeply.

Chapter Twenty-two

"You have not yet satisfied me, Cluain."

From behind her, Ewan paused only the length of a heart-beat as he strung a line of kisses along the column of her neck. "God's teeth, woman, I've only just begun."

"But we . . . you must . . . I demand you ex—"

Madlin's command ended with a moan just as he knew it would when he focused his attention on the sensitive spot beneath her ear. He was rewarded further by the delightful way she arched her back and brought her magnificent breasts dangerously close to spilling out of her bodice.

Explanations and apologies could surely wait until tomorrow. She'd had a long day full of excitement, tensions, and even a threat to her life. The oblivion to be had from lovemaking would do her good. It would surely do him good!

He'd been wanting to get her alone, preferably in bed and splendidly naked, since he'd first seen her garbed in the stunning emerald and gold gown. No, it had been long before that, he amended as he slipped his hands under the edge of her bodice and freed her breasts. He'd wanted her back in bed the minute he'd seen her luscious body wrapped in a fur this morning.

Renewing his onslaught on her sensitive ears and neck, he cradled her breasts in his hands and felt the instant rise of her nipples against his palms. As he caressed her, he heard her whimper before she abruptly pushed out of his embrace. He groaned inwardly when she yanked her bodice back in place and then put several feet between them.

"Why did you keep your title a secret?"

His sigh was loud and full of frustration. Dropping his head backward, he gazed at the ceiling and sighed again. "You, madam, are fortunate I am so thoroughly besotted that I'm prepared to indulge this whimsy," he muttered more to himself than to her.

"Whimsy? You think my question mere whimsy? I assure you, sir, your title is not such an insignificant factor that my demand for an explanation is prompted by mere caprice!"

She was visibly quivering. By the stubborn lift of her chin, the fire in her eyes, and the tone of her voice, he doubted it was wholly from the sexual excitement he'd aroused in her moments before. He took a deep breath to help calm his raging desire and organize his thoughts.

"I choose my words poorly; I beg your understanding, my sweet. My mind is not ever functioning at its best when I have you in my arms."

"Then you will keep those arms safely at your sides, sir. We have much of import to discuss, beginning with your deception regarding your complete identity."

God's teeth! She had the way of a commander about her. He felt he ought to pull himself to straight-backed attention and execute a sharp salute.

And yet, with her cheeks flushed with arousal and the way she flicked the tip of her tongue along her pouty lower lip, he'd never seen a more seductive woman. The quicker he supplied the necessary explanations, the sooner he could return to giving her the kind of "satisfaction" she deserved.

"When first we met, secondary only to my desire for your lovely body . . ." he began, immediately gratified to see a blush rise on her cheeks, ". . . was my aspiration to clear my clan's name by discovering who had started the hostilities in the first place.

"It has been my experience that people are far more open in their conversations with a stranger when they're unaware of any lofty titles that stranger might possess. Though I was unable to discover who was responsible for instigating the hostilities, I knew that, given the location of the seat of my title, it was best not to reveal it to the MacKendricks until I was sure such a disclosure would not cost me my life and set off even more hostilities."

Confident he'd explained himself, he started to move toward her, but she backed up, her arms protectively stretched out before her. "No, do not think to resume your lovemaking in hopes of diverting my attention from the important issues that lie between us."

"Surely you cannot accuse me of something so devious."

"Humph." She rolled her eyes and dropped to the settle beside the hearth. "You have spoken much of trust and expected— no, demanded that I trust you, but I see little evidence of your extending the same courtesy to me. While I understand your reasons for withholding this information from others, why did you not trust me? I believe there was opportunity. The morning I confronted you with the Stewart sword, for one."

Cautiously, lest he send her flying across the room, he approached the chair facing her. Seating himself, he linked his fingers and rested his hands between his knees. "That, sweet wife, was a mistake for which I have no excuse."

The imperious lift of her brow warned him that she was far from appeased. If anything, his excuse seemed to fan her anger to a level commensurate with that she'd displayed earlier in the evening.

"You had other opportunities."

"When? The second day of our marriage? The third?" Remembering how worried and angry he'd been during her progress through her territory added more harshness to his voice than he wanted. But once the crack in his control opened, his anger began to match hers. "Need I remind you that you ran away?"

"I did not run away!" She jumped to her feet. "Need I remind you that I am laird of the MacKendricks? Duty called me away, and you well know it!"

"A thousand pardons, my lady laird of Dunfionn."

The sarcastic edge in his tone negated any possibility she'd think him sincere. "You talk of rewards, usually implying they are the result of trust. Trusting you, specifically. I did trust and what reward? I've been made to look a fool, falling right into a trap neatly laid by your father and aided by you."

"I did not aid—"

"You most certainly did. Glendarach knew of your title. All of the Frasers knew it. But I, your wife, did not. You should have taken me aside and told me."

Taking a deep breath, she pounded her fist against the mantel. "If I had only known . . ."

"If you'd known when? From the first when you captured me? What would you have done had I told you I was Baron Cluain?"

"I would not have married you," she admitted, squeezing her eyes shut against the thought that she would never have known the joy of being in his arms. I must rule with my head, not my heart, she reminded herself. Though her heart was wounded by the trap Glendarach had laid for her, her head admired him for his cleverness. And it was her head that told her that Glendarach would not break the peace.

"Your having a title equal to mine complicates the peace. Even endangers it. Though my people respect you, there will still be many who will never accept a Fraser as their laird. Perhaps . . . perhaps Francis is right. We should have this marriage annulled. 'Twould solve many problems I see stretching before us."

Ewan threw his hands up in exasperation. "Francis!" His anger brought him out of his chair. "That priest is nothing but a troublemaker. I swear I'll have him expelled from Dunfionn at the first opportunity. Tomorrow morning would not be too soon. He can leave with that base cur Munro. At sword point, if necessary."

Her eyes wide with horror, she rushed across the room. Her face was pale and the fingers she pressed to his lips shook. "Say no more, I beg you. Francis is a bishop. 'Twould be most unwise to treat him with less than respect."

Ewan turned his head away from her touch. "I am to be

commended that I have so far managed not to plant my fist in his face."

"No! You must not ever do such a thing, not even think it!"

If possible, her face had lost even more color. There was a look in her eyes he'd not thought ever to see in her.

"My God, you fear him. What has he done now? Priest or no priest, he'll answer for it." He turned and strode toward the door, intent on retrieving his sword, any sword, and confronting Francis.

"No!" Madlin clutched his arm and held on. "No, please. He's done nothing."

"If the bastard holds his tongue, I'll merely escort him and that other miscreant to Dunfionn's gates before the hour is ended."

"But it is near midnight, and the weather is bitter. You cannot turn them out this night. 'Tis unthinkable. And . . . and dangerous."

Holding his rage in check, he asked, "Dangerous to whom, madam? To them? I care not for their safety."

"No, the danger would be to you. Me. Everyone here at Dunfionn. These are perilous times, and Francis would be justifiably angered. He has always been a gentle, loving brother but . . . but if he should mention such an affront to someone else in the Church, I fear the consequences. He is a bishop."

Tears were falling down her cheeks. "Again, this brother of yours has caused you to weep. For that alone, he does not deserve to live, but I shall not be guilty of adding to your tears, nor will I forsake the vow I made never to raise my sword against a MacKendrick. I shall bow to your wishes and not disturb the priest. But this is the last night he spends under Dunfionn's roof for a very long time. If ever."

"How? Francis chooses his own comings and goings. None here dictate them to him. Though the Church is his home, 'twas Papa's wish that Francis always be made welcome here at Dunfionn. I must abide by that wish."

"Though it frustrates me to see you so loyal to that troublemaker, I admire you for honoring your sire's wishes."

He swept his arm around her waist and pulled her close, breathing deeply of the scent that so defined her. Fresh, innocent, and yet intoxicatingly arousing. It calmed him considerably.

"On the morrow, I shall merely suggest to Francis that he keep the Munro company when he takes his leave. I shall be at my most diplomatic and express my deep personal concern that the Munro should not be separated from the comforting counsel provided by such a qualified spiritual adviser as his bishop."

Madlin felt his grin against the top of her head and could not stifle her giggle. "Perhaps you should spend the remains of this night on your knees in the chapel begging God's forgiveness for even contemplating such a colossal lie. You care not one whit for the Munro's spiritual well-being."

He tipped her face up to him and planted a quick kiss on her lips. "My sweet, if I spend any time on my knees, it will not be in Dunfionn's chapel. It is your forgiveness I seek most this night, and you I shall worship.

"Let us not talk of Francis MacDonald anymore this night, nor ever again mention his advice. You will never rid yourself of me, nor I of you. After last night, or this one . . ."

He kissed her again, lingering a bit longer than before. "Or perhaps after the following night." His next kiss merely tantalized her to want more. She looped her arms about his neck and brought his head down to hers. His lips hovering just above hers, he said, " 'Twill not be long before you are carrying my son and heir."

His words doused her flaming desire as effectively as a wave of icy water from the loch. "*Your* heir? What of sons for the MacKendricks?"

"Ah, yes, that most charming of reasons for your choosing me as your husband." His grin was full of rakish devilment as he gently pulled her back into his embrace. "Madam, I promise to attend to that . . . ah . . . *duty* most diligently; I propose to provide sons enough for both Cluain and Dunfionn." He pressed his lips against her forehead and murmured, "And probably some extras. Perhaps four or more just in case—"

The rest of what he might have said was silenced by Madlin's fingers across his lips. "Do not even voice worries for their lives. 'Tis bad luck. If the faeries should hear you—"

He silenced her with a long, deep kiss. "Such superstition, my sweet," he teased as he lifted his lips from hers. "You, the sister of a priest, talking of faeries. If there is a faery anywhere about Dunfionn, 'tis the one I'm holding in my arms, for she has surely cast a spell upon this mere mortal and stolen my heart away."

His words thrilled her, but she refused to let him sway her so easily. Spreading her hands against his chest, she let them linger against the hardened hillocks of muscle that comprised his chest before gently pushing herself free. "You are too much the courtier, husband."

"Perhaps not enough," he remarked as he let her go. "Obviously, I am too clumsy with my words, for they have failed to soften your heart toward me."

If only he knew how soft her heart was toward him, had been since probably that first moment in the glen when she'd looked upon him, but she must not listen to her heart. She must lead with her head. Her heart had led her down the wrong path and made her trust when she should not have.

"Have you else upon your heart that you ought to confess to me? Any other omissions?"

He did not answer immediately. His expression grew serious, and he appeared deep in thought. A long moment passed during which she steeled herself for something very grave indeed. "I believe I have failed to state that I believe myself far more than enchanted by you. I now count the day you captured me and forced me before a priest the luckiest of my entire life. Quite simply and most honestly, I love you, Madlin of Dunfionn."

Totally flummoxed, Madlin could only stare at him. Thoughts of anything else completely fled her mind. "You love me?"

"Yes, I do. Those are no courtier's words, I promise you.

You exasperate me, challenge me, sometimes enrage me, and always excite me. But in your arms, I also find peace."

"Oh . . . oh, my lord, Cluain."

"No, not 'my lord,' " he said as he curled his arms around her once more. "Or Cluain, or Fraser. Ewan. Say it, please."

"Ewan," she whispered.

"And Madlin. In our bedchamber, we are only Ewan and Madlin. Here, we are but a man and a woman, husband and wife. Titles do not identify us and will not divide us. Not anywhere, least of all here," he declared before covering her mouth with his.

This time his kiss was all she wanted and more. When he started to lift his head, she reached up, thrust her fingers into his hair, and brought him back so she could kiss him just as thoroughly. She heard him groan before he pulled her hard against him. But it was not close enough. She needed to feel his flesh against hers, explore with her mouth and hands the fascinating terrain that was his body, and have him deep inside her.

She tore at the laces that fastened his shirt, whimpering her frustration when she could not free him of his garments fast enough. Ewan was suffering in similar fashion, but soon their garments were scattered across the floor. Lifting her into his arms, he carried her to the bed, where she was soon mindless to anything but the pleasures their hands, mouths, and bodies could bring to each other. When at last he joined his body with hers, she was quivering with need and could think only of rushing with him to that summit of pleasure where he had taken her the night before.

He drove into her and she met him thrust for thrust. Sweat slicked his body and mingled with the moist sheen upon hers as they rocked together and apart, then strained and clung to each other at that last glorious moment when they hovered in paradise.

"Madlin, my love," he cried just before he collapsed on top of her, completely spent. Madlin held him, his weight the welcome foundation she needed for stability. All her senses were attuned to him. His taste remained upon her tongue. There was no scent but his, that wild, musky mix of pine, sunlight, maleness, and their passion.

She both heard and felt his breathing, shallow and rapid, then gradually slowing and deepening. His heart beat against hers, a steady throb that was echoed where they still joined.

Another echo, just as strong and impossibly sweeter, sounded within her mind. *My love.*

His love. And he was hers. Her heart was fair bursting with it, but her strength was so draining from her, she could but sigh his name.

The effort of sound cost her the last of her reserves. Her legs unlocked from around his hips to fall limply to the mattress. Her arms loosed from around his waist. She struggled to resist the mists threatening to envelop her. There had been something, something of great import she'd needed to tell him just before he'd swept her mind away.

With considerable difficulty and reluctance, Ewan lifted himself up and away from her. It was a humbling thing, this insatiable thirst he had for her body. He nestled his head against the pillows and tucked her against him.

A surge of warmth expanded in his chest as her head burrowed against his shoulder. Her palm came to rest over his heart, and her thigh slid over his. Her glorious hair, dampened and tangled, flowed over his chest. Her lush body lay trustingly in his arms. He felt the richest of kings holding her thus.

He fit his palm to her belly, wondering if even now a babe lay within, a product of their love. She'd not said the words, but he knew she loved him. She was too honest to give herself so freely without love. It was the most delightful of "duties" to ensure that she would be swelling with his child by the time the snow melted and the passes through the mountains were cleared for travel. By Lammas next, surely his babe could be suckling at her breast.

That idyllic image was immediately shattered by a surge of guilt that jarred him to the soul. *Jamie!* His blasted orders and that cursed earldom.

Softly, he swore. Madlin stirred, lifted her head, and asked sleepily, "Is something wrong?"

"Nay, love. All is right and as it should be."

He pushed her head back upon his chest. The trusting way she settled against him increased his guilt. She was right in her accusations. He did not trust her as he expected her to trust him. It was not well done of him, for he knew she'd have every right to be furious with him if she ever discovered the mission Jamie had given him.

But did she need find out? Was it so wrong to keep something a secret if the knowing might hurt her? Give her reason to question his love for her? No, it was not wrong, and the solution was so obvious and simple, he nearly laughed aloud.

He'd write to James and tell him he'd not only married the MacKendrick's daughter but fallen deeply in love with her. He'd ask him not to reveal the conversation they'd had concerning her. Jamie would understand. Madlin need never know the king had all but ordered him to marry her and dangled an earldom as reward.

As for that reward for fulfilling a royal command, even if Madlin were swelling with his child when he presented her at court and peace was assured throughout the Moray, James might not bestow an earldom upon him. There was no guarantee.

Through the ages, sovereigns had been notoriously forgetful of their promises. Why not James? The man had a lot on his mind, trying to put his kingdom back to order. He might forget a brief conversation six months prior. Besides, if anyone deserved the reward for bringing about peace between the two clans, it was Madlin. She should be elevated to countess in her own right.

In the end all would be as it should be. He'd make sure of it. It was a husband's duty to protect his wife. He wasn't deceiving her, merely protecting her.

"You're awfully quiet this morning, my sweet. Are you not feeling well?"

"Just a bit tired, I think," Madlin admitted.

Ewan sent her one of the leering grins that begged for retribution. She sailed one of the bed pillows in his direction.

Propping her head in her hands, she enjoyed the enticing view of Ewan's tight buttocks flexing beneath the length of linen he'd wrapped about himself. She loved their mornings together almost as much as their nights. Watching her husband shave while they discussed the plans for the day was one of the great delights she'd discovered in the past fortnight of being married to Ewan Fraser.

She plucked at the fur robe spread beneath her, not quite knowing how to begin a long-overdue confession of her own. She should have told him the night of the banquet when she'd demanded he reveal any and all deceptions, but he'd distracted her. And since then, the moment had never seemed quite right.

She could not put it off any longer. But how? *Start at the beginning.* That's what Aunt Liusadh had always told her.

"Ewan . . ."

"This sounds serious. As long as it's neither that you've ordered a cessation of sweets with the meals or are crying off from tomorrow's excursion, I promise to forgive you."

"No, I . . ." She sighed. Ewan had finished shaving. A slightly amused expression on his face, she had his full attention. She sighed again.

"Do you remember the night we returned to Dunfionn when both of us were weak and injured? Aunt Elspeth put us immediately to bed and assured that we would stay there by spooning sleeping draughts down our throats."

"Aye, though it is the morning after that is more memorable." He sent her a leer and waggled his eyebrows exaggeratedly.

His antics did not alter her seriousness nor even bring a blush to her cheeks at the reminder of her boldness their first morning together. "Seamus Munro arrived sometime after we were both fast asleep. He was so angry when he was told I'd married, that Gordie posted a guard on him."

"Wise of Gordie." Folding his arms across his chest, his expression was no longer amused. "And then what happened?"

"Nothing really, Seamus left before dawn the next morning. But Gordie and Hugh thought his coming here so late, alone, and rather disheveled looked rather suspicious, so we sent someone to Dubhfireach to spy on him." Looking up, she admitted, "We've heard nothing from her, and I'm worried."

"*Her?* You sent a woman to spy on that miscreant?"

"I felt the same as you when Gordie and Hugh suggested Beatha. But they said she'd spied before. Also she has both a sister married to one of the Munros and a sweetheart there herself, so no one would think it strange if she went for a visit. And she is Daidbidh's granddaughter, as fierce a warrior in her own way as Daidbidh ever was." Breathless, she had to pause. "Or, so I was assured. Oh Ewan, she should have been back by now."

"Perhaps the weather is keeping her at Dubhfireach," Ewan suggested.

"Perhaps."

From the way she was worrying her bottom lip, Ewan knew she was far from convinced of Beatha's safety. "So, it's Munro you suspect of starting it all?"

"I'm not sure, but that's no excuse for having not shared my suspicions of him." She shrugged. "Gordie and Hugh do not think the Munros would follow Seamus on any kind of raids, especially not ones committed to such atrocities. Perhaps they are right."

She looked up at him and smiled wanly. "Poor Seamus, he did so disgrace himself at the banquet. And before two clans. He will not be able to ever show his face here again."

"And that would be a blessing." Ewan scoffed. "The man's a miserable excuse for a human being. 'Tis a miracle no one has yet murdered him," he remarked as he sat down on the bed beside her. Despite the weeks that had passed since the night of the banquet, his blood still froze when he thought of the Munro's attack upon Madlin.

"Mark me, someone will soon run him through, and there'll

be naught but rejoicing once the deed is done. The man's a menace to his clan and all the Highlands. Since first you told me of him, he's been a suspect. What else have you not told me about him?"

"There isn't really much else. His ascension to laird of clan Munro was shortly before the beginnings of the troubles. But perhaps that is mere coincidence."

"The desire for power can be a powerful motivator," Ewan offered as he stretched out beside her. "Your sire turned him away, but still he persisted in presenting his suit. 'Twas more than clear the night of the banquet that his desire to have you for his wife was not motivated by any affection for you or attraction to your person."

His scowl was replaced by a grin that was markedly lascivious as he gazed boldly upon Madlin's naked backside. Reaching a long, muscled arm across the expanse of mattress between them, he ran a caressing hand down the length of her back and rested his palm on her silken bottom. "More proof of the man's inadequacies if he did not find everything about you and your person utterly delectable."

"You thought me naught but a half-naked hoyden when first we met."

"Aye, but a delectable one." He rolled to his side and pulled her close so that their lower regions were pressed together. "I happen to have a great liking for hoydens, especially naked ones."

Sliding his lips along the silken column of her throat, he delighted when she squirmed and arched her back. The action brought her glorious breasts against his chest, just as he'd hoped. Palming the heavy weight of one of them, he prepared to enjoy the sumptuous feast it offered.

Since their first joining, Madlin had been as eager to explore and delight in his body as he was in hers. But as delicious as were the ministrations of his lips and tongue upon her breast, she resisted being swept away.

"Please . . . no," she managed, her words sounding like more of a plaintive moan than an order even to her own ears.

Pushing away from him, she scooted off the bed and slipped on a linen shift. Touching Ewan or being touched by him always scattered her thinking. "We need to discuss the next visit from Francis."

"Francis! God's teeth. Even when he is not here, the man plagues us. Do not tell me you expect him soon."

"No, but I rarely know when he'll arrive. Promise me you will be civil the next time he is here?"

With a heavy sigh, Ewan heaved himself up against the headboard. "I'd prefer we lower the gates at the first sighting of him, but aye, I shall endeavor to be civil."

"It would be best. As I said before, it would be unwise to anger him."

Bolting upright, a scowl sharpened the planes of his face. "You do fear him, then?"

" 'Tis not fear I feel for him, but I was uncomfortable in his company last time," she admitted as she pulled on her stockings. "I doubt I am the only one who was uncomfortable around him. Have you noticed how much stronger Alys seems these past two weeks? She was so pale and seemed to grow more sickly by the day during Francis's last visit." She made a mental note to question Alys about Francis. Had she been subjected to pious harangues as well?

"Humph, Francis would have that kind of effect on anyone. And in her delicate condition, 'tis not surprising her health would be affected by his gloomy presence."

Madlin could not chastise her husband for that remark. "I vow I did not understand the Francis who last visited here. Mayhap, I never did," she added so softly that Ewan was not so sure he'd heard her aright.

Turning back to Ewan, she admitted, "In truth, I feel no eagerness to see him again, but since his appointment to bishop last year, he has been at Dunfionn more than ever before."

She thought for a moment. "Mayhap, 'tis his greater responsibilities that make him so somber and overly pious," she said before opening her trunk and pulling out a warm woolen gown.

Swinging his feet off the bed, Ewan gave up the notion of making love to his wife again this morn. As they dressed, he considered the question that had been forming since first he'd met the priest. It might hurt her, but it needed asking. "As your sire's eldest and only surviving son, could Francis think himself more deserving than you to be chieftain?"

"Nay!" Madlin's denial was quick and fierce as he expected. Surprisingly, however, she calmed almost as quickly as her denial had come. "He had no place in the succession and always did he know it. 'Tis a cruelty but a reality of life for the baseborn.

"Papa would have trained him for knighthood. But Francis was small and could never have made his living with the sword. 'Twas why Papa gave him to the Church so that he could make his way with the strength of his mind, not his body.

"Papa was right to give him to the Church. He has done well in it, rising so quickly to bishop." She shook her head slowly. "Nay, Francis would not give up what he has to lead clan MacKendrick. If it is power he wants, he has more as Bishop of Beauly than he would have at a small barony like Dunfionn."

Her reasoning made sense. Dismissing MacDonald as a suspect, he remarked, "Then we are back to Seamus Munro as our sole suspect."

"If only Beatha would return soon."

"I'm sure she will." He opened his arms and beckoned to her. "Come, sweetling. One last kiss to hold me until we can be alone again."

A wary look on her face, she moved slowly toward him. "Just one kiss, for we are already late to break our fast."

Wrapping her in his arms, he groaned as she melted against him. "Perhaps we should have food sent up to us each morning."

"Nay, we would spend all the morn here, and then you would suggest we have the noon meal sent up and then—"

He stopped her with a deep, lingering kiss. As always, the taste of her sweet mouth and the feel of her in his arms incited him to soar beyond himself. It was with the greatest of will that he ended the kiss and set her away from him.

Opening the door, he pushed her through it. "Let us go slay today's dragons, my love," he teased.

Praise God, winter had descended so heavily upon them. There had been no more attacks on the MacKendricks since the snow and ice had begun to fill the mountain passes. The clogged passes precluded any communication with Glendarach. He could but pray that the Frasers, too, had been granted the same reprieve.

"Now who is being overquiet?" Madlin asked as they began their descent to the hall. Pausing on a step, she turned and brushed her fingertips across his brow to smooth the furrows there. "I'm sure all is well at Glendarach just as it has been here."

Startled that she should read his thoughts so clearly, Ewan raised his brows at her. "You are a witch, woman."

Standing a step beneath her, his eyes were level with her chest. The gold chain of her pendant glittered against the creamy column of her neck. Running a finger along the edge of her bodice, he hooked the chain and lifted the gem-edged disk from its resting place between her breasts, then tilted it one way and another until it caught the light from the brace of candles on the wall.

"It glows. 'Tis the source of all your powers and wisdom, am I right?"

With a playful grin, Madlin snatched it from him and tucked it back inside her bodice. "Only the wisdom in the words etched upon it does it share with me." Sobering, she added wistfully, "And strength sometimes."

Her last word ended with a yawn that Ewan found infectious. "Are you sure we should not march right back up these stairs and into bed? The strong and very wise woman who placed that pendant about your neck would surely counsel that we get more sleep."

"She would suggest we be abed early tonight and quickly to

sleep. You will need to be well rested for the morrow. As I recall, Cluain has determined it the day he shall go out to the forest and choose the yule log for Dunfionn."

Ewan grinned. "Cluain does have a very special tree in mind for it, too. Will the MacKendrick accompany him to a meadow high in the heart of his lands?"

"Aye, she does think he might need her to find this meadow."

Sliding an arm around her waist, Ewan forced his feet down rather than back up the steps. "And she would be right, for always, Cluain will have need of the MacKendrick."

Chapter Twenty-three

The farther they rode into the disputed lands, the more nervous Madlin became. No, not the disputed lands, she reminded herself. Cluain.

Turning in the saddle, she looked back to the men following behind. Colley, Hugh, and Gordie were all carefully scanning the forest surrounding them. Their merry expressions and high spirits had sobered with each passing mile. Her unease grew. They were close.

The trail had broadened enough that she could nudge her mare abreast of Ewan's stallion. Pasting a smile on her face, she said, "There are many fine trees here, Ewan. Nearly any one of them would make the perfect yule log."

"These?" He swept his arm to encompass all around them. "Too ordinary, my love. Trust me, I shall provide Dunfionn with a tree fit for the royal hall at Stirling."

"I begin to think it's Stirling where you expect to find this tree," she grumbled, shifting to ease the stiffness in her backside.

Ewan grinned. "Your discomfort will be rewarded, my sweet."

She gave him a disgruntled glare. He leaned across the space between their mounts and lowered his voice. "I shall be delighted to administer a soothing balm to your soft bottom when we get back to Dunfionn and expect the same in return from you."

Madlin gasped. "You, sir, are an insatiable knave!"

His grin was even wider. "Aye, and are you not thankful?"

Warmed to the tips of her toes by the images his remarks had incited, she was unable to form a fitting setdown. Quickly, she glanced over her shoulder to assure herself that no one had heard his remarks. Oh yes, she was thankful, but she was not about to admit it to him. He was cocky enough.

At the edge of the forest, Ewan reined his mount to a stop. "There." He pointed toward the middle of the broad glen spread out before them. A majestic fir soared proudly toward the heavens, its base as broad as five men standing at arm's length. "It's even finer than I remembered."

" 'Tis a grand tree, Ewan," Madlin said, her eyes scanning the ridges surrounding the glen. This was it, she knew it. He'd led them straight to the very glen Colley and Malcolm had described upon returning from patrol duty. Her stomach knotted.

"I'll race you to it," Ewan cried and made to spring Triese through the drifts.

"No! Stay back!"

Turning Triese sharply, Ewan struggled to bring the animal around. Tossing his head and pawing at the ground, the stallion was eager to run. Madlin's new mare responded to the stallion's excitement and began sidestepping nervously and fighting the reins. She had to pull hard on the reins to hold her in place.

"Why did you call me back?" Ewan demanded as soon as he had his stallion calmed.

"There are but five of us, and we know not what lurks amid the boulders and trees up there. Out in the open, we would be vulnerable."

Looking sheepish, Ewan admitted, "I fear I let my excitement override my judgment. 'Tis inexcusable. But the snow appears undisturbed, and all looks calm in the ridges." He grinned at her. "I doubt there's anything but red deer, foxes, and coneys up there."

Astride the big bay mare, Gordie grumbled, "Anything else has tucked itself away till the spring."

"Let us pray so," Madlin said as she continued to study the trees and boulders studding the ridges. "If I'm not mistaken, this is the glen Colley and Malcolm described. The one where they found the cave that they think the raiders used as their base."

Frowning, Ewan looked beyond her. "That so, Colley?"

"Aye, my lord, I fear it is the very one." He guided his pony past the others and drew up beside Ewan. Rising in his stirrups, he pointed to a spot high on the ridge to their left. "Up there, that's where the cave is. It didn't look like it had been used for several weeks, but it has been more'n a fortnight since we patrolled here."

Madlin moved her gaze slowly over the ridge, watching for any color, flash of light, anything that would not be natural amid the boulders and snow-laden conifers. She saw nothing, but still she felt uneasy about moving into the open. "We are . . . what? Half a day from Dunfionn. Less in fair weather. How long to Glendarach?"

"About the same, mayhap a bit longer than half a day," Hugh supplied. "I haven't traveled it in many a year, but that's how I remember it."

Looking toward the spot Colley indicated as the location of a cave, Ewan asked, "Is the summit of that ridge broad enough for a fortified manor?"

"Aye, 'tis broad enough and would command a good view. 'Twould take a good bit of clearing, but the timber could be useful in the building. Oaks enough are scattered through the pines and firs," Colley supplied almost absently as he, too, studied the ridge.

Madlin sat her new mare quietly, scanning the ridges while at the same time thanking God for the respite. Excited to be on their way, Ewan had awakened her long before dawn and set a hard, fast pace as soon as their party had been assembled. The trip had been arduous, but the chestnut had a smooth gait and handled easily. She should not feel so tired after a half day's ride but she did, plus what little food she'd put in her belly was not sitting well.

To add to her unease, she'd had a sense of foreboding since they'd left the village that had increased her worries about their ultimate destination. A single set of tracks from the village had appeared to be those of a woman. Another set had joined those, slightly larger, the stride more like a man's. The tracks had merged with those made by a horse's hoofs, and then only the tracks left by the hooves had led into the forest beyond.

A tryst between two lovesick young fools was what they'd all decided. Certainly only the lovesick would be venturing out in this cold. And I am surely that, she thought with chagrin. Only a wife totally besotted with her husband would venture so far from a warm hearth on a day such as this.

She shook off her unease and interrupted the men's discussion. "Much more nattering about the Cluain fortress and the sun will be gone from the heavens long before we see Dunfionn's gates. If the cave was empty when Colley saw it, it undoubtedly still is. Since we are at last near the tree his lordship was so insistent was all would do for this Christmastide at Dunfionn, let us set to it."

Ewan gave the ridges one last glance, then smiled mischievously, "Think you ready to test your lady against her lord, now?"

Letting his high spirits infect her, Madlin returned, "Princess will be long to the tree before that hulking brute has taken ten strides."

"Princess," he repeated. "So you have finally named her."

"Aye," Madlin patted the mare. "She has shown herself to be as fine a lady as any in the kingdom. And most spirited," she cried and, without further warning, sprung her mount.

Madlin had a sizable lead before Ewan had even set his stallion in pursuit. But the huge sorrel destrier was more than a match for any horse. The snow spraying up high and wide with every stride of his great, muscled legs, Triese cut into his mate's lead and had pulled abreast long before they were halfway to the tree.

Though Ewan reached the tree before Madlin, she was off Princess's back and inspecting the tree before he dismounted. "Boughs there are aplenty to deck Dunfionn. Aunt Elspeth will be pleased." Pushing aside the fir's heavy branches, she peered at the trunk and announced, "A fine, thick trunk. 'Tis very straight and nearly perfect."

"Be quick about it, men," Ewan called to the others. "Let us get this tree down before the MacKendrick decides that there is a more perfect tree for the stealing even deeper in Cluain's territory."

"Stealing?" Madlin's eyes matched the mischief in her husband's. "My good sir, the MacKendricks are a most honorable clan," she announced haughtily.

A broad smile upon his face, Ewan tipped his cap to her. "My apologies, my lady. All of the Highlands know the honor of my baroness and the MacKendricks, especially their laird." Too late, he saw her draw back from the tree, a ball of snow in her mittened palm. The cold missile hit him squarely in the face.

Sputtering, he wiped snow from his eyes just in time to see her grin of triumph before the "honorable" baroness turned to head for cover around the tree. About to scoop up some snow and begin retaliation, he heard the scream of a horse behind him and saw a bolt drive into the ground a few feet from where Madlin had just stood. Another fell harmlessly a yard from his own feet.

"Attack!" His bellow was still upon his lips as he sprung toward Madlin and rolled with her beneath the tree.

"Get off me, so I can help defend us," she cried, her voice muffled in the snow.

"Stay down," he ordered, his tone harsh with rage. Carefully, so as not to give away their hiding place, he pushed a bough aside to assess the situation.

The bay mare had taken a bolt to her haunch. Gordie already had her upon the ground and quieted as best he could, while Hugh dug the obscene bolt from her. "God's teeth, men. Keep yourselves down," he yelled. "I would you sacrifice the mare before yourselves. Colley?"

"Here, my lord." Colley called from their right. His voice sounded strained, his breathing audible from the distance as if he were panting. " 'Tis . . . only two, I think. The cowards are not . . . close enough to do so verra much damage . . . yet," he managed between gasps that grew more lengthy and loud with every word.

A rustling sound from Colley's direction preceded the landing of the bow and quiver that had dangled from Princess's saddle. "The laird is our best archer, my lord Ewan." Another set landed beside him. " 'Tis mine . . . devil take them, but they managed to hit me in my left arm."

"Let me up, now!" Madlin's struggles to free herself from his weight intensified. "I can help ward off our attackers, Ewan, if only you'll get off me."

Ewan swallowed hard. It was against everything he believed in to let a woman put herself in danger. But he had no choice. Madlin was not just a woman. She was a warrior. If Colley said she was the MacKendrick's best archer, he had to trust it was the truth. Trust her.

"Ewan . . . please . . ." Muffled in the snow, her voice carried a plea that he could not ignore any more than he could ignore the archers hidden somewhere on the ridge. Two men with crossbows, no matter how unskilled, could cut them all down if there were no retaliatory fire. A man and a woman, if skilled enough with the longbow, just might succeed in mounting a counterattack. God help them, there was no other option.

"Careful now, and keep your head down," he said as he rolled off her.

She met his gaze and held it for a long moment before squeezing his hand. "I know what I'm doing, Ewan."

"I know you do, Madlin," he said, and realized then how fully he believed it himself.

"Just as I know you do, too." She reached for her bow and quiver. "How bad are you, Colley?"

"I . . . I'll live . . . just no . . . good to ye in this fight."

"Keep yourself well hidden, Colley. You've done enough by getting my bow and quiver to me." Using her elbows and feet, she started scooting on her belly toward the back of the tree. "Ewan, I'm headed directly back. Can you take up a position on the other side?"

He was already moving toward that point. "Do not leave your cover until I tell you. And cover that bright head of yours." Keeping his voice just loud enough for her to hear him, he directed, "On my signal, step away just far enough to make the shot, then drop, roll under the tree, and wait for my signal again. If God is with us, they'll shoot, and we'll know where they are."

He paused briefly beside Colley. The bolt was still in his arm, but not in too deeply. "Praise God they were not closer," he muttered as he tore off a strip of his plaid and tied it around the man's arm. "Stay still and keep packing snow around the bolt. It should slow the flow of your blood until we can do more for you."

As he crawled toward the back of the tree, Ewan assessed the situation. If he and Madlin could catch sight of their assailants, and if there were only two as Colley thought. And if their attackers were not adept with their crossbows. And if they had not moved forward. Then, and only then, they stood a chance.

Arriving at his destination, he pulled off the cap that covered his own head and shed his plaid of crimson and green. Rolling out to a crouch, he set an arrow to his bow's string, and looked to Madlin. Her glorious eyes were upon him, the light of battle shining brightly. Her cheeks rosy from the cold and the excitement. *God protect my warrior queen.*

With a quick nod of his head, he rose and stepped out into the open. Not wasting time taking aim, he loosed his arrow quickly. As planned, he dropped immediately and rolled back to the dubious safety afforded by the tree.

Out of the corner of his eye, he saw Madlin drop and roll. Drawing himself into a crouch once more, he watched for her to be ready for the next round. To his horror, she was rolling not back to the tree but further into the open. Suddenly, she was on her feet again, loosing an arrow, dropping and rolling yet farther into the open.

Understanding of what she was doing came quickly upon the heels of his fury that she should put herself in such danger. Loading another arrow in his bow, he anticipated and feared two bolts flying in her direction. With all attention on Madlin, he was afforded the time to find his first quarry. When he saw a man step away from a boulder to crank his weapon's bow once more, Ewan stood, took careful aim, and released his arrow.

The man made an easy target, Ewan thought, as his arrow found its mark. The fool wore a bright cloak of crimson. The first assailant's scream pierced through the quiet of the snow-blanketed glen as he clawed at the feathered shaft driven through his chest. Pitching forward, his limp body tumbled down the slope. Bouncing from tree to tree, it finally came to a stop at the base of the ridge.

From near the front of the tree, Hugh's, or perhaps it was Gordie's, voice came low, just loud enough for Ewan to hear. "To yer right. A great jagged stump. Get him, lad, afore he gets our brave lass."

Ewan needed no urging. Having already left his cover and moved to the front of the tree, he scanned the ridge for the other assailant. One of Madlin's arrows flew toward the ridge.

And then, Ewan saw him.

Cloaked in black, he rose like the specter of death himself from behind a ghostly stump. So sure of his safety, he stood with his back fully exposed as he took aim at Madlin.

Ewan loosed his arrow and prayed it found its mark in time. His arrow was just making its downward arc when his attention was caught by a flash of color. "No!" he roared as Madlin rose to shoot again. Swiftly, he sent another arrow toward the cloaked figure. Another. And another.

Running forward, Ewan yelled and bellowed between shots to turn the man toward him. A howl, more rage than pain, was followed by an anguished wail that echoed long and eerily through the glen. Ewan could no longer see the black-cloaked man and could only hope that he was dead or so wounded he was no longer a threat.

His heart pounding so loudly that he could hear naught else, Ewan ran toward the still figure sprawled facedown upon the snow. "Noooo!" He was on his knees beside her, reaching his hand for her shoulder, when he saw her body shudder and heard the sound of her sobbing.

"Praise God, you are alive." Gently, so as not to cause her more pain, Ewan turned her over. Her features were agonized, tears flowed down her cheeks in a torrent while her body shuddered with her sobbing. "Where?" he asked as he looked for the bolt.

"Nay." She batted at his hands with remarkable strength. "Do not touch me. Save yourself. Leave me."

He caught her hands and trapped them against his chest. Sliding his arm under her shoulders, he lifted her up against him. "The danger is past. We need not fear any more from them. They are both dead."

All the while he talked, he kept up a frantic search for the bolt, blood staining her clothing or the snow where she'd lain—anything that would show him where she was wounded. He could find no evidence she'd been hit, but still she shuddered and writhed, sobbing out her agony.

"Shh, shh, my love," he crooned as he tried to cuddle her close. Inwardly, he wailed, "Oh God, oh God, please do not let her die." Aloud he forced a calm he hoped would reassure her. "We will have you to Dunfionn and under Elspeth's care soon. If I could but take your pain, I would."

"You cannot!" With surprising strength, she wrenched away from him. He reached for her, but she held up her hand to ward him off. "No! Please. Go! Save yourself. Leave me!"

"Lass, lass," Gordie cried gently, falling to his knees beside her. "Where is it?" He reached for her, and she fell into his arms, muttering incoherently between her sobs. Over her shoulder, Gordie shook his head toward Ewan. "Let us help you, lass."

" 'Twas Francis. Why?" she wailed. Much of what she managed between her sobs was unintelligible, save for "Francis" and "traitor."

Helpless to aid her, Ewan's blood chilled and his heart ached as he listened to her cry as if her heart had been torn asunder. "Francis? She cannot want that priest."

Gordie shrugged, then went back to rocking and crooning to his godchild.

"Come, lad, we need to make sure there's no more danger from the curs." Hugh placed a hand on Ewan's shoulder. "I doona think the lass has taken a wound to her body. 'Tis more a deep fright to her soul. Facing death and mayhap causing the death o' another, no matter that he would have taken her life, is not an easy thing. She is a brave one with a warrior's heart, but killing is not a natural thing for any lass."

Ewan could not leave her. He reached out to her once more but stopped his hand midair. Fisting his hands upon his knees, he dropped his head to his chest. *Not again, Lord. Not again.* "My fault. She did not want to come so far. I paid no heed to her warnings. She knew there was danger. All my fault."

"No. No, 'tis no one's fault but those devils that shot at her." Hugh rested his hand on Ewan's shoulder.

"She won't even let me touch her."

"Och, she is not herself. Later, she'll be wanting ye. 'Tis natural in a time like this, she would turn to one she's known all her life. Like a father, Gordie is to her. Ye can do no more for her for the nonce. Come. Let us see who the bastards were."

Ewan pushed himself to his feet. "I'll do it by myself. See to Colley, then round up what horses you can so we can leave this place as soon as possible." Unable to stop himself this time, he laid his hand gently on Madlin's head. " 'Twill be all right, my love."

Ewan came across the body of the red-cloaked assailant first. It had rolled almost to the bottom of the slope and was an obscene blot of bright color against the pristine white of the snow. From the color of the cloak, he'd guessed at the identity even before he turned him over. Still, he felt an element of surprise that it was indeed Seamus Munro. From the beginning, he'd suspected him but had allowed himself to be convinced that the man was too cowardly for such perfidy. If only he'd run him through that night at the banquet. Then there would not be a woman's weeping piercing the glen and wounding his heart. "Rot here, Seamus Munro, for you deserve no better."

Farther up he found the body of the second assailant. Two of his arrows protruded from the bastard's back. Ewan turned the body over and swore long and viciously when he recognized the man.

MacDonald stared sightlessly up at him. His mouth was curved in a snarl that even in death was menacing. If the bastard had not yet been dead, Ewan would have slit his throat.

She must have seen his face when he stood and stepped so boldly from behind his cover to fire upon her. The bastard must have been so hate-filled that he had wanted her to know it was him who was about to take her life. "Damn you, Francis MacDonald, for the black-hearted traitor you were and the pain you have caused!"

Another arrow had struck the body, one of Madlin's. Cursing the dead man again, he yanked it from the priest's bloodless heart and pushed its point into the ground. He could not be certain as to which arrow had ended the bastard's life. But he would die before he let her know there was any chance that hers had dealt the mortal wound. Her heart was broken enough that the man she had called brother would seek her death. She did not need the guilt of his blood upon her hands.

"May your soul burn for all eternity, Francis MacDonald." Ewan turned away and started back down the ridge. With each foot of ground he covered, his conviction grew stronger. Behind him lay the source of the great evil that had swept like the Black Plague through Fraser and MacKendrick lands these past months.

What had driven Francis MacDonald to such lengths to rid himself of the family who'd accepted and provided for him, he could not imagine. But the reasons could be sorted out

later. Before him wept a woman who would be a long time recovering from such treachery in one she had so honored that
she'd called him brother. Her safety and recovery were foremost, and to those he would devote all his energies.

Just how the black-hearted devils had known to lie in wait
in this place and upon this day, Ewan wondered as he trudged
through the snow. More than a fortnight had passed since the
pair had taken their leave of Dunfionn. MacDonald had to
have had a confederate within Dunfionn's walls. Who?

Darkness was upon them before they reached Dunfionn,
but the village was alight with torches. Two bodies had been
discovered in the forest in midafternoon. The first was Mairi,
one of the kitchen maids. Her throat slashed, her clothes torn,
and her body used roughly, she'd not died quickly.

All that was known was that the pretty young maid had
dressed with special care that morning and left her father's
cottage long before dawn. She had told him she was meeting a
special friend before she took up her day's duties at Dunfionn.
He had supposed she had a sweetheart, possibly one of the
lads who had accompanied the Munro on his last visit, for it
was shortly afterward that a series of assignations had begun.

Near the edge of the village, not far from Mairi's body,
they'd found Beatha. Her satchel was still gripped tightly in
her hand. Clearly, she had been on her way home. Her throat,
too, had been cut. That she had not been abused as had poor
Mairi was some consolation to all who'd known her.

Whether young Mairi had been unwitting in her chatter or
been threatened for information, no one could know. That
somehow Beatha had been found out, they were certain. It
would never be known whether it had been Seamus's or
Francis's hand that had taken the women's lives. Only prints
from one man's boots appeared in the snow, but the prints of
two horses cut clearly northeast from the women's bodies.
Toward a glen at Cluain's edge where grew a magnificent fir,
Ewan was sure.

Chapter Twenty-four

He stood in the middle of the broad meadow all golden in the sunlight from the top of his fair head to the spurs on his booted feet. An honorable knight, as pure of heart as he was fair of face and form. He opened his arms. "Come, my love."

Her heart leaped within her breast at the sound of his voice and the sweetness of his words. She started to run toward him, but a dark, cloaked figure moved in front of her. She could not see his face, but a horror like she had never known gripped her. It raised its black-robed arms wide in front of her, blocking the warming sunlight and her way. She tried to move around him, but her feet and legs were suddenly leaden.

"Honor, Maddie, lass. Honor in all things."

Papa's words, but not Papa's voice. The sound was harsh, strident in its tone, and filled with condemnation.

"Always. The laird must lead with honor."

A cold wind swirled about her, chilling her to her very soul. She tried to move away from the specter. Toward the sunlight. Toward the golden knight, but still her feet were too heavy to move. In frustration, she cried, "Go away. Leave me!"

"Yer actions have disgraced yerself, me, and all of the clan. 'Tis shamed I am to claim ye as a daughter o' my house."

Papa's words again. Spoken to her long ago but of other things, another deed of far less gravity than today. Tears stung her eyes and flowed freely down her cheeks. Deep sobs welled up from the deepest part of her. "I'll not shame you again," she said, but it was not to Papa she made this pledge. It was to the golden knight.

* * *

"She still sleeps?"

Ewan brushed his palms down his beard-stubbled face. All through the night, he'd watched Madlin struggle in her sleep. Each tear that had flowed from beneath her lashes wounded him. Every cry that had passed her lips pierced him. "Aye, she still sleeps, but there is no rest in it."

Elspeth set a linen-covered tray down upon the trunk beside the bed. She brushed her palm lightly across Madlin's forehead. "There is no fever, but a sickness rages within her. Yesterday was too much, even for one as strong as our Madlin."

She frowned as Madlin tossed her head from side to side and began moving her legs restlessly once more. "Curse Francis MacDonald's black soul," she muttered beneath her breath.

"That my brother's kindness should be repaid with such viciousness." Elspeth's shoulders slumped, and she buried her face in her palms. "Too much heart had my brother, and too much does his daughter."

He'd known her only a few weeks, but never had Ewan thought to see Elspeth MacKendrick Ogilvie brought to such a state. Only a day before, it would have been unthinkable that he would fold his arms around her and feel her tears dampen his shirt. "Great hearts do mark all the MacKendricks," he said as he patted Elspeth's back. "Most especially the women. 'Tis why I love your niece more deeply than ever I thought possible."

"You are a good man, Ewan Fraser, " Elspeth said at last, drawing away from him. Straightening her shoulders, she wrapped herself in the dignity that so marked her character. Except for the redness about her eyes and the moisture on her cheeks, she was once again the formidable chatelaine of Dunfionn.

Briskly, she moved about the chamber, stoking the fire, pulling back the heavy draperies over the window. A pale wintry sun struggled to light the skies and chase away the black gloom of both the night and the spirits within Dunfionn. She whisked the cloth from the tray to reveal a bowl of stew still steaming from the kitchens, fresh bread, and a tankard of ale. "You will eat. Then you will clean yourself up and get some rest. I have enough to look after without adding you to my list."

"I shall endeavor to keep myself well," he said with the hint of a smile. God's teeth, it was good to see some normalcy return in a MacKendrick woman. He prayed that soon he would see the golden sparkle in his wife's eyes that boded mischief. Or the way her eyes darkened to the deep shade of the dark center of the forest when she wanted him. Even if it was anger darkening her eyes and putting patches of bright color upon her cheeks, he would welcome it. Anything would be preferable to the broken-spirited woman they had brought home from that glen.

From beneath her lashes, Madlin watched her husband bathe. How beautiful he is, she thought. The sight of his firm, muscled body made her ache.

Holy Mother, grant me the courage for what I must do.

When he had finished and was dressed again, he came to the side of the bed, bent over her, and brushed his lips against her forehead. Her resolve nearly shattered. How very much she wanted to open her arms and pull him down to the bed with her. She steeled herself to remain still, pretend she still slept. What she had to say to him could wait until he settled himself upon the chair he'd pulled to the bedside.

But a moment passed and yet another, and he did not take up again the chair where he'd spent the night. Instead, he remained bent over her and said, "I know you're awake, sweetling."

Startled by his statement, Madlin's eyes flew open. "How?"

"I've watched you sleep too many hours not to recognize the signs when you are merely pretending." He smiled tenderly and curled his palm gently against her cheek. "Yours is an open heart, my love. There are many things you do exceedingly well, but dissembling is not one of them."

He brought his face close again, and Madlin both feared

and yearned for his lips upon hers. A sudden wave of nausea decided for her. Pressing her lips together to hold back the bile, she turned her face away. Ewan's closeness made even breathing difficult. She pushed at his chest with both her palms to give herself more space to breath.

"Leave me." Seeing the confusion on his face, she quickly added, "I . . . I beg some privacy to . . . to bathe and dress for the day."

His soft chuckle sent a shiver through her body. "I have seen and kissed every inch of you, sweetling," he said as he slid his hands beneath her as if to lift her from the bed. "Come, I think the water is still warm enough. As I recall, you don't mind sharing bathwater."

Instantly, her body remembered how very much she enjoyed sharing bathwater. Of the many joys he had introduced to her, sharing a large copper tub was one of the best. She pressed her lips together tightly to stem a moan. Every part of her tingled at the memory of how they had solved the positioning of their bodies within the confines of one tub. And, how many towels it had taken to mop the floor of all the water sloshed there from their vigorous "bathing."

She stiffened in his arms and pushed again at his chest. "No! I prefer you take yourself off to the great hall and break your fast there with the others. I . . . I'll join you later," she said, though for the first time in her life, the very thought of food made her ill. "There is much that must be attended to this day."

Ewan's smile was replaced with such a look of pain that Madlin wanted to call back her words. "Aye, there is much to be done this day. I shall take my leave." With obvious reluctance, he let go of her, but not before he brushed another kiss upon her brow.

The door had scarcely closed behind Ewan when Madlin swung her legs over the side of the bed and raced to the chamber pot. Though her belly was long since emptied, she was still bent over it when Elspeth entered the chamber. Her aunt raised a speculative brow, then poured a cup of water and pressed it in Madlin's hand.

"Perhaps you should return to bed," she suggested as Madlin rinsed her mouth. "You do not look at all well, and yesterday was an ordeal. Your body needs time to revive itself."

"No . . . I shall be fine," Madlin said with more conviction than she felt. Still light-headed, she leaned against the wall for support. "Colley? How does he fare?"

"He is already on the mend and up and about."

"Daidbidh?"

In the act of handing her a clean chemise, Elspeth paused. "You know about Beatha?"

"Aye. And Mairi." She pushed away from the wall and reached for the chemise. "I must go to Daidbidh and Mairi's father. I was too much within myself last eve to offer either of them any comfort. 'Twas not well done of me to put my own grief ahead of that of others."

"Do not grieve for Francis MacDonald!"

"I do not grieve for *that* one, but for all those who were his victims. Even Seamus, I think, was a victim, and I am sorry for it and that clan Munro is left without a laird."

Elspeth scoffed. "There is a cousin. Douglas, if I remember aright. A man more like Nairn than was his own son. Clan Munro will be the better for having Douglas at its head." She started to hand Madlin a dark green woolen gown, but with an almost imperceptible shake of her head, she placed it back in the trunk and pulled out the black velvet.

It was fitting, Madlin thought as the black gown slid over her body. A dark, bleak color for mourning. For Beatha, whose brave loyalty had been rewarded with death. Madlin squeezed her eyes shut to keep more tears from falling. She should not have sent her. Nothing was gained by it, and so very much lost.

Mairi would be mourned this day as well as many to come. Madlin shuddered. So unfair that her young life had been taken so very cruelly.

By the time she was dressed and her hair arranged to Elspeth's satisfaction, Madlin's light-headedness had left her and the clenching in her belly felt only like complaints of emptiness. "Why, Aunt Elspeth?" she asked as they descended the stairway. "Why did Francis betray us, his only family?"

Elspeth's immediate answer was a sharp shake of her head. They'd reached the landing. Wordlessly, she hustled Madlin toward the counting room and away from the great hall.

"Sit," she ordered, directing Madlin to the comfortable cushioned chair pulled up next to the hearth. "You'll not enter yon hall with concerns for Francis MacDonald weighing so heavily upon you. I cannot know what caused him to do the things he did. Surely they were the acts of a twisted mind. Someday, perhaps, we will know the answer, but perhaps we will never know, and his reasons will accompany him to the grave. For now, you must put him out of your mind and not allow his poison to color your decisions in the coming days."

Madlin shuddered and moved her hand to her belly.

In the process of stoking the fire, Elspeth saw the protective action. "You are carrying Ewan's child?"

"No. I mean I do not know. 'Tis too soon to know for certes."

"Have you had your monthly courses since your marriage?"

Madlin shook her head. "But . . . but since Papa, Bram, and Airic were killed, they have not come every single month."

Elspeth nodded and put down the poker. Coming to Madlin, she squeezed her hands reassuringly, then patted her gently on the shoulder. "You have had much to deal with for one so very young. 'Tis natural your cycle might be upset. How long have you been rushing to the chamber pot upon awakening?"

"Only this morning."

"And the light-headedness? Has that bothered you only this morning?"

"Yes," Madlin answered, then quickly changed her answer. "It has happened on other mornings. I thought 'twas only from . . ." She blushed scarlet. "From fatigue or mayhap hunger."

Elspeth raised her brows and studied her niece for a long moment. At last she said, "Mayhap, you are right. 'Tis too soon. But you must take care of yourself, Madlin. Not only for the babe, but the clan *and* your husband need you well and strong. If you are not yet carrying Cluain's heir, you soon will be."

"No, and pray you that my womb remains empty!"

"I will do no such thing, nor will you!" She caught up Madlin's hands again. Holding them fast, she dropped to her knees so that her face was level with Madlin's. "You are wrong to be thinking as you are. Your blood is not tainted. Francis MacDonald's actions were his and his alone and have naught to do with any MacKendrick blood he may have been carrying.

"Out of the great kindness and love my brother had for all children, he chose to accept that child as one of his own when his mother brought him here, but there was never a certainty he was of Toirlach's blood, for that woman had lain with many before and after my brother. But whether he was Toirlach's or not 'tis of no importance. Neither you nor any MacKendrick is to blame for Francis MacDonald's actions. Any bairn you bear will be as good and fine as his parents, and a blessing."

If only she could believe Francis had not been Papa's child. Then, perhaps, she could let go of her guilt. But as long as there was a chance, she could not risk thrusting such a child upon Ewan and the new house he was forming. *Cluain*. It was to be a place of such sunshine and happiness. She would not be the instrument that would bring shadows to those high meadows and the future of such a fine and honorable house. It would be an act of pure selfishness to do so.

She bit her lip against the grief that swept over her at the very idea of the course she must take. She crossed herself quickly and pressed her hands together. "God forgive me for what I must do."

"Would you be kind enough to find Cluain and send him to me?"

The flatness in her tone Elspeth liked not at all. Nor the formality Madlin used in referring to her husband. "As you wish," she said with a sigh.

It seemed Elspeth had barely closed the door behind her before the clatter of crockery preceded Ewan's voice. "Elspeth told me you have eaten little this day. The noonday meal is long over, and I know you to be a woman of hearty appetite. Edana has heaped this tray with enough food for a small army. There is a hearty stew she kept warm for you, bread, cheese, pippins. All she could think of to tempt your palate."

The fragrance of the stew wafted to her nostrils. Her belly growled, and she thanked God it was naught but emptiness causing it. Gathering her courage, she turned toward her husband.

Carefully, she kept her gaze from resting overlong upon him. He was so achingly handsome this morn and was all that was good and fine. A man far too fine to be deceived.

"Thank you. 'Twas kind of you to bring this." She looked at the food with far less longing than had been engendered by the brief glance at her husband. Perhaps she should eat first, for surely she did need strength.

She plucked a pippin from the tray and took a bite. She knew the fruit to be sweet, but it tasted like vinegar to her soured palate. She tore off a piece of the bread and popped it in her mouth. "I see Edana has sent along a plate of fruit tarts," she remarked. Despite the moroseness of her thoughts, she set them aside. Grasping at just one more moment of happiness with this man was perhaps selfish, but it would have to last her for her lifetime. "For me?" she asked in a teasing tone. "Or mayhap they are for you?"

Ewan shrugged. "I suppose 'tis possible she knows how much I appreciate her pastry artistry."

Madlin rolled her eyes and snorted in mock disgust. "You will grow fat and toothless if you persist in eating so many sweets with your meals . . . and in between."

"And will you still love me if I grow fat and toothless?"

His query, so blunt and abrupt, took her aback. No laughter colored his voice, for he'd spoken in the deep, rough tone he used when at his most serious.

Her gaze flew to his face, seeing not the merriment twinkling there that so warmed their blue depths when he was teasing her. Instead, his mouth was set in a straight tight line. His eyes were dark with intensity, their gaze unwavering.

Nonplussed, she could not pull her gaze from his. "Do not think to dissemble," he warned. "Not on this. Not between us."

Madlin swallowed hard. "I . . . I would still love you if you grew fat and toothless," she vowed truthfully, knowing she would love this man until the day she died and beyond if it were within her power. "The love I hold for you is not at issue. 'Tis honor that compels me to free you of the vows I forced upon you. I did present myself and the reasons for marrying you falsely."

In the process of moving around the desk with the intent of sweeping her into his arms, Ewan stumbled. His mouth fell agape, and his eyes widened in shock. "Honor compels you? More like lunacy compels you."

Madlin drew herself up to her most imperious. "There is no need for insults."

" 'Twas no insult, madam, but statement of fact. God's teeth, woman! What else but lunacy would lead you to tell me you will love me even if I grow fat and toothless and in the next breath suggest releasing me from our marriage vows?"

"I could not bear to live without honor."

Having slowly made his way around the desk, he stood inches from her. Bringing his face so close to hers their noses nearly touched, he roared, "You? Without honor? What about you is so false I would be compelled to save your honor by casting aside the woman I love to the very depths of my soul?"

"I cannot give you a son for Cluain!"

His response was a lift of one golden brow. "The matter of the MacKendrick heir, I suppose." Madlin opened her mouth to disabuse him of that thought, but he gave her not the chance.

"I foresee many sons and daughters from our union. Our second son, perhaps our first daughter, will be MacKendrick's heir. Is that what this is about? You know the babe is a daughter, then?" he asked with far less volume than he'd been using. A sentimental smile lifted the corners of his mouth.

"No," she answered, her anger considerably quieted. "I do not know of a certes that I am carrying a child, male or female."

"I do," he announced quite smugly. "Old Meta told me just this morn and told me I would know it by your thinking being peculiar. I do believe she is most correct, especially about your thinking."

He silenced the protest she might have voiced to such an insult by quickly leaning forward and kissing her. "As for the child she claims you are carrying, she claims 'twill be a son and we shall name him James. But I already knew that."

"And just how is it that you think to know that I am carrying a son and his name will be James?"

Color rose from Ewan's neck and he looked to the ceiling, then busied himself stirring the bowl of stew he'd brought her. "I . . . ah . . . confess to a small deception that . . . ah . . . I think does balance whatever falseness you think misrepresented when we stood before a priest," he said, and promptly shoved a spoonful of stew into her mouth.

Madlin could do aught but chew and swallow before asking, "And just what was this small deception on your part?"

Ewan did not answer immediately but sat down upon the chair behind the desk and pulled her onto his lap. He spooned more stew into her mouth before saying, "I'm warning you right now that no matter how grievous you think my deception, I'm not letting you out of this marriage."

He fed her another spoonful of stew. "I want to make it perfectly clear that I do love you and 'tis a most honorable love I hold for you and I believe just as strongly that your love for me is right and honorable."

He made to pop one of the berry tarts into her mouth, but Madlin batted it away. Pushing away from him and onto her feet, she cried, "No. No. No. You must hear me out. You deserve fine sons and daughters. I will not be the instrument to taint your blood and all the generations to come. Do you not understand?"

Tears blurred her eyes, and her voice rose to a shriek as she beseeched, "You must put me aside and seek out another to give you those sons. I am not worthy of you. And I can never face your father, Lady Guenna, your brothers, or any of your clan. How kind they all were to me, but how they must hate me and all my kin now."

She began to pace and wring her hands. "All those months we MacKendricks blamed Frasers, and all the while it was one of our own who directed the murders and burnings. How righteous we were in our belief that we were too honorable, too good to ever commit such atrocities. And all the while we harbored a villain to our breasts.

"We cannot bring the dead back, but we can assure it will never happen again. Toirlach's line will die with me. There can be no more. The madness will stop. I am not fit to lead this clan. I will turn it over to another, someone not of my father's line. Colley, perhaps. He is a good and fine man. A good MacKendrick, born of another branch stemming from many generations beyond my grandsire. His blood is surely pure. He is strong and—"

Ewan grasped her by the shoulders and gave her a shake. "You will do no such thing. This is utter nonsense! I'll not listen to another word that is clearly naught but hysterical ramblings brought on by shock, fatigue, grief, and even that guilt you think to wrap around you. I'll allow the first three, but the last is groundless.

"Listen well, Madlin of Dunfionn and Baroness Cluain. You are the laird of the MacKendricks by right of succession and by the proof of your fine leadership."

Madlin lifted her gaze to his, and the look in her eyes was chilling. They were utterly lifeless. "Leave me, Ewan Fraser. Leave this day and do not come back," she said in a tone so cold and bitter he lifted his hands from her and took a step away.

"I will leave you but only because I do not want to upset

you further in your condition. But do not think you have seen the last of me, my lady wife. I pray that Meta is right and that your thinking is peculiar right now only because a babe so newly formed is making it so."

"There will be no babe of my body," she announced as he reached the door. "It . . . I will not allow it."

He spun around and glared at her. "Madam, do not try my patience further. You will do nothing to cause harm to yourself or to my child. *I* will not allow it."

He started moving toward her. Madlin cringed and took a step backward, then another. The light in his eyes was like nothing she had ever seen there before, and it frightened her.

Chapter Twenty-five

Grasping her arm, Ewan started her toward the doorway. "You, Lady Madlin, laird of the MacKendricks, have duties, and you will perform them in the manner of the good chieftain that you are. I will be at your side making sure you do not overtire yourself and risk harm to you or the babe. And I will remain at your side until you have regained the good sense I believe still lurks within your beautiful head."

Madlin tried to wrench away from him, but his grasp was too strong. "You may remain at my side this day, as my people have suffered enough shock. Some show of normalcy will be reassuring. But tomorrow, you will leave here, Ewan Fraser."

"Tomorrow, perhaps, we shall discuss it," he told her curtly as he dropped a heavy cloak about her shoulders and handed her a pair of gloves. "Today you have visits to make and people to console. Your grief shall wait," he said as he lifted the hood to her head and fastened it securely.

"Do you not think I know that? Know that my personal feelings must be put aside on behalf of those of my clan?"

"I am beginning to wonder," he muttered as he shrugged on a mantle and pushed open the door to the bailey.

Within minutes, they were mounted upon his stallion's broad back and clattering across the drawbridge, heading for the village. "I should be upon my own horse," Madlin said angrily. "I do not need such coddling, and the weight is too much for your horse."

"I believe you do. Triese is more than enough horse to carry two. 'Tis a bitter wind blowing across this causeway; I would

301

shelter you within my arms to guard against your taking a chill. And sitting across the saddle is less jarring for you and best for the babe. Now relax, compose yourself. You have your people to think of."

She had no choice but to do as he bid. For the next several hours, she visited the families in the village. They stopped at Daidbidh's cottage last. The old man was beside himself with grief, blaming himself for letting his granddaughter go to the Munro's fortress. "Nay, Daidbidh," Madlin soothed, holding his large, gnarled hand within hers. "The fault is mine. I should not have sent her," she told him, but he would not accept her claim of responsibility. "I filled her mind with tales of heroism, of being a warrior, because I no longer had a son to tell of such things. I was proud, too proud, that she would take on such tasks. She was ever so eager to please me, to seek my praise."

He began to weep, his great bony shoulders shaking with the deep sobs welling from his heart. Madlin put her arms around him and rocked him as if he were a bairn. "Placing blame will not bring her back; we must think on the joy she brought us all. The treasure she was to you and to all who knew her."

After a time, the old man was able to lift his head and say, "Aye, 'tis the living that we must think on." He placed his other hand over hers and held it there firmly. "Ye're the best of Toirlach and his Aislinn, my lady. 'Twas an old fool who said ye are not fit to lead us."

"But I failed Beatha and Mairi. I should have kept them from harm," Madlin argued.

"Och, ye could not know what lurked in Francis MacDonald's heart. I've lived far longer than ye, lass, and I did not guess at it." He stood and rubbed the tears from his face. "I thank ye for coming to my cot. Ye're tired, lass, I see it in your face and eyes. Ye must get back to Dunfionn before 'tis too dark to cross the causeway safely."

She would have said more, but Ewan pressed a hand to her shoulder and gave a quick shake of his head. "Daidbidh, I did not know your granddaughter, and I am the less for it, I know. Will you accept my condolences for your loss?" he asked.

Daidbidh nodded and clasped Ewan's hand. "Take care of our lady, Cluain. Even one as strong as her needs someone to watch over her."

Madlin was speechless, hearing such from Daidbidh. No longer did she harbor biting anger toward Ewan for his high-handedness. At Mairi's father's cottage, it had been much the same as with Daidbidh. Douglas, the elder, and his son would not allow her to place blame upon herself. They had just been glad to see her and share their grief for a bit.

"Daidbidh is right, 'tis time I got you back to the keep," Ewan remarked as he lifted her to Triese's back. "There are no more cottages to visit, are there?"

Madlin shook her head. "When word spreads, some of the cotters and herds from beyond will come into the village and to the keep. I will meet with them then."

"They'll be burying the women on the morrow?" he asked as he settled himself behind her.

"Aye, if a priest can get here from the monastery by then." She tipped her face toward the darkening sky and felt the wind and snow upon it. "Mairi's da will be more comforted if there is a priest to pray for her before she is put in the ground. 'Tis a long ride to the Moray. Pray Malcolm can get there and back with a priest by the morrow."

"If not the morrow, then perhaps the next day," Ewan said as they drew closer to Dunfionn's gates. " 'Twill be soon enough."

He'd been right in pulling her out of herself and forcing her to meet with her people, Madlin thought as they rode through the barbican. And it had been right for her people to see him by her side.

Tomorrow, or perhaps the next day, would be soon enough to send him away. She must talk to Colley, too. Tomorrow, or perhaps the next day, would be soon enough to turn over the reins of clan MacKendrick.

* * *

It was four days before the priest arrived to perform the burials of Mairi and Beatha. During the wait, Ewan hovered by her side, day and night. He held her safely within his arms each time she wanted to ride to the village, and each night he held her as she slept.

" 'Tis time, Cluain," Madlin said the fifth morning as she tried not to watch him go about his morning ablutions.

"Time, my sweet?" he asked as he wiped the last of the lather from his face.

"Do not play the dolt, sir," she grumbled as she slipped out of bed. A wave of dizziness broke over her as soon as she was upright. Her stomach threatened, but she pressed her lips tightly as she held on to the bedpost. Ewan was beside her immediately and guiding her toward the chamber pot in the corner. He rubbed her back while she emptied the contents of her belly and handed her a moistened cloth to wipe her face when she was finished.

When she was seated upon the settle by the fire, he tucked a blanket across her lap and handed her a cup of mint tea. "Your aunt and the lady Alys both say this will pass in another few weeks," he said as he offered her the tin of wafers Elspeth kept in good supply for her.

She glared at him over the rim of her cup. "Would that I could rid myself of you so quickly. Or might my prayers be answered and you are leaving this day?"

He chuckled, and Madlin nearly threw the remains of her tea in his face. Folding his arms across his chest, he propped himself against the wall and said, "Are you still persisting in this foolish belief that your blood is tainted and my only hope of sound heirs is to put you aside and seek another wife?"

"You know good and well I am. And 'tis not foolish!" She bit into one of the wafers and then washed the crumbs down with the last of her tea. She refused to look at him, for he was wearing nothing but a scrap of linen wrapped around his loins. Barely enough to cover him. Damn the man for flaunting himself so! And damn her own wanton spirit for still wanting him.

"I am not leaving, for you are not yet in your right mind. 'Twould by most unchivalrous of me to desert a wife when she is ailing."

"If not for you, I would not be ailing," she snapped and tossed the lid of the wafer tin at him. He caught it and laughed. Laughed!

Every morning he awoke in a fine humor, but this morning he seemed in even higher spirits than usual. She could not bear it. "Ewan Fraser, you are the . . . the . . . most exasperating, doltish, insensitive, obtuse man ever placed on this earth, and I want you gone from my sight today! This hour! This very minute!"

"No, you don't, sweetling," he said with amusement twitching at the corners of his mouth. "Who would hold your head each morning and put up with the tantrums that inevitably follow? No one, that's who. Only the man who loves you and is responsible for your current state."

"Oh, Ewan." She shook her head slowly from side to side. "When will you accept that this child cannot be Cluain's? You cannot want it to be. Leave me and let me live out my days with some honor at least."

His expression sobered as she'd hoped. Wordlessly, he went to the chest that he'd commandeered for his belongings. From it, he extracted a small book. He dropped it in her lap. "This was found on MacDonald when his and the Munro's bodies were recovered yesterday. Read it and discover the truth of the man you called brother. 'Tis his journal."

Repelled by anything Francis might have touched so intimately, Madlin shoved the volume from her lap. She shuddered and moved her hand to her belly.

Ewan picked up the book and replaced it on Madlin's lap. "Read it. I will leave you to it and make sure no one disturbs you." Without another word, he left her alone for the first time in days.

Madlin stared at the book for a long time after Ewan left her. She poured herself another cup of the herb tea and stared at the fire until finally curiosity impelled her to open the book and begin to read. Hours later when she had finished, she tossed the small volume into the fire. As she watched the pages rapidly turn to ash, she symbolically cleansed her heart of all that it had ever carried for Francis MacDonald.

Baseborn the bishop had been, but not of Toirlach's blood. The innkeeper's daughter who had birthed him had merely named Toirlach, for he had been the only nobleman among the many men she'd lain with that summer. Francis had known the truth of his origins from the very day he'd been deposited at Dunfionn's gates.

Shamed and embittered that he had been born to such a slattern, he had gradually re-created the woman. By the last year's worth of entries in his journal, Francis described her as a virtuous woman, nearly saintly, who had been cruelly wronged by many, Toirlach MacKendrick above all. Thus, he'd rationalized all his actions as a son's righteous duty.

The early writings had been executed in a fashion akin to that of a seneschal with the hand of a trained scribe. Meticulously, he'd detailed how he'd hired a crew of mercenaries from the gutters of Aberdeen, even including a full accounting of the supplies and expenditures provided for them. With cold detachment, he'd outlined every raid, from the planning to its execution and finally the results, tallying the dead as if they were no more than sheep in the annual autumn slaughter.

With each raid, he'd fully expected the two clans to declare war upon each other and the far larger clan Fraser to triumph, finishing off the MacKendricks for him. That neither Toirlach nor Sir Cameron had retaliated with murderous raids to match those executed by Francis's minions was a source of growing frustration. Discovering the desertion of his coterie of cutthroats had angered him, but it was her marriage to Ewan and the alliance for peace that followed that had put him into a frenzy.

With his goal slipping away from his grasp, his writings became more disjointed in their composition and less legible in execution. Since the final entry had been made before the

Munro's last appearance at Dunfionn, and there had been no mention of him prior, Madlin was convinced that it was as she supposed. Seamus had been but one more of Francis's many victims. It had to have been when he journeyed to that black granite mountain, from which the Munro's stronghold, Dubhfireach, took its name, that he'd drafted Seamus into his scheme.

She was standing at the window gazing sightlessly through the glazed pane when Ewan returned. A heavy weight had been lifted from her heart in the reading of the journal, and another important concern was remedied. Or so she hoped.

"You have finished it?" Ewan asked.

"Aye, and I do thank you for forcing me to read it. Someday, mayhap, I will find it in my heart to feel pity for him," Madlin said, though in her mind's eye she saw Francis's face as he aimed his crossbow at her. There had been nothing but hate contorting his features and driving him to kill those who'd treated him with kindness and acceptance.

"Waste no pity on that bastard, for he had none for you that day he thought to take your life." He came up behind her and curled his arms around her middle. Pulling her back against him, he brushed a kiss upon the top of her head. "I have never prayed so hard that my aim be true as I did that day. Praise God, my arrows flew straight and strong."

She let herself relax in his arms for the first time in days. "I have not thanked you for saving my life, for I did not think it was one worth saving. Until now."

He turned her and swept her up tightly against him. "Always it was worth saving, and if any should feel guilt, it is I. 'Twas I who put you in danger, insisting on that particular tree and announcing that destination for days before. I once accused you of being impetuous, but 'tis I who stand guilty. If only—"

"Shh . . . shh." She placed a quieting finger across his lips. "You are guilty of naught but wanting to bring cheer to this keep and all within it. You have been telling me for days that I could not have known about Francis or Seamus, and now I charge you to take your own advice. Shall we make a pact?

I shall release my guilt over Francis if you will relieve yourself of all guilt for that day."

"I will if you also promise to talk no more of sending me away from you or ever thinking again of ridding yourself of me as your husband."

She smiled, the first true genuine smile she'd given anyone in far too long. Draping her arms over his shoulders, she played her fingertips through the hair at his nape. "I suppose I will have to put up with you for the rest of my days."

Rising on her toes, she pressed a kiss to his lips that was quickly returned and deepened. It was several kisses and ever hotter caresses later before she pushed out of his arms. "Nay, do not think to woo me onto that bed just yet. I need my wits, for there is more that needs be decided between us."

His desire for her still so clearly evident, Madlin nearly relented. Moving away from him lest she succumb, she said, "I want all concerns settled between us before we share that marriage bed again."

"All right." Folding his arms across his chest, he leaned against the wall and waited for her to continue. It was a pose she knew indicated his impatience, but she resolved not to hurry through the concerns she had. They were far too important to be dismissed quickly.

"I must do all within my power to assure that nothing like Francis MacDonald's evil ever threatens Dunfionn, Glendarach, or even Cluain again," she began. "No child of the house of MacKendrick or Cluain will feel he or she does not have a place of legitimacy and honor."

Ewan visibly bristled. "I assure you I have not nor do I plan to cast my seed indiscriminately."

"Forgive me, 'twas not you I was referring to but another, my brother Bram. And 'twas not indiscriminate that he planted his seed but within his formally betrothed, the lady Alys, whom he did love most deeply."

There was a gleam in her eyes. A rather zealous gleam that Ewan found most unnerving. "Where is this leading?"

Brushing her hands down the sides of her face, Madlin

clasped them beneath her chin. "The solution has been right before us since the very beginning, and I was blind to it. If only I, Aunt Elspeth, Alys, or someone had thought of it earlier."

"What should you have thought of earlier, and exactly what problem have you solved?"

She began to pace about the room, but not in the nervous, hand-wringing way that had been her habit of late. Instead, she seemed almost to dance as she told him, "While at St. Margaret's, I read much, including a book of laws of Scotland. I was especially intrigued by the passages outlining marriages and the rights of primogeniture."

"And?" he asked, beginning to suspect where her thoughts were leading.

She whirled about, such a gladness on her face, and clapped her hands in joy. "When a couple lay together after all the formal declarations of intent to marry have been made, in the eyes of both Scotland and its Church, they have a legal and sanctified marriage. Not a handfasted marriage, mind you. But a legal one. Children born of their coming together even before the final vows are made are considered true and legal heirs."

Smiling with her, Ewan still had to ask in order to assure he understood her completely, "Does this mean that the very minute Bram's child is born, he or she is the MacKendrick?"

"Aye," she answered, and pulled him into the middle of the chamber intent on dancing about the room to show her joy.

Sobering just a bit, Ewan planted his feet and held his excited wife in place. "That would mean you will no longer be the MacKendrick. Are you so willing to give up that title so soon?"

"Aye," she answered sincerely and soberly. "I never expected to be laird and took no joy in it." Then, she grinned almost impishly. "But even a child as precocious as Bram's assuredly will be must have need of his aunt for a few years. I will lead the MacKendricks and hold Dunfionn secure for him or her."

He thought to ask her about Cluain's heirs and if she would be able to guide them as well but decided that discussion could wait until another time. Problems enough had been solved this day. He joined his wife in her dance about the room, steadily twirling her closer and closer to the bed.

It was several hours before they left their chamber. Only their duty to apprise Alys of her child's status caused them to pull on clothing and spare even an hour away from each other's arms. The door had scarcely closed behind them before their clothes were scattered about and their bodies lay intertwined once more. Another hour passed before hunger compelled them to attack the contents of the tray Ewan had commandeered from Edana's kitchen.

"I want to make it perfectly clear that I do love you and 'tis a most honorable love I hold for you."

Before she could say aught, he popped one of the berry tarts into her mouth. Serious indeed, Madlin thought with a giggle, if Ewan was parting with one of his favorite tarts to keep her mouth so full she could not talk.

"You do believe that, don't you?" He watched in fascination as dark red juice trickled out of the corner of her mouth when she nodded. Bending his head, he licked the juice from her chin, and then the crumbs from around her lips.

"I do so love all things sweet," he murmured before he savored the sweet honesty of his wife's mouth.

Madlin's last coherent thought was that there was only honor in remaining married to one so good and fine as this golden knight who held her so tenderly.

Epilogue

May 1425
Stirling Castle

The royal gaze was riveted upon the doors at the back of the great hall. The crowd of courtiers and noblewomen ceased their chatter the moment Sir Ewan Fraser, Baron Cluain, and Lady Madlin, Baroness Cluain, were announced. James had not even tried to keep it a secret that he had summoned his newest baron and his lady to court. Thus, the court had been abuzz for weeks in anticipation of at last viewing this woman who was rumored not only to be laird of her clan but to have held a sword to Cluain's throat and forced him to marry her.

It was said the woman was a veritable Amazon who'd herself slashed her right breast from her body so she could better wield the huge claymore she'd inherited from a fierce Viking ancestor.

A hardened warrior was this Madlin of the MacKendricks, more man than woman. So scarred from her many battles she was a fearsome thing to look upon.

A reincarnation of the legendary Medb, and Cluain feared for his life every night when he was forced to bed her.

At the very least, she was a tattooed Highland barbarian who stained her face blue with woad.

Poor Cluain. In public, men and women alike had sighed in despair that such a man as Ewan Fraser, battlefield commander and hero of the wars in France, had been forced before a priest by such a one. In private, the women had plotted ways of "consoling" the tall, golden-haired knight who'd set their hearts aflutter with his dramatic entrance eight months before.

The wide doors swung open to admit the fabled pair. A collective gasp was the immediate response to the stylishly attired couple who stepped forward. More than a few feminine sighs rippled through the court when the baron was sighted.

His golden hair brushed to a gleaming shine, his body attired in a black velvet jacket and snug-fitting trews, Cluain's broad-shouldered, well-muscled physique was shown to its best advantage. The severity of his attire was alleviated by elaborate gold stitching at the high collar and sleeves of his jacket, the golden spurs jingling at the heels of his shiny black boots, and the scabbard holding the famous Stewart sword.

Beside him, Madlin, the MacKendrick, Baroness Cluain, glided in a rustle of heavy silk. She was tall, yes, but gloriously formed was the male opinion as she moved toward the dais.

Her hair was a fiery mass, barely confined within a gold net beneath a short veil of gold sarcenet that was held in place by a simple chaplet of gleaming gold. A nimbus of errant curls framed a beautiful face with large green eyes, a perfect nose, and a luscious mouth that made men ache.

If her chin was a bit stubborn in its appearance, that was the only part of her that made any man retain the slightest sympathy for Cluain, Sir Ewan Fraser. Envy was the dominant emotion sweeping through the assembled males.

Her gown, dyed the deep hue of the forest, was of the very latest fashion, sparking envy in many of the ladies and appreciation in the men. Long flowing sleeves and a deep squared bodice displayed the flawlessness of her ivory skin and the perfection of her full breasts. A chain of intricately worked gold hung about her neck and drew many a male eye to the shadowed place just above the bodice edge where it disappeared between her breasts.

The whispers rippled through the court as the striking pair moved past them. Though the deep folds of extra fullness in the front of the lady's gown did hide it when she stood still, as she moved it was immediately apparent to everyone that the baroness was swelling with child.

Ewan and Elspeth had prepared her well for this introduction to the court. Madlin paid the whispers no mind, nor the whisperers so much as a glance. She kept her gaze upon the king and queen.

A handsome couple, she thought as she neared the dais where the two thrones sat side by side. The king's red-gold hair and ruddy complexion were in sharp contrast to Queen Joan's dark hair and ivory skin. James appeared tall and athletic even seated, whereas Joan was petite and quite pretty, the delicate English rose he'd brought home to Scotland and his throne.

Upon reaching the foot of the dais, Ewan swept the royal couple a deep bow. "Your majesties, I am most pleased to present my wife, the lady Madlin, Baroness Cluain, and regent laird of the MacKendricks."

Madlin bowed her head. Keeping her arm firmly curled around Ewan's, she swept into as deep a curtsy as her thickened waist would allow. With Ewan's arm steadying her, she wobbled only slightly when she rose. She sent her husband a small smile of gratitude when she was once again upright.

"We bid you welcome, baroness," James said, his gaze speculative as it swung from her to Ewan. "Regent laird? Explain this. We were given to understand that Lady Madlin is laird of the MacKendricks."

"Sir, my brother's wife has given him a son, posthumously." Nervous that she might make a misstep in protocol, Madlin nonetheless gamely offered a shaky smile and took a half step forward. "The laird of the MacKendricks of Dunfionn is a wee lad of just one month. If it pleases your majesty, I will serve as his regent until he is old enough to lead the MacKendricks."

James leaned forward, propping his elbows on the arms of his throne. "Lead the MacKendricks, train her nephew, bear and rear Cluain's heirs, and oversee Cluain's household." James ticked the list off on his fingers, a grin playing about the corners of his mouth. He winked at the queen before centering his gaze upon Ewan. "Your countess will not have the time."

"Countess?" Madlin's query rose higher than that rippling through the assembled court.

With a satisfied grin, James leaned against the back of his throne. "Aye, countess, my dear lady." In a voice that carried to every corner of the great hall, he announced, "Sir Ewan Fraser, you did perform each and every task I charged you with last autumn and have most assuredly earned the title I will confer upon you today."

Caring not for protocol at all, Madlin narrowed her eyes upon her husband. "An earldom? You told me nothing of an earldom. You . . . you—"

"Deceiver," Ewan supplied sheepishly. "And a surprised one, I must add to my defense."

"Surprised?" With a flash of the temper that was making him infamous at court, James demanded, "You dared to doubt your king's word?"

Catching up his wife's hand, Ewan squeezed it as a warning to keep quiet. "Nay, sir, never that. 'Twas just that I consider myself unworthy of the honor. If reward is due for the peace that now reigns along the northern banks of Moray, 'tis to my lady it belongs."

James tipped his head to one side and subjected Madlin to a thorough visual assessment. "You are carrying Cluain's heir, Lady Madlin?"

Involuntarily, Madlin smoothed her hand across the top of her belly where Ewan's son had just kicked her as if to answer in his own stead. "Aye, 'tis my husband's son."

James laughed heartily before chiding Ewan. "At least you have performed one of the stipulations I laid down for you."

Shocking the court, Madlin had the temerity to ask, "Just what were these stipulations, sir?"

Neither Ewan nor the king were certain as to of which of them she was demanding explanations. Ewan hesitated and the king answered her in a near apologetic tone. "My lady, this knave was told by his king to bring peace to the Moray by the most expeditious manner possible—marrying the Mac-Kendrick's daughter. Further, 'twas suggested that if Cluain's heir was swelling that woman's belly by the spring when he was summoned to court, an earldom would be conferred upon him."

He rose and stepped down from the dais. Enclosing Madlin's hand in his, he patted it and said, "I do know your husband quite well, and I vow to you that 'twas more than the promise of an earldom that did compel that knave to marry you."

Madlin raised a brow and actually scoffed. "A sword at his back, more's the like."

James laughed again. "So we have been told, madam. You are indeed a most extraordinary woman, and Ewan Fraser is the most fortunate of men to have been captured by you."

To Ewan, he ordered, "Hand me that great sword you carry at your side, Ewan Fraser. I have need of it." The sword in hand, James ordered them both to kneel before him, then asked, "Tell us, Sir Ewan, how is it that one lady, even one as extraordinary as your lovely wife, is going to carry all the responsibilities fate has thrust upon her?"

Ewan's voice rang as loud and clear as his sovereign's when he declared, "Sir, Lady Madlin Fraser née MacKendrick can do anything she sets her mind to, for she is a woman of great wisdom, talent, and, most of all, honor."

It was a most unusual title conferment, for the sovereign did tap the shoulder of both Sir Ewan Fraser and Lady Madlin Fraser before ordering, "Rise Countess Madlin and Earl Ewan of Cluain." Above their heads, James glared darkly at the silent assemblage until the appropriate applause began. As the sound rose, he leaned toward the new countess and for her ears alone whispered, "The queen and I will be honored to stand as godparents to young Jamie Fraser when he does make his appearance."

* * *

Autumn had painted the Highlands bright with color to welcome the royal progress. Among the entourage was the Lord High Archbishop of Scotland, come to bless the manor house rising in the middle of a sunny meadow high in the very heart of Cluain's lands. Beneath a clear blue sky, he stood at the spot where one day a chapel would grace "Dunàgh" and did christen the infants held in the arms of the king and queen of Scotland. James Ewan Fraser and his sister, Joan Elspeth Fraser, younger by ten minutes, were then presented to clans Fraser and MacKendrick. It was a joyous occasion for all the gathered, an omen that Dunàgh would most certainly be a fortress of happiness and prosperity as the name implied.

A handsome lad was young James, with his father's blue eyes and a hint of red glowing in the blond fuzz that covered his head, testifying to the MacKendrick blood he carried. Wee Joan was declared a beauty, a feminine replica of her brother.

It was her mother's prayer that her spirit might liken itself to the gentle grace of her royal namesake and one day be a lady possessing all the womanly skills of her great aunt.

It was her father's prayer that she have all the fire of the woman who'd borne her. A small bow and quiver were already being made for her, as well as a wee sword like the one being made for her brother.

If you loved HIGHLAND BRIDE
by Janet Bieber,
you won't want to miss her next book,

In Name Only

Coming in summer 2000

*Turn the page for a sneak peek
at this wonderful new historical romance.*

September, 1833

Lily Patterson was dead.

The day she and her tiny stillborn child were laid to rest dawned as bleak as the hearts of those who mourned her. Most of Cleveland turned out for her funeral.

They patted the survivors, mumbled their condolences, and wiped their eyes as the parents, sisters, husband, and children of the "dear departed" said their final good-byes. Though the family had long since left and the sky threatened rain, the crowd was reluctant to leave the cemetery. Huddled in little groups against the bitter wind blowing in from Lake Erie, they talked in hushed tones.

Her pa had preached a fine service for her. His voice had faltered now and then, but that was expected, as he'd been mighty fond of his eldest daughter. Her husband and children had borne up well all things considered. The four little mites looked so lost standing there with their pa, grandma, and aunts. In shock, most likely. It was not surprising; everyone was shocked.

"I saw her Tuesday. Pretty as ever, she was, and the very picture of health. I surely did not think to be attending her funeral by Friday. So sad. So, very, very sad."

"The Lord giveth and the Lord taketh away."

These and similar remarks were met with sighs, slow shaking of heads, and muttered *tsk, tsk, tsk*s.

As tragic as Lily's sudden passing had been, the cause was

not so unusual as to merit much discussion. Women sometimes died in childbirth. It was a fact of life.

What was really keeping everyone gathered at the cemetery was what had happened immediately after the funeral.

The Reverend had cast the first handful of dirt upon the smooth cedar casket holding Lily and the tiny child's remains before offering up the final words from *The Book of Common Prayer*. "Earth to earth, ashes to ashes, dust to dust; in sure and certain hope of the Resurrection unto eternal life. Amen."

The family had followed his lead, first Rose, then Ian and the children. Instead of a handful of dirt, Rose and the children had tossed floral nosegays fashioned from the last of the flowers blooming in Rose's vast garden behind the parsonage. Valeriana, Laurel, and Primula had stepped up and added more flowers. Then the family had turned away and slowly begun to wend their way through the crowd toward the carriages waiting at the edge of the cemetery.

The crowd was quiet as one by one they each gathered up a handful of the soil and cast it into the grave. Quiet and solemn, the custom matched the mood. Suddenly, crying, "Beauty is gone from this world! I cannot bear it. I must leave it, too!" Anson Phillips threw himself into the grave.

The gravediggers had a devil of a time getting the man out so they could finish their work.

"Always thought that painter man was a bit odd," someone finally had the courage to say, breaking the silence that had been weighing so heavily since Phillips had been led away.

"Heard he painted Lily's portrait more'n once and was teaching her to paint, too. Said she was the most beautiful woman he ever painted and a promising pupil, too."

"Still no cause to make such a spectacle of himself."

"Well, artists are a sensitive bunch, I'm told."

"Best he move on. Won't be many folks in these parts wanting him to paint their pictures or teach their children after this."

"Shoulda' left the fool in there and thrown the dirt on him.

Never did think he was much of a painter, or much of a man, neither."

"God be thanked the family wasn't here to witness such a thing."

Finally, the heavens opened and rain began to fall, effectively putting an end to the discussions—for the moment.

As certain as the sun would come up tomorrow, the day after, and the day after that, Lily Patterson's funeral would be discussed for weeks, perhaps months. At least until something more interesting occurred.

At the Patterson house on Euclid Street, a pair of black-ribboned mourning wreaths hung on the wide double doors. Having deposited the family safely at the door, two carriages were just pulling away from the wide portico that sheltered the main entrance of the house. The family had arrived just as the rain began.

Inside, the Marys, as the family called the two maids, Mary Flick and Mary Cunningham, had just finished lighting the lamps and stoking the fires in the hearths. It was only midday, but the light and warmth chased away some of the gloom and damp, as did the scent of cinnamon and other spices that wafted from the kitchen.

The cook and housekeeper, Gerta Hosapfel, had been baking almost nonstop since the night her mistress had died. What she hadn't prepared, others had. A steady stream of visitors had been arriving bearing linen-covered baskets since word of Lily Patterson's passing had spread.

Helpless in the face of death, the women found their own comfort in the preparation of nourishment for the living. And so they had come, until the kitchen was full and both the sideboard and the long table in the dining room were fair groaning with every manner of food. During the wake, a sizable dent had been made in the potages, cakes, pies, and heaping platters, but several more crowds of visitors could have been sustained by what remained.

Having been in an understandable daze until now, Ian

looked upon the largess as if seeing it for the first time. Running a hand through his hair, his deep voice cut through the awful silence that blanketed the house. "Rose, take some of this food home with you today. I know there are people in and out of the parsonage all the time. And, if you could draw up a list of those who could use some of this, I'll have it packed up and distributed."

"I'll see to it, Ian dear. Here, now, you must keep up your strength." Rose thrust a heaping plate of food in his hands.

"Where are the children? They must be hungry." He took the plate but didn't look at it. Eating was the last thing on his mind.

"Ana has taken them upstairs to the nursery. Laurel and Primmy are with them, too. I'll ask one of the Marys to take a tray up to them."

"I must go to them."

Rose slipped her plump arm around Ian and guided him to a chair at the table. "You will eat something first, dear boy. John? You, too." Having settled her son-in-law, Rose pushed her husband down in a chair on the opposite side of the table.

Needing to keep herself busy, Rose fluttered about the dining room preparing a plate of food for her husband. After serving him, she pushed through to the kitchen, ostensibly to order pots of tea and coffee. In reality, she could not bring herself to sit down in her daughter's dining room. She knew once she stopped moving about and seeing to the needs of others, the depth of her sorrow would overwhelm her. When she did sit down, it was to make the list she'd promised Ian. She did it at the kitchen worktable, a place she found infinitely more comfortable than the lavish ostentation of the formal dining room.

In the dining room, but for the occasional clink of a fork against china, silence prevailed. Ian didn't know or care what was going on in his father-in-law's mind. All he hoped was that the man would leave soon and take all his family with him.

He was genuinely fond of Rose and her two younger girls,

Laurel and Primmy. If they shared John's narrow piety and philosophies, they didn't go around advertising it. However, Valeriana, or Ana as the family called her, was her father's daughter through and through. If she wasn't evangelizing about one thing or another, she was censuring the lesser beings of the world—namely, any male over the age of fourteen as well as anyone who didn't follow the strict teachings of Calvin. The less time he had to endure in that woman's company, the better.

Mainly, he just wanted the house to get back to some sort of normalcy. It was a relief to get the funeral over with. Having their mother lying in a coffin in the parlor and all the people trooping in and out for her wake had been an ordeal for the children. He wasn't sure Jessie or Rob quite understood the finality of death. He knew the little ones, Maara and Joseph, certainly didn't.

He supposed he ought to say something to John. John being such a voluble person, it was odd to experience such a length of silence when in his company. But then the man had just buried his daughter. Lily had been Ian's wife, and he was sincerely sorrowed by her death. However, it was one thing to bury a wife, quite another to bury one's child. He grieved for the little one who'd died before it could take its first breath, but knew it to be but a small fraction of the grief he would suffer if fate should be so cruel that he should ever have to bury one of the others.

Unable to think of anything else, he broke the silence by saying, "That was a fine service you gave for Lily, John. I know it was difficult for you. I admire your strength. Mine would have surely failed me under similar circumstances."

"The Lord God grants strength when His children are in need of it," MacPherson said, though his voice lacked its usual power. With a shaking hand, he reached for the cup of tea Rose had set before him, started to lift it to his lips, then changed his mind. He replaced the cup.

"Couldn't have borne it if anyone else had done my Lily's funeral. I baptized her, welcomed her into the Church, married her, and baptized her babies. Had to do her funeral. Had to. No one else. I had to be the one."

MacPherson's pallor grew more ashen as he spoke and his eyes appeared unfocused. "Had to do it. So beautiful. Gone . . . gone . . . my hopes with her." His voice hoarsened and his speech rambled until he was muttering unintelligibly.

Alarmed, Ian rounded the table and grasped his father-in-law's shoulder. "John?"

MacPherson seemed not to hear him and continued his disjointed muttering. Gently, Ian shook him again, but Mac-Pherson was in a world of his own.

Hating that the woman should have to be further burdened, Ian went in search of Rose. He found her washing dishes in the kitchen. She'd made Gerta sit down and rest. He wasn't surprised. Rose MacPherson was that kind of woman, always seeing to the needs of others.

"I'm afraid John is not himself, Rose," he said, then marveled at her calm as she took over the care of her distraught husband. But then, that was Rose. Always calm no matter how grim or shocking the event. She'd been that way throughout the night of Lily's suffering, delirious ravings, and eventual death.

"I'll come with you and help get him into the parsonage," Ian said a short time later as he helped Rose load her husband into the carriage.

"Thank you, dear, but your place is here. I appreciate the use of the carriage and your Mr. Ferguson to drive us. Laurel and Primmy will be help enough."

Ian took in the anxious faces of his two young sisters-in-law seated on either side of their father. He smiled gently, hoping to reassure them. "With the inestimable MacPherson ladies attending him, John is a fortunate man," he remarked, and meant it.

Laurel and Primmy were young, neither yet twenty, but each was remarkable in her own way. Dainty and raven-haired like their mother and eldest sister, each showed the promise of becoming the great beauty their sister had been. Laurel was only seventeen or perhaps eighteen, he really couldn't remember right then, only that it was Laurel who called upon the sick and often stayed to nurse and comfort them. Primula was the family delight. A couple of years younger than Laurel, she was usually bubbling with joy and chatter. Except for the past few days, he'd rarely seen her serious.

And Valeriana was . . . Ian frowned. Where was Valeriana?

He turned to find his eldest sister-in-law, sans cloak and bonnet, embracing her mother in the open doorway, as if saying good-bye.

"I'll send someone around for James Cooke," Ian offered, watching with growing dismay as Rose patted her now eldest daughter's cheek and started toward the waiting carriage.

"Oh, don't bother the doctor, Ian dear. I'm sure all John needs is rest. He'll be better tomorrow, I'm sure."

The way MacPherson was hunched down and continuing to mutter to himself, Ian was unconvinced. "I'd feel better if a physician were to look at him."

Rising up on her toes, she pressed a kiss to Ian's cheek. "You're a good man, Ian Patterson," she said, then climbed into the carriage.

Ian closed the door and said, "I'm sure it'll be a comfort to you to have all your daughters at home, Rose. Once the children are settled for the night, I'll see that Valeriana gets home safely. She's been a great help these past days, but I know her place is with you and John."

"No, no, all her things are already moved, and John wants her to stay here."

"Stay? Here?" A sinking feeling settled into Ian's midriff. Desperation prompted him to say, "That's very . . . uh . . . thoughtful, but she's done so much already, and I do know how much John relies on her to help him with his sermons and other church business. I couldn't impose any longer."

"Doing for family is never an imposition, dear. Now we really must be getting John home."

Speechless, Ian watched the carriage move down his driveway. All her things? Just how long was Valeriana to stay? When she'd arrived the morning after Lily's death, portmanteau in hand, he'd assumed her stay would be but a few days. If there had been a trunk or any other baggage accompanying her, he hadn't noticed, but then his greatest concern that morning had been how to tell his children that their mother was dead.

To think he'd actually been glad to see her. With all the arrangements to be made and the stream of people in and out of the house, he'd had little time to spend with his children. It was a comfort to know that someone who loved them was there to care for them and stay with them constantly. They needed a familiar face and their aunt was that. Since their very births, he'd more than once speculated that their three aunts had spent more time with them than had their own mother.

Turning at last, he took in the drawn look on Valeriana's face and the way she was worrying the handkerchief in her hands. "Sister, I know you're worried about your father," he began, hoping he could appeal to her good sense. Rose had clearly been more addled than he'd supposed.

"I simply cannot impose upon your kindness any longer," he said, deciding to appeal directly to the source. "Please, gather up what you might need for tonight and allow me to see you home. I can have the rest of your things sent over tomorrow. It just wouldn't be fair of us to keep you here when you are clearly needed at the parsonage."

Ana shook her head, the movement sending the black ribbons of her cap swinging and his hopes plummeting. "No, Mr. Patterson," she said. "Thank you for your concern, but Mama is right. It would be best if I remained here. It would only upset Papa if I were to return home."

With a rustle of taffeta over starched petticoats, she moved briskly into the vestibule and headed for the stairway. "I left one of the Marys with the children, but I must get back to them. Do come inside, Mr. Patterson, you're letting all that cold and damp into the house."

Her peremptory tone grated and briefly Ian considered standing out in the rain with the door wide open just to spite her.

Lord, help me, he thought as he followed in her wake,

closing the door with more force than was necessary. The heavy door shuddered as it came to rest and the sound of the latch clicking into place echoed through the large vestibule.

It was a childish thing to do, akin to stamping his foot in a show of pique, but it had felt good to slam that door. He felt even better when he saw Valeriana pause in her progress at the sound.

"I'll be up to see the children in a little while," he said as he headed for his study at the back of the house. He didn't hear an answer and assumed she'd continued on up the stairs. Good, he could use a little time alone.

In the smallish room that was his very private sanctuary, he opened a cabinet, pulled out a bottle of brandy, and splashed a small portion into a glass. Swirling the rich amber liquid in the snifter with one hand, he picked up the poker and stirred the coals in the hearth. He took a sip of his drink, savoring the taste on his tongue and the warmth that spread down his throat as he watched the flames come to life in the grate and begin to lick along the logs stacked there.

Images of Lily flitted in his mind. It was too soon for any of them to be pleasant memories. He took another sip of the brandy and rubbed his forehead, easing the ache and wishing the memories were as easy to erase.

He lifted the glass to his lips, draining the remains in one swallow. She'd given him four beautiful children and they were joy enough for any man. He tried to concentrate on their innocent little faces. Each had a tight hold on a special place in his heart. He'd fight until his last breath to protect them.

"Mr. Patterson! Would you stumble up the stairs to your children with that evil on your breath?"

Startled, Ian nearly dropped his glass.

Valeriana glared at him from the doorway. The full-blown censure of the diehard temperance leader was written all over her. If her hair weren't secured so tightly beneath that silly little cap she wore, he was sure it would be standing on end.

He let out a loud sigh of exasperation. "Sister, a few sips of brandy never hurt anyone. I promise I shall not stumble up the stairs nor shall my children be tainted in any way by my presence."

He set his glass down on his desk. Leaning against it, he crossed his arms over his chest and asked, "What brings you to my study? Have you changed your mind about going back to the parsonage?"

"Certainly not!"

Her answer came quickly and vehemently. By the way she was eyeing his empty snifter and the bottle still out on his desk, he could almost read her thoughts. Leave those precious ones in the care of a drunkard? Why, it was not to be considered while there was a breath in her pious body. He almost laughed.

"Well, if it isn't an announcement of your imminent departure, just what is it that made you so courageous as to beard this lion in his private den?"

Valeriana tightened her lips and seemed almost to shrink within herself. He was immediately sorry for his sarcasm. He was feeling surly but had no right to take it out on her. An apology sprang to his lips but she spoke first.

"I regret that my presence here causes you such discomfort, but I shall endeavor to stay out of your way as much as possible. Papa believes the children need a woman, preferably a relative, to watch over them and I agree."

Sure that she must be choking on her professed regret, Ian managed to stem another sarcastic comment. He didn't like himself very much for descending to such tactics. It wasn't usually his way. "I'm sorry, I'm afraid I'm not quite myself today. Now what was it that brought you here?"

"Joseph and Maara are down for a nap. The rain has stopped, and I thought Jessica and Robert could do with some activity. Perhaps you'd like to take them for a walk or a ride in the carriage?"

Her gaze strayed to his empty glass and then the bottle again. "That is, if you're able."

His anger barely in check, he informed her, "Valeriana, I am more than able to walk or control a team of horses." He observed the tightness of her features and the rigid way she held herself. "You seem inordinately tense today. Perhaps you'd like me to pour you a glass of brandy. I'm sure it would do you a world of good."

Her look of horror and loud gasp were the last he saw or heard from her for the rest of that day.

PRINCESS
by Gaelen Foley

Darius Santiago is the king's most trusted man, a master spy and assassin. He is handsome, charming, and ruthless, and he has one weakness—the stunning Princess Serafina. Serafina has worshiped Darius from afar her whole life, knowing that deep in the reaches of her soul, she belongs to him. Unable to suppress their desire any longer, they are swept into a daring dance of passion until a deadly enemy threatens to destroy their love.

LORD OF VENGEANCE
by Tina St. John

Set in majestic medieval England, this is the story of two valiant people who struggle with the sins of the past to forge a love as turbulent as the land they live in. Devilishly handsome Gunnar Rutledge has spent years plotting against the man who nearly destroyed his life. He seeks the ultimate vengeance on Raina d'Bussy—his enemy's daughter—a proud beauty who will be slave to no man. Gunnar sets out to break Raina's glorious spirit but instead finds himself bewitched by her goodness and strength.

Published by Fawcett Books.
Available at bookstores everywhere.